T0365919

ANGEL

SAMANTHA HARTE

DIVERSIONBOOKS

Also by Samantha Harte

Cactus Heart
Timberhill
The Snows of Craggmoor
Kiss of Gold
Hurricane Sweep
Sweet Whispers
Autumn Blaze
Vanity Blade
Summersea

Diversion Books
A Division of Diversion Publishing Corp.
443 Park Avenue South, Suite 1008
New York, New York 10016
www.DiversionBooks.com

For more information, email info@diversionbooks.com

First Diversion Books edition March 2015.
Print ISBN: 978-1-68230-041-1
eBook ISBN: 978-1-62681-656-5

To my friends
and those I love
who helped me.

—S. Harte

Part One

One

For me and mine the journey to Kansas Territory was dogged with sorrow. Not ten days out, my baby sister Becky met with her end. For most that would've been enough to high-tail it back to Missouri, but we was of mule-headed stock.

I begin this account of my life in the gold country with Becky's death, though it brings to mind days long past. I'm told a tale such as mine must've started off somewheres, so I must recall Becky's sweet face and, in turn, tell how I come to be called Angel.

Becky and me had been down by the river, spinning dreams that spring when I turned fourteen. "I want lots of dresses and petticoats with lace," I'd said. "We'll live in a white house with a picket fence."

"And a swing in the yard, too, Angie. And flowers!" Becky was scarcely four, you understand.

We was still dreaming when we got home and found Ma roasting a goose! We'd lived so long on beans my mouth set to watering so's I thought the Missouri River was running through it! On the table we spied dress goods, ribbons, tobacco, and new shoes.

"Are we rich, Ma?" Becky cried, her eyes round as cups.

"Yep," Ma said, crouching to hug Becky. She pulled a peppermint from her pocket and popped it into Becky's mouth. Then she tied a blue ribbon in Becky's silky black hair. "I didn't bring you candy or ribbons, Angie," Ma said to me. "I'm hoping to give you something more."

I would've been glad for just a bit of that candy.

Pa come dragging in later, saying, "What's all this?" and scratching the stubble on his chin. Pa always looked like he couldn't understand why life dealt him such a poor hand. Folks said he had an alley-dog look that made mean men want to kick him. In the same breath they'd say Ma was fine-looking baggage.

"I was down by the courthouse today, Frank," she said, her eyes shining. "Saw a notice with my name on it—Lillian Jacobs. My grandfather left me five hundred dollars!" She poured some coins into Pa's trembling hands.

"Put the rest in the bank, did you?" he asked, counting under his breath, his narrow chest heaving with excitement.

"Spent it on a wagon, three yoke of oxen, and a horse. We're going West, Frank."

Pa looked like his eyes hurt. "You said I'd dragged you far enough. You was planted for good."

Ma just smiled.

Within two days we had a wagon and joined up with the Lewises, three other families, and a half-dozen jakes. We didn't know how far Kansas Territory was or how long it'd take, but we set out just the same. Jim Lewis rushed us along saying every nooning and every evening, "Got to reach the mountains 'fore the snow."

I couldn't imagine no place that far. Day after day we climbed hills, slid into valleys, bumped over rocks, and fell into ditches. The wagon wheels squeaked. Our feet blistered. The cooking was terrible and the sleeping worse. The fordings was hardest. Pa invented mighty fearsome cuss words when Jim Lewis would say, "Cross and be done with it." Jim was bent on sinking somebody.

One afternoon we come upon a wide shallow stream. We'd made twelve miles that day, and I'd walked every step. Ma sat high on the wagon seat, swallowing the day's dust, while Pa worried out a spot to ford. Becky looked bright, peeking out the back of the muslin top, her pretty blue hair-ribbon fluttering in the breeze.

When Pa layed on the whip, our wagon plunged down the bank

so fast Ma shut her eyes. Them dumb oxen got bogged right off. Cussing, Pa got back down to lead them across. Inside, the flour barrel began coming loose of the ropes.

"Hold it, Ma!" I yelled, throwing my arms around it.

Becky leaned over the tailgate, calling hello to the wagon behind us. "Here comes the water," she squealed, as it seeped into the wagon box.

"Sit down!" I cried.

Becky scared me, hanging so far over like that. She yanked the ribbon from her hair and waved it. "Yippee!"

I fell back, yelping when the barrel slid onto my foot. I threw out my hand to catch the back of Becky's skirt, but Ma cracked the whip. The oxen jerked the wagon forward, and Becky flopped over the tailgate!

I sprang flat out to catch her. "Ma, stop! Becky fell in the water!" I held my hand over the tailgate, expecting to see Becky splashing below. Nothing but curls of mud rose in the current.

Two men on horseback galloped in to save her. I couldn't figure where she disappeared to. The stream wasn't that deep I kept expecting her to bob up laughing, but the seconds crept by. My heart began pounding so I couldn't breathe. I pulled up my skirts and jumped in. For a blinding second my ankles hurt so bad I couldn't move.

Ma fell face first into the stream, stood up spitting water and dragged herself toward me. "Where is she? Where's my baby?"

When Becky surfaced downstream Ma shrieked and tore at her hair. She tried to run, but the mud and current held her back. The sun went under. A chilly breeze whispered through the grasses. The gurgling water rushed on.

Not 'til Pa got the wagon to the opposite bank did he realize why everyone was either in the stream or running along its edge. He splashed across just as one of the men laid Becky in Ma's arms. Ma smiled down at Becky like she was going to whisper her name. Then her neck corded, and she wailed.

"She's just stunned!" Pa panted. "She'll come around." He

looked so downright empty-headed, I wanted to shake him and say, "Look what you done! Look what coming West done!"

There was Becky's long black hair trailing in the water. Her dimpled hand hung limp. She wasn't playing possum and she wasn't stunned. She was dead.

Cornelia Lewis pulled me to shore and forced me not to look, though she couldn't keep me from hearing Ma's cries. "Say a prayer, child," Cornelia whispered. "Your ma's going to need the Lord's help."

"Don't know no prayers!" I sobbed, slapping at Mrs. Lewis's gentle hands. "Ain't no God!"

Cornelia turned my face west where the grasses was pale gold and green, not a tree to be seen, and lonely, oh so damned lonely. She said words from the Bible, though I ain't sure 'cause I never read a book, good or bad. She said something about still waters and my soul, but the waters of my life and those that took Becky's weren't still. If I had a soul, it seemed damned.

Everybody pulled at Ma to leave Becky and come away. "Take your hands off my child!" she screamed. "Don't touch my baby, Goddamn you."

Even Pa tried to calm her. Ma turned on him, tearing at his face, beating his chest 'til her grief was spent and she fainted.

I kept thinking it should've been me.

At dawn we buried Becky on a hill overlooking the crossing. Thanks to some potion Mrs. Lewis gave her, Ma was silent. Nobody gave me no potion. All night I relived them awful moments 'til I thought I was coming unhinged.

I couldn't believe them folks was going to bury forever my little sister with that hair so much prettier than mine, that smile so much brighter. While Jim spoke fancy words over her body, I waited for Becky to wake up. I waited 'til the last bit of dirt was patted in place and the cross with her name scratched on it was pounded in the ground. I couldn't even read it 'cause the only word I knew was my own name.

Afterwards, Cornelia pulled Ma up the bank to follow the wagons. I looked across the stream, thinking thoughts best left unspoken—even now. Then I saw something laying on the opposite bank and fought the current to the spot where Becky lay the day before.

Half buried in the mud lay her ribbon. I smoothed away the dirt and imagined her waving it, smiling, shining like the treasure she'd been. The ribbon felt smooth and cool against my lips—like a kiss. I turned my face west and started walking.

Come August we reached the South Platte fork and headed south. One night a couple fellas playing a fiddle and mouth organ started up a dance. I watched Jim Lewis's seventeen-year-old daughter, Effie, dance with every pair of boots in camp. She had the face of a horse and the laugh of a harness-sore mule.

Ma danced a few, which surprised me. She'd grown thin and pale, her eyes empty as the sky, but she was clearly the prettiest woman there. Pa was behind some wagon, betting on anything that moved, backing it with whatever came to mind.

After the dance Ma sat by the campfire, waiting for him. "Jim says we'll find Pikes Peak soon. Frank'll go looking for gold right off." Yellow fire reflected in her eyes. "I met Frank when I was sixteen. We was both poor, but..." She rubbed her temples. "... but I loved him." She began pacing, her arms folded tight against her breast. "Me and Frank never had more than we got right now. He's spent his whole life dreaming. I've spent mine working. Frank will never know how hard I've tried." She threw her head back. "*Remember*, Angela. Remember what keeps your babies alive. Work. Dreams are for fools and children."

"I'll work, Ma. I'm old enough."

She whirled, her eyes swimming. "I better bring him back else we won't have enough money to buy goods in Denver City. This time we're starting off right. Nobody'll ever know how hard it was to come by that money for the new start."

I climbed into the wagon and settled under the musty blankets, listening to yipping coyotes that made my hair stand up prickly. If that money hadn't come easy from Ma's dead grandfather, where did it come from?

Like a crack of thunder, a pistol shot split the night. A minute later I heard footsteps, but they wasn't Pa's. That time of night he'd be holding onto wagon wheels to keep hisself up. These come fast and stopped sudden by our wagon.

"Angela? Your ma needs you!" Jim Lewis was still pulling up his suspenders as I peeked out. He clutched his rifle, looking like he'd tasted bad meat, which wasn't such an unusual expression for him.

Hurrying to the wagon where men had been playing cards, I found Ma standing over a man face-down in the grass. "Pa!" I screamed, falling to my knees beside his body. Blood had pooled on the ground under him. "Wake up," I cried. "Wake up!" His pale blue eyes stayed fixed on the stars, the light gone, the hopes, the dreams…"Look what you done now! Look what you done!"

The men backed away, their sunburnt faces squeezed up tense, not wanting to hurt Ma none, but not wanting to get shot, neither. Jim Lewis caught me up and whispered, "Think you can get the pistol from her? She don't seem right in the head."

I was ready to throw myself at her…'til I saw her face. Never had her eyes been rounder or her teeth clenched harder. "You know how long I worked to get that money?" she growled, waggling the pistol. "I even let him gamble some!" She turned on the men. "*You* let him do it! You let him bet his horse, his team, and finally the whole kit and caboodle!"

"Pa lost our wagon?" I whispered.

"I should've done it sooner." She threw the pistol into the dust and stood up straighter. "Come on," she hissed, strutting into the midst of the men. "String me up. Without a wagon I'm as good as dead."

ANGEL

The men looked like maybe they might hang her! "Ain't nobody going to do nothing to you!" I said, dragging her away from them. Already I could see Pa's grave and hear them final solemn words that would lay in my heart like cold stones.

So it was next morning, after laying Pa to rest only miles from his dream, we headed on alone, Ma facing the wind, her chin high and proud. I trotted alongside, trying to be just like her.

Two

Fall 1860

Even in her state of shock, Ma looked excited when we walked into booming Denver City a-ringing with hammers and rasping saws two days later. "The gold's farther south and west," the jakes shouted, clearing out.

Cornelia stayed behind with the wagon while Jim went to the land office. "Please, sit up here, Lillian. I'm weary worrying about you," she said from the wagon seat.

Ma sighed and then almost smiled. She looked small, climbing up next to Cornelia, a tall, raw-boned woman with iron-colored hair. Cornelia's face wasn't much better than Effie's, but she had warm eyes. I felt better just being near her.

"Them mountains is something, ain't they?" Cornelia sighed, squinting into the sun so's her eyes looked like raisins. "Jim wants a piece of one." She chuckled and patted Ma's hand. "Men! We bear their children and start out on treks like this—they give back mighty peculiar thanks. I'll be darned if I know what I'll do with a piece of a mountain. I belong in a kitchen, tending grandchildren. Now that we're here, Lillian, what do you think you'll do?"

I wondered if Ma had even been listening. "Work," Ma said after a bit.

A supply wagon lumbered by, and the driver tipped his hat at us. "Too familiar hereabouts," Cornelia huffed like an angry hen.

When Jim come back, he swung up on the seat, near to bumping

Ma off. "A fella called Snowy Ray says there's land south of here near a new road going up a pass. I like the sound of that." He stopped and gave Ma an ornery look. For a God-fearing man there weren't much pity in his eyes. "You're welcome to take up with us, Lillian." With unyielding eyes Ma stared back. Then she gathered her bundles. "Thanks, but I won't burden you. Me and Angie'll do just fine right here."

I threw good-byes over my shoulder as Ma rushed me along to a bake shop she spied. When we walked in, the miners swarming around them sweets drank in the sight of Ma like a stiff shot of whiskey. "The proprietor, please," Ma said, taking notice of nobody.

"That's me, Ma'am," the man behind the plank counter said. "We got here the best baking in Denver City."

"I ain't here to buy. My daughter and me can bake anything you got supplies for."

We worked there a week. Every crumb sold for double. Mr. Tucker knew his fortune was in his shop, not out under some rock. Then one morning a woman from our train come in. She'd endured same as us but, at the sight of Ma, she turned right around and left. By night fall word had it Mr. Tucker was employing a husband killer.

"I can't believe it, Mrs. Jacobs!" he said, addressing Ma by her newly chosen name.

Not even bothering to look at him, Ma slapped the flour from her skirt and motioned for me to get our things from the back room, where we'd slept on the floor by the ovens.

Seeing his fortune about to take her leave, Mr. Tucker got a sight agitated. He spat a chaw into the spittoon clear across the room. "I'm just asking that you tell your side."

Ma stared at him. "What folks say is close enough to the truth." She shushed me with a harsh snap of her head and walked out, clutching her bundles with white-knuckled hands and holding her chin high. She pushed through knots of miners, disregarding all manner of leers and smiles.

"No women here," the owners of every boarding house told us. "Just men in my rooms. Wouldn't be proper." Every hotel was full, too. Miners and emigrants was sleeping in halls, under tables, and fighting for chairs.

At a drafty eating house, Ma asked, "Got any work for women hereabouts?"

The bearded man serving us sour meat rubbed his tobacco-stained beard and smirked. "Depends."

Ma got me out of there quick! By sundown the only lamplight come from saloons and dancehalls. Ma looked up and down the street, like she was shaking her head. She'd always steered me clear of saloons before. Suddenly she was leading me within smelling distance of the whiskey!

"I'll be back," Ma said, leaving me in a shadow.

"I'm going, too!"

She grabbed me and held me planted, her face hard. After she slipped away I got down on my haunches and gathered my skirt around my legs. Soft voices drifted from open windows. Doors slapped shut. Bedsprings squeaked.

When Ma come back, my legs had gone numb. She helped me none too gentle behind some cabins 'til we come to a store. A man motioned us inside. "Keep down and don't go to the window," he whispered, laying out a bedroll. Ma made me crawl in. I woke later when she lay down beside me, shivering.

We lived like that from hour to hour, sweeping or cooking when we could. Hiding got mighty scary. At night I'd wake, drenched with sweat after swimming halfway 'round the world after Becky's body. Or I'd be shaking Pa, and shaking him 'til his head fell off. One night Ma stroked my bushy hair and whispered, "We'll connect with something good soon."

"If we was men we could get ten jobs," I said, dashing away tears.

"I met a man called Snowy Ray the other night," she said. "He knows of a job near his trading post that I can have if I want it. Ray sold Jim Lewis some land down that way and is taking him there tomorrow. We could go, too."

"I'd like that, Ma!" I said, hugging her.

ANGEL

• • •

So next morning when Cornelia saw me walking into their camp north of town she smiled like the sun. "Angie! How you been?"

"Pretty good. And yourself!" I burned my lips on the coffee she offered, but drank it down nonetheless I was so hungry.

"Can't shake this ague, but I told Jim I can travel."

"We're thinking of going with you if you'll have us," I said.

She laughed and hugged me. "We wanted you all along!"

Looking sour-mouthed, like her pa, Effie whispered plenty loud, "We ain't got room with all them new supplies."

Cornelia pinched her. "Tell your ma to hurry. We're leaving soon."

About then a man on horseback thundered into camp. His curly brown hair danced in the breeze and his eyes snapped. Sweeping off his gray hat, he jumped down from a mighty smart-looking Appaloosa and strutted around, measuring us with a critical eye and calculating smile. "Morning, ladies." He cocked his head and fixed his eyes on us like a beast of prey. "Fine day for anything, wouldn't you say?"

Cornelia conjured up a face of stone.

"Seeing as how you're so talkative and helpful," he smiled. "I'll get right to the point. I've been hearing about two beggar women hiding in town. Heard anything of the like?"

"Injuns?" Effie cried, her eyes popping.

"No, my dear. White women. I'm a newspaperman, here in this glorious western wilderness, seeking stories for the tabloids back East. My readers have had their fill of gold fever and Indian raids. Now I need tragic trail stories to whet their bloodthirsty appetites." Suddenly bowing toward me with a dazzling smile, he said, "How do *you* do, Miss? You're the smartest thing in shoeleather I've seen all day!"

"Be off with you, young rascal!" Cornelia shouted, shooing him away with a stick from her campfire. "You can't talk to a decent young lady like that!"

"My humblest pardon, Ma'am. She just looked so pretty I

couldn't help myself. Think of it, my dear. Two destitute women begging miners for…"

Cornelia flapped at him 'til he turned away chuckling, mounted his horse and galloped to the next wagon, hailing the folks there as he had us. "Arrogant young pup! Curb that bold eye, Angie. Close your mouth, Effie. He's too old for either of you."

"He was *so* handsome, Mama," Effie hawed, setting her long chin on her arms. "Who was he?"

None of us knew, but that was the famous Travis Saunders who wrote hot and scandalous stories of the West. He was known as far as London and San Francisco. I'd hear tell of "The Savage" and his bloodcurdling stories as the years wore on, though I'd never read one.

After three days skirting the foothills to the south, we come upon El Dorado City, hid by a bunch of peculiar red rocks and nestled among boulders, pines, and pretty yellow trees that shimmered in the sun and spoke a comforting song in the wind. The doors of every saloon stood open at midday and looked to be pulling in more gold than the richest mine.

Jim struggled through a blue-blazing knot of wagons to keep up with our guide, Snowy Ray, who was on horseback. The fat little man forged ahead, paying no heed to Jim's problems with the wagon tires axle-deep in red mud.

Bearded, sunburnt miners watched us go by and might've jumped us quicker than Injuns. The only reason they didn't was 'cause we was driving oxen, an animal they had little use for, and we looked like an ordinary band of trail-worn folks. None knew about Jim's wealth of supplies. If they could've laid eyes on Ma we would've been of considerable more interest.

"There ain't no bridge!" Cornelia gasped as we neared the mountains.

I climbed forward and there ahead of us saw the gap in the

rocks called a pass. The mountains rose high on either side and down between them raged a narrow creek that sounded mighty pretty, tumbling over the boulders.

Effie leaned back, closing her eyes. "I'm faint."

"We better stay the night in town," Cornelia whispered.

"We got to keep going!" Jim yelled, his eyes round. The man was near to being scared out of his drawers!

He fumed nearly ten minutes before Snowy Ray pounded back and yanked hisself to a halt beside the wagon. A wet stogie hung from his mouth. He swept off his hat, and what hair he had was white and jutted at all angles around his collar. "What's keeping you, Jimmy boy?"

"How are we supposed to get over that gorge?" Cornelia cried.

"Gorge!" he whooped. "Greenhorns! Don't know why I put up with 'em. Get your whip up, Jim, and move them dumb beasts. You're holding up a mess of muleteers that wouldn't think nothing of stringing you up just to get you and yours out of the way."

Sure enough, some mighty fierce-looking men was shouting curses over the bray of their straining teams. "How long will it take?" Cornelia asked, gripping her seat.

"Just up the road a piece. Nicest little valley you ever did see. We'll stop for supper in Tempest. I'm hungry, so move 'em, son!"

Jim plunged the team across a soggy bed of pine boughs, and as we started up the grade, the wagon gave out with groans from every joint. We went over the tailgate best we could.

"Do I have to walk all the way?" Effie moaned, gasping for breath when we rounded the first bend and saw how high the narrow road snaked.

Cornelia pinched her and pushed her on. We worked ahead, clearing the road of fallen rocks, mindful of the wall-eyed oxen behind. Snowy's horse got winded, so he hung back, conversing with Ma. From what I could catch over my own heavy breathing, Tempest was growing up along the creek we was following. It hadn't been a recognized place more than a summer and was the last settlement up the canyon. After that was Snowy Ray's post and Jim's land. Only trappers and prospectors knew the mountains beyond that.

Tempest turned out to be a disappointing assortment of tents and shacks. Everything looked like it might blow away in a light wind. The only solid building was, naturally, a saloon. Its windows was covered with painted words but, it being a place of sins and vices, Cornelia wouldn't let Effie read them to me.

Next to it was a tent with plank tables out front, boasting the worst mess of gobbling miners I ever saw. Seeing we wasn't laying to jump their claims, they turned back to their tin plates. We took supper there.

"Best hurry," Snowy said after a bit. He wiped his mouth on his sleeve and gave a hardy burp that set Effie to giggling.

Jim's eyes slid across the table. "Lil, are you sure you're doing the right thing?"

Snowy's eye flicked over me and Ma. "Changed your mind?"

Ma shook her head.

"Maybe we could settle right here or go back to that other town," I said. "Buy supplies off Jim. We can set up a bakery."

"Only one kind of woman stays in places like this," Cornelia said, her usually kind eyes narrow.

Ma left her food uneaten and started back for the wagon.

"Ain't we got enough money, Ma? Ain't there nothing we can sell...?" I whispered, trailing after her.

On the far side of the wagon Ma grabbed my shoulders. "I ain't buying nothing off Jim Lewis! Cornelia's right. Only one kind of woman stays in these camps. First chance we get we'll go back to the States, but right now we got to make-do. We're going to work for Snowy's friend Dalt, and that's it!" Ma walked away, her mouth set.

"I didn't mean nothing, Ma. It just seems mighty lonesome around here. What's it going to be like off in some cabin?"

By the time we reached the road camp at the end of the new canyon road early the next morning I felt lightheaded with hunger. The high meadow was as pretty as any place I'd ever seen.

"You come up Buffalo Canyon in the dark?" a roadman cooking coffee over a blazing campfire whooped. "Hellfire, you could've gone over the edge in half a hundred different places!"

"Seen anything of Snowy Ray?" Jim asked, accepting a cup of coffee. "I lost him in the night."

"That old reprobate! He brought a fella named Jackson up here last year. That greenhorn near to froze. It's for sure Snowy ain't brought you here out of the goodness of his heart. You're better off going back where you come from. It's for damn sure this ain't no place for them womenfolk."

"Seen him?"

"Don't get your dander up. He come through last night."

"Jim Lewis is the name. We're here to stay—me, the missus, and my girl, Effie Mae. Them two is headed someplace else."

"Dalt's," Ma said, her chin out.

The roadman grinned. "Hellfire, Ma'am! It'll be good to eat female cooking again. Dalt don't know flour from salt."

Ma sighed deep. She'd been more worried than she let on.

Snowy showed up by noon. "I been to see Dalt and he'll have the both of you, but his sleeping room is for paying customers only."

"We'll take what we get, Snowy. Thanks," Ma said.

As Snowy led us along the grassy trail beyond the cleared road, he told us how buffalo used to come up the pass that way. I could just hear ol' know-it-all Jim repeating them stories someday as if he'd seen the buffalo hisself. The trail meandered beside the creek, then veered up the mountainside. Silver Peak shimmered in the afternoon sun to our left. Pikes Peak rose to the south, majestic solid pink granite with its crest in the clouds.

After Jim made camp, Ray led me and Ma on up the mountain 'til we come upon a squat cabin laying flush to the mountainside. A few tethered horses stood outside.

"I best get back and show them folks their land," Snowy said, throwing our bundles down. "It ain't dawned on them yet that's all there is—land."

"They'll be safe, won't they?" Ma asked, fretting over Cornelia's delicate state of health.

"Safe as any, I expect. They can come stay with me if that fool can't get up a lean-to before the snow. He's got—oh, two or three hours yet." He chuckled, patting Ma's backside. "Fix some of that good cornbread when I come up later." Then he thrashed his horse 'til he was out of sight.

The hush of whispering pines closed in around us. Ma looked all around, her eyes wary. Just when we thought we couldn't stand another moment of the silence, the cabin door fell open and a man shaped like a bear, wearing red johns so thin and full of holes they fit like a second skin, stepped out.

"I told Snowy to bring me something good from civilization," the man called Dalt grinned. "Ain't you two something to look at! Can either of you cook?" His clean-shaven cheeks rounded up pink as he smiled, and he was as bald as a babe.

Though close to forty, he looked strong and wily as a wolf. His unnerving "Heh-heh-heh" set every hair on my body to prickling. His lips was, by far, his most arresting feature. Behind them sparkled clean square teeth, rare in a man so plainly used to tobacco and drink.

"My name's Lillian Pallard," Ma said, extending her hand, having taken up Pa's name again. "This is my daughter, Angela. We both cook, clean, and sew."

"*Fine*-looking woman!" he chuckled, looking Ma over from her raven hair to her dusty boots. "Best thing I've seen in five years. And the little lady…" His coffee-brown eyes twinkled as he cocked his head. "How old is this one?"

"Fourteen," Ma said, her eyes as cold and unblinking as a snake's. "She's just a child."

We stepped inside his smoky cabin, feeling his eyes on our backs as he closed and latched the door.

Three

Early Spring 1861

I dropped another armload of kindling along the outer wall of Dalt's cabin and kicked big puffs of snow ahead of me as I went back to the door.

"Say one more word like that and I'll leave!" I heard Ma hiss from inside.

"She's the kind any would want," Dalt chuckled.

"Don't let nobody lay a hand on her!" Ma snarled. "I'm warning you. I'll do what I have to, but you leave her out of it."

"You're warning me?" he laughed.

What was they talking about, I wondered. We'd been getting on well enough the past couple months, though sometimes Ma wouldn't say a word after one of Dalt's customers left. I wondered if I'd been too friendly to the one eating inside just then.

Hearing nothing more, I pulled open the door and peeked in. Dalt was bending over the cookstove in the lean-to kitchen, lighting a stogie. I didn't see Ma. When Dalt felt the cold air sweep in, his head come up sharp. "I thought I told you to gather more kindling."

A soft gasp come from back in the sleeping room where the cabin met with the rocks. "Where's Ma?" I yanked the door shut behind me, thinking he'd hit her maybe—and she was back there crying.

Ma appeared in the doorway, plucking nervously at the throat of her bodice. "Can't you do any chores like Dalt wants?"

Ma and Dalt looked at me like they couldn't stand having me around. I stomped back into the snow, grabbed up the bucket and headed toward the lake for water. I'd stay out 'til I froze!

That customer galloped away about the time I reached the lake. When my rear-end got numb from sitting on a snowy rock, I started back. Silence heavy as cook smoke hung in the air as I tiptoed inside the gloomy cabin. Looking in the sleeping room I near to fainted dead away!

Dalt was kissing Ma and his big hands was covering her breasts. They heard me gasp and jerked apart, looking guilty as thieves. "Get out before I take a strap to you!" Ma whispered. Flashing hate-filled eyes at Dalt, she yanked her bodice closed. "I said get out! I thought you knew enough to stay away." She made a face like her belly ached.

"I'm sorry, Ma. I got cold."

"Go away!" she shrieked, balling her fists and beating the air with little cries. Dalt grabbed her hands and she struck him!

I ran out, feeling so crazy I didn't know what to do. I started running down the trail and didn't stop 'til I saw a thin curl of smoke rising from Snowy Ray's chimney.

A rangy young fella with a weak-looking chest like Pa's stood in the doorway of the post. I fell into his arms, sobbing so hard I couldn't get no words out. He wore buckskins of a handmade variety I'd never seen. His black hair was as straight and long as mine was wiry. I pulled away careful. My tears dried up from the shock of realizing Snowy Ray's boy was half Injun!

Snowy pushed past him, a mouthful of food evident on his lips. "Trouble?"

"Dalt—"

"Hurt hisself, did he?" Snowy pulled up loose suspenders and reached for his rifle.

I grabbed his arm. "He's got Ma! He's going to..."

Snowy put his rifle back. "Bring her inside, Pike."

Their post was bigger than Dalt's cabin, but smokier and colder. I guessed the peculiar smell in the air to be Snowy's stocking feet 'cause he applied hisself to a rocker by the fire and propped his toes

on the hearth.

"Ain't you going to stop him?"

"Cooking wasn't all your ma was hired for. I'm surprised Dalt ain't using you, too. Must be getting old. It's a good thing you showed up 'cause Pike's no good with a needle. As you can see, I got more holes than toes. Make yourself useful, and I'll tell my boy to go easy on you when the time comes."

Suddenly the hair on my neck rose like the hackles on a cat. I looked into Pike's low-lidded black eyes and near to ran out screaming.

"Take them wet things off," Snowy said with a smirk as he went in search of his mending. Pike brung bear steaks fresh from the shed back of the post and hung them over the fire.

"If you won't help, I'll go back myself and…if Dalt's hurt Ma, I'll kill him!"

"Lil can take care of herself," Snowy said, pushing me onto a bench alongside the table. "Her kind always gets along."

I stood up to that fat little man. "What kind is that?"

He didn't even look up. "Got it in your head to scratch out my eyes, do you? My Injun boy will cut out your heart. You know damn well your ma's kind, young missy, so don't go trying my hospitality. You'll come a lot farther in this life, acting nice and pretty to match your face."

"We ain't no special kind. We're just doing the best we know how."

"Doing damn well of it, too! Sit down. You ain't got half your ma's sense. She wouldn't stick her chin out at me. She'd kiss my boots and thank me for letting her in out of the cold. The law here is, them that gots, keeps. Them that don't, asks, and asks real nice. Smile pretty for my boy. He might take a fancy to you. Elsewise, I'll chuck you out in the snow."

"My ma don't kiss nobody's boots, leastwise yours!"

"I'll check the horses now, Pa," Pike said from the shadows.

Snowy looked disgusted. "I'll do it. Talk some sense into this scrawny brat."

After he disappeared outside, I stood shivering and crying. What was the use? Ma didn't even want my help.

Pike turned me around with hands that felt kindly on my shoulders. "Don't listen to him." I was so surprised that half Injun wasn't tearing away my clothes, I just gaped. Pike didn't sound like no Injun, didn't even smell like one if Effie's stories was to be believed. "Pa forgets I was raised in a mission," he said. "I've never lifted a scalp. I'll take you back tomorrow and see if I can help. Soon as you're done eating, climb into the loft. You'll be safe with me," Pike whispered, his black eyes watching the door. "Pa ain't too old to be tempted."

"Thanks," I whispered, raising my eyes slow to meet his.

I was half asleep when Pike come up later. He crawled in bed beside me and I near to jumped out of my skin! I lay stiff as a starched shirt as he pressed against my back. "Don't be scared," he whispered, sliding his arms around me. Safe, he'd said.

He opened my shirt and reached inside. I figured if I ever got struck by a thunderbolt it'd feel like that first hand closing over my breast. I didn't breathe again 'til he took it away. Then he rolled me over and kissed my forehead with lips cool as a snowflake and fell asleep! Snowy's snores got softer after that. I figured the snake had been listening!

Was that all Dalt was doing, I wondered. Was that all any man did? It wasn't nothing to get so all-fired upset about. In fact, it had been mighty nice. I snuggled down to sleep, glad nobody could see my smile.

After two days of heavy snow, Pike rode me back to Dalt's. The cabin door was drifted over and not a print marked the snow. "Suppose they went somewhere?" Pike asked, his ruddy face sharp against all that white.

"I shouldn't have left!" I wailed, running through hip-deep snow toward the cabin.

ANGEL

The door swung into the drift. Bare-chested and grinning, Dalt swaggered out. "Thought maybe wolves got you."

I stopped short. "Spent a lot of effort looking, didn't you?"

Ma pushed past Dalt. "Angie?" She let out a cry and laid her head against Dalt's arm. "She's safe!" Clutching a blanket around her bare shoulders, she said, "Are you Snowy Ray's boy?"

"Yes, Ma'am. Brought your daughter back safe and sound."

"Where'd Jim Lewis settle?" She stepped into the snow.

"About ten miles from the freight road. I'm dropping supplies by in a few weeks. I'll give him your regards."

"You can do better than that." She jammed her money pouch into my hand. "Tell Jim this is what I owe for the ride from Denver City."

"I gave Snowy a price to bring me a woman!" Dalt said, pulling her back. "Lewis got a cut."

With sick eyes Ma said, "Please, Pike. Take Angela. Make sure she'll be kept."

"Ma! I ain't going no place without you!"

"You'll go because I said. You'll stay, and I ain't arguing." Ma looked like she did when she'd stood over Pa's body. "I don't want you with me no more, Angie."

Pike swung down from his horse, his eyes narrow and harsh. "Your ma knows what she's about."

"I don't even like Jim or Effie!"

"Lil's just been worried," Dalt said. "Looks like Pike took good care of you though. Real good—for two nights."

"I ain't done nothing!"

"Tell Jim I'll send more," Ma whispered. "Go! For me."

"I'll see she gets there, Ma'am," Pike said, taking the pouch.

When Dalt pushed Ma back inside and shut the door, Pike boosted me onto his horse, swung up behind me and plunged us down the trail.

"Don't make me go!" I cried.

• • •

27

The Lewis place sat on a hill near a shallow, ice-edged creek. Only the chimney smoke curling from the snowy mound showed folks lived there. "Hello!" Pike called out, giving me a hand down.

Cornelia opened the door, her dressing gown flapping in the wind. A shotgun lay heavy across her arm. "Oh God, Angie! It's you! Come on in! Set yourself down and get them wet things off. Are you hungry?" Cornelia pulled us into her bitter cold cabin. "Effie and me are crazy lonesome here! How's your job? How's your ma?"

I began chattering about the roadmen we'd served and complained about the work. With a silly smile Cornelia drank in every word. She looked thinner and older with her iron-colored hair straggly down her back. "Keeps me warm," she laughed, though I suspected she'd been spending her days abed. And she moved with an odd stiffness. Effie just stared into the fire, paying no mind to the Injun at her table, or me. For sure, she'd growed fat.

"Where's Jim?" Pike asked at dusk when we'd seen no sign of him.

"Hunting…in a manner of speaking." Cornelia smiled feebly as she divided the quilts on her bed. "I'm glad you're here, Pike. I need a man around. Twice wolves tore through our lean-to. Lord, will I be glad when Jim gets back!"

I nodded toward Effie. "Scared her, huh?"

Cornelia didn't answer 'til Pike finished his coffee and went to sleep by the fire. Then she pulled me aside. "You ain't said a word about your ma."

"She give me this and said pay Jim what she owes. I know she don't owe nothing. This here's payment so I can stay with you, if you'll have me. I'll work hard for you, Cornelia."

"Lord knows I could use some help. With Jim gone and Effie…" She leaned closer. "Effie mixed herself up with the fella who helped us build this cabin. Foreman of the road crew, he was. He heard Snowy Ray brought us here with no shelter, and got his men together. I'm mighty grateful, mind you, but I don't thank him for luring my girl into an assignation." She leaned closer still and whispered, "She's expecting, come July. Jim beat the daylights out of her when he found out! Now he's gone to find that fella and a preacher if he can—gone two weeks already."

"Well, it looks like Ma's got herself mixed up in…what'd you call it—an assignation?" I looked away. It was hard to imagine Ma taking up with any man but Pa.

Pike stayed a few days, fixed the lean-to, brought in two deer, sharpened the ax, and learned me how to split kindling. I kept my mind off Ma best I could by working. As time wore on, only the nights was hard. I took to sneaking a sip of Cornelia's potion to help me sleep.

Jim rode in one day a few weeks later while I was stacking, of all things, kindling. "What the hell are *you* doing here?" was his words of greeting.

"Morning, Mr. Lewis. Caught yourself a son-in-law, I see."

Following at a distance, a tall young fella led three snow-matted pack mules. I stopped smiling and my mouth went dry when I looked up at him. Effie's shotgun husband was a golden boy!

He grinned slow. "If she's the girl I compromised, Mr. Lewis, I'm real sorry I tried so hard to outrun you." He tipped back his broad-brimmed hat exposing russet-gold hair.

"I asked what you're doing here," Jim said, his lip curled like he smelled something.

"Ma sent me." I didn't offer no other words. I just handed up the pouch. Near as I could count, there was twenty-five gold dollars in it, enough to make even *me* welcome.

Jim dismounted. "How long do you mean to be here?"

"'Til spring, maybe. If you figure I ain't needed though, I'll go tomorrow." My chest began to swell with confidence. I had Jim by the short hairs! He needed Ma's money. He needed my work, and he needed lots more than Effie's fat belly to make that handsome jake stay!

"In the morning start building a shelter for the horses and mules," Jim said to his captive. "As for you, Angela, if you stay, you work. Ain't nothing else for you here. Nothing."

We settled in at the Lewis ranch with that understanding. Effie come out of her melancholy like someone raised from the dead when she saw her fella. Being a high-handed man to begin with, Jim spoke his own brand of marriage ceremony over her and that golden boy, Rusty Kennings. That necessitated the building of a new bed.

Their cover rustled near half every night, while Cornelia and Jim slept in the other bed across the room never moving. I felt right comfortable by the fire. Though I missed Ma, I liked being around Cornelia. She made me feel good and smart no matter what I did. That made up for all Effie's mean looks and Jim's aggravating Good Book quoting.

Come spring, Rusty set to fencing a corral. Effie grew bigger by the day. About the time she had nothing left to wear and was drilling our ears with her bellyaching, Jim decided to find a preacher again.

"I can't keep staying here," Rusty said, following Jim all around the barn the day Jim readied for the trip down the canyon. "I mean to make a name for myself. Don't you want your son-in-law important?"

Me and Cornelia was clearing a garden patch nearby. Effie was just standing there, looking hot and ugly.

"I wouldn't trust you across the creek," Jim snarled, cinching his horse tight. "If you're gone when I come back, your *name* will be over your grave. Soon as a preacher makes this legal, then you can go back to your crew."

"Pa, let him go if he wants."

Jim hardly glanced at Effie. "I'll go as far as Denver City this time," he said, riding out of the yard.

"Go inside and rest," I told Cornelia after Jim was out of sight. I knew working in the garden pained her, though I didn't know where. "Help Effie with that knitting."

Cornelia sighed. "You're a good girl, Angie. Leave some hoeing for me, though, hear? I'll do some later. And look out for Rusty."

I felt shamed knowing she'd seen how often he looked my way. He was digging post holes nearby. After an hour of casting smiley looks my way, he come over and brushed against me. "What's ailing the old lady? She looks ready to drop."

"Get away. I don't like you talking like that." He'd never come so close before. I felt addled and couldn't get enough air.

"Pretty girls like you get more with honey than vinegar."

"Get on about your business."

"Bothers you when I'm close, doesn't it?" He nudged me, winking. "I got one more hole to dig on the far side of the shed if you're looking for me later. You might be lonesome. I've seen how you look at me."

"I don't look at you at all! You belong to Effie."

"I must've been out of my head the day I took her into the trees. I'm not staying just because she's pregnant."

"Jim's rifle is holding you," I snapped. Sweat poured down my back though it wasn't that hot.

"He's gone," Rusty smiled, heading for the shed.

For months I'd been eating beside Rusty, hearing his snores, watching him pull off his shirt and flex them muscles. I wished I *could* have one little kiss from him before he belonged to Effie forever.

"Haven't you guessed what's keeping me here?" Rusty whispered, grabbing my hand and pulling me after him. His lips come down on mine like two coals.

Much as I hated to, I pushed him away. "I feel sorry for Effie," I said, rubbing my lips. "You ain't even trying to be a good man to her."

He kissed me again and thrust his hand inside my shirt. "If I don't get what I want, I'm leaving. I'm not saddling myself with an ugly girl who doesn't love me. I feel how you move against me. Say you want me. Say it!"

If Rusty cleared out, I'd get blamed, I thought. If I gave in...

Rusty pulled me to his chest again and opened my shirt wide. A fire started deep in my belly. He surely was a good-looking fella...

The soft crunch of footsteps come up behind us. "Rusty, the damn horse went lame. Saddle up the..." Jim choked into silence.

Pushing me away, Rusty glared at Jim. "It was bound to happen."

"Turn loose of that whore! I'm going to blast her where

she stands!"

"Are you crazy?" Rusty squawked.

Jim charged so fast, Rusty couldn't duck the rifle. He fell with a gash in his temple. Don't guess Jim had ever seen such a sight as I was, standing there with my shirt open. His whole face sagged. The rifle, too. "You're just like your ma," he said, fixing his eye on me and swallowing. "I hear she's laying for two bucks up at that cabin. Whores, the both of you!" He stepped over Rusty. "I won't have my wife hurt by what you're doing." He pushed me backward with the rifle barrel. "Cover yourself. No decent girl would stand like that, muddling a God-fearing man's thoughts. Ain't you got no shame?"

I wouldn't cry in front of that bastard—I'd die first! I tried edging past him to collect my things, but he caught my chin and held me bent so I thought he meant to break my neck. "Effie don't even love him," I said between my squeezed cheeks.

He let go and slapped me. If I hadn't scrambled away, he would've kicked me. "Run while you can, whore!"

I ran.

I ran blind scared across the sage to the mouth of the canyon. I wanted to go to the road camp. My bruised face might make the men go after Jim, but...as I tried to close my shirt, I began coughing out sobs. They couldn't do nothing. Maybe they'll call me whore, too, and pass me around camp like a canteen. All I could do was go back to Ma and Dalt. After that, my course was set.

Four

Fall-Winter 1861

"I never seen Ma so sick," I said, heating another pot of water. "Maybe some of Cornelia's potion would help."

Dalt looked up from mending the snare. In his eyes was the same fear I felt. "Think Cornelia's medicine would make her better?" Dalt asked, rubbing the back of his neck.

"Something's got to work." I turned away so he wouldn't see my chin tremble.

Ma'd felt poorly since I come back from the Lewises' in June, but wouldn't say what ailed her. I never told her about Jim and couldn't bring myself to ask if she'd been doing what he said.

At first Dalt thought Ma had eaten some bad meat. Later he said, "Must be mountain fever." As the weeks passed, though, she got worse. Dalt made her take to his so-called fancy bed back in the sleeping room. While it was a kindly gesture, a pine frame and horsehair tick didn't help much.

Now she was delirious, talking to folks I'd never heard of, crying over things she'd done that I knew nothing about. She called for Pa often enough to make Dalt jealous. 'Til then I'd worried on how to cure her. Now I wondered if I could. My belly knotted around the cold fear of seeing the light go from Ma's face, too.

Some of Cornelia's potion would've helped me get through the fearsome nights, too. She wasn't there to pray for me, and I didn't put much store in it anyway, so I took Becky's blue ribbon from my bundle of out-growed clothes and looped it around my neck like a charm.

After Dalt left for the Lewises' I sat with Ma night and day. I'd fall asleep and dream of muddy water or playing cards blowing through sagebrush. I'd wake chilled with sweat, feeling a nameless fear clutching my heart.

Finally Ma rested easier though her cheeks was flushed and her lids purple. I put my cheek close to her face to tell if she still breathed. She opened her eyes and smiled. "You looked tired, Angie."

I near to cried for joy. "I made soup, Ma! You got to start eating. The way you've wasted, you look little as me." I gave her a gentle hug. "I knew you'd get better."

I spooned soup against her dry lips, but she pushed it away. "What day is it?" she whispered.

"I ain't sure. October, probably. It's so warm out I still keep the door open. Smell the pine needles? Come sit in the sun awhile. It'll do you good. You feel kind of cold now that your fever's broke. When you're better we'll visit Cornelia and see Effie's baby. It must be three months old by now."

I paid no attention to her head shaking. For the first time in weeks I felt I could help her. As I eased Ma up, her shoulder blades dug into my arm. She floated along beside me small and trembly like an old lady. In the sunlight her skin looked kind of waxy though the sun's warmth made her smile. I sat her on a log where she could see through the pines to the meadow and I pointed out the road crew almost lost to sight on the far side of the valley. The men didn't come up to eat no more. It was too far.

"Dalt's bringing some of Cornelia's potion. Then you'll feel good," I said, jumping up to get the soup and a blanket.

Ma took my hand and wouldn't turn loose. "I feel fine."

"Dalt ain't going to work you so hard no more, Ma. Maybe we won't get back East this year, but in the spring..." She looked so puny perched there I started shaking. "One thing's for sure. You ain't sending me off no more."

"No more," she whispered, smiling, her eyes shining and sad.

"No more." She touched my hair, nodding. "My, but you're getting pretty. I always knew you would be. Said to myself the day you was born, God, look at this beautiful child you gave me. I got to do right by her." She shut her eyes tight and pinched her lips together. "I thought coming West would be good. Thought I'd bring you to some place clean and new so you'd grow up decent. I didn't lead a good life and wanted better for you. Those times I sent you off…" She lifted her chin. "You know now what I was doing, don't you? I quit after Becky come along. Swore I wouldn't go back to it, but Frank…Frank wanted to come West so bad. I thought it'd be good…for all of us. Only one way we could afford it, only one way I knew. Don't hate me, Angie!"

I slipped to the ground and laid my head in her lap. My heart hurt so it was killing me. I needed Ma strong so she'd take care of me.

"You ought to take my money and go back East," she said. "If you stay, you better marry up quick."

I forced a laugh. "Pike's nice, Ma."

"If you marry a breed, you'll be cut off from regular folks."

"Heck, Ma! Why we talking like this?"

She winced. "'Cause I ain't got long to go."

"It ain't so!"

She rubbed my shoulder. "I had my first man at your age. I was poor trash with seven sisters. Every one was pretty and quick like you. One by one we married and had babies—and starved. My oldest sister took to gathering favors from men after her husband run off. We all done it when times got hard. I did when Frank couldn't find work. Yes, I did, Angie."

"I don't believe it!"

"I been running from myself almost as long as you've been alive. You always thought I followed your pa and his hopeless dreams. I did, after a fashion. I was willing to so's he'd never find out what I did on the side. I hope he didn't. I'm sorry I killed him."

"I would've done the same!"

She looked at me long, her gray eyes solemn and luminous like the moon on a cold night. "I lost Becky because of what I done, Angie. I lost Frank. I couldn't lose you, Angie. You're so pretty now. So pretty. I tried to protect you…and just kept hurting you instead."

I pressed my face into her skirt, trying to swallow a lump choking my throat. She even smelled old. "I'm proud to be your daughter, Ma." When she didn't say nothing, I looked up. The sun caught a single tear rolling down her cheek and made it sparkle. She slipped her hand around my neck and pulled me close to kiss my forehead. I closed my eyes to fix that moment forever in my memory.

"What's this?" she asked softly, finding the blue ribbon around my neck. "Why you wearing this? This was Becky's!" She almost looked scared.

"I kept it 'cause it made me feel better, Ma. I'd always looked after Becky real good for you, and then that one time…I'm sorry, Ma! It was my fault she died. I know how you loved her."

Ma grabbed me and her fingers were sharp. "If it was anybody's fault, it was mine! Angie, look at me! Becky was a dear baby to be sure, but you, you were my special baby. You come from Frank's and my love. Maybe that love faded, but in the beginning when we was young and happy, it was mighty strong. God, Angie! Don't you know how important you've always been to me? Becky wasn't even your pa's child!"

Looking into her wild eyes I began shaking to my very bones. She untied the ribbon and smoothed it between her thin white fingers. Then she slipped her hands under my hair and pulled the ribbon up behind my ears tying it with a bow on top. She fluffed my wild black curls and patted my cheeks with hands tender and cold.

"I got Becky a ribbon that day so she wouldn't feel left out. I didn't bring you one because I was giving you something I thought was more important. Everything I did last summer was for you. You couldn't see my gift, and now it's lost forever, but I did it all for you just the same. Guess I was a fool." She smiled, her hands trembling. "Don't cry, Angie. I ain't got Frank's bright future to give you now, so you wear this ribbon proud. I am a fool! I dreamed just like Frank. Thought I was so much better. I hope he forgives me for being so stupid. Angie…if you ever have to do what I done, do it because you got to live. Don't look back."

"I won't."

"Dream, like Frank. Work hard, like me. When the right man comes along, get yourself married. Get your children book-learning and church-learning. Take 'em as far as you can. Don't look back."

I put my arms around her and held tight. If I kept her close she couldn't leave me. "I'll make you so proud of me, Ma!"

I thought of all them times she sent me off so she could earn the money Pa gambled away. I felt so downright empty-headed and selfish for hating her hard work and looking down on her when she forgot to smile. I'd never be that dumb-ignorant again. I'd show Ma I understood. I'd make her rest easy and be happy again.

I squeezed Ma tight, rocking her, kissing her. Then I had to ease her to the ground. One sharp cry come out of my throat. Then I covered my face and screamed.

Ma was gone.

There in the fading sun, I sat with Ma a long time. When I carried her inside, I warmed water and bathed her careful, like I'd seen Cornelia bathe Becky. I dressed Ma in the blue calico she'd bought back in Missouri for the trip. Her hair flowed like black silk through my fingers as I brushed it and smoothed it over the pillow.

I'd been mad 'cause Dalt took so long bringing the potion, but now I was glad to be alone with Ma. Crossing her hands at her breast, I finally bent and kissed her full on the mouth. For a moment I hurt so bad inside I couldn't straighten up. "Rest easy, Ma."

Near as I could figure, she was only thirty-two.

When Dalt rode up the trail later that day with lots of bundles sticking out of his saddlebags, he didn't see me up in the pines. I was hacking at the red dirt, trying to kill my grief with a spade. Seeing him go in the cabin, I sank down. My arms shook so bad I had to hug myself. I pictured him grinning silly as he walked in, expecting to

find me still tending Ma. I imagined him looking down at her body…
When he come charging out, I'd dried my burning eyes. He crashed
up through the pines and grabbed me up. "What happened?"

I couldn't say nothing 'til he turned loose of me. "Got any
wood for a coffin?"

"She died!" Dalt kicked the spade into the hole. We glared at
each other, the both of us hating each other's guts clean through.

"I figured you'd be put out," I muttered.

"Didn't you watch her careful?"

"*I* didn't take my sweet time fetching something that might've
eased her passing! And…" I added when his mouth dropped open,
"she told me everything."

"I'll just bet she did," Dalt barked, his nasty grin returning.

"Soon as I bury my ma, I'm leaving this stinking place."

"Back to Jim Lewis, I suppose. Hand me that spade. The grave's
got to be deeper. I wouldn't want wolves…"

Laying my hands on the handle, I swung with all my might. Dalt
caught it, pushed, and sent me sprawling. I leaped right up and hit
him square, sinking my fingers into his throat and drawing blood
before he pinned back my arms. I cried, bit his shirt, and cussed him
'til I was so tired I just wanted to lay down beside Ma. "Where's her
money?" I said, pulling free when the urge to kill him left me.

My neck almost snapped when Dalt slapped me. "You ain't
going no place. What your ma and me had going was our business,
so you don't talk against her. We had to survive."

I swung to slap him. He caught my wrist and about squeezed
the bones flat. "I ain't talking against Ma. I'm talking against you!"

"You're as stupid as that Effie. God, I hope I never spend
another day listening to her bellyaching. I went all the way to Tempest
for real medicine, not that laudanum Cornelia guzzles. She might as
well drink whiskey few all the good it does her. Didn't know your
upstanding Cornelia can't last an hour without it, did you? You really
think I would've taken so long if I'd known Lil was dying?"

"Get out of my way."

"Your ma would want you to stay with me."

"She wouldn't! If I stay, folks'll call me names. Ma wasn't bad, but Jim Lewis said…He ain't never worked as hard as Ma, but he's a man, an important man hereabouts, and what he says is what folks'll hear."

"Jim Lewis is a jackass."

"He called Ma a whore!"

Dalt pulled me back toward the cabin. "If you was a man with a shovel, what would you do?"

"Dig."

"And a man with a rifle hunts. I sell whiskey, though I grant you, it ain't much. Last summer prices went sky high in Tempest. Your ma could earn more money than me. And we needed it. Stand still and listen! Jim's calling names so nobody'll notice his stupid ugly daughter got herself married and three days later birthed a nine-pound boy. Folks are laughing out the other sides of their mouths. Hell, Angie, don't spit fire at me. I cared for your ma."

I pushed through the door and sank onto a stool. "What am I to do then?"

Dalt fingered the ribbon in my hair. "Stay with me."

I yanked the ribbon out and hid it in my fist.

I never got to see Effie's baby. As winter come on I don't know what folks thought of me living in Dalt's cabin. If they thought anything at all, they kept it to theirselves.

Dalt made another trip to Tempest and bought new johns and a fine shearling coat. For me he got boots and woolies. He was content to mind his manners 'til one night in December when a blizzard hit. Then he began drinking his own whiskey to pass the hours. When he ran out of easy talk I felt something in the air like the hush before a thunderclap. His eyes strayed my way. I knew then he was over losing Ma.

For every stitch I took in Dalt's socks, for every tight nervous breath I drew, I knew my time had come. At fifteen I still didn't

SAMANTHA HARTE

know more awaited me in the arms of a lusty man than looking
and touching.

"Come here and sit with ol' Dalt," he said from the chair by
the fire.

The wind howled across the face of the mountain, freezing me
where I sat. My cheeks burned soon as I neared him. Dalt drained
his bottle and tossed it. Though I could smell his breath, it wasn't
unpleasant I'd growed to expect it in a man.

He laid me across his lap and pushed up my woollies. His palms
felt rough as pine bark. I didn't like him pulling my drawers down
or hustling me back to the sleeping room where the wind didn't
reach. Then in the orange shadows I noticed something about Dalt
had changed.

Pushing me back on the tick and taking my clothes, he began
unbuttoning his johns farther than they'd ever been undone before.
He laid on me and something new and terrible began happening,
something painful that I couldn't stop. Dalt moved against me,
breathing hard, whispering and pressing me into that horsehair tick
'til he moaned and fell spent. The fullness and pain went away. When
he rolled away, no strange shadow tantalized my ignorant eyes.

"My first virgin," he chuckled softly. "I'm forty-two years old
and never had one. Damn! I'm going to teach you things that'll make
you the best damn woman this side of Missouri."

After he got up and pulled up his johns, I lay shivering, touching
myself where he'd touched me. I was sore and tingly, like maybe I'd
get used to what he'd done!

When he come to me again before I woke, pure naked and
ready for more, I curled against his warmth before realizing what was
happening. "Oh, no!" I said, trying to wriggle free of his caresses.
"You ain't making me your whore, too."

He froze. His body crushed me. "Who said anything about that?
Whoring means taking money for this. Am I giving you money? No,
I ain't and don't intend to. I'll care for you, protect you, feed you. In
return you warm my bed. This is what men and women do together,
all men and all women, except dried up pious old goats like Lewis,

40

sick ones like Cornelia, and maybe spinsters. Your ma and pa, Effie and Rusty, all men and women healthy and having a need for each other just naturally want to hop into the nearest soft place and horse around. Last time, it hurt 'cause you was a virgin. I honestly figured Pike took care of that. Seeing as how he didn't, it's up to me to teach you. It ain't whoring unless you do it with a stranger for money."

He didn't give me no chance to protest. He just used me again, longer, but gently. There was moments I thought I might stay. What he did felt mighty fine, but in the cold clear dawn, I thought on what I'd done. While he slept I gathered my things and lit out.

Down past the pines I stumbled through snow two feet deep. The wind drove icy bits in my face so I couldn't see. I scarcely made three miles before my legs gave out. Snowy Ray's post seemed to have disappeared in a howling mass of white fury.

By afternoon I knew Dalt wasn't following me. I was a bit sorry, fearing I meant nothing to him after all. Hopelessly lost and feeling foolish and scared, I crawled under the drooping boughs of a big spruce to wait out the storm. Snow fell most of the next day. The wind couldn't get to me, so I slept awhile. By morning I was so cold and wet I knew one more day there would kill me.

I slipped in and out of a numbing sleep, wondering if I'd really left Dalt 'cause I'd liked what we'd done but didn't want to think I come natural to such wickedness. I wanted to talk to Effie, too. She'd got herself laid out, just like me. Was Dalt right that folks come by that need naturally? Did Effie?

For a time I slept near death under that tree. Being dead, just drifting off like that, had to be easier than deciding what to do. Should I go on or crawl back to Dalt and try leaving him in the spring?

Guess I'm trying to say I didn't choose the easy way. My toes grew warm with frostbite. My mind grew weak and cloudy. What got me to my feet and back through the pines wasn't hunger or the fear of death.

I lifted each leg and stepped into snow so deep sometimes I got stuck. I'd lay back to pull my legs free and then throw myself forward. Each step was all I could think about. Pull free and fall forward. Pull free and fall.

The chimney smoke curled high into the clear night sky. Coyotes cried back and forth in the timber. I wondered if I was being stalked by wolves. I'd been gone near three days but the snow around the cabin sparkled in the moonlight pure and untouched. I plunged the last few yards, thinking maybe I'd come back all that way to find Dalt drowned in his own whiskey.

I didn't have the strength to knock. I just fell against the door and butted it with my hip. The door fell open. Dalt hadn't shaved and, indeed, smelled so high of liquor I wondered what kept him standing. He began laughing so hard he had to hold onto the door. "Don't nobody in the road camp want a high and mighty puss like yourself? Price too damn high?"

I didn't have the strength to look mad. I knew what I had to do. "I'm sorry."

"You're sorry! You hear that?" he yelled out, his voice echoing across the valley. "This little lady is sorry!" He sneered. "I take you to my bed like my own woman, scrawny and ignorant as you are. You run off to tell the whole world I raped you. Now you're sorry."

"I ain't been to the camp," I panted. His face grew dim and swam before my eyes. "I didn't even make Snowy Ray's." Holding to what honor I had, or knew enough about to abide by, I said, "I won't leave again 'til you throw me out. I want to be with you."

That snuffed his smile. "I thought you came to eat and get warm and pay with your inexperienced brand of charms."

"I am hungry," I said, my knees folding. "And I'm so cold I'll be dead soon if you don't let me in; but if I got to die, I want to die with someone I know."

At that, the wolves that had been following me, attacked, their red lips drawn back over gleaming yellow fangs. Dalt jerked me inside and bolted the door, a look of shock on his face that told me he cared—if just a little. Sprawled at his feet, listening to claws rip the door to splinters, I knew I was where I belonged.

Dalt carried me to the fire and stripped away my wet clothes. He opened his shirt and laid my blue feet on his hairy chest; then my hands; then my cheeks. By then I guess he figured the full treatment was called for, so he carried me to bed, laying his warmth full length against me.

Life's pain come back to my limbs as he kissed me. I gave up wondering if other women liked lying close to a man. I did. I opened my arms to learn how to keep Dalt wanting me.

Five

Spring 1862

"I ain't no Injun wife you got to hide!" I cried, climbing out of bed.

Dalt's eyes narrowed. "You ain't no wife at all. I never had one and sure wouldn't pick you to be it. You're nothing more than my woman; and I ain't taking you to town, looking like that."

"I could wear a full skirt. Nobody'd notice how fat I'm getting."

Dalt snorted. "Fat goes in a corset. What you got will just cry like a coyote. I won't have the whole valley knowing about it."

I opened my shirt and spread my hands over my round belly. "Then I figured right. I'm expecting."

"If you didn't know that already, you're a pretty dumb-ignorant girl."

I marched up to him and poked my finger into his chest. "I don't call you names or go off leaving you to the wolves."

"The wolves are in the high timber, so quit your squalling." Taking up his supplies, Dalt headed for the door. The sun was baking through the roof, bringing the smell of rotted timber and wet pine needles inside. Frowning, Dalt turned. "Close up your shirt, Angie. Ain't you got no shame?"

'Course I did, but by then I knowed the power of my body. I could get Dalt to sweet talk me, saying I was the best he'd ever had. I could get him to hunt up fresh meat if I was hungry. He'd have a hard time, refusing to take me to Tempest, if I let his eyes wander over me.

Dalt sighed and held out his arm. I rushed to hug him, pressing my face into his coat, smiling to myself.

"I still ain't taking you, Angie. I ain't being mean. I'm just not taking you."

I jerked away.

"You want me thrown in jail? You ain't near old enough to be in my bed, much less carrying my child."

"Marrying up would change that," I said, tugging on his arm like a spoiled child.

"For the last and final time, no. I ain't marrying you."

"This here will be a bastard!"

"I'm a bastard myself. It ain't hurt me none."

"It give you a thick skull." I turned away, buttoning up, not knowing how much anger I dared let him see.

Dalt went out and swung up on his horse. He fixed his hat over his eyes. "I'll bring you something, Angel."

I slammed the door. Only a bit of sunlight got through the chinks in the logs. I was supposed to patch them. I was supposed to jerk elk and bear meat, cook up berry jellies, mend the bed tick, and make him a new shirt. When the hoofbeats died away I burst out crying. Two years in the mountains! Every time I tried to get away I was stopped by snow or some damn fool man.

After Dalt had been gone a month, I was crazy for the sight of another person. At night I feared the howling wolves and the possibility of a stray man happening on me. I worried about running out of food. Worst of all, I missed Dalt—and his loving. My dreams would've set timber afire. I'd wake sweating and aching and go to the door, listening to the wind, the far-off rush of water, the crack of twigs. The sky would be dusty with stars. Sometimes the moon would look so close I thought I could reach up and touch it.

As my belly swelled, it didn't seem possible a little creature could be growing in there, a child the result of me and Dalt bedding. I felt small and helpless, full and hopeful, all at the same time. I guess I loved Dalt as much as any girl almost sixteen and birthing her first baby could. I didn't want to think he'd abandoned me.

So the day I did hear hoofbeats on the trail I pushed my wild hair out of my face and pinched my cheeks. With the first knock, I knew it wasn't Dalt. Taking up the shotgun, which I couldn't shoot worth beans, I crept to the door. "Who's out there?"

"It's me, Angela. Pike."

I quick put down the shotgun, looking for a place to hide!

"Angie?" His voice sounded so delicious. I couldn't resist opening the door a crack. I needed to talk to somebody more than I feared being seen in the full flower of my predicament.

"Remember me?" he grinned.

"Your hair's shorter," I said, thinking he didn't look nothing like his former self. He wasn't scrawny or weak-chested. His skin looked redder, his eyes more fiery and snapping. "You look taller."

"I am taller. You going to let me in?"

I just plain wanted to crawl away and die. Pike had growed into a fine-looking man. I opened the door just enough to let him in. The firelight glowed on his grinning red face in a way that sparked me.

"What you holed up for when it's so nice out?"

"I'm cooking," I lied. (I'd been sewing a baby dress.)

"You're still the prettiest girl in Buffalo Canyon."

"Ain't much choice between me and Effie," I said, giggling. "Least, I hope not. Seen Cornelia?"

"Yep. She's got herself a regular house now, upstairs bedrooms and all. Effie lives in the cabin. Her boy's a fat little rascal."

"Almost two, if I count right. Dalt told me Rusty took off," I said.

"Jim'll find him."

I laughed. "Sit down. I'll get some coffee."

Pike followed me into the lean-to where more sun got through the chinks. "Nobody's heard a word from up here in over a year," he said. "Cornelia would visit, but she's been sick. Where's Dalt and your ma?"

I poured coffee, wishing he'd turn away. I couldn't think. Suddenly he grabbed my shoulders and kissed me full on the mouth! I dropped the pot and stood shaking. By thunder, he had changed!

"I been wanting to do that so long!" he grinned.

I backed away not trusting myself. "Ma's dead...since last fall."

Pike sighed and shoved his hands in his pockets. "I'm sorry, Angie. Cornelia will be mighty sorry to hear that. If I'd known, I wouldn't have been so bold." A new thought formed in his head and he looked hard at me. "Has Dalt been good to you?"

"He went off to Tempest last month. I hate being here alone."

"You should've gone with him. There's all kinds of new towns springing up, some as high as timberline. Folks are pouring in. Did you know this is called Colorado Territory now? It's got its own governor and militia. I tried to join up, but they don't want breeds. They're fighting Indians and Confederates."

"What's that?"

"Haven't you heard about the war? The South's trying to secede from the Union. Had a big battle south of here to keep Colorado Territory for the North. Big battles back East."

"I'll fix some supper," I said, not understanding or caring.

"Aren't you glad to see me?" Pike pulled me close. "I figured you and me...I figured we liked each other some." He held me so tight I was scared he'd feel my belly. I tried to ease away, but darned if I didn't start pressing against him as hard as he did me. "Didn't you think about me at all?" His hands found their way inside my shirt as we kissed.

"I thought about you," I whispered angrily. "I wanted to find you last winter, but the snow stopped me. I had to come back."

Pike pushed back my shirt baring my breasts to his hands and lips. When he kissed me deep and then held me pressed against his neck, I thought I'd die from the pure pleasure of it. He smelled so good of pine and leather I wanted to hold him forever. "When's Dalt coming back?" he whispered.

"I don't know."

"He shouldn't have left you alone," Pike said, looking down

at me, his eyes growing wide with desire. Suddenly his bottom lip come up tight. I saw hurt in his eyes.

Hanging my head, I said, "He didn't want nobody knowing about this." I spread my hands over my skirt to show what I'd hoped to hide before.

"He raped you?"

I couldn't look at Pike square. Maybe thinking of something else would keep me from crying, I thought, reaching for a bag of meal.

"Did he take you by force?" Pike's voice was cold.

"I didn't really know what he was doing." That was true enough, but it come out sounding like I'd been guiltless. I should've told Pike flat out I was Dalt's woman, but Dalt was gone. I was lonely. Maybe Pike would marry me.

When I served up supper—listening for trail sounds—I let my shirt hang open just enough to keep Pike's mind where I wanted it. He told me about his travels in the mountains, the towns, and mines he'd seen. All the while he looked on me with longing. When he pulled me to his lap, I was ready. I let him carry me back to the bed.

Pike loved me slow and easy as if enjoying me like a good meal. He brought me to tears with want, pulled my heart out and wrung the desire from it 'til I quivered in his hands like a helpless creature. He spent hisself inside me, crying out some word I didn't know, then kissed my face as if thanking me for the joy of it. I clung to him, telling myself what I'd done was right.

But all night I lay awake beside him—crying. I wanted Pike to marry me and I'd asked with my body. That was wicked.

Next morning he was up early. I hurried to warm some coffee. When he didn't say nothing I began feeling uneasy. I watched his arms rippling with power as he stoked the fire. His gentleness the night before seemed all the more appealing.

"With your hair cut you don't hardly look like a breed."

"Sometimes it's easier to hide it," he said, looking sad.

"Is your pa still running the trading post?"

"Nope. He took off," Pike rubbed sleep from his black eyes. "He's probably still selling land, though he has to look farther to find greenhorns. Fellas like Saunders write in newspapers about speculators. Folks stake claims more careful now and register with land offices."

"You're not leaving already?" I cried, seeing him pull on his boots.

"You're coming with me," he said. "Dalt's left you."

I backed away. "He just didn't take me 'cause he didn't want to get throwed in jail. He'll come back."

"Folks would've made him marry you. Then, at least, after they strung him up you'd get his property." His eyes flashed. "That's what I'd do."

"String him up! I'm sixteen, Pike! I buried my own ma, saw my pa killed and my baby sister drowned. I ain't to be treated like no child."

"I'll take you to Cornelia's, then." He pulled on his shirt. "I wish you'd stayed there."

"Jim hates me."

"That don't make no sense."

"Does to him. He called me a whore and throwed me off his place! I wouldn't ask him for help if I was bedded up with the devil hisself."

Pike glared at me. "Why'd he call you that?"

"'Cause Dalt made Ma earn money from his customers. He would've made me, too, if he'd got the chance."

"Would you have?"

"I'd have died without Dalt!"

"Would you?" My arm hurt where he grabbed me. The firelight threw Pike's face into a scary mass of red and black shadows.

Pike was a mighty handsome fella and I would've dearly loved crawling in bed with him again, but he had a way about him, a way that reminded me a powerful lot of Jim Lewis. He could look mighty cold and pious in the face of a girl's ignorant reasoning. Seems church-learning put matters of judgment in men's minds. I didn't look to be judged by no half-breed Injun, or any of Jim Lewis's breed. I intended to live best I could, sinning and not sinning as life saw fit to deal me.

"Dalt ain't planning to marry you."

"I know, but he's honest about it. Are you figuring to?"

Pike only thought about it a second, but it was pause long enough. "I'll marry you," he said.

Them was the saddest words I'd ever heard. "I wish you'd rode up last year," I sighed, my heart aching. Seems I could only taste happiness before I had to spit it out. I wanted to press myself to Pike's chest and feel his arms across my back once more, but it was no use. "I ain't going."

Sorry as I felt, a weight lifted from my heart. I smiled as he ducked out into the sunlight. I waved as he rode away. I didn't cry, though my throat ached. I went back in the dark cabin and washed up. I done right, I told myself over and over. Only once did I stop to put my hand on my belly and remember the love I felt for that breed.

The rain and cold in August must've put a damper on Dalt's carousing in Tempest 'cause he showed up late one afternoon after I'd resigned myself to living alone. "Angel?" he yelled from the trail. "I'm back!"

I couldn't believe my ears! He rode a big black stallion, sitting on a tooled saddle trimmed in silver. His Stetson and shiny black knee-high boots made him look taller and younger. As he swung down and swept me into his arms, the fringe on his leather coat danced. He had to be the finest piece of man-flesh I'd ever laid eyes on. "You been gone so long I thought you died!"

"I'm rich, Angel! Richest damn dude in Tempest, Colorado Territory."

"You went prospecting?" I cried. My hands itched when he ripped open a brown paper package and pulled out a length of yellow calico.

"Hell, I ain't dumb enough to dig for gold. I just let little cards make my fortune."

"You was gambling?"

"I drew four pretty ladies and fooled them bucks. I bet this damned hole, my horse, my clothes—and won."

"You bet the roof over my head?"

"I won."

"You could've lost and I'd be birthing your bastard in the snow!"

"I ain't stupid like your pa. I knew I'd win. I don't do it 'cause I can't help myself. Right now there's more money in Tempest than a decent man can carry. Figured some ought to be mine. Get that high and mighty look off your face. You look like a skinned cat. You been pining for me?"

I went back inside the cabin.

"I'm sorry, Angel honey. I thought maybe you'd be gone. It took a long time to hit the jackpot, but I did. Wait 'til you see what I brought."

I couldn't talk.

He stomped out, cussing his pack mules, throwing packages down so hard the wrapping paper busted open. I didn't like making him mad right off, but I didn't like thinking I'd given up Pike for a gambling man.

Dalt set something heavy by the fireplace. "Dammit, look at it. I had it made special. I went through hell getting it up here."

Warm firelight bathed a polished pine cradle. It rocked so gently I could almost imagine the wave of a tiny fist, a little face like Dalt's…I busted out laughing and a flood of tears poured down my face. I couldn't stop even after Dalt cuddled me. "Don't you like it?"

I punched his chest. "You damned snake! I'm hungry and tired and scared. I'm crazy lonesome. I hate you. Oh! how I hate you. I thought you'd left me!"

By late November I looked like I was going to bust. I didn't recall Ma looking so big when Becky was expected. For once I could stand by while Dalt did all the work. "I don't suppose Tempest has a decent doctor," I said, getting a perverse pleasure feeling so helpless and female.

"You don't need one." Dalt paused over the chopping block,

licking sweat from his upper lip.

"You planning to help me?"

"I seen a squaw have her baby by the trail once. Nothing to it."
He swung again and split the pine log clean through.

"Supposing something goes wrong?"

"If it'll make you feel better I'll fetch Cornelia." He set up
another log and swung at it.

I didn't think she'd come, but I said, "Fetch her today. Bring
anybody. I ain't no squaw."

"When it's time I'll go."

"You was ready enough all them times you wanted to bed me!
Now you can't get on your fancy horse when I need something. I
could die, you know. It's been known to happen."

Dalt squinted at me and set down the hammer and wedge.
"You expecting trouble?"

"I'm only sixteen. I ain't come this far to die in childbirth. And
I don't want my baby dying 'cause I'm too ignorant to birth it right."

He left next morning. In my efforts to hurry him along, I scared
myself. The least little twinge from my kicking belly sent my heart
a-racing. By sundown I realized I hadn't felt no more movement.
I paced away the hours, worrying like never before. If I knew just
one prayer…

My pains started just as the moon rose over Silver Peak. They
was light at first, but by dawn I was wore out from walking back and
forth to the door. At noon my belly ached long and hard, wearing at
my strength, filling my throat with fears I could only half imagine. I
tried telling myself birthing was as natural as breathing and wound
up crying into my apron for Ma.

Near dusk I heard the creak of a wagon. I couldn't get up no
more so I laid there, straining to hear who Dalt brought. The cabin
come alive with noise. Not only had he brought Cornelia, whose
voice I heard saying, "Take me to her," soft and sicklylike, he'd
brought mule-mouthed Effie and the loudest squawling child I'd
ever heard.

"We would've come sooner if we'd knowed you was expecting,"

Cornelia said, smiling as she tiptoed in. "How you feeling, honey? How long's it been hurting?"

I grabbed her hand. "It ain't stopped for hours. Cornelia, I'm dying! My baby won't come out."

"All babies come out sooner or later." She pulled the bedcovers back and opened my legs. "You ain't even broke water. It'll be a sight easier if you let up on my hand and relax. Ain't nothing to ease the pain but taking command of your fears and saying, 'I'm in the hands of the Lord.'"

Having no answer to that, I laid back, my belly clenched and the pain between my legs like nothing in this world.

Cornelia put a kettle to boil and soon as she'd washed, put her hand in to see what she could figure of my situation. "Rest now," she said, wiping the blood on the sheet. "I'm going to let Effie help you and I'll quiet Todd. He's been crying all day."

"Thank you for coming, Cornelia."

"Nothing could've kept me away, Angie. Rest easy now. Effie will be just as much help as me. She's strong enough to wait it out."

"Am I going to die?"

"Not if I got any say with the Almighty. I know more prayers than you can shake a stick at!"

Soon as she left, my waters broke, soaking the tick and shaming me 'cause I didn't understand it. Effie settled herself on the bed with a sigh. "Got yourself in a pretty fix, didn't you?" she snickered. I marveled at how much uglier she'd growed. "Get them candles in here. I ain't working this miracle in the dark," she called.

Dalt set three candles on a stool near the foot of the bed. In the dancing yellow light his face looked tight and sickly. I knowed the red dust was calling me. Them candles burned to stumps as I writhed far into the night. Effie fell asleep only to wake when I screamed.

"Damn you," she muttered. "Scared me to death. I didn't scream once. Why'd you get yourself mixed up with an old coot like Dalt? Best you could get? My husband is the handsomest man in the valley. Spread your legs there, Angie. Push. Now, hold still. Damn it all, I don't know nothing about this. I got to wake Mama. Stay right there and don't scream. I don't want Todd waking up."

Cornelia hobbled in, washed, and checked my progress while I held the pillow over my face and screamed my lungs raw. "Sure enough," she whispered to Effie. "Wrong end first."

"She needs a doctor, Mama," Effie hissed. "Did I bleed that much?"

"Hush!"

"Mama, do you know how to get it out? Send that no-account man for a doctor!"

"She ain't getting no better help than we can give her. Wash up and reach in there to pull that arm free. It's that or watch Angie die."

"I can't! You do it!"

Cornelia pushed Effie toward the washbasin and poured steaming kettle water over Effie's hands. "I'm scalded!" Effie yowled.

A delicious wave of hot pleasure pulsed through me. Arching up to meet my pain, I smiled at the wall. Cornelia didn't wait to dry her daughter's flaming hands. "Free that baby's arm," she hissed.

By then I didn't care if Effie pulled me inside out. As soon as she withdrew her bloodied hand, though, I felt the pressure give.

"Don't go blaming me if I broke it," Effie whimpered.

"Here it comes, Angie. Hold on a little longer."

Effie and Cornelia was so busy I didn't know or care what they was doing. I just thanked whatever God there might be for setting me free of the pain. For sure I figured I'd died and didn't much mind the idea.

Softly, though, came a gurgly mew. Cornelia raised tear-filled eyes. "She's alive!"

Cornelia packed me with all the clean rags I had, then sank to her knees at my bedside. I felt cut away, floating in a painless fog, not knowing why she prayed so feverishly.

"Mama, get up. Go back to sleep. I'll look after Angie."

"Amen," Cornelia whispered.

"There you go, Angie," Effie sighed, laying my baby in my arms all wrapped cozy in a little quilt. Then she brushed at her bloodied skirt. "I hope to God you don't have no more babies any time soon. I'm wore out."

Cornelia pulled herself up and was heading out the door when Effie passed me, muttering, "Just what this world needs, one more hussy's bastard brat." Cornelia's hand striking Effie's face sounded like a pistol shot.

I saw Dalt grab Effie's arm and twist it. I hadn't realized he'd been near all along, sweating and drinking steady. I was too weary to watch if he'd wring Effie's neck there or take her outside to do it. Next morning he just took them back to their ranch and made record time returning to see if I still lived.

Three days passed before I opened my eyes to the world and the whimpers of my pale child. When I put her to nurse, she knew what to do even though I didn't.

Oh, she was small! I marveled at her beautiful smooth face and downy curls. All she did was sleep or mew, beating the air with curled fists no bigger than a kitten's paw. I never got tired of all the funny faces she made. To have her suck at my breast made me feel wonderful. I was everything in the world to her. After a week, though, I could still almost see through her skin.

All that time Dalt never came to my bed. "I can't sleep in here," he'd say, hurrying out soon as he brought food, clean rags, or the chamber pot. "The air smells...thick." He meant to say it smelled of blood.

"I need you," I whispered. My voice was so quiet the December winds near to swept it away. "Look at her, Dalt. She's yours, too."

"I can't, Angel. I don't know what's wrong with me."

So me and baby Lillian, as I come to call her, slept alone. Ice formed on the rock walls. The snow fell, drifting against the walls, filling chinks I'd neglected. Eighteen sixty-three come in on the tail of a howling blizzard. Dalt spent hours tending his horse and mules to keep them from freezing.

I grew stronger and made plenty of milk though baby Lillian didn't drink enough to suit me. I cared for her from the bed, dressing her in the calico gowns I'd stitched, petting her, admiring her, talking to her of the day I'd take her into the spring sunshine.

"That'll pink up your cheeks and make you fat and sassy," I'd say. "If Dalt don't want us, then I'll do for you what Ma done for me. I won't never send you off. We'll be together, just you and me." I held her close to give her all my warmth. I'd look down on her as she slept and try to send my strength into her. I still didn't hold much store in praying, but if there was a God, I asked Him real nice to give my baby a chance.

Soon, I could get up and answer nature myself, but I never strayed far from my child. She was my very own, with black hair as silky as Ma's and my pa's sky-blue eyes. I dreamed of the day she'd call me "Ma." And though I worried she wasn't growing much, I knew if I watched her close and kept her warm she'd be with me always.

One night she let me sleep 'til dawn with out a single cry. I woke refreshed, feeling well for the first time. Near as I could figure, it was February. I hoped Dalt would go for fresh meat. I was hungry.

As it turned out, he left the very next night.

He left straight from the mountainside behind the cabin, where fresh-turned frozen red dirt lay stark against knee-deep snow. He left, and I wanted him to, 'cause that morning I woke feeling so good…baby Lillian lay beside me still and cold, her delicate life having left me while I slept.

Six

Summer 1863

I threw logs on the fire 'til flames leaped halfway up the rock chimney. The heat seared my face and made my breasts, rock hard with undrunk milk, tingle with pain. I had no potion to ease the sorrow, nothing to kill the pain. Warm blood seeped onto my rags as I lifted the cradle and dropped it with a grunt into the fire. Red tongues licked the sides, turning the golden pine black. I held tight to my belly as my chest heaved with unshed tears. I'd make myself forget.

Suddenly, I let out a howl and dragged the smoking cradle into the cold room, smothering the glowing rockers with water. I fell to my knees curling over 'til my forehead touched the frozen floor. By thunder, I'd never call on Cornelia's God again!

Dalt come back about April. I went right to making coffee as if he hadn't been gone three months. He come in and dropped his pack and a mess of pelts across the table. "Feeling better?"

"I'm mending. You?"

He ran a scratched hand over his shaggy beard, looking so old I felt a mite sorry for him. He smelled worse than a skunk and looked like he'd been through mud, briar, and maybe a couple of Injun wars. His hat was ruint from the rain, and his clothes was so tore up I'd never be able to mend them. "I come back for one reason," he said.

"I ain't healed enough to bed with you. Don't know if I'll ever be. The point is, I ain't ready in my heart, neither."

"I got more on my mind than that."

I did think he looked disappointed. "I'll fix you something to eat."

After a couple of minutes of clearing his throat and fidgeting, Dalt sat. "I'm sorry about everything," he said, his eyes growing soft. "You're keeping them graves up real nice."

I went to him and touched his shoulder. He laid his head on my flat belly, his hand trembling across my back. After we ate, he said, "I can't live here no more. When I came back from Tempest last, I didn't tell you I won more than money. Now I'm figuring to go take a look at the business I won, maybe sell it. I'll give you enough money to catch a stage for Denver City, and you can go back East."

"Don't you want me in Tempest with you?"

He chewed his lip. "It's a wild place crawling with greenhorns, old-timers from California, and hard rock miners—no place for a lady."

"I never been accused of being a lady. What's the business?"

"A dancehall. I guess you could stay there if you wanted, maybe make a couple of friends, have some good times."

"A dancehall is just another name for a whorehouse."

Dalt shrugged. "Every saloon has a few girls to service the customers. It ain't a real cathouse—just a business like any other. If you ever had a hankering to be rich, that would be one way to do it."

"Am I hearing you right?" I cried.

"Decide what you want. I'm going to Tempest."

The canyon had changed so I hardly recognized it. A rickety rail built along the steep edge kept greenhorns on the road. Them bright-eyed emigrants didn't look much different than we had three years earlier. Tempest had growed into the worst mess of buildings I'd ever seen. Except for the main street following an old trail straight up the mountain, there wasn't another track you could call a real street. A conglomeration of stores and buildings had sprung up on either side; some two stories, some brick or stone, but mostly raw pine.

Cabins and tents dotted both sides of the canyon. Wagons, buggies, and logging carts choked the street. I almost laughed to see wheels mired in red mud, hear cussing and see the faces purple with anger. Three years fell away. I felt like that wide-eyed girl from Missouri seeing a boomtown for the first time.

Dalt grinned as we started up the steep street. He pointed out the emporium, land office, and bathhouse, where men stood six deep. "Must be dressing up for Bess's tonight," Dalt said. "She's got enough rules to be a schoolmarm. A man's got to be wearing scraped boots and a necktie to walk in her place. You'll like her."

At the top of the street we could see the whole town. Its life pulsed in me, bringing a cautious smile to my lips and a spark of hope to my heart. I hugged Dalt's arm. "I'm glad I come."

Across the street stood a two-story false-fronted saloon of weathered gray pine. It was smaller than I'd expected. Lacy curtains fluttered in the three open upstairs windows.

"What's them words?" I pointed to the white lettering across the front windows.

"Says, 'Bess's Dancing Salon.' The little sign by the door says, 'No drunks allowed. Dancing 50¢. Gentlemen preferred.'"

"Says all that, does it?"

When we walked in the dancehall's double doors, I saw Bess herself. That's when my education began. It was mid-afternoon, mind you. She'd been awake all of an hour. Hunched over a wobbly round table, she poured whiskey into a coffee mug to cool the thick black mess I supposed actually was coffee!

"Nobody's allowed in here before five o'clock! Get the hell out 'fore I blow off what you sure would hate to part with." Bess turned slow. A shotgun lay across her lap completely hid by the width of her.

"Didn't I tell you I'd be back?" Dalt grinned, taking a spread-eagled stance.

"Damn, Jack! I'd hoped never to see the likes of you again. You still think this here's your place! Hell! Get some cards and let me win it back real quick."

"I'll sell it back to you," he said, grinning like I'd seen him the very first time. His eyes glittered hard and unnatural, at least it seemed unnatural to me 'cause I knowed the kind of man he was inside.

Bess raised herself out of the chair slow as a sunrise. She dropped the shotgun on the table and threw back her hair. "The hell you will."

She stood near as tall as Dalt. Her hair was brown, yellow, and gray in little waves all down her shoulders. Her wide, flat cheeks came almost even with the tip of her nose, and her lips was still tinted red at the edges.

She smelled high of liquor and dusting powder. Her morning wrapper was a color and design I'd never seen in all my life, partly red, purple, and green. It clung to her soft sloping shoulders by some kind of magic and her pillow-sized breasts flowed and wiggled with each step, as did the rest of her. Sticking out the bottom of that ruffled wrapper was a pair of sturdy miner's boots.

"And *what* have we got here?" She prowled around me, her eyes swelling. "Where did you find me this darling girl?"

Dalt kept hisself just enough between me and Bess so she couldn't touch me. "This is Angela."

"Not the little lady you been keeping up at your cabin? Why, you old dog. She ain't more than twelve. Thirteen, maybe."

"Almost seventeen," I said, disliking the way she eyed my shape.

Bess laughed, looking at Dalt out of the corner of her eye. "You old devil. You been bedding a child."

He drew me aside. "Sit with Bess. If I don't get a bath and shave, she'll throw me out." He rubbed his stubble. "I think she could do it!"

I edged closer and sat across from her. Bess's slithery eyes shined as she gulped her coffee. "He brung you here to work."

"He brung me here to cook. I can sweep, sew, make beds, empty slop pails, and scrub, too. I ain't here to lay with men."

Her eyebrows shot up. "I got me a Yankee freed slave sweeping up. A California Chinee cooks and changes the linens. They work so damn cheap I figure I'll roast in hell for what I pay them. You ain't the dumb beasts they are. You'd tire of the arrangements real quick. Nope, I keep things like they are. You want to cook, go to the Red Rock Restaurant. You want to sew, see Molly James. You come here, you work upstairs like the rest."

"No."

"Then git the hell out! You're giving the place a bad name. I don't give a hoot in hell if Jack thinks he owns this place. He don't and that's it. Thinks he can bring me his...what the hell are you, honey, if you ain't a whore? Jack Dalton's goddamned wife?"

I gave her a look of pure hate and walked out. I found Dalt jawing with a bunch of fellas out front of the bathhouse. "Show me a restaurant or dress shop."

Dalt looked at me like I was a stranger. "Eating house is right across the way, Ma'am. Can I help you across the mud?" He took my arm and led me between the wagon traffic. "They won't let you work here. The cheap labor's going to freed slaves and Chinamen. If you stay in Tempest, the only place to work is Bess's."

I gave him a smart kick in the shin, "I think you're a snake and I hate you."

"Afternoon, Ma'am," he said, tipping his hat when we reached the far side of the street. The smell coming from the eating place near to turned my belly. "You're supposed to work in Bess's kitchen," he hissed. "Dancehall girls eat as well as..."

"Then you talk to that old sow. She says that ain't your place and unless I work upstairs, I don't work." I marched into the restaurant past the hungry red eyes of a couple dozen slobbering miners and got throwed out, nice as you please, five minutes later.

The fella there paid his blacks and yellows six bits a week. Me, he expected to pay "warming space in his bed back by the woodpile."

He was so filthy I caught wind of him every time he lifted his arm to cleave a piece of meat.

The dress shop wasn't no better. The widow-woman there had her two daughters, who weren't no older than fourteen, sewing eighteen hours a day. Her little ones did chores for near every store in town. They had about as much decent work for me there as a stray dog.

By nightfall my feet was sore, and my belly ached. I didn't have the strength or will to stay clear of what I'd been born to. I was already a whore but too damn proud or stupid to admit it.

I stopped by an apothecary for something to quiet my mind when the time to step upstairs come. "I'm looking for a certain brown bottle of potion my ma used to take for her spells," I told the man with the spectacles and white apron. He was the first clean person I'd seen all day.

"A pain killer?" he asked, inspecting my face. "You probably mean laudanum, my dear. You have enough cash for a small bottle," he said as I produced my only gold coin. "I do have larger sizes if your…" he cleared his throat, "…toothache, or what-have-you is a big one. Doc Granger might be able to help if you're in need of medical attention. Folks don't give him credit, but he's a fine young fellow." He brought forth a bottle I'd seen Cornelia use many a time. "Just a bit now," he said. "Too much could be fatal."

He displayed the writing on the label. I gazed at it, hoping I looked like I was reading. After paying him, I hurried up to where the lamplight shined from the dancehall's windows. I wanted to get there 'fore that greasy back kitchen and the starving girls in the cramped sewing room faded from my memory.

Taking a sip from my bottle, I walked through the doorway. Six girls sat at little tables along the bare walls. They was dressed as sober and respectable as I'd ever seen Effie. Corseted tight, their hair neatly coiled and their faces unpainted, they looked pitifully ordinary. After years of seeing mostly men, so many girls all in one place kind of gave me a start. I wondered if it struck the men the same.

Dalt sat back in the office with his new boots resting on the edge of Bess's desk. He looked mighty respectable dressed proper. It was hard to believe I'd borne that big, fearsome man a child.

The black piano player looked up from his stool and then went on dancing his long fingers over the ivory keys. Two miners followed me in and hung their hats on pegs. Their hair was slicked down, their cheeks shaved shiny and red. Their clothes was ragged but clean; and their boots, scarred up as they was, was scraped. Handing over a nickel each, they chose two girls to dance. I would've sworn it respectable enough even for the Lewises.

When he saw me, Dalt got up and bowed with a smug smile, sweeping his arm so I'd join him. If I hadn't known it was Bess behind the desk I would have sworn she was a lady. She wore a black silk gown covered with jet beads that caught the dim lamplight as she pulled herself out of the chair.

"I told you she'd come back," Dalt said, puffing on a long cigar.

"You got a job, if you want it," Bess said, her eyes brittle.

Dalt excused hisself, offered a nickel to the prettiest girl and danced away. A jealous beat pounded in my heart as I turned to Bess and braced myself for her cussing.

"You didn't tell me you just had a baby," Bess said, settling back in the groaning chair. "Every girl here tells me if she's married, pregnant, wanted by the law—everything and anything—no matter what."

"It weren't your business."

"Honey, everything in this town is my business. My girls tell me everything that goes on upstairs and I keep it to myself. Everything goes into me. Nothing comes out. If you need work but can't work upstairs yet, that's my business. I don't turn girls away. This afternoon you struck me as a high and mighty piece of baggage. Fact is, there ain't no place for you here at all if you're thinking yourself better than us. We're all the same under our corsets. Working upstairs, bedding a husband, it's all the same. We women got to stick together. Ain't one girl here who don't want to be, so get it out of your head I'm some kind of witch luring you to the devil's ways. Try your hand working anyplace else you want. Write the territorial governor, asking to open a school, for all I care."

"I can't read."

"Hell, I doubt that makes any difference!"

My mouth began turning up despite myself. "Do I have to tell a sob story like Dalt says the other girls do?"

"Maybe I do let my girls use every weapon they got. Considering the hand life's dealt most of us, I figure it's fair using pitiful looks, tears, and innocent misfortune to our advantage. I'm just a poor widow-woman myself. Got to make a living best I can." She looked at me with such sincere, helpless eyes I laughed out loud.

"You're worth something if you work here," she said. "We women get used and abused right down the line. When you decide to go upstairs, you're not the one getting used no more. Remember that. Here, it's the men that gets used. They got an itch no amount of gold or adventure can scratch. This is where you get even."

"I ain't holding no grudges."

"Only alley dogs and stray cats deserve what most women get."

My chin come out. "I ain't no alley dog. I ain't going to starve when I can eat. I ain't going to sleep on no more dirt floors if I can have a real bed. I ain't going to sleep with no man and get nothing if I can get something I can use." I stood up and made a fist. "I take what I get, and I work with it. That's what my ma taught me."

Bess smiled.

Stomping boots thundered across the dance floor as Bess and me moved to watch from the doorway. Slicked down men eager to dance a nickel's worth with a pretty girl filled the hall. One spied me and bolted for me so fast he near fell over his feet. He was young enough to have a face full of blemishes, and a careless barber had given him agony.

"Hello, Davey!" Bess said, hugging the skinny boy. "Ain't seen you lately."

He blushed up to his hair. "Got took in a poker game, Miss Bess. May I dance with this young lady?"

"Why, Angela honey, don't that brighten your day? Davey, may I present Miss Angela of Lancaster, Pennsylvania. Angela, this is Davey Whitehouse all the way from New York state. Miss Angela just got in town and is dead on her feet. You know," she whispered, leading us toward the back, "she was one of the last survivors of a massacred wagon train. She'll be rested soon enough," Bess smiled.

Davey gazed at me with doe-eyes. "I'd be mighty honored if you'd consider me, Miss Angela," he said, shaking my hand.

When Bess steered me back to the kitchen, I said, "I ain't from no place called Lancaster."

"It don't matter. I lie like a dog most all the time. Tell the jakes that there story. I got to see to my customers now. Try teaching Cing Loo to make American coffee. I think he uses mud."

Cing Loo, a Chinaman half my size with curious eyes and a long black braid, made coffee thick enough to use for axle grease. We couldn't talk to each other, but once I showed him how to do it, he made coffee easy as anything. He'd learn all I knew about cooking in a day.

All evening I watched the dancing, reminding myself those plain-faced girls in the tight laces was whores. I was beginning to wonder just what that meant when it got right down to the bare naked details.

I taught Cing Loo the secrets of sweet biscuits and sourdough bread and waited for the sinning to begin. I think I expected them females to act like bitches in heat and the men to act like Rusty Kennings had when he was after me. One girl in long yellow curls disappeared from the floor for maybe a half-hour at a time. Two others went about as long and returned still fully dressed and fresh-faced as they'd been at six o'clock. Nothing in their eyes showed they'd lifted their skirts for a man they didn't love.

Whoring was supposed to be the worst of a woman's sins, worse than husband stealing, worse than adultery. From where I stood, it sure didn't look that bad.

About midnight the laughter was high, the dancing ever faster. The piano player worked up a fine sweat. Cing Loo, who knew enough English to show he understood American money, told me the black got four bits a night and a glass of beer every hour. Cing Loo admitted he got four bits, too. And "no beer!"

"How much do the girls get?"

"Half," was all he'd say. "Half."

The plainest girl come into the kitchen for coffee while Cing Loo nailed the heel of her dancing slipper back on. She was about my size, squeezed into a dress meant for a girl less buxom. Her brown hair was knotted pretty at her neck.

"You get half, working here," I said. "Half of how much?"

"You wouldn't like this place," she said, looking me over. "If you need work, you work. You don't ask the pay. Hell, Jessie gets a buck, favors extra, and she knows them all. She makes five bucks every time she lays down. I get six bits. What them toads don't know about they won't be asking for. Bet you never done nothing Frenchy." That brought light to her pale eyes. "Being young, you might go for six bits, maybe a buck a throw. I, personally, hope to hell you work someplace else. Bess may want you 'cause you'll bring in more customers, but remember, every penny you make is a penny out of somebody else's pocket."

"Half!" Cing Loo said after she pulled on her slipper and marched out.

My head reeled. Walking upstairs four times in one evening I could make more than Cing Loo or the piano player in a week. Four times! After a week I'd be rich. In a month I could go anywhere! The promise of a new dress, pretty shoes, and a soft bed with real linens and blankets lured me on just as gold fever had lured my pa. When the last miners left and the girls climbed the stairs to sleep, I set myself down across from Bess.

"Your girls don't like me and I don't even work here yet."

"Jealous tarts," Bess grunted, pulling off her boots. "You want to see fur fly, wait 'til my star attraction gets here from St. Louie. The hall won't close 'til dawn."

"How much would I make…working upstairs?"

Bess's eyes narrowed. "For the little 'widow,' first time this side of sin, a dollar. That'll be the first month or two. After that, six bits. Later, four, unless you got a specialty. In the end it boils down to about two. Everybody gets old. None of *my* girls are that low, but life's hard and it happens. You turn your money over to me and I keep it safe 'til you need it. Thursday afternoon you have off. Don't expect to be welcome about town, though. My girls usually send Cing Loo's boy to pick up goods."

"I changed my mind," I said, my belly turning cold. "Any objections?"

She laughed like a jackass. "You look like a stray cat. Maybe babies like Davey think that's appealing—that boy's simple-minded. Can't be a day over sixteen and ain't been upstairs yet. Hell, you need a good night's sleep and a real bath. Then you'll bathe Thursday mornings like everybody else. Thursdays we're closed and you can receive callers. It's a nice rest for my girls. You'll like it.

"I'll get you fitted for some new dresses and lots of drawers. Hell, Angela, you're better off wearing 'em out than sewing 'em! You'll sure as hell make more money! I'll show you what to do with that hair, too." She laughed again to herself. "We'll get Davey upstairs yet. He'll wish to hell he'd stuck with poker. These young ones got appetites that cost 'em dearly. Not more than twenty minutes, though. Hear? You tell 'em that. They finish their business in twenty minutes or they pay more."

My jaw sagged.

She laughed. "I'm tired. Cing Loo, fetch hot water. I got to soak my feet again. I only got one room empty just now, Angela. I saved my best for that St. Louie sweetie pie. You can fill it 'til then."

Cing Loo poured a basin of hot water and helped her set bulging feet into it. "Think it over careful, Angela. The first week's the hardest. They all want it new, and you ain't new long. Figure ten a night. I ain't kidding. They'll wear the skin right off your back. If you was to meet one on the street, though, he'd look at you like trash. You'd best be sure. There's no turning back."

"What else is there? Jack Dalton don't want me."

"Hell, Jack's forty-five years old, at least. He won't wait around for you to leave him for some young buck with stamina."

Two days later I found myself standing with the other girls waiting for the first customers. I was in debt to Bess near twenty dollars for my clothes and linens. My hair was brushed back and held with combs. I was scrubbed cleaner than I'd ever been and footsore, thanks to poorly made dancing slippers. My heart swelled and pounded the first time a man walked in. He headed straight for Jessie, the tall beautiful blonde.

Then a group of prospectors come to the door. Bess promptly tossed them out, cussing like a muleteer that if they couldn't clean up they belonged down the hill in a pig hole with girls fit for nothing better.

"Git that piano going, Banjo," she said to the black piano player. He gulped his beer and commenced to filling the hall with the call of his tunes. One by one they trailed in; miners, prospectors and strays; the grocer, the tinsmith, a livery boy. With hats in hands, eyes sparkling, their whiskers smelling of hair-washing soap, each man stood at the door, gawking.

I picked up dancing from various fellas easy enough, but didn't do more than stare at their ragged coats, wondering if they had a dollar. A whole dollar. I wasn't even sure what it'd buy.

When I heard them first stammering words, I near to fainted. "Evening, Miss Angela," Davey Whitehouse said, handing me his nickel and taking me in his trembling arms. "I been thinking about you all week. You know, I ran away to the West two years ago. How long you been out here?"

"Three…" I gulped and hung my head feeling ages older than him.

"Three whole weeks. Must seem like mighty strange country to a young lady like yourself. I'm eighteen. Got me three claims staked.

I don't hold to working placers. I'm going right for the mother lode. Soon as I'm rich I mean to take me a wife and buy land, build me up a first-class ranch. Miss Angela, you're the prettiest girl I ever seen. I'd be right honored if I could take you up…" His face got so red I thought he'd bust. "Excuse me for insulting you, Miss Angela!" he cried. He fled the dancehall, forgetting his hat.

"What the hell happened?" Bess yelled, seeing me standing alone amid the laughing dancers. "You ain't supposed to tell 'em the cost 'til you're upstairs. Don't you remember nothing?"

I remembered. Oh, how I remembered the things she told me to do, to watch for, to guard against. "He ain't ready," I cried. "And I ain't ready for him."

"He's just another customer."

"But I'd be his first. I ain't…" I rushed into her office in tears. "I ain't good enough for him!"

Bess slammed the door. "You'll get 'em young, old, fat, thin, handsome and ugly. All I can guarantee is clean boots. Don't be a fool, Angela. He's just scared to drop his drawers."

I glared at her, hating her.

"There'll be another chance. But next time Davey or any green kid comes in here, you lead 'em upstairs and convince 'em they're the best on earth. You owe me money, honey. I don't give nothing away free."

As it turned out, Davey wasn't my "first." A hard rock miner with a face like Pikes Peak granite handed over the first dollar. Leading him upstairs, I felt the eyes of the whole world on my back. My room was in front, one with curtains. The night air rushed in the open window, filling me with a longing for home. The unpapered walls seemed to close in as I shut the door. The sagging floor made it hard to walk casual to the bed and turn it down. A candlestick stood on the floor in a corner, the wavering flame dancing shadows across the walls.

The miner, whose name I never caught and whose face I never saw again, peeled down to patched johns. There was no mistaking what he'd come with me to get. I don't know why I felt surprised.

"Rules is, everything off," I choked out as I shed my clothes. I sounded like I'd been doing it for years. "Washbasin is over there."

Bess had warned me: "Some'll think you're being insulting, but don't set an inch of yourself on that bed 'til they're washed. If you're smart, you'll do it for 'em so's you'll know if they got clap. If they do, my girls just take sick suddenly and offer to call up a friend. That 'friend' will be Banjo or me to escort them out the back way. Ain't no two ways about it, Angela. No washy, no fucky."

Hesitating only a minute, the miner dropped his johns to his ankles. He wasn't much to behold. I let out my breath. He let me soap, rinse, and dry him. I no sooner sat on the bed than he was on me, going about the business he'd paid eight bits for, and doing mighty well of it, considering his age.

It pained me some, but not as much as I'd figured and not as much as I deserved. I thought more about his bones rubbing me raw than anything else. In no time he was done and slipped into his johns, smiling from sideburn to sideburn. Soon as he left, I pulled another basin from under the bed and washed the way Bess told me, using strong soap and a syringe. I felt cold, picturing that rock-faced man the father of my next child.

A hour later I was back. Cing Loo had put fresh water in the basin under the bed and had changed the linens. This red-faced prospector thought the bathing so pleasurable he didn't get no farther. Without unbuttoning my bodice I sent him away smiling, too.

I turned over eight dollars to Bess my first night. Twelve the next. Thursday morning I was so wore out and sore I didn't want to move from bed, much less bathe in the kitchen tub, watched by a gaggle of girls who hated me. They looked forward to the day my value dropped, for it was certain I was the sensation of Tempest that week, dancing like I'd been born to it and going upstairs with no more qualms than it took to dress a deer.

Thursday, refreshed, clean, curled, and near out of debt, I

never expected a caller. It struck me odd any man would call on a
dancehall girl and treat her like any other sweetheart; but there was
Davey expecting only to walk out back past the privy and garden
patch to enjoy the colorful aspens. He clutched a bunch of posies
and smelled of soap. I thought he'd come to propose.

Seven

Late Fall 1863

Dalt stayed clear of me after I began working for Bess. I only thought of him or our dead baby in the lonely hours before dawn, though raking over my sorrows was a task I preferred to avoid with a gulp of potion. I was relieved when Dalt sold Bess her dancehall back and left town, though I missed him.

At last I had everything I could want; a man to hold me six or seven times a night, fancy food, a fine bed and a town noisy enough to make anybody forget their sorrows. I should've been happy, but one day I counted all the gold coins collecting in my money pouch. It took ten minutes to get the numbers straight, considering I was limited to ten fingers. Fifty-seven dollars—and I had no place to go.

I had no use for the East. I heard Denver City was so civilized it published newspapers, was negotiating a railroad line, and boasted circuses, operas, and real grand balls. I didn't long for the sunny side of respectability; the shadows treated me kinder.

I was stuck there at Bess's, it would seem. We girls got along about as well as six yoked oxen; hard-headed, single-minded and dumb, all hitched together in a cramped building with no more privacy than a cow in a corral.

Jessie had beautiful golden curls. Evalee was slow-witted. Louise understood all about mining districts and legalities. Abigale, who'd told me so kindly how welcome I wasn't that very first night, had left town in September.

ANGEL

Plump, jolly Maybelle could make a rock laugh. Even Nana, with her hair so long somebody else had to brush it for her, was popular, though she was as homely as a spinster. She could cry at the drop of a hat. I figured she had some fine and mysterious speciality with them tears.

I caused a lot of mean-eyed looks when I come upon the scene, but Bess's special attraction upset the applecart altogether. Sara rode into Tempest at dusk on a Friday—sidesaddle! She held a ruffled parasol over her narrow shoulders and a cloudburst of petticoats showed under her hooped skirt. Hand embroidered pantalets peeped from under all that fluff, enough to let the gentry know she was a high-priced dumpling of the finest variety.

Bess stepped onto the walkway to get a better look and her jowl sagged. "Help her down!" she yelled to Banjo, who stood in the doorway enjoying his first beer of the evening.

Looking dignified in a new ruffle-breasted white shirt and shiny red vest made special by Mrs. Molly herself, Banjo stepped into the mud to help the confection to the walkway.

"Evening, Miss Bess," the little lady-doll drawled.

Bess smiled and winked. Her competition promptly hated her more—for her high standards, her lace curtains, and her piano!

Sara's calico-blue eyes twinkled. I'd never seen hair such as hers, a soft golden copper, smooth as molasses. It lay tucked up careful under a hat dancing with plumes and teasing ribbons. I took sick right off, hating her and admiring her. She looked so elegant in them bone-colored kid gloves and fine wool cape trimmed with a braided cord, I couldn't see how she'd fallen on hard times.

"If that ain't sugar-candied baggage," Nana hissed, "then I'm a school girl and never been kissed."

"Must be from New Orleans," Jessie whispered as we watched from the windows. "Big city whore."

I didn't believe that. No girl that beautiful *had* to be a whore.

"My name's Sara Sweetwater," Sara said, bestowing her smile on everybody within hearing. "What a fine place. May I come in?"

Evalee, having a weakness for liquor, sneaked herself a gulp.

"We're all done for," she groaned.

Banjo started playing. Men come up the street in droves, tucking in shirttails, slapping back cowlicks with a handful of spit. Bess stood at the door, greeting the goggle-eyed fellas with a broad smile and high voice. "Come on in! Big dance tonight. All the beer you can hold!" But before she let them pass she had Louise paint over part of the little sign by the door.

"Where's that new little lady?" the first man to hand me a dime asked.

"Bess is talking to her in the office," I said, dodging his boots, sizing him up as to the amount of encouragement I'd give him. The other girls went upstairs with whoever asked. I still played favorites. Some rated only a smile and cool laugh. Others rated a meaningful caress on their necks. Others still rose to the call when I tickled their ears and whispered, "You're a mighty fine-looking, hard-working man. I'll bet you're strong as an ox."

All evening the men stared at the closed office door. Now and again I'd hear Bess bust out laughing. Cing Loo came and went with coffee and cakes twice. I danced my feet raw before getting a request for "a little relaxation" upstairs from a fella who'd sold out and was moving on in the morning.

He had a drooping brown moustache and sun-streaked hair. His eyes was gentle and full of mischief. His hand lingered on my backside as we mounted the stairs.

With relief, I closed my door and kicked off my dancing shoes. I pulled off my dress and opened the strings of my corset cover to whet the fella's appetite. "Something special tonight?" I asked softly, pulling down the shade.

Lights from saloons down the way looked like stars. When I turned, he'd pulled off all them worn clothes. I led him to the basin and soaped him, always nervous 'til I'd found no disease.

He was a fine example of manflesh, built powerful and lean. He smiled down on me with lips as full and pink as my own. I offered my price. He made his needs known. We mounted the bed.

I took to thinking of new dresses and supper since the evening was young. I didn't have the strength to get worked up with my first tumble. My high time was over, I kept thinking. Though still prime stock, I was "one of the girls" now. That Southern belle would get my brass bed, and I'd get Abigale's lumpy cot.

Wind howled under the shade, sending it flapping. I wrapped my arms around that fella's neck, feeling tears come sudden—and hard. Much as I needed him, I near to went crazy as he pumped and puffed. I wanted to push him away and spit on him, yet I held tighter, thinking I was wore out as a dancehall girl at seventeen! In that awful moment I found satisfaction for the first time since before my baby had been birthed. I'd near forgot that special fire that used to pulse in me, that terrible reminder of what it meant to be a woman loved.

Waiting for the throbbing to pass from my legs, I held onto that poor stranger and cried into his neck. Oh, it had been so very long 'since I'd really held another person close! There was a mighty big difference between that and laying skin to skin with a customer.

I kept my face turned away while he dressed. I knew I had to squirt myself clean but couldn't move. I wanted to lay close to that tall fella's back all night. His coins clattering on the washstand gave me a jolt. I'd forgotten to get his money and could've been cheated! The door closed and I was alone. Always alone. Even after I dragged myself off the bed and counted five dollars in silver, I didn't feel no better.

Whoring wasn't no life of sin, no endless lusting after the flesh as the Bible-thumpers preached in their halfbuilt church. Whoring was baking bread that didn't rise, building houses that fell down, and birthing babies that died.

No daughter of mine would ever sit alone with the warmth of a man's touch still leaving an ache in her belly, knowing to the bottom of her soul she was worth nothing! Yet I dressed, painted on a bright new smile, and went downstairs.

Within days Sara took over in the front bedroom. For the next several months she brought in more business than if gold had been jumping out of the creek like trout. In February all that gray rock that had been clogging the sluices turned out to be high grade silver ore! Overnight Tempest busted at the seams.

By summer three new girls found their way to Bess's back door. When Bess announced it was time we doubled up, Jessie's eyes glinted. Weren't nobody going to sleep in her bed except paying customers! Maybelle and Nana agreed to double. Two of the new girls agreed to. The third looked at Louise and resigned herself to sleeping alongside a stranger of the female sex!

"Angie can come in with me," Sara Sweetwater said.

I coughed up my potion-laced coffee and stared at her in surprise. All those months Sara hadn't been much of a talker. She only bubbled with charm for pay. I felt a mite special that she picked me and was mighty glad to get back to that fine bed.

After a month Bess knew she'd struck her own mother lode. While one of us danced, the other stepped upstairs. Cing Loo had to trot to keep up with the water basins! Most times we ran out of linens, so Bess's standards slipped. Nobody noticed or cared except us.

At dawn Sara and me would fall into bed so tired we couldn't sleep. We would've gone on living as strangers, but one snowy November night after we'd turned in I lay staring at the ceiling unable to sleep. Suddenly, Sara, who'd been sleeping sound beside me, sat bolt upright. Clutching the cover to her chin, she stared off into nothing, looking so terrible scared her neck strained like she was lifting a heavy trunk! She leaped from the bed and ran flat out into the wall, knocking herself silly. I scrambled after her and gathered her up. "What's got into you?"

"Damn!" She patted a knot growing on her forehead. "Done it again. Let me up, Angie. Did I scare you?"

I shook my head. She'd scared the drawers off me!

"Did I scream or hit you?" Where was the sugary voice, the helpless eyes, the pouting mouth fellas loved better than whiskey or gold? She staggered to the bed. "We should sleep while we got the chance." Looking up, she added, "You don't look like you're sleeping at all these days."

I slipped back under the covers, eyeing her. "I think I'm pregnant." I hadn't dared put my fear into words, yet saying it out loud somehow made it less terrible.

Sara rolled sleep-swollen eyes. "This dirty town hasn't got a decent doctor for fixing, unless you count that little fella Granger. I don't think he'd do it anyhow. What'll you do?"

"Die, probably. Are you all right now?"

She made a silly face and laughed. Honestly, it was the first time I'd seen her do more than crack a polite smile, except while working when she near to ran over with giggling. "I'm fine. And you won't die."

"Almost did when I birthed one wrong. My innards took six months to get right."

"You don't look old enough to be here much less a mother. Are you working on your back to support your baby?"

"I ain't no mother. My baby died. I ain't nothing but a wore out whore carrying some son of a bitch's child."

"Maybe it's better you die then, huh?" she smiled hopefully.

"No."

"Then quit complaining. As long as Bess has this famous idea of making money off us we've got to live together. So far you haven't been half bad to put up with. You're quiet and pretty clean, and you don't snore."

I felt like pinching her. "If you hate it here, why not leave? You must have enough to set yourself right again," I said.

Sara smoothed back that pretty taffy-colored hair. "What'd Bess tell you girls, that I was an innocent down on my luck? Hell, I'm a twenty-five-year-old pro. I been earning my way since I was nine."

I busted out laughing. "You're a liar!"

"No lie, Angie. Nine years old my step-pa and two brothers used me. I had my first baby at thirteen. I was lucky. It died, too. Since then I've been fixed three times. Now I don't have to worry."

"How come?"

She settled under the covers and stared past the ceiling like she could see right through it. "Working girls catch things. Doctors do things. One or the other fixes you good. I been safe from babies six years. Emptiest feeling I know. I've put a pistol to my head twice that I recall—have to be drunk, you see. Never can do it, though. Haven't got the guts."

"That's crazy talk!"

She laughed that musical laugh that bewitched the miners.

"I hated you when you come into town 'cause you was so pretty."

She laughed some more. "I've got to be prettier than a princess and fancier than the highest paid actress. I've gotten as much as a hundred dollars. What's the most you ever got?"

"Five dollars in silver."

"What'd you have to do? Sometimes men ask me for unnatural things I don't enjoy, but I set a price and generally they pay."

"Don't know what I did. Maybe I gave it more than usual."

"I used to send them off too weak to walk," Sara giggled. "Figured I'd enjoy myself in the bargain, but I lost all my pretty fat and got circles under my eyes. I cut that out quick! How old are you, Angie?"

"Eighteen."

"I'll give you money to go to California. Tell folks your husband was skinned by Indians. Then keep your eyes down 'til the marrying kind comes along."

"Ain't you saving up to go home?"

"Nowhere to go!" she laughed. "I don't need all I got. You take it. Bess'll throw you out soon as you show." Her eyes blazed.

"Bess'll take care of me!"

"Bess will look out for her own personal self. Anybody else be damned."

"I can't believe you been whoring since you was a kid," I whispered. "You got book-learning!"

"From the time I was twelve I worked in a brothel. I learned everything there, *including* reading and writing. I probably had an easier life than you. Out here, though, I'm likely to get killed. Bess doesn't protect us."

"Banjo throws out the rowdies."

Sara chuckled. "Rowdies I like. It's the rich 'gentlemen' that scare me. Some men…they're usually fat and old with shriveled wives, spinster daughters, and mothers who look like spiders…they hate women, especially prostitutes. They come for their needs and then…" She shuddered. "One such man got me. I was dreaming about him again. I've got scars to prove my story, Angie. I guess I'm crazy, wishing I was dead. I fear death and pain so much I've sunk this low to stay alive."

"This is the best place in Tempest!"

"I feel like a teacher. The best place is opening up across the canyon. Next summer they'll have pros from San Francisco and New Orleans. The rich men in this town are dying to part with their silver! Big Bess and her laced girls doubled in bare rooms will sink as low as the rest to keep up. You watch. Next June you'll be down to a half-dollar."

I threw off the bedcover. "If you're so damn special, go on over to that new saloon and wear your fancy dresses!"

Sara shook her head. "My scars haven't healed enough. Maybe they never will." She went to the looking glass, smiled at her hair and stroked the silky white smoothness of her throat. Untieing her camisole, she spread it open to show low full breasts. An ugly scar eight inches long ran down each one! She arranged her hair over the scars and went on smiling. "There's something about riding into a town for the first time, watching the way men turn and stare, that makes me feel powerful. When I'm alone with them they belong to me."

"You like bedding?"

"I hate sex more than I fear pain. I don't enjoy any of it any more. My body doesn't need men, my mind needs them. If I quit, I'd have no power. I'll bet you've never noticed how plain I am." She pulled back her hair revealing a simple face with large troubled eyes. "I'm really very ugly." Her eyes darkened. She closed the camisole and turned away. "I'll go on living for that power…" Sara said, "…until the next crazy man comes along."

. . .

Taking Sara's advice, I left the high rocky walls of Buffalo Canyon for El Dorado City a few days later. The stage come through the pass over a log bridge that near to rattled my teeth right out of my head. Seeing the snow-covered prairie, I felt like I'd come into the light of day after a three-year night in the mountains.

I stepped off that stage, dressed sober enough to pass for Effie Kennings's sister. Sara had writ some letters on a piece of paper for me. I stopped now and again to match them up to the signs overhead. By the time I'd passed an apothecary and barber, I was at the grain and feed store at the end of the street. Next to that was a livery and smithy a-clanging with hammer against iron. The smell of horse was enough to bring tears to my eyes.

I stopped by the corral and watched a beautiful chestnut mare spread her hind legs and shoot a steaming gush into the snow—and laughed. Damn, if some mighty odd things didn't strike me funny! Turning away, I saw an Appaloosa getting shod back of the livery. His owner paced in the barn, smoking a cheroot and scrawling on a tablet.

My heart quickened at the sight of that curly dark hair. I'd know him anywhere. I sure wasn't the smartest thing in shoe leather no more. I bolted across the street, starting my search along that side for the sign: D-o-c-t-o-r. By the time I got back where I started, I was puffing and cussing myself for falling so soft in my months on my back.

As I stomped the slush from my good high-topped shoes, that fella on the Appaloosa reined right in front of me! He swept off his white hat and smiled. "Afternoon, Ma'am! My name's Travis Saunders. Begging your pardon, is this the way to Tempest? I heard of a silver strike up that way."

His name had a fine ring to it. I'd forgotten what a belly-stirring thing his voice was, too. He wore leather and fringe, tooled boots and silver spurs. How I wished *his* kind visited Big Bess's place!

"That's Buffalo Pass all right," I said. Damn! I never could talk fancy to gentlemen. "Tempest is ten miles up. You won't miss it. It straddles the road."

"Is the silver as good as they claim?" His eyes twinkled as he smiled down at me.

"Better than the gold ever was." I wondered if he recalled my face yet. "Planning to write yourself a humdinger of a newspaper story, Mr. Saunders?"

He sat back. "So, you know me! I seldom forget a pretty woman. I most humbly beg your forgiveness. Tell me we've met. I hope not just on the pages of a newspaper."

I laughed, feeling powerful, seeing how a person like Sara could get to liking it more than anything. "Would you believe I've never read a word?"

"You wouldn't be interested in my words anyway," he said, not knowing I meant any word, not just his. "I write foul and disgusting stories of Indian raids, wagon train calamities, and mining hoaxes. I've just come from Denver City, where there was laid out in the very street a whole massacred family! It was enough…" He swallowed hard, stretching his lips back over clenched teeth as if trying to clear his mouth of a bad taste. "Tell me where we've met."

I wished I could dimple like Sara. I wanted to lure him from that fine horse and look in his eye. I wondered about a man who could chase after and write about things that pained him.

Just then, though, a man rode up the street hell for leather. "Mr. Saunders! Come quick! Word just come in on the Denver stage. They done what they said they would!"

Mr. Saunders spun his mount to meet the man on the lathered horse. "The militia?"

The man nodded, gulping. "Kilt every Injun in the camp. Took 'em near all day!" Mr. Saunders was about to whip his horse up to speed when the other man grabbed his coat sleeve so hard I figured he'd rip it right off. "There weren't no braves, Mr. Saunders! They was a band of friendlies flying the Stars and Stripes—and a white flag of peace! The militia blew 'em to hell, kilt every one and left 'em to rot same as Injuns leave whites—mutilated! God-a-mighty, Mr.

Saunders. Why'd they do such a damn fool thing? Ain't no squaw ever butchered a soddie family."

"Don't bet on it," Mr. Saunders said, galloping away.

The next day I boarded another stage for Denver City. I'd decided to go back to Missouri after all. Carrying a stranger's child weren't half so bad as fixing it so it'd come out too soon, like Sara said I should. I couldn't rightly "fix" a child of my own flesh anyhow. Ten miles out we swung along near as sick and cold as we could get. I sat squashed between two gents and across from a woman no more respectable than me, just smellier. The driver yelled, "Injuns!"

Out the stage windows we saw riders kicking up snow and mud, coming from the north. The stage cut right off the road, made a wide circle in the sage and dashed back toward the red rocks of El Dorado City. Both gentlemen was busy at the windows, their pistols shaking so bad they couldn't hit nothing except by accident. The woman screamed and pulled at her hair as the driver fell past the window with an arrow through his neck.

Some time during that bone-breaking, head-knocking ride my little stranger decided this life wasn't worth the trouble. My belly began cramping. I grew so faint I don't know how we got back to town. When the stage door fell open, the men and woman spilled out, sobbing their tale of terror to the miners and storekeepers gathering about. I lay on the stage floor, my skirts heavy with blood.

I woke to the babble of creek water. My belly hurt so bad I wondered if it was an open wound. A squat man tucking his shirttail into his trousers came in the room where I lay abed. "Dora! She's awake." He pulled back my cover and pushed my knees apart. "Bleeding's let up. Had yourself a miscarriage, thanks to them heathens. You're lucky. I don't like to think what them Injuns would've done if they'd got you, being in the frame of mind they was."

"Ain't Injuns hereabouts friendly pretty much?" My voice

sounded faraway.

"Not no more. After what they done to some soddie family, a damn fool official up in Denver City figured to scare them off with a show of force. They took volunteers and wiped out a whole village of squaws and papooses. Ain't a worser thing they could've done. We'll be wiped out before Christmas."

"That's no way to talk to this poor thing," a plump woman with sorry eyes scolded. "Your people send you to town alone?" she asked me.

"She's got a right to her secret, woman," he said, winking. "You'll be up and about in a few days." His small eyes slid over me before he waddled out, adjusting hisself and patting his belly.

The woman lifted me and began spooning salty broth into my mouth. "Didn't see no wedding band on your finger there. You folks on the stage wasn't robbed, so I take it you ain't married. Right, dearie?"

"Not married." I pushed her away, dizzy and filled with an ache that didn't come from bleeding. "Not pregnant no more, neither."

"That's something to be grateful for." She dabbed at the spills down my neck. "Ain't nothing worse than an unmarried girl saddling herself with a young'n. Be more careful next time your fella has his way with you. S'pose your people will take you back now that you're out of your fix? Nice and natural it was, too. You can tell 'em that."

I just looked at her. She couldn't know how I felt, the sorrow, the hope...now the emptiness. "Are you a nurse?" I asked.

She laughed so big I counted seven missing teeth. "Just ol' Doc's friend. Doc ain't no real doc, but then I never did meet a real one. I just sit on folks while he tends them. He worked in Tempest 'til they run him out. They sent back East for a graduated fella from some medical what-dya-call-it. Doc knows plenty of females, though." She laughed hard over that one. "He owns the best sporting house in El Dorado City. You're lucky you lost that baby natural. My ma used to say it was better to fall off a barn than get fixed. 'Course, if you got to get fixed a doc is better than a midwife. Them old crones dirty you up with their poking sticks. Vermin gets in you and kills you dead."

"You'll bring up that broth with your fables," the doc said, poking his head in the doorway. "Dora's trying to tell you not to listen when I say there's a place for you at Eloise's if you can't go back to your people. Eloise will treat you proper and the work's easy."

"Easy!" the woman howled. "Did an Irish railman ever jump on top of him?" She dabbed tears away. "Ain't nothing harder than trying to please one man, much less five or ten or a thousand. You stay clear of Eloise! A sweet young thing like yourself don't know about life's sins, only its pleasures and…little consequences. Lie back and sleep. You had money enough in your satchel to stay here a few weeks. Doc's already relieved you of it."

"You ever let a man hop on you?"

"Such a question! Don't go considering the sporting house! I seen what girls go through once they catch pox. Ain't no hell worse for man nor beast. Go to sleep."

"Have you? For pay?"

"Just where the hell you come from?" she snapped.

"I'm one of Big Bess's girls."

"Holy hell! Dancing and whoring. No wonder you're so damn skinny. Doc! We got another of Bess's girls here! We done Abigale last fall. She come through safe and sound. Doc knows his way around the innards of females. She's working at Eloise's right now. I'll send for her. Damn, I would've taken you for a preacher's daughter. Would've bet money on it!"

After they left, I lay contemplating my turn of luck, studying the streaking sunshine coming through the window. It was better the baby was gone. Better for both of us…The gurgling creek water lulled me into a half sleep. As evening fell, piano tunes echoed between the walls of the pass. The same high laughter filled the night as in Tempest, but in Tempest the carousing had somehow belonged only to me.

Eight

Late Fall 1864

"I'm so pleased to meet you, Angela," Eloise said, her voice deep and rich. "May I ask how old you are?" The jeweled combs in her white hair gleamed bright as her teeth.

"Eighteen." I hung back, scared to go in her fancy parlor. Her brothel looked like a mansion house and scared me witless.

Miss Eloise's sharp eyes went over me. She made a beautiful smile and settled herself behind her stately desk. "Abigale tells me you were the sensation at Bess's last year."

Grinning, Abigale pushed me closer. I stumbled over the thick carpet. "Some thought so," I said. I would've felt more comfortable facing a hungry timberwolf.

Abigale perched on a red plush chair, smiling at me like a queen. I wondered how she kept her breasts from falling out of that low-cut gown. She'd growed long nails and her face was colored to the high hue of good health.

"Did you enjoy work at Bess's?" Eloise asked.

"I ain't much at dancing, but then most the men ain't either."

"How much did you make? Come, come. Don't be coy."

My arms broke out in gooseflesh. "At first a dollar. Then six bits. Sometimes I get tips. Bess bet me a ten dollar gold piece if I can get a certain fella upstairs…" Why'd I tell her that? I looked away.

"Show Angela our specialty room later, Abigale. She needs a proper education. Fifty cents, indeed! As you can see, we're a high-

---

class house. We employ only the best. Would you be interested?"

"Working here?" I cried.

"We'll talk again if you find us to your liking. I'd advise getting free of Bess before she wears you out."

Giggling, Abigale led me up the grand staircase and showed me each of the rooms, even one with sliding panels and peepholes drilled in the walls. They was beautiful, decorated with red or gold velvet wallpaper and carpets so soft I wanted to lie down and wallow. The beds was wide and bouncy, some with curtains or canopies, some with brass bedsteads a-gleaming in the lamplight. The bedclothes was so snowy white and inviting, I longed to stretch out and discover if bedding was any different on a tick scented with rosewater than one smelling of whiskey.

In some rooms beautiful ladies sat at dressing tables, fussing over curls of every shade and hue, painting on ruby lips, dusting rice powder over swelling bosoms. They smiled as if I was so far beneath them they had no need to feel jealous.

"Here the men pay for the room and the favor, not who's new or not," Abigale said, leading me into her room where a pine tree laid whiskery branches against the windowglass. "I can't work but a week or two before my time comes. Doc says I'll always have trouble now that I been fixed. I wouldn't wish fixing on my worst enemy. Dora said Doc fixes best of any she's seen, too." Abigale's pink face paled at the memory.

"Fixing can't be worse than birthing," I said.

"It is! Doc takes pleasure from his work, too. Has he bothered you?"

"In my condition?" I laughed. "I'm flowing like a fresh dressed deer."

Abigale eased herself onto the bed. "You're a gruesome little creature. Learned any specialties yet?"

"One fella says I ride him better than he rides a bronc, and longer!" My cheeks grew hot. "With younger ones I get a secret pleasure soaping them—drawing them off before they're ready. 'Course, then I ride 'em out and make 'em pay twice. I'm no fool!"

Abigale shook her head. "I like Eloise's place. It's warm, and the pay's better. I only got one specialty and that's how I keep my place here when I'm flowing."

"How's that?"

"I wouldn't tell you! You already drove me from one place."

I didn't have no idea what other specialties amounted to. Frontwards, backwards, and riding in the saddle was the only ways of coupling I'd learned—and them from insistent customers thinking I was a tease making them "show" me what they wanted!

As long as I was there, Eloise figured I ought to join her girls that night in the parlor. Abigale helped me dress fancy in a white gown so sheer everything I had showed right through it!

"Am I really good enough to work here?" I asked, gazing at the looking glass. With my gray eyes smudged dark, my lips rosy with paint and my hair a wild mass of curls around my pale face, I looked downright...handsome!

Abigale adjusted her neckline and splashed on eye-stinging toilet water. "You're just a bill of goods."

I cast her a low look.

Descending the staircase and walking into Eloise's parlor that night made me think I'd found the place I'd been longing for. Gentlemen filled the parlor. Their fine clothes, heavy rings, and soft talk all spoke of riches I could only imagine.

One had a gut so big the ladies swarming about couldn't get close unless they stood at his side. His boots sported Mexican spurs. His fine cut tan trousers and leather coat with foot-long fringe made him look rough and cultured all at once. No such gentleman had ever set foot in Bess's dancehall! Spying me, he opened his arms wide and welcoming. I thought his booming "Howdy, girlie," was for Abigale beside me.

Eloise took my arm. "May I present Silver Stan Sampson, the richest, handsomest man in Colorado Territory." She smiled wickedly and winked. "Stan, this is little Angela."

"Richest, maybe," Stan bellowed. Offering his elbow like a Thursday afternoon beau, Stan led me into the next parlor where the piano player looked so much like Banjo I almost called him by name! "My, my, little Angela. Where do you hail from?"

I felt befuddled. He sat me down on a velvet settee and dropped heavily beside me. Had Eloise forgotten I was in no shape to go upstairs? I cringed when he took my hand in his big white paw.

"New at this, are you?" he chuckled. "Ol' Stan will go easy on you. Are you free now?"

My mouth went sour. "You'd best check with Miss Eloise."

He wetted his lips with a flick of his tongue. "I'll do just that."

As he swaggered away Abigale walked by smiling through her teeth. "You dirty little bitch."

I clamped my teeth. Silver Stan must've been hers. Hers he'd be again, I thought. He chilled my bones!

Eloise signaled with her eyes. I scurried after her, expecting to be sent away where I'd cause no more trouble. Mr. Sampson stood just beyond the doorway.

"Not a penny less than fifty," Eloise whispered.

My belly quickened.

Silver Stan Sampson steered me toward the stairs, humming with anticipation. We was halfway up when Eloise turned, her face stricken. "Dollars!"

I stumbled. Fifty dollars?

Stan steadied me, turned me down the seductively lit hallway into the finest bedroom. I'd forgotten if it had the peepholes or wardrobe full of whips. As the door closed I felt that same over-the-cliff feeling I'd had facing my first customer at Bess's.

"How *many* dollars?" Stan asked, hanging his coat and shirt on the clothestree, revealing the fleshy chest of an older man. Whipping off his belt, he grinned over some great secret.

"Fifty," I squeaked.

His lower lip stuck out. "Fair price. Catch!"

A coin sang through the air and landed at my feet. I stooped to pick up the silver dollar. Another glittering silver coin rang by and landed on the bed. I took it and undid my front buttons. When my breasts was near bare, he flipped more and more coins. I scrambled all over the floor, gathering them into my hands 'til they began spilling out.

He laughed. Oh, how he laughed! The floor shined with his silver. I let my breasts swing free, figuring the man needed something for his money. I knew I couldn't count to fifty muddled as I was. At the painted china basin he soaped hisself. When he'd dried, he stood before me, sporting the finest erection I'd yet to see. In his manicured fingertips he held still another coin. "Eloise tells me you're fresh as a daisy."

I was kneeling on the floor. He stood so tall and proud, naked as a jay, his shoulders broad as mountains, his eyes wide and burning. "Mr. Sampson, Eloise misled you. Kind as you are, I'm not fit for entertaining tonight. I just began my…time." I hung my head. Fifty dollars.

He lifted my chin. "I know." He placed the last coin on his erection. "I know you're not a virgin, but, my sweet, I know of another kind. I see it in your eyes. I want you to take this coin from me with your lips."

Fifty dollars.

He held my head and kept me kneeling before him 'til he took his money's worth. I think the look on my face pleasured him most.

Bidding nobody good-bye, I left El Dorado City the next morning. I hoped when my flow stopped and the tiny rips at the corners of my mouth healed, I'd be ready and eager to coax a lamb like Davey Whitehouse into my bed.

Nine

Early Spring 1865

"You're a damn fool!" Bess smacked her desk. "Don't you know nothing?"

"I didn't want to get pregnant!" I yelled, rubbing away bothersome tears, squirming 'cause I hadn't had time to change my rags. My petticoat was getting spotted.

"You think I'm some evil woman who'd throw you out?" Bess's face puckered into a stormy frown. "Jack came looking for you a couple weeks back. I said it wasn't none of his damn business where you was, but he knowed you'd run off. Told me you're noted for leaving folks to worry."

She paced, waving her big arms and hollering, but in the end she hugged me. "I'm glad you're all right. Get on upstairs and wash your face. Tell that bitch, Sara, not to scare you into running next time."

I tried to smile. "Thanks, Bess. I'll go back to work soon as I can, but…I don't want no more next time. Ain't there some way…"

"Hellfire! You didn't know what to do?" She pressed her fist to her bosom as if she was pained.

"There's a lot more than that I don't know."

"Meaning what?"

I told Bess about the doc in El Dorado City, Abigale, Eloise, and then Silver Stan Sampson's fifty silver dollars. Bess stampeded in a raging circle. "Fifty dollars, hell! No man pays that kind of money unless he's…What'd he do that sent you back so damn fast?"

When I told her she let out a whoop.

"That ain't nothing like he could've done! There's so much you don't know it'd curdle your water."

I hung my head.

"Hell, I thought you didn't offer no special favors because you didn't like to. That's generally what men are looking for, you know. Special pleasures. 'Course, here in these mountains, just *seeing* a woman is pleasure enough for most. I figured you weren't going upstairs so often 'cause you didn't want to."

"They ain't asking!"

She smacked her desk again. "It ain't up to them! You're the one working. Tell me, missy, if you was running that bake shop I hear you dreaming on all the time, would you keep customers with one kind of pie?"

I giggled.

"And would you stay in business if that one kind of pie was half baked? That's right. Your bedding is half baked. Now I know why Davey ain't been upstairs. Jack Dalton done wrung the heart right out of you."

"I don't much like bedding no more," I said. "I hate them dirty miners and their whiskers."

"That's how it'll be most all the time," Bess snapped. "Ain't no reason to open your legs and turn your face to the wall. If a man wants that, he can use his wife. He can marry some female like Molly James who probably never screwed without a Bible in her hand! You're working a business here, missy. Hellfire! First chance I get, I'm clearing out! I'll open the riproaringest cathouse you ever saw and I won't hire no dumb-ignorant girls who don't work for their four bits."

She hurried upstairs. When she waddled back in, her lips tight with anger, she shook a bit of sponge hanging from a string in my face. "Just beforehand, when you're washing, stick this in. Wet it first with water and lemon. It ain't a sure thing, but it works better than crossing your fingers. Use it every time, hear? You're watching out for fellas that is dirty, ain't you? Doc says he's seen three cases in the last month." She pushed me out of her office and poured a stiff whiskey. "Dumb-ignorant girls…"

Though Sara didn't look so glad to see me, I told her everything that had happened since I left. Then I sank onto the bed with a groan. "Got some extra rags?"

"You ought to see the doctor. Women sometimes die from miscarriages." She sat spread-eagled on a stool before her new dressing table.

"I really needed to hear that."

She got up and patted my shoulder. "I was hoping you were starting your new life. You don't belong here, Angie. You were meant to be a wife."

"I don't care if I never see another man much less his private parts," I snapped. "Husband or otherwise."

She lifted a pile of rags from one of her trunks. Though they'd been washed and ironed, the stains still made odd matching patterns along the folds. "Then you're better off a wife. Lots of whores like sex. Plenty, like me are just tired of it. *All* wives hate it."

"I used to like it!"

"So bad you had to cross your legs to ease the ache?"

I thought back to that summer Dalt left me alone and pregnant. "Yep," I nodded. "Best damn dreams I ever had!" A lump grew in my throat. "But whatever made me want a man is gone. Can I work feeling like this?"

Sara shrugged. "I have all these years. If you can't, you'd better leave for good. Bess expects you to work. You won't bleed forever."

But I was still flowing after another month. I felt too weak to eat and could near see right through my skin. Dr. Billy Granger had an office just across the freight road. Curious posters of muscles and bones covered the walls of his surgery. In the middle of the room stood a high table where he pulled teeth, dug out bullets, and set bones.

"Morning, Miss Angie," Doc Granger said when Bess and Sara pushed me in his office. "I hear you're feeling poorly. Please, come in. Don't be afraid." He was a slight man of maybe thirty-five with wire spectacles, a soft, gentle face, and bright brown eyes. "Wait outside for Angie," he said to Sara. "We won't take long. Keep handy, though. I wouldn't want this little lady thinking I was taking indecent liberties." He winked at me.

I didn't appreciate his teasing. "I ain't undressed for a man in months," I said from behind his screen, wishing my voice would stop trembling. "I've been warned about doctors with knowledge of females."

"Bess says you've been bleeding a long time." He kept his back turned as he assembled a tray of ugly instruments.

My belly churned. "I lost a baby. That's the honest truth. No fixing for me! You can ask the doc in El Dorado City. He took care of me."

Doc Billy straightened stiffly. "The one who owns Eloise's cathouse? I hear he's pretty good if you're already dead." He turned, no speculation in his eyes. "Hop up on the table. I'll try not to hurt you."

Clutching a loose chemise around my shivering shoulders, I stepped from behind the screen. As I climbed onto his table, my heart hammered. He laid me back and pulled up the tray. His eyes grew serious as he bent between my parted knees.

I yowled when he pressed my belly. I grabbed my mouth and my chemise slipped. I felt so foolish, considering he was one of the few men in town who hadn't seen me raw.

"Sara said you were once delivered of another baby. When?"

"Almost three years ago. I was sixteen. Cornelia and Effie helped me."

"Cornelia Lewis?"

"You know her?" I half sat. His hands and instruments was bloody. I fell back dizzy and scared.

"Cornelia came to see me just a few weeks ago. The Lewises moved to Tempest for the winter. I hear they decided to stay. It'll be a shame to lose her. She's a fine woman. I don't see how she's lasted this long. Her kind of cancer isn't pretty."

I didn't know the ailment.

"Angela," he said, washing up. "I hate to think you'll go back to work after I straighten you out. You shouldn't get pregnant again."

I didn't say nothing to that.

He sighed. "This'll be painful. How about some of my best whiskey?"

"I ain't much on liquor."

Doc Billy smiled. "Looks like there's something I can teach you then!"

Next morning, abed in Doc's back room, my head spun like a whirligig. I understood why Pa used to look so pained after a night with the skull varnish. The slightest move brought stabbing pain to my head. My belly threatened to crawl out my mouth so I hardly noticed the dull throb deep in my innards.

When Sara visited I scarcely opened my eyes. "You sure I ain't dead?"

Sara held my hand. "You'll feel better soon. I stayed with you all night. Davey's been asking for you."

"Let him make eyes at somebody else."

"I'll go now," she whispered. "Get some rest."

After she left I lay watching the road through the window. A white-topped wagon went by with folks trailing after it. I closed my eyes and could almost picture Ma walking along. There sat Pa driving our wagon. I opened my eyes before letting myself see Becky waving from the back and pressed my face into the pillow.

"Did I leave you in much pain, Angie? I could let you have a bit of laudanum." Doc Billy came in and sat beside me. His hands was near as small as mine. I wondered if he was small all over. Then I felt ashamed. With such warm, comforting eyes, I knowed he was a good man. "Would I be a dirty dog if I kissed you?" he asked. A tear squeezed out of my eye as he kissed my forehead with warm lips. "You had an incomplete miscarriage. You're weak and hung over, but you really will be better soon."

I kept my face turned away.

"I've cared for a few prostitutes in my day, but…" He rubbed his eyes. "I hate to see you throw your life away."

"I ain't even good at it," I whispered. "I ain't good for nothing."

"That's not so! Look at me. Please?" he said. "You're as good as you believe you are. I'm afraid for you only because whoring will harden your heart. Not for any other reason."

He lifted me into his arms and held me, saying nothing more, just hugging me tight like maybe he could squeeze all the sorrow out. I sobbed against his shoulder 'til my eyes was wore out and dry.

Davey come by the next day. "Miss Sara told me you were back," he stuttered, standing in the doorway, clutching wild daisies, Injun paint, and columbine. "She said you took sick and had to come back for good. Hope it wasn't something you ate."

I was sitting up, wearing a ruffled bed jacket Sara brung. I'd brushed my hair and pinked my cheeks. I made a smile and watched Davey light up. "How you been?" I asked, patting the tick so he'd sit by me.

He perched hisself on the spot I patted, his face flushed.

"Did you have a drink before you came?" I scolded, my eyes twinkling.

"I'm scared of doctors," Davey grinned sheepishly.

"Are you still scared of me?"

"No, Ma'am!"

We stared long into each other's eyes. For a homely, scrawny boy, Davey looked mighty appealing to me as he leaned close and kissed my lips.

"Why, Davey!" I cooed.

"I kicked myself for not…going upstairs with you all them

times I wanted to. I know you wanted to, but I was jealous and didn't understand."

A cold hand touched my heart. "Understand what?"

He went to the window. "Did you hear we'll have a postmaster soon? Maybe a telegraph line, too. I went up to the Silver Star Hotel just to see what it's like. What a place! It's got gambling wheels and...women. I paid for one before I heard *you* was back. I ain't had a woman yet, Miss Angela. I want one 'fore I go crazy and ruin myself. I wanted you, but...Hell, I don't know what kind of jackass I am. I seen Bess's girls go upstairs. I seen you. I knew all I had to do was pay the price. The fellas told me that, just a dollar to step into heaven."

"Was she good?"

"I didn't use her, Miss Angela. I wanted a special woman to teach me to be a man! She didn't even look at my face. I was paying good money. I wanted to feel..."

I held out my arms. "Kiss me again, Davey."

He bolted for the door. "I'll be waiting, Miss Angela!"

I laid back smiling. I wasn't wore out yet. Not by a damn sight!

A few days later, Doc Granger threw me out to make room for a fella who'd ate bad meat and was yelling with belly pains. "If you don't leave I'll be crawling in your bed myself," he said over the fella's howls. "I'll sure be glad to get Whitehouse off my heels. All week I couldn't take a step without him asking if you were well yet. You must be quite a gal in the sack."

"Anytime you want a taste, Doc," I smiled, "you'll know where to find me. Thanks." Stepping into the sunshine, I felt like I'd been gone years. The air smelled so good. Wagons, mules, and people filled the street. Miners went in and out of eating houses, saloons, and land offices. A familiar looking man in a white apron loaded the back of a farm wagon with sacks of flour, sugar, and corn meal.

Picking my way across the street, I come upon a new barber

shop where nine men stood lined up. They all stared like they knew me; I stared back and couldn't remember a one. Remembering the man in the apron brought me a shameful sense of relief. At least I'd looked at *one* I'd been with.

"Afternoon, Ma'am," he grinned when I reached him.

I didn't know his name and wondered if I ever had. Smiling my best, I watched dazzling wonderment cross his face. "Will I be seeing you up at Bess's soon?" I asked, sounding like Sara.

"Maybe Saturday night, Miss Angela!" he whispered, his cheery blue eyes sparkling.

I laid my hand on his arm. "I'll look forward to it."

Stepping down to cross to the next building, I saw Dalt watching me from a saloon down the way! I hadn't seen him in a year! He struck off across the traffic, pushing fast toward me, a tight mean look to his face. I don't know why I suddenly felt so mad. Just when Dalt was within earshot, the storekeeper called to me. "Oh! Miss *Angela!* I heard you was sick."

"Had a touch of the ague." I coughed delicately. "Terrible winters hereabouts. And you just call me Angel! Remember now, Saturday night. I'll be looking just for you."

"Oh, yes! Miss Angel!"

I near to walked right into Dalt's chest. He glowered like a hungry bear. "Afternoon, *Miss Angel.*"

I wouldn't let him take my arm. "Afternoon, Mr. Dalton. Back in Tempest for long?"

"Where have you been? I've been trying to find you…to warn you."

"I just come from my sick bed, so don't get me upset or I'll up and faint right here!" I lifted my hem and stepped away.

"The Lewises are in town. I'll take you to…" Glancing up, a sick look crossed Dalt's face. "Afternoon, Mrs. Kennings. Nice to see you again. I heard your husband's back. What road company was he working for?"

I whirled. Standing in the store's doorway, Effie paled and near to dropped her bundles when she saw me. She was uglier than sin.

A little boy, the spit 'n' image of his golden-haired pa, tagged at her side. Her parting words rang in my ears, "One more bastard brat..."

"Angie!" she said. "Mama's been asking for you."

"Tell her hello for me." I hurried off before she could say more. Giving Dalt a sneer, I rushed up the street faster than I should have. My lungs ached and I felt faint when I reached Bess's. Turning, I saw Effie watching from the edge of the store's porch. Dalt had disappeared again.

Henry Albertson, the general storekeeper, was one of my first customers when I went back on the job two weeks later. I intended to do the best I could, even if it killed me. That included remembering names, faces, and preferences. I liked Henry. He was as eager as a pup. That scared me 'cause I didn't recall it from before.

"Where was my head?" I asked Sara as we lazed about in the morning.

"Go easy before you wind up at Doc's again. This time dead."

Oh, I was careful! I was so damn careful I scared myself. I was just so glad to be alive, glad I wasn't bleeding, glad laying didn't hurt.

Then come the night Davey was ready to go upstairs! I'd been back to work awhile and was clearing a good five bucks a night. He held me tight as we danced, a special new light in his eyes. "I can't wait no more," he whispered.

"Ready to step into heaven?" I asked and giggled when sweat broke out on his brow.

I led him upstairs feeling as beautiful and wicked as ever in my life! We stood together in my room, looking into each other's eyes, smiling. "What do I do?" he asked, trembling.

I'd seen a lot of nervous greenhorns, but he was the worst! I sat him down and pulled off his boots. He cringed when I worked the buttons on his shirt. "Help me with *my* buttons," I said, thrusting my bosom toward his thin awkward fingers.

He shook as if he had the palsy. Never saw a man so slow! My breath come quicker as he exposed my breasts. I let my skirt down and dropped my three petticoats. Then I turned, letting him enjoy me in my corset and drawers.

Davey licked his lips and drew a ragged breath. I shut my eyes and sighed when his hands closed over my breasts and he kissed me. He shed his shirt and let me help with his trousers, boots, and socks. After he opened his johns to all that pure untouched flesh, I soaped him, marveling at the miracle growing to full size in my hand.

I trickled the water over him 'til his head wrenched back, the muscles in his neck like corded cables. "Lay back now," I said, washing quick and poking my sponge in. "Want to take off them johns?"

He shook his head. "Please hurry, Angel!"

Trembling, I laid beside him. "Sh-h-h. I want to enjoy you, too."

I hardly touched him before he crawled on me, panting, almost crying. "Now, Angel? Now?"

I showed him the way, expecting he'd go off quick, but, by thunder, he had stamina! Davey Whitehouse was my first virgin man, first I knowed of, anyhow. I clung to him, hearing my own cries of delight and thought *this* was how it should be! *This* was what I longed for.

"You're wonderful!" I panted, feeling him build to his peak. He took me there with him, released the fountain of pleasure deep inside me, poured wave upon wave of mystery on me like I hadn't knowed in ages. I'd forgotten how blinding it was, how it ripped me open and left me almost screaming for the pure enjoyment of it!

He pumped and pumped and suddenly, with a soft gasp, drove me deep into the tick. We quivered in each other's arms, moaning and laughing. Davey let out a whoop. "Damn!" He hugged me tight and laughed. "Damn!"

I rolled off the bed to wash, expecting him to watch me walk about.

He laid grinning at the ceiling with his hands clasped behind his head and wiggling his toes. "I'm going to get drunk!" He hopped up.

"Dry off first," I laughed, feeling wonderful, beautiful, special. He pulled on his clothes. "How much do I owe you, Angel?"

Then he grabbed me. "You *are* an angel! The most beautiful, most desirable female on this earth!"

I felt bold. "A dollar."

He slapped the cold coin in my palm and kissed me. "I love you!" Then he waltzed out, whistling loud enough to rouse half the town.

I opened my hand. It was a mighty pretty gold dollar. I dropped it on the bed and douched three times.

Davey come upstairs six more times. Each time he paid with a kiss, a whistle, and a gold dollar. Bess let me keep them coins for good luck, laughing when she heard Davey's whistle 'cause she knew where he'd been.

In July, Davey married Mary Drake, the new postmaster's seventeen-year-old daughter.

Ten

Summer 1865

"I hate him! Sneaking bastard."

"No, you don't. Come this fall, he'll be back with his smile and gold dollar. You'll bring him up here same as before." Sara smiled into the looking glass to examine her teeth.

I jerked the brush through my hair. "I'd spit on him!"

"You didn't think he'd marry you?" Sara cried. "Davey's like any other man. He wants a whore for his bed and a virgin for his wife. I guarantee he'll be back every Saturday night once you give him a French delight. Men love it more than just about anything," she giggled wickedly.

"I'd sooner bite it off."

Sara shook her curls. "You're still pretending you're better than the rest of us."

"I suppose you're not?"

"*I* won't ever fall in love with a dumb red-haired boy—or anybody else."

"I don't love him. I hate him!"

Davey met that sly piece of baggage the night word reached the postmaster that somebody kilt President Lincoln. She'd been so upset she just "intruded upon his heart."

Keeping my bitterness to myself, I started working harder and longer than ever before. I went on charging a dollar and some didn't like that. To them I'd say, "You want cheap, you enjoy cheap."

Bess liked the idea. "The price of coffee's gone up. Land's selling for a fortune. Why shouldn't you girls charge more?" And she'd roll with laughter, growing richer by the hour.

One night I sat in the kitchen, drinking whiskey and coffee with Bess. Rain pelted the back of the dancehall so hard it oozed under the window. Banjo swept the empty dance floor, watching in case some fella ventured out in the downpour. Sara, Jessie, and Maybelle was sleeping. Annie and Clair, the newest girls, stood on the porch watching red mud course down the street.

A clap of thunder rattled the windows and echoed off the canyon walls. A frantic knock at the back door made us jump! "Bet that's some husband out to 'tend the stock,'" Bess chuckled, easing her bulk out of the chair.

Cing Loo opened the door. Rain slashed at him, soaking the floor. "New girl," he squawked.

Bess sighed. "They turn up at the worst times." She lumbered to the door, holding back her skirts. "Come in here, girl! I ain't wetting my drawers for the likes of you. Come on! We don't bite."

"I *ain't* coming in!" someone yelled over the howling wind. "I'm looking for Angela Pallard."

I joined Bess at the edge of the rain's reach.

"Who *is* that, Angel? A friend of yours?"

"Angie, is that you? Oh my God, I didn't believe it!" The girl cleared her eyes. Effie Kennings's wet hair stuck flat to her face. Rain poured off her skin and her shoulders sagged under a soggy blanket. "Mama's sick!"

Grabbing Cing Loo's slicker, I plunged into the torrent, following Effie around to the street. There sat Jim Lewis in their wagon just as mean-eyed as I remembered. I climbed up and threw myself against him hard, just to be a bother. Effie squeezed up beside me.

Cussing a blue streak, Jim turned the wagon in the mud and thrashed his mules. We jolted down to the canyon road and crossed over. Up past cabins and garden patches awash in mud, the road snaked higher. Had Jim kept on, he would've come out on the mesa where the Silver Star Hotel looked out over the canyon. I hadn't knowed so many families lived in Tempest, but then I couldn't see the whole town from my window no more.

Jim pulled to a stop alongside a cottage and Effie jumped down. As I climbed down I heard little Todd squalling. He surely was his mother's son!

"I'll take you back when Cornelia's finished with you," Jim said from the dripping shadows under his hat. I shuddered hearing that low voice. I glanced back over my shoulder as I headed for the door. He didn't move.

"Every woman in the valley must be here," I whispered in amazement as I stood in the doorway, shaking mud from my dancing slippers.

"When Mr. Albertson told me where I'd find you, I didn't believe it!" Effie hissed, toweling her face. "I wouldn't let you in here except Mama insisted I find you. Thank *God* you're dressed half proper. I thought I'd have to wait *all night* for you to come away from one of your..." Her voice choked into silence.

"Effie?" come a soft weak voice. "Did you find her?"

"Yes, Mama. Stay put. We'll be right in."

Under the haughty stares of eight or nine women, I brushed at my wet red skirts. They was all in black or brown and frowned up plain faces, their eyes shocked wide. I lifted my chin. Staring back, I silently cussed them old biddies.

Cornelia appeared in the doorway of a dim sleeping room, standing hunched forward, a kind of gladness in her eyes that spoke much of sorrow. I rushed to her but she held me off, kissing my cheek with papery lips. "Don't hug me, Angie. The pain...You know most of these ladies, don't you? Mrs. Albertson. Her husband owns the general store. Mrs. Drake, the postmaster's wife. Helen Gilbert, she married the bathhousekeeper. Lottie Myer's husband is an assessor. Lizbeth Corning is new in town and a bride of three months."

I stared at Cornelia in panic. She probably thought I was baking bread in some eating house! "If I'd knowed you was sick I would've brought some cakes," I said, wishing it was true.

She smiled a bit. "You used to bake the best bread. Ladies... Oh, I forgot Molly James there. She's a widow and runs her own dressmaking business. Cathy Johnson works for her now. I'm sorry, ladies. I didn't see you sitting there."

When I come in, they was the only two who didn't stand. They knew what I was.

Cornelia didn't notice their stiff nods. "This is little Angela Pallard," she went on. "She come across the prairie with Jim and Effie and me back in '60. Her baby sister drowned in the Little Blue. Her pa got killed on the trail. And her ma, she was a dear, dear friend of mine. We was up to put flowers on her grave last summer." By the look in her eyes I suspected flowers rested on baby Lillian's grave, too. I thought I was going to bawl in front of them all!

Effie turned away. "Lord give me *strength!*"

Cornelia sagged. Taking her on my arm, I led her back to the sleeping room. Effie helped her into bed. The bare room was cold and smelled odd. Effie poured a spoonful of potion. Cornelia swallowed it and closed her eyes as if it tasted sweet as honey. "Leave Angie and me alone," Cornelia whispered.

Looking wounded, Effie crept out. When the door closed, Cornelia uncorked the brown bottle and drained it!

"Don't!" I cried.

"Sh-h-h. I need it, Lord, forgive me. I'm weak and afraid." She reached for my hand. "Effie won't believe I'm dying."

"Don't talk like that!"

"She'll carry on when I go. There won't be nobody to pinch her and make her mind."

I giggled as if I was coming unhinged.

"Thank God, Rusty came back to her," she whispered. "He showed up in December—late one night—like he was running." Pausing, she rubbed her eyes. "Effie's expecting again, did you notice? I wish I'd live to see this one. Rusty ain't much of a husband, but he sure gave her a fine son." She licked her lips and sighed deep. "You ain't married?"

I shook my head.

"Not to that man…Dalt?"

"He just happened on me that day I saw Effie at the store."

"Pike came by our place last year asking after you. He looked…
wild." She shook her head.

"I ain't seen him since before my baby Lillian died."

"Oh, Angie…" she sighed. "You poor thing. You should've
come to us." She seemed to forget what she was saying. "I told Jim
we'd look after you. He said you'd been after Rusty, so he drove
you off."

"I wasn't! Please believe me, Cornelia!"

She lifted her hand. "Men are foolish. *I* know you were doing
your best. Get my Bible—over there."

I found it on the dresser, three inches thick with gold on the
edge of each page. It fell open to a picture of a bearded man in
the clouds, pointing his finger at a naked woman. I closed that
book quick!

"Read to me."

"I can't," I whispered. "I thought you knew."

"Call Effie."

I went to the door. Effie burst in, her face streaked with
tears. "Mama?"

"Read."

The pages creaked in a strange ancient way as Effie opened the
book. "The Lord is my shepherd…" She whimpered, "I can't. Oh,
Mama, try to be strong. Let me get Doc Granger!"

"Show Angie the words. Teach her."

Effie bawled.

Cornelia opened her weary eyes. "Angie is to have my Bible…
and those things I made for her. Get them."

Giving me a wet look of one-hundred-proof hate, Effie opened
the trunk at the foot of the bed. She lifted out a pile of baby dresses
embroidered and tucked with the finest stitches.

"I made these before we knew…Angie, you've known more
sorrow than you deserve. Keep those for the next baby." She
waved Effie away. "You'll find a good man, one who'll understand

everything. I promise."

Effie ran out, slamming the door.

"If she ever needs anything…"

I stared at Cornelia. "Effie wouldn't come to me! You don't know…"

"Yes, I do. If she needs help…promise. And help Effie keep her husband. He's not worth it, but…Effie isn't strong or brave like you."

"How could I help? I ain't seen Rusty since that day Jim run me off!" I clapped my hands over my loud words.

"She ain't pretty and she ain't willing."

Cornelia knew! I felt light-headed and grabbed the bedpost. Effie was sobbing in the bosom of Tempest's respectable ladies. Jim sat in the rain ready to make sure I got took back where I *belonged*. I was with Cornelia, and she knew!

"Go," she sighed.

The Bible laid like a stone in the crook of my arm. The baby dresses felt soft as kisses against my fingers. I backed out quickly, thinking if I got out in time, she'd never be dead to me. Cornelia looked across the room as if seeing a great vista from a mountaintop. Her face glowed with eerie white light. She smiled…and the light went away.

I opened the door and stumbled out. I couldn't get my breath. I wanted to scream. Did I dare faint in Effie's parlor? I ran out, thinking I'd get so drunk I wouldn't suffer this loss. As I climbed aboard the wagon with Jim, Effie yowled so much like a coyote the hairs on my scalp stood up.

"Pa!" she screamed from the door. Jim whipped his mules as if he didn't hear her. The wagon lunged down the narrow winding road like he meant to outrun death.

Mud flew up and struck me in the face. The wind tore at the things in my hands. The rain hid my tears and washed me clean by the time we reached Bess's. Jim looped the lines over the brake lever, jumped down like a man half his age and come around to lift me down. I couldn't look away from his red-rimmed hollow eyes!

His arms went around me! He pressed me against the muddy wheel and his rain-wet lips hit my face! "How much?" he hissed.

"What? Cornelia only gave me…"

"How much do you charge?" He thrust hisself against me, showing what he meant. "How much?"

I couldn't believe it! "Ten dollars. In gold!" I tore free and started for the back door.

"Where the hell'd you go?" Bess said, appearing in the doorway.

Jim grabbed me and jerked me back. "Are there back stairs to your room?"

I threw off his hand. "Get away from me!"

Bess took the Bible and baby dresses. "What the hell are these things?"

I didn't have time to answer. Jim pulled me back toward the wagon. Though I struck his face and scratched his neck, he wouldn't turn loose.

"Bess!" I cried.

She reappeared with her shotgun. By then Jim was trying to push me back on the wagon.

"I ain't going nowhere with you. Bastard!"

Lightning fast he tore my bodice from throat to waist! Cold rain pelted my breasts making my nipples stand up pert. He'd thought on me since that day he caught me with Rusty, I could tell. His eyes got full, his jaw slack. Them big hands come at me slow, closing over my breasts. I fixed myself for pain. I thought he meant to kill me!

Jim Lewis kissed me! And it wasn't no kiss of a pious man. He pulled me down the gully behind the privy through Jessie's garden patch. There, on a hill running in mud, Jim threw me down and straddled me. I kept rubbing my eyes as he loosened his belt. I wanted to see Jim as he should be, but he kneeled over me, his teeth bared. Opening his trousers, he displayed a fearsome weapon of flesh. I pressed my knees so tight together they hurt. He got hold of them and forced them apart.

So help me, I did not want to feel what he made me feel, holding me wide and looking…looking…

SAMANTHA HARTE

Then he was in me, driving in his hate, pushing me deep into the mud. If I'd been anything but what I was, he would've hurt me bad. I closed my eyes and rode him out, forgetting who he was. My nails cut my signature in his arms. I took all he gave, took it and took it 'til he filled me with his fury and grief with a cry.

As if he'd turned to stone, he fell on me. I made one small move against him to get my release. A little cry of pleasure filled my throat and I chuckled. In a gasp of horror, he rolled off me, looking stunned, struck dumb with surprise. The rain filled his face and beat his chest, washing away the evidence of his sin.

Jim jumped to his feet and closed his trousers. He stumbled in circles, searching for his hat. I lay there, smiling just a bit, feeling blazing power throbbing in my legs. Bess's giant shadow filled the back door as Jim tried to turn his wagon in the mud and couldn't.

"I'd help you," Bess called to him. "But you don't need help with nothing. You just take 'em where you find 'em!" She laughed and laughed. Even the thunder couldn't quiet her.

Jim beat his mules mercilessly. In a flurry of groaning wheels, braying, and flying mud, he was gone. Cing Loo hobbled out to pull me from the muddy hill. I stumbled in the kitchen, soaked to the skin, my skirts heavy with mud.

"Boil water! Get the tub!" Bess shouted to Cing Loo. "Holy hellfire, I ain't seen nothing better in twenty years! You had him plain crazy, Angel! Makes me hurt just to think of it!" She stripped me as Cing Loo filled the tub with bucket after bucket. I slipped into the warm water and let Bess rinse the mud from my hair.

"I told him ten dollars," I said through chattering teeth. "He didn't pay."

"Don't you worry," Bess cackled. "He'll pay. Damn, you're something!"

"You could've stopped him!" I yelled.

"And cheat you of that pleasure? If I ain't mistaken, that was Jim Lewis hisself. I heard he wants to clean up this town and be our first mayor!"

Cing Loo poured another pot of hot water in the tub. I shivered more. "A minute ago I felt like the best in the world."

"You was! Hellfire! I wish one man wanted me that much."

"He didn't want me. He was punishing *me*!"

"You're so dumb you don't know *what* men what. He can't admit it, but he wants you. The hell he don't. Where'd you get that Bible? And them baby dresses—you ain't pregnant again?"

"Cornelia Lewis just gave them to me—on her deathbed. Bess! I feel like a whore! First Jim Lewis called me one. Now he's made me one. Will I go to hell for this?"

Bess laughed 'til her eyes watered. She had to sit down to get her breath. "Hell and damnation, girl! You ain't going nowhere but up to bed. It's that widow-man who's going to hell!"

Eleven

Winter 1865

Bess got mighty particular who she let in when, by winter, a bunch of no-account, suspicious fellas took up residence in Tempest. They come west after the war of the rebellion. Some had been with that notorious militia that kilt all them Injuns. Always there was talk of them riding up the pass to mutilate folks like they was doing on the prairie. Decent folks spent hours worrying, while more sensible folks spent their free time at Bess's and the like!

'Long about that time more than one miner began grumbling that Jim Lewis's preaching in the new church was giving Tempest a bad name. Whenever I heard of Jim's sermons against the sins and vices infesting the respectable folks' fine mountain community I thought on that rainy night Cornelia died. Jim called hisself a lay preacher. He wanted his grandchildren growing up strong and clean-minded in God's pure air, but I knowed. I knowed Jim Lewis right down to his last cry.

Under that profusion of Injun trouble and Good Book quoting, we girls bedded down to each winter dawn. The sun would creep over Silver Peak bringing gold light to the rooftops, chimneys, and mine shafts. Rattling wagons and stages would fill the morning silence. One such November morning Sara and me was trying to sleep.

"Lay still," Sara muttered.

I punched my pillow. "I wish I could read Cornelia's Bible. Then I'd know what to think about Jim Lewis's preaching I keep hearing about."

"Since that bastard got you, you keep worrying on your damn soul. Jim's worried about *his*, you damned ninny! If it makes you feel better, tell yourself he was crazy drunk."

"He was ice cold sober."

"Go to sleep. I'm tired."

"I can't. It's too quiet."

"It ain't quiet! If it'll ease your ignorant mind, I'll admit we're all going to hell. Why you care is a puzzle to me. I'm the one raised by a family quoting scripture. If I didn't know you couldn't read a word, I'd say you'd been raised a nun."

"Don't know what that is."

"A religious woman. A virgin married to God Almighty. Leave your soul for when you're old and ugly."

"It *must've* been my fault! Why are we called the sinners, but not the men?"

Sara sat up balling her fists. "When you get like this I could hit you. Is it time for the rags?"

"No," I sighed. "My last fella tonight…he said something about one of Jim's sermons, how sin can be seen in the eyes. If I had church-learning, I'd know if he's right!"

"That's just fine! Now I have to listen to you fret. Did you tell that guilty bastard to spit in Lewis's face? That pious old dog raped you, though no judge would ever admit a whore can be raped. Does that sin show in his eyes?"

I snuggled into the lumpy pocket on my side of the tick. "I said if he closed his eyes while he was with me, come morning nobody'd see nothing in them."

Sara clapped her hands. "You're good, Angel!" She patted my knee. "Was your ma educated? Did your pa talk God to you?"

"Gold was Pa's god. Ma just talked of starting over and becoming respectable."

"See that? You got religion at your ma's knee. If you're really worried about your soul, dress up fine Thursday afternoon and ask Jim Lewis to preach to us sinners. *I'll* keep his eyes popping!" She squirmed with glee. "Oh, I'd love to do that! Ask him, Angel!"

"Go to sleep," I said, turning away, imagining Sara spread-eagled in a front pew! Downstairs a spittoon got kicked across the hall.

Not more than an hour later I woke feeling as if I'd slept sound 'til late afternoon. Tempest was in full morning clamor. I tiptoed across the icy plank floor. From the window I watched a lumber wagon wheel higher and higher to where a new saloon was going up. The double clap of hammering and its echo off the canyon walls should've convinced me nothing was wrong.

The last time I'd woke feeling bright and alert, though, I'd been laying beside my dead baby. Unnerved, I hopped back in bed, grateful for Sara's warmth.

Next thing I knew, Banjo was shaking my shoulder. "Wake up! Bess is gone." I'd never seen him in a flannel shirt and work pants. He seemed bigger, more a man. "She's not dead," he whispered. "Just gone. Piano and all. Cing Loo was fetching water to start breakfast. She's cleared out."

Wearing only a corset cover and drawers, Sara leaped from the bed and threw open one of her trunks. Collapsing on the floor, her arms buried in layers of ruffles, she sighed. "I still got my cache!"

I pulled the enamel chamber pot from under my side. My pouch was safe.

"Seems you ladies is well set," Banjo said, rubbing his neck. "But I'm out a week's pay and a job."

Sara patted his arm. "It's time we all moved on, Banjo. Go show them folks at the Silver Star how good you play the piano."

"If you please, Bess give me that dumb name. My name's John Harrington, and I'll see you girls get situated before I take off. You'll need an ass-sist with them trunks."

Sara grinned. "I could pay, John. With more than money." She curled her fingers around Banjo's thick arm.

"You want I should carry them trunks up Silver Peak?"

"We won't be a minute, Angel," she giggled. "Course, if you want to stay…What you say, John? Got the stamina for two lusty ladies?"

"I need coffee before I indulge," I said, slipping out, too unsettled to think on bedding. I set water to boil and threw in a handful of grounds. Bess's office was bare to the walls. So was her sleeping room upstairs. How she snuck off in those early hours since we'd fallen into bed—and why—I couldn't figure. For sure, the next time I woke to the notion something was wrong, I'd pay attention!

Our bedsprings needed greasing. As I crept down the hall, I might've given in to the temptation to peek in to see Sara's snow white limbs entwined with John's black ones, if I hadn't caught sight of something odd in Jessie's room. Leaving passionate cries behind, I stepped in. It was bare, too, except for her fine bed and linens—soaked with blood!

I ran to the foot of the bed, clutched the post and stared down into dried pools as if I might fall into them! My head reeled. The stain smeared across the linens and across the floor to the side window. Leaning out, all I saw below was wagon tracks in the muddy snow.

The bedsprings stopped their telltale serenade. "Smell's like the coffee's burning," Sara called in a full-throated, dreamy voice.

Swallowing bile, I presented myself in the doorway and looked on a pair of mighty contented folks languishing in the fullness of their pleasure. "What is it?" John asked, seeing my face. He followed me into Jessie's room. As he leaned out the window I figured the light of day did a man's backside justice.

Sara toddled in, pulling on her wrapper.

John pushed us out. "Get dressed! Any cold water downstairs?"

"Two buckets," I said.

He was already in our room, poking long dark legs into white johns. "I'll clean up. Soon as you're ready, we clear out."

"What happened in there?" Sara whispered, her face drained.

"We don't want to know," he said, tumbling down the stairs. "I heard Angel's old friend Dalt is working the greenhorns in the Placer Saloon," John called, lugging the buckets up the stairs. "Go to him."

• • •

When we walked in the Placer Saloon an hour later the boy sweeping up looked me and Sara over so careful his ears blushed. "Mr. Dalton's in number three. I expect he's still sleeping," he said.

Sara chucked the boy under his chin and winked. "Fetch him some strong coffee, and I'll thank you right proper later."

The boy beamed.

Upstairs, Dalt lay snoring in a tousled bed, his arm around the naked back of a dark-skinned girl. "Morning, Dalt," I said.

Dalt sat up, his eyes half crossed. After a second he blinked and frowned. "Clear out, Marie." She slipped from his bed, muttering under her breath, and jerked on her clothes so hard her breasts bounced. "I ain't seen you in months," Dalt said. "What is it?"

"Bess cleared out," Sara said. "We'd like to work here now."

"Somebody got kilt there last night!" I whispered. "John's back there cleaning up blood!"

Dalt rubbed his lips, chin, and nose. Then he swept his hand over his bald dome as if dusting it. "Just what I need. Who the hell is John?"

"Banjo," Sara put in. "Can we stay?"

"Marie won't like it, but I could use the business. Working here, though, you'll have to fix up better than that, Angel."

"Still the gentleman," I snapped, sorry I'd been glad to see him.

"Still a huffy little lady." He pulled on his trousers.

"You offering to stake Angel for a new wardrobe, big man?" Sara smiled, dimpling.

He eyed me and grinned. "Yeah. Get yourself a halfdozen things that'll pop eyes out. You got the build for it now, honey. Put it on my tab."

"*You* got credit with Mrs. Molly?"

Dalt buffed his boots with the corner of the bedlinen. "I got credit everywhere."

• • •

ANGEL

Mrs. Molly was doing a brisk business in woollies and shawls 'til I
come in. Two ladies I recalled from Cornelia's dying was there, but
I disremembered their names. "Morning," I called, inspecting a blue
calico dress in her window. "How much for this?" The ladies walked
out, looking like they was downwind of a privy.

"Morning, Angel. You're up early," Molly said wearily.

"Got me a new job and need six new dresses."

She brushed dull hair across her forehead. "How soon?"

I smiled. "Today."

"All I have is catalog dresses and what I make. Find someone
else to sew for you. I can't hold up my head in front of my friends."
Molly rubbed her neck.

"Ain't hungry enough to welcome my money yet, is that it?"
I smiled.

"Folks help us out."

"Mighty nice to have folks about when you need them," I said.
"How many you feeding? Five? You sew much for Effie Kennings
and the others? Do they buy six dresses in a year?"

"I don't mean to insult you, Angel. If Cornelia thought highly
of you, she had good reason. I just don't feel right sewing clothes…"

"…I take off," I finished for her, "Take 'em off for half
the men in this town. It might keep some respectable man from
marrying you."

Molly hung her head, but her eyes snapped.

"Visiting me don't change a man's feelings one bit when he
fixes to marry," I said. "I'll get six dresses, but someday you'll marry
up again."

"The dress is six dollars."

I snapped a ten dollar gold piece on her counter. Beside it I put
down two more, slow, so she'd taste the vittles they'd buy. It was all I
had at the moment. "Finish three this week and three more soon as
you can," I said. "I want new petticoats, more French drawers with
buttons and long lace, and two corsets, the kind with whalebone and
pink ribbons. The very best. Put it all on a bill and send it along to
Jack Dalton at the Placer Saloon. Room three."

"But, Angel…"

"I'll pay you three more ten dollar gold pieces when you finish." A warm charge went through me. "Tell them biddies I don't like paying your high prices. I'm wishing I could go to some other dressmaker as good as you. I think you're a hard-hearted woman charging me more than you would a regular customer. Be sure and tell 'em that. Tell 'em you mean for me to pay ten dollars a dress, and you're thinking of charging fifteen. It's only what a woman like me deserves. And you charge twice over for all them drawers and corsets."

Her eyes softened.

"If times get hard I'll order up another mess of dresses to keep you in victuals and firewood. Can you fit that blue dress for tonight?"

Molly motioned to her back fitting room. "What other styles would you like?"

I tried to describe what Sara'd been wearing the day she arrived in Tempest. Finally I took Molly's pencil and put down my ideas on some brown wrapping paper.

"You sketch very well," Molly smiled.

I hadn't held a pencil since I was eight. "Didn't know I could do that," I grinned.

"Won't you get cold with your…shoulders so bare?"

I smiled wickedly. "I ain't never cold!"

Mrs. Molly cut down that blue calico so my bosom almost fell out. I felt mighty special 'til I got back to the Placer and saw Sara sitting on the bar.

"Where's Dalt? I'm hungry," she said, her eyes sparkling, one dainty foot swinging. "He's taking us to the Silver Star for supper!" Her voice sounded the same. Her hair shined as pretty, but her face was creamy and pink. Her gown was as beautiful as a flower.

"I hate you all over again," I said, taking the whiskey she poured.

"Come on," she laughed. "We'll do you up proper, too!"

...

"Are you ladies ready?" Dalt asked when he arrived driving a rented buggy. He wore a new black suit and white ruffled shirt. He looked good though the years off the mountain was telling on him.

He drove us across the canyon up between cabins crouched under giant pines. Children played shoot-'em-up in barren yards with yapping dogs and squawking chickens underfoot. Wash flapped from ropes slung between trees. We come out on a mesa high enough to look over half the canyon.

The Silver Star Hotel, backed by Silver Peak, stood a full three stories high with a veranda busy with strolling couples and groups of men smoking and talking. Properly it was known as a restaurant and hotel. Folks come from El Dorado to visit and dine. Men owning rich mines lived there. Gamblers and a string of fancy Eastern whores worked there.

Sara walked in with her head high, a coy smile to her lips and a swing to her bustle that drew all eyes. I felt dumb-ignorant stumbling up the steps, gawking at the pretty colored glass windows, exclaiming over the chandelier glittering overhead.

At a table set with silver and china, we ate beefsteak. Dalt ordered up champagne and got me drunk! We visited the gambling rooms, did a lot of talking and laughing, tossed around a lot of money, and set a lot of eyes to smoldering.

"Would you laugh if I told you I mean to own this place someday?" Dalt asked near dawn.

"I'd say you're every bit as drunk as me."

"I stake prospectors all over these hills and have part stock in half the claims in the district. When the railroad comes, Tempest will boom like never before."

"I heard a fella say no railroad can take the grade."

"A narrow gauge can. You wait, Angel. Soon I'll be so damn rich I'll eat off gold plates." His lips spread full, sparking my desire. "I got us a room, heh-heh-heh," he smiled.

"Ain't Marie enough?" I whispered. "What about Sara?"

"Sara found herself a gentleman long ago. Marie just keeps me warm. I've missed you, Angel honey. You'll always be special to me."

"Even if I could count good, I couldn't know how many men I've bedded since you."

He chuckled. "Learned any new tricks?"

"There was plenty *you* didn't teach me!"

Sara and I worked the Placer Saloon the next couple months and got along fair, considering the slower trade. One night we come downstairs to find Davey Whitehouse and Rusty Kennings sipping beer! My heart stood still as Sara nudged me. "Didn't I tell you Davey'd be back?"

I made a smile. Acting like nothing had ever happened, I strolled to their table, but I felt cold deep inside. Rusty was still full-faced and good-looking, a man busy making a name for hisself with important townsfolk. Having Jim Lewis for father-in-law made it a sight easier. He looked like he wasn't so sorry he'd saddled hisself with the ol' mare, Effie, after all.

Davey's skin had cleared, and he'd developed a good set of arms, thanks to the smithy's hammer—he sold his claims and took up honest work to support his wife. The responsibilities, though, had done away with his doe-eyes.

Alongside Rusty and Davey sat a third fella they introduced as Ben Corning. He wasn't no special sort of man, not that good to look on, not even promising much under his clothes. And oh, he had solemn eyes, but Sara grew pale under her paint. Her lips parted as if she could almost taste him. I was never to know if Ben reminded her of somebody, or if he just melted her heart that very night. I never saw her look like that before, and she was never quite the same afterwards.

Pulling my eyes from her stare, I curled up to Rusty. "If it ain't the husband of my very dearest friend!" I toyed with his curls. "You're looking good, golden boy. How's Effie?"

"Pregnant." He pinched my thigh and had a mean look I didn't remember and didn't like.

I bounced up and hugged Davey. "How's my favorite fella? Got a family started yet?" I felt like strangling him. Instead, I ran my hand inside his collar and made him shiver.

"Mary could be expecting in the spring." He grabbed my wrist. "I've missed you, Angel."

"*You* know this little lady?" Rusty asked, drinking slow, staring low at Davey as if refiguring his opinion of him. "Have you worked here long, Angie?" Rusty near to laid me out right there with his eyes. The flesh along my back crept up to my neck.

"I been in Tempest near three years. I broke in more men then you've cleared road. What you bet I have?"

Rusty licked his lips. "Remember..."

I forced my eyes to sparkle. "Want to look again? I'm reasonable, ain't I, Davey?"

Davey gulped his beer and ordered another. His hand shook.

Sara floated across the floor and trailed her hand across the back of Ben's neck. He broke out in a sweat! She pulled up the nearest chair and sat so close her knees pressed against his leg. She wetted her lips slow and then draped herself over his shoulder. "Hi, Ben."

Ben swallowed, clutching his drink so tight I wondered if he'd squeeze fingermarks into the glass. Sara played with his collar and whispered in his ear. He stood up so fast I thought he was going to run. Tripping along, tossing her hair and smiling oh-so-sweet, Sara led Ben toward the stairs.

Davey tipped his chair back farther and farther, watching 'til they disappeared above. "He wasn't meaning to do that!" Davey said, his chair hitting back hard on its four legs. "Lizbeth won't like it. She didn't even want him drinking."

"What Lizbeth don't know..." Rusty snickered.

Before I could take Rusty's hand, eager to get that golden boy upstairs and wring his pockets dry, Davey said hoarsely, "Working tonight, Angel?"

Power rose in my chest. I leaned over, giving him full view of

Mrs. Molly's genius with a neckline and whispered, "Want to try something special?"

He ran his hand over his mouth. "Well, hell," he said to Rusty. "If Ben can, so can I!"

"And leave me drinking alone?" Rusty said with a sneer. That's when Marie walked in. Dressed for work, she was a handsome woman.

Closing my door, I had to keep my eyes down for fear Davey would see my hate. "Two bucks…" I said, rolling a ball of scented soap in my hands. "…for a French delight." I didn't touch him 'til he dropped the coins down my bodice.

"I don't know what that…French de-light is," he said, kissing me. "But if it's worth two whole bucks I'll bet it'll tear my head off."

"You won't miss it," I giggled, soaping him.

Watching me undress, he sprawled on the bed, smiling like he'd forgot he married that postmaster's daughter. I ran my hands around my breasts and thighs. I was going to try Silver Stan Sampson's favorite sport on him and wanted him to love it, but not 'cause I wanted to pleasure him. He was going to know just what he was missing every time he laid his respectable wife.

Soon as he knowed what I was about, he doubled in size! The first touch of my tongue made him crawl backwards up the bedstead. "Oh, Angel!" he cried, tangling his fingers in my hair.

Judging from the moans, folks might've figured I was torturing the poor newlywed man of six months, but when Davey come off his peak I figured every soul in Tempest knew I'd just delivered two dollars worth of pure heaven.

After that I never took less than two gold or silver dollars. I was the best whore in Colorado Territory. Davey Whitehouse would testify to it on a Bible!

Twelve

Summer 1866

"How come you're going to scratch in your garden patch and get all sweated up?" I asked.

"I want to feel the sun baking my hair and pretend I'm back of a cabin, growing greens for my family instead of back of a saloon biding my time 'til the evening's trade," Sara said, wearing the faraway look that had haunted me for weeks.

I watched her go down the stairs, holding the banister tight. She paused at the bottom to push back her pretty reddish-gold hair with a pale hand. A shiver ran up my back as I followed her. I felt scared, scared something was wrong. Sara had closed herself off from me and there weren't nothing I could do.

I found Marie in the kitchen, searing tortillas over the cookstove. "What's ailing Sara?" I asked, watching out the back door as Sara stooped to look at her scraggly vegetables.

Marie looked at me with them black eyes set in a thin face all shadowy with hollows and sharp bones. I felt a breath away from a knife in my ribs every time she looked at me. "Ben ain't coming around much longer."

"'Cause of his wife?"

Marie's eyes flashed. "Ben loves Sara, but he ain't fixing to marry her."

"Did he tell her that?"

"Stupid," she muttered. "He didn't have to! Besides, he's flat broke busted, living off the charity of friends. Ain't nobody going to give him enough money to support his wife and a whore."

I watched Sara struggle across the yard with a water bucket. It was more work than I'd ever seen her do, discounting climbing stairs. I liked my Rusty, but sure wouldn't mope around if he stopped seeing me. I guessed I didn't know how love felt.

As usual, our lucky trio, Rusty, Davey, and Ben, come by that night. They sat laughing and drinking, talking of the bid for statehood, the price of gold and silver, and the prospects of Ben getting a paying job. Sara hadn't come down yet. Marie was already upstairs with an early customer, a lanky fella who worked at the livery and was on his supper break.

"Come keep us company," Davey called when I come down.

I smiled, feeling a bit nasty. "How's your little wife?"

"Fat," he chuckled. "Complaining all the time. Cabin's too small, cookpot's too heavy, weather's too hot. How come wives don't act like pretty gals?"

I curled onto his lap and toyed with his kerchief. "All wives have to be is good."

Rusty and Davey hooted. "That's for damn sure! Good and ornery. Got the time for me tonight?" Rusty asked, running his hand down my arm.

"I always got time for you," I smiled, still a bit done in by that sweet face. 'Course, in bed he was no lamb. Rusty took his pleasure rough and tumble. "Marie will be back down soon," I said, kissing Davey's cheek. "You like that hot pepper, don't you? What's Mary think of your new skills?"

Davey blushed blood red.

I pranced around behind Ben's chair. He was a peculiar one to figure. His brooding face and hard mouth didn't match his sad soft eyes. I could see why Sara wanted to ease his torment. I slid my arms around Ben's neck and giggled. "Sara's upstairs getting ready just for you."

He went stiff and reached for his beer, tipping some into his lap.

Davey and Rusty whooped and slapped their legs. "You got his eyes popping, Angel!" Rusty laughed. "Hell, Davey. Let's treat Ben this once. Looks like he needs some, bad!" He slapped a gold dollar on the table.

Davey reached into his shirt pocket, smirking.

Ben come off his chair like it was hot and bolted for the door.

"I'm sorry!" I said, running after him and grabbing his arm. "Don't run off. Sara would be broken-hearted. Don't let them two snakes bother you none."

Ben's face looked hard as granite. "They're buying my beer, too."

"You could be a muleteer," I said. "It's good pay…or a drover."

"Lizbeth says I got to work in town. You say Sara's expecting me? I hoped she wouldn't notice if I didn't show up this once."

"A working girl don't often find someone special like you."

Realizing he was standing in the doorway of the Placer Saloon with a whore on his arm, Ben Corning broke free and bolted. I felt like hell. Sara would kill me!

A minute later she come down the stairs, wearing a pale green watered silk with creamy lace all over the neck and sleeves. Her stockings showed dark under her petticoats and short skirt, and she was wearing new high-button shoes. Seeing only Rusty and Davey, her smile faded. She grabbed the banister and steadied herself.

"Sara?" Marie called from the upstairs hall. "Somebody's hanging around out back. Tell Dalt to check on it."

Dalt served up a couple more beers and then went out back. "Ben's waiting for you, Sara," he whispered, coming back moments later, his face stormy.

I didn't see Sara again 'til I come downstairs with Rusty an hour later. She lounged in the lap of a fella who ran the bathhouse. Seeing me, she gave her customer a quick kiss and got up. "Don't worry when I don't come up tonight," she whispered. "I'm meeting Ben." She shushed me. "Don't scold, 'cause I won't listen. Ben's my fella now. I'm not charging him any more."

My legs got wobbly, and not 'cause of Rusty's workout. "Does Dalt know?"

"He's not my whoremaster! And you're not telling me I can't!"

She went back and coaxed her customer to his feet. He paid for their drinks and followed her upstairs.

We did a fair piece of business that night. Henry Albertson and Andy Dempster, a fella from the grain and feed store, come in early. Tex, a muleteer in once a month, paid me three dollars to ease an itch he'd nursed near a month! Kendall, a Yankee sergeant who still wore his army blue trousers, wanted me on the floor instead of the bed. I thought the night would never end!

Sara only went upstairs once more with a fella I knew she didn't like a whit. Then she was gone. As the black morning sky turned pale lavender, Dalt closed up. "Where's Sara?" he asked, rubbing his stubbly chin and pressing at his back. "I'm too old for this all-night business."

"In the privy maybe," I said, hoping I looked innocent. "We ain't had trade like tonight in weeks." I handed him twelve bucks. "Put it in the strong box for me. I'm going to bed."

"Feel like coming in with me tonight?" It had been a while since he'd asked.

I gave him a hug. "Got to catch me a little earlier, Dalt."

"Did you hear? Jim Lewis is pretty certain to be the new mayor. Ain't another man in town to challenge him."

I smirked. "Why would folks want to ruin a perfectly good town?"

Sara's and my room had lots of pictures on the walls and lace doilies on the tables. We always laughed, wondering who made our braided rug and if the poor woman knew it rested under the legs of a whore's bed. I laid awake more than an hour waiting for Sara, trying to figure a way to set her straight. She was giving away free from the goodness and stupidness of her heart what she'd sold for fifteen years.

Fifteen! Sure as hell she had to be tired of it, but she was asking for trouble. Townfolks didn't tolerate girls "working" any place but inside a saloon. They kept our "dens of sin" pushed up the hill as

ANGEL

far from respectable society as possible.

One time Sara read me an editorial from the *Tempest Telegraph*: "Our fair community is in need of radical changes," it said. "Tempest has thirty-seven drinking and gambling establishments but only one church. Ninety-three ladies of the night practice their contemptible trade within the town's limits, while decent men can only boast forty-two women of virtue."

Ladies of the night. I sighed. True, I knew the passage of the moon between the ridges the way others knew the sun. I readied for my monthlies when the moon grew full, judged Tempest's growth by lamplights.

I got up once and leaned out my window. The night air felt cool on my cheeks. The smell of pine made strong by dew was fresh and clean compared to the stink of cigar smoke and whiskey downstairs. Sometimes I wished...

A wagon rattled to a stop beside the saloon. I heard chickens squawking. Sara and Ben rounded the back of the saloon—each carrying chickens by the legs. Feathers thick as snowflakes followed the chickens to the ground when they let them go. Sara began throwing out feed, calling softly to her brood and giggling like she was drunk.

Then Ben took her in his arms. They stood so close no light peeked between their bodies. My heart hurt in a lonesome kind of way. Breaking apart, they held hands swinging back and forth back to the wagon. Ben swung onto the wagon seat and hissed to his mules. Sara stood watching and waving long after the sound of his wagon was lost in the growing dawn traffic. I expected her to come upstairs and fall into bed, giggling about her adventure. Instead, she began throwing out feed again.

There was eight chickens.

Bess clearing out so sudden never seemed unusual to folks in Tempest. The new owner turned the hall into a saloon, naturally,

125

and brought in a load of ladies from Mexico. I seldom thought on them bloodstains in the front bedroom 'til a couple Saturday nights after Sara got her chickens.

Rusty and Davey come to the Placer as usual. I'd just come downstairs ready for a hard night.

"Don't know how long he was down there," Rusty was saying when I come up to him. "Doc says it could've been months."

"Evening, fellas. Hot, ain't it?" I said.

Davey squeezed his temples and didn't look at me. "Next time you need help for a job like that, ask Ben or somebody else," he said to Rusty. "It made me sick, dragging that body up to the road and hauling him back to town. Angel, give me a whiskey, and leave the bottle. I'm getting pig-stinking drunk tonight."

Smirking, Rusty slipped his arm around me. "This boy's got one weak belly, I'll tell you!" He caressed my hip. "Bring two glasses, Angel. A couple muleteers found a body dumped in a ravine up the canyon."

Dalt ambled over and put down the bottle. "What's the news on the dead man?"

"Some prospector probably stole his clothes," Davey said. "It wasn't Injuns."

Rusty tipped back his chair. His smile made me feel spiders walking down my back. "You want to believe somebody from around here slashed him like that? He must've bled something fierce," Rusty said, screwing up his lips, his eyes glinting. "I say a razor done it. He was a gambler maybe. Doc says he was fat, at least 'til he wasted."

Dalt glanced at me with uneasy eyes and went back to his bar.

"Could've been anybody," Rusty went on. "The way he was wedged in the rocks I say he was dumped stripped, cut and dead."

"I can't listen to no more!" Davey groaned. He bolted his whiskey and gritted his teeth. Two big tears swelled in his eyes.

"Send him up with Marie. She'll make him forget," Rusty laughed.

"Marie's resting this weekend," I said, unable to get up a smile. "Me and Sara is taking the trade, though it's sure Sara's heart ain't in it." I didn't add she was meeting Ben later.

Rusty looked up at me quick as he unfolded a newspaper sheet. "Says here, we also got us a thief in Tempest."

I set myself down, paying more attention to Davey's sorry eyes than Rusty's reading. "How's Mary?" I asked him.

He ran his hand over his mouth. "Nigh onto her time. S'pose we could go upstairs for a bit, Angel? You mind, Rusty?"

Rusty's eyes grew dark. "I suppose I can wait."

I gave his golden hair a tug though I was feeling so crawly I could scarcely bring myself to touch him. "It's your fault I'm here instead of watching over a cookpot, wondering which saloon my husband's dallying in," I teased, the truth of my words hidden under my false smile.

"Aw, you like it here better. Ain't it so?" Rusty grinned.

"I'll tell you, if I was minding a cookpot, my husband wouldn't be at no saloon. He'd be in bed, waiting for me!"

Rusty's eyes went over me and then he settled back to read. Davey poured hisself another whiskey and gulped it. "Says here," Rusty said, jabbing his finger into the newspaper sheet. "Lizbeth Corning lost eight chickens from her coop couple weeks back."

Davey hiked his trousers and gave me an impatient tug toward the stairs. I paused. That varmint, Ben Corning! He gave them damn chickens to Sara! Night and day she was out feeding them and refused to let Marie or me dress one for supper. She kept Doc Billy locked out of our room and spent hours abed, pouring whiskey down her gullet.

"Angel…" Davey whispered. "I ain't got all night. If Mary has that baby while I'm gone I'll never hear the end of it."

That snake, Corning, telling his wife them chickens was stolen, I kept thinking. Marie would have to burn any newspapers left around so Sara woudn't read that. I was tired of her reading to me anyway. What did I care about the bid for statehood getting denied 'cause President Johnson didn't like Republicans? I wasn't sure what a Republican was and I sure didn't know what the hell a president was supposed to do.

"We got to use Dalt's room," I said. "Sara ain't worth a sack of salt since Ben stopped coming around."

"I never thought girls like you got sweet on fellas."

"We love you all," I giggled, closing the door. "What can I do for you tonight?" I slid my arms around his neck. He'd filled out some. His Mary must've been a good cook at least.

He gazed into my face with a softness I hadn't seen since the early days. "You was my first, Angel. How come you want me, but my Mary don't?"

"Come on, we're up here for fun. You fellas can't make me believe every girl wearing a wedding band hates crawling into bed, not with a fine fella like yourself."

"Sometimes I wish she'd make one single sound. Why can't a good woman enjoy it?"

"Bible-thumpers like Jim Lewis say only whores do."

"Guess I shouldn't complain. Mary, at least, tolerates me. Ben says once Lizbeth's with child he'll have to keep to hisself."

"Lizbeth don't appreciate a good man like Sara does. Maybe your Mary feels less inclined 'cause she's expecting. Wait 'til spring. She'll be so hungry for bedding she'll be after you all the time."

"Now, don't go talking about my wife like that."

I let loose of his neck and walked to the washbasin. Something hotter than whiskey fire pumped through me. I'd never felt quite like that before, like maybe if I turned I'd go after Davey with my nails, maybe even a knife!

I wanted to kick myself. I kept forgetting my customers was just men with an itch. I scratched it for a price, got talked down to by every so-called good woman in town and lived a life of loneliness as thanks. I kept hoping them fools cared about my feelings. Damn the lot of them!

"What's your price tonight for a trip around the world?" Davey asked. "It might be a spell before I can come back." He'd stripped to his johns and was pulling off his boots.

I started unbuttoning my dress as I had hundreds of times before. Sometimes I'd been tired, sometimes needful of love, sometimes scared...Why I bothered thinking at all when I closed

ANGEL

myself in with a fella, I couldn't figure. Damned if I wasn't expected
to ease their sorrows, make 'em feel important, and haul their ashes
all at the same time. For two bucks they was getting a bargain! "I'll
knock you ass-over-teakettle for five bucks," I said, my voice so
much like Bess's I almost looked around to see if she'd ghosted
herself up into one of the room's corners.

"That'd buy a lot of beans and coffee!" he cried.

"Some thief could hold you up on your way home to your wife
who's fat as a sow and won't give you no pleasure. You could be
robbed of them five bucks and wind up rotting naked in a gully. As
pious ol' Jim Lewis says, we're all living on the brink of eternity."

Davey's face drained. He put five dollars in coin on my dresser
and climbed out of his johns.

"Come on over here, big fella. I'm going to make you wish you
could climb out of your skin."

Davey squirmed and moaned with pleasure so loud it sounded
like I was bedding a sick coyote. I pleasured him every way I knew.
Silver Stan Sampson would've been jealous! Davey was a hair's
breadth from going off like an Independence Day firecracker when
I heard giggles out back. Can't figure how I heard them over all
the noise.

"Hold it right there. I'll get a mouthful of whiskey," I told him.
It'd make him last a bit longer and was a good excuse for me to peek
out the window. The canyon looked as dark as the inside of my
heart. Suddenly I saw Sara and Ben dash toward the bushes behind
the privy below.

"Angel..." Davey groaned. "Hurry..."

Hoofbeats hard and fast come 'round from the front. Sara and
Ben darted from the bushes for better cover. A woman on horseback
stopped smack in the middle of Sara's garden patch and pranced in
circles. Ben climbed over a rim of boulders behind the saloon. From
there he could creep along a sluice and get back to the street where
no one would know where he'd been. I saw him doing it and didn't
think nothing of it at first.

Moonlight caught Sara buttoning her bodice as she stepped

129

from behind the privy. I saw her face, cool and innocent. The woman on horseback reined so hard her horse reared.

"Git the hell out of my garden!" Sara yelled.

A pistol glittered in Lizbeth Corning's hand. "I want my chickens!"

"Sara! Sara, watch out!" I yelled, banging on the windowglass.

Sara strolled to her makeshift roost, lifted the screen and scattered the chickens. Grabbing up the nearest one, she rushed on Lizbeth.

"Sara!" I tried to lift the sash but it was stuck fast. The lumpy glass warped the shadowy figures below but didn't distort the flash from the pistol! The explosion broke the night sounds clean off like maybe I couldn't hear no more.

Sara's shriek sliced through me. I hit the glass hard. I snatched back my smarting hand and pressed it into my belly. Holy hell, was Sara screaming. I grabbed my wrapper and ran out.

"What's happening?" Davey cried, sitting up blinking, his erection like a shaft pole.

I wanted to kill him. I wanted to kill them all! Sara's shrieks filled my head and made me crazy. I half fell down them stairs. The men downstairs was headed back toward the ruckus, but stopped dead when they saw me flying down them steps, wearing only a corset and wrapper, all other vital areas free for the viewing.

A couple fellas smiled. I smacked and punched and slashed as I went. Pushing through the kitchen, I tumbled out the back door. Sara lay on the ground, shrieking so loud I couldn't figure if she was herself or Ma grieving over Becky, or me birthing baby Lillian.

Marie appeared beside me, a butcher knife in her hand. I took it from her just as if I'd sent her for it and she'd expected me to take it. The cold handle felt comforting as I walked toward Lizbeth. I would open her...

"You'll roast in hell!" Lizbeth shouted. She didn't see me. "No tramp is going to ruin me! I hope I tore your heart out, you dirty bitch. I hope you take a year to die! Whore! *Whore!*"

I slashed—and, damn my eyes, was so crazy mad I missed her!

Her horse shied away. Lizbeth screamed and kicked at me. I saw her eyes, wet, red, wild. The horse reared. Suddenly she lay grunting on her back in the dirt.

"Angel! Don't!" Dalt yelled. Marie tried to hold him back but he slapped her. She let fly with Mexican cussing.

Lizbeth scrambled backwards trying to cock her pistol again. I raised the knife…

Sara stopped moaning.

Dalt come up behind me, took my arm and spun me around fast. I fell hard. He stepped on my wrist and took the knife. Yowling like a mountain cat, Marie leaped on his back and sank her teeth into his scalp!

Lizbeth ran for her horse, hiked her skirts and flung herself up. In seconds the hoofbeats faded into the clamor of piano and nickelodeon.

I began crawling toward Sara. Like in a nightmare, the distance between us grew and grew 'til I thought I'd never reach her.

Some men pulled Marie off Dalt's back. He slapped her quiet.

I rolled Sara over and brushed bits of gravel and dry grass from her bloody lips. I shook her and her head wobbled. Her thin plain face was twisted from those last moments of agony. "Aw, Sara," I wept. "Why'd you have to be such a damn fool?"

I let her fall limp beside me and wiped my sticky hands on my corset and breasts. The thick smell of blood filled my nose. I got to my feet and fell into the nearest clump of sage. My belly emptied 'til I thought my eyes would come out.

It ought to rain for funerals. Seems the sky ought to cry for a lost soul. Sara got put to rest the day after Lizbeth Corning shot her dead, and the weather was fine. I saw folks picnicking across the canyon behind the Silver Star.

Dalt hired a buggy and drove me and Marie to the graveyard on the sundown side of the canyon. The first burying place the miners used in Buffalo Pass was generally thought to be Tempest's potter's field. Upright folks, like Cornelia, got buried up the other slope behind the half-built church.

Damned, if it wasn't one of the prettiest days I'd ever seen. The sky looked like pure Injun turquoise. The mountains was thick with dark pines and soft green aspens. The sun was a blazing knot that brought up the high odor of all us dressed in mourning black.

A shiner covered half Marie's face. Holding her mouth so tight her cheekbones looked high as an Injun's, she stepped down from the buggy and made a motion over her breast.

Dalt's neck sported fiery red teethmarks. Hollows I'd never noticed before circled his eyes. The sun showed up his pale skin and the lines by his mouth. He'd gone and growed old.

Damned near every man, dancehall girl and whore in Tempest stood there in the graveyard. The road and hillside got so crowded with wagons and hired buggies it looked like an Independence Day celebration. Only, there weren't no children. And there weren't no ladies.

I'd had enough potion to float a mule. The night before, as Sara lay on the Placer Saloon's bar in her fine watered silk and high-button shoes with that fine hair flowing over the polished pine, I'd kept expecting her to get up and giggle. No woman, decent or otherwise, could just ride up and kill my only friend, I kept thinking.

"Take my arm, Angel," Dalt said, leading me toward the hole.

Tempest's undertaker had a mighty fine black hearse decorated with plumes and fringe. The bowed sidewindows had fancy designs etched right into the glass—but it sat back in his shed. No amount of money, threats, or begging got him to bring out his best for a whore. So, we stood about, waiting for that blackhearted undertaker to roll Sara up in the back of a feed wagon.

I was ready. I'd seen Becky go under the ground wrapped in Ma's only pieced quilt. I'd laid Ma out with three planks and a pine bough over her head. Baby Lillian had gone to her reward in a flour sack. While that don't sound elegant, no greater love ever went into placing a body in a grave. Now come my friend Sara in a pine box.

Dalt helped lift it to the graveside.

Lizbeth Corning had shot her right in the gut. Doc Billy said there couldn't have been a worser way to go. At the wake, only hours after she died, I'd drunk the Placer dry, but could still see. I could still think. I could still see that silhouette of Sara and Ben a-kissing in the garden.

I began trembling. I looked about at the bowed heads. The men's faces wasn't much different from weathered rocks. Us women was too pink and pretty for daylight, our skirts too short, our hair too curly, our eyes like mine pits, deep, black, and empty.

I felt that hole, pulling at me! I tried to imagine Sara's pretty face as she laid in that box, her eyes closed, looking like she did if I got up first and looked down on her. All I saw was a tangle of black hair!

I saw my own face, my own eyes closed, my own mouth shut for all time. My ears heard the nothingness of death! A noise come from my mouth. Some men looked over at me. Others looked away. More weeping, more snorting into kerchiefs, more clearing of throats and coughing—it was like we all saw ourselves sinking into that grave!

There weren't no preacher.

Dalt stood beside Sara's coffin a minute and then clapped his hat on and marched back to the buggy. I saw John Harrington—Banjo—come through the crowd. He wore his best red vest and white rufflebreasted shirt. His sleeves was held up with lacy blue garters and his trousers was black and shiny new. He swept off his derby and looked over the crowd. He was the only man standing with his head high and his eyes clear.

"We're all grieved to be here today," he said, his voice ringing strong, his fine dark skin gleaming in the sunlight. "Sara Sweetwater was a beautiful, generous woman who brought pleasure to many. Her killer will go unpunished..." He paused for the respectable men murmuring in the back. "Except she'll know a human life got lost. May God have mercy on her soul."

Everybody watched John walk toward me as if they'd expected

more. Whose soul, all the eyes asked.

"I'm sorry I wasn't at the wake last night. News didn't come 'til dawn."

I couldn't talk.

The crowd thinned. Dirt began falling on pine boards. Doc Billy come up. "Can I see you privately?" he whispered.

I scarcely noticed him. "Don't go," I said to John. I looked over the crowd. Except for the postmaster and Jim Lewis, Rusty, Davey, and Ben were the only men who didn't come.

"Morning, John," Doc Billy said. "Heard you play at the Silver Star the other night. You play a fine tune."

John stared him down.

Seeing as how John wasn't to be dismissed, Doc Billy ambled along toward the buggy with us. "You'll hate me for saying this, Angel, but I have to. You and Marie need to come to my office tonight."

I looked at Doc Billy low.

"Maybe Dalt, too." Doc took off his spectacles and polished them. "I know it isn't kind to speak of it now, but Sara was ...infected."

"What the hell does that matter now?" I shouted.

John interrupted. "She gave it to Corning?"

Doc Billy nodded solemnly. "Lizbeth came to see me yesterday. She's been trying to get pregnant a long time. Now she's three months along. I had to tell her I found a sore. I'm sorry, Angel, but I've got to check you. I hope the women in town just think Lizbeth did what she did because of the chickens—Lizbeth wouldn't want it to get around that..." Doc looked sick. "Will you come?"

I nodded. I felt like I was slogging through mud three feet deep. John helped me to the buggy seat. "What'll happen to the Corning baby?" he asked.

"I'm praying that fall from the horse will..." Doc put his spectacles back on. His eyes got big and made him look sadder. "Or maybe I can try the cure on her."

My gut twisted. Pox. A shiver of revulsion went through me. I felt dirty. I felt sick. I pulled out my brown bottle and popped the cork. Dalt tried to stop me from draining it.

"Go easy on that, Angel," Doc Billy said.

"Go to hell," I whispered. "We'll be down after dark. All of us."

Marie looked at me with murderous eyes. Dalt swallowed. "I'll be there, too," John said. That made ol' Doc Billy's eyes pop.

Marie was clean. Dalt hadn't been with Sara, so he was, too. John seemed okay, but he wanted the cure just the same. I was fine, too. Jim-dandy.

"I'm sure Sara didn't realize she could pass it on," Billy said as I stared out the office door late that night.

"That don't make it no easier," I said. "And that don't make Lizbeth Corning no saint."

Doc put out his hand, but I wouldn't take it. "Give it up before you get it, too. Leave town before someone puts a bullet in you."

I walked out.

Wind raced up the black canyon. Storm clouds skittered across the moon. Horses snorted in the livery nearby. A wagon rattled up the street. Some men come out one saloon and went into another. I didn't hear much laughing. Shadows I'd once felt was friends pressed on me making me afraid.

"Angel?"

I whirled and near to fell against a tall dark man. "Damn, you scared me!"

"I'll see you back to the saloon," John said. "Dalt ain't thinking straight, leaving you to walk alone."

"He ain't never wasted a lot of worry over me."

"Would you share a drink with a black man?" He held out a flask.

"Did you ever want something real bad, John?" I asked, taking a gulp. "Hell, I still think of you as Banjo. Where'd Bess go? Who kilt that man they found up the canyon? Was he the one dumped from Jessie's window? Why'd Sara have to die like that?"

"You're mighty full of questions."

"I think I'm losing my senses. Is Sara burning in hell?"

John laughed. "Can't be worse than dying with your guts all over the ground. We're all sinners. We die a sinner's death."

"You got church-learning, John?"

"Enough to keep me awake nights talking to God."

"What's a bearded man in the sky got against me? I didn't let my little sister die or make Ma sick. If there's a God, He done them things and put me where I am."

"You ain't to blame?"

"I ain't so sure no more."

"I was born a slave. God did that to me, I suppose. I used to pick cotton 'til the bones in my back froze and I couldn't straighten up. I'd walk around like that, saying to myself, I'll be a bent-over black man all my life. They'll sell me south when I can't stud no more. The day President Lincoln made me free, I stood up straight and walked clean out of that state. Didn't look back. Been standing straight ever since."

"Ma said don't look back."

"Ain't easy."

"You wasn't scared?"

"Scared as hell. I figure God give me that chance to start over."

"Some chance, working in a dancehall for four bits and beer."

John roared. "When you've had nothing your whole life, four bits and beer is everything. If you ain't happy doing what you're doing, clear out."

"I thought I was happy."

We stopped near the Placer Saloon. Cigar smoke curled out the door. Dalt was chuckling. Marie was swearing.

"Thanks," I said, shaking John's hand. "Say a prayer to your God for Lizbeth's baby."

Part Two

Thirteen

Summer 1866

I started up Buffalo Pass three days after Sara's funeral. I wore an old hat over my tied-up hair, a flannel shirt and trousers. I looked like a prospector trudging up the freight road, panting and a-tugging on my mule's neckrope.

I camped by the creek the first night. Wasn't no use bothering myself worrying over coyotes or timberwolves. I had a Henry rifle and intended to kill anything that looked crossways at me.

The clouds that had gathered all afternoon gave off a mist that wasn't too bothersome, just cold. I expected to hear a bit of Tempest's noise, but not so much as a whisper touched the air. No bursts of laughter, no creaking stairs, no boots close behind, no bedsprings squeaking faster and faster, no water dribbling in the basin—nothing.

I heard only the soft splash of a fish in the deep part of the creek, some night creature's footsteps up in the pines and the drumming of my heart. The next morning I woke cold and stiff, hearing Sara scream in my dream. My fire had gone out.

Mule and me made poor progress that day. Beans, tack, and coffee surely did taste good after not eating for hours. It was still raining when I woke the second morning to another dead fire. By the third day I'd lost track of how far I'd gone. The clouds hung low and grumbled as mule and me walked in the creek some, crossing from side to side when boulders blocked our way. I began to weary of the trek.

On the fifth day the sky cleared some. I reached the meadow where the canyon spread out. The road curved south toward Pikes Peak. Silver Peak looked pretty much as I remembered it. I kept thinking I'd come upon Snowy Ray's post before nightfall and expected to be at Dalt's old cabin by morning.

I wandered farther and farther, sometimes heading into the pines, other times going back, hoping to see the trail to Dalt's cabin. Darned if I could find the post or trail. Then the next afternoon it poured. I followed the creek 'til it veered up a gulch. I couldn't figure how I'd forgotten the way and hadn't the sense to camp and rest proper. The rain smeared the sky, rocks, and muddy ground into a scary gray wash. I thought the sky would crack, the thunder ripped so loud.

Lightning struck a pine on the ridge and set it afire for a few minutes, before the torrent doused it. I stumbled over boulders, slogged through mud, cried some, and cussed myself plenty. I kept going, stubborn scared, drenched to my drawers, wanting only to find that cabin.

I'd been climbing steady for hours when finally I did stop to catch my breath and shake the heavy mud from my boots. I heard a low roar, like the whole mountain was coming down on me. A tree ahead in the mists toppled like a giant stepped on it. A wall of water appeared out of the shadows and swallowed me whole before I could take a step!

I grabbed at my mule and hung onto the saddlebags. The mule had sense enough to turn around. In the blink of an eye darkness closed around me. The cinch began to give as the mule dragged me down the gulch. When the saddlebags come away in my hands, I fell face down in the rushing water. I fought for air and solid footing. Lightning lit nothing but water, rock, and pine in stark black and silver.

I tumbled for what seemed like a lifetime 'til I saw the meadow in a flash of lightning. I fancied I saw window light and a building silhouetted against a looming black mountain. Sheeting rain stung my eyes. I tried turning myself toward them lights but the water rushed ever faster. I kept going under, kept getting swept against boulders and the pain and fear addled my mind. After a spell, breathing didn't seem so important.

I smelled bread baking.

Something heavy sat on my chest. My arms was too weak to move it. I was warm and dry, but dizzy. The muscles in my neck hurt. I smelled linen sheets, camphor, lamp oil, and pine.

At last my eyes opened. I lay in a low room with walls of split pine. Painfully bright sunlight poured through a window trimmed in red calico. On my chest only inches from my face lay a monstrous black cat with large green eyes. He was purring.

A woman wearing a ruffle-shouldered apron come in carrying a tray. She was tall and thin, her face heavy with bones and weariness. "Solomon, you bad cat!" she scolded, smiling. "Get off the poor child! You've scared her. Get down!"

She set the tray on a pine table next to the bed. The cat hissed when she lifted him. "Solomon doesn't like me," she grinned, setting him on the window sill. She pulled up a ladder-backed chair and sat. "Howdy keeps Solomon around to catch mice. The rest of the time he lazies about in the sun. I wish my life was as easy! Try some of this broth before you waste away to nothing."

It tasted pure as gold!

"You've got such pretty eyes, kind of gray with sparks of blue," she said. "My eyes are just hazel, but I can see. That's about all a body can ask for." She laughed and kept spooning.

I thought her eyes was beautiful. They smiled.

"Your fever's down," she said, her hand cool on my forehead. "Howdy said either you'd die or pull through. Isn't that silly? Don't try to talk. I can carry on a conversation with myself just fine. Been doing it close to three years. That's how long Howdy and me have been married. We do a fair piece of business here, not enough to make us rich, but not so poor we should close. We're fifteen miles from Cold Water City. It's a good spot for an inn."

She dried my lips. I laid watching her lather a cloth after she fetched hot water. Without so much as a if-you-please, she pulled back my cover and washed me up one leg and down the other, one arm and then the next. Them skinny limbs didn't seem mine.

"Doesn't that feel better? Some folks don't hold to bathing, but I do. You got a nasty bruise on your hip, so take care when you start moving about. You must've met up with a boulder in that flood.

"You hear me this time, don't you? The other times I don't think you understood. You had a fever so high I had to sponge you with creek water. That was some flood all right. Our root cellar took water so I had to put up vegetables. With all the cooking I do for the travelers, I hardly had the time.

"Howdy found you laying out by the creek and took you for a log. Then he thought you were a miner 'til he rolled you over. That's not fair—turning out to be so pretty! My hands are full keeping Howdy as it is!" She winked. "Feeling better? Hope you didn't lay out there too long. We couldn't figure where you came from. All you had were the clothes on your back and the saddlebag. Why you were dressed in men's clothes, I don't know. I suppose it's a safer way to travel. You're so pretty, men would forget themselves and take advantage.

"Don't you worry about your things. Hope you don't mind me washing them. We wasn't sure you'd pull through and I wanted your name in case we had to put up a marker. Didn't find a thing, though. The Bible was almost ruined. I dried the pages, but some are stuck together for good. Even if you can't read all of it, it's mighty comforting to have around. I put it right here in the chest.

"The baby dresses will always be a bit pink. The red mud is something, isn't it, the way it gets into clothes? My petticoats will never be white again. I couldn't figure what a young girl like yourself would be doing with fine baby dresses. Did you sew them? I've never seen such fine work! Howdy said you must've had a baby. I said that was foolish. You weren't wearing a wedding ring, and if

ANGEL

you'd had a baby, you sure would've been clinging to it instead of a saddlebag! These must've come from your hopechest. There ain't a poor, helpless infant laying out there, is there?" Her lips trembled.

It took all my strength to turn my head from side to side.

She smiled and dashed away a tear. "Praise the Lord. I told Howdy you were too young. Your cloak is still hanging outside. Wet wool smells so, you know. I've got some things you can wear 'til we stitch you up a new dress. The gold dollars are right here, safe and sound. Now, I can't figure what this is."

She held up a bit of sponge tied with a string. "I've never seen a trinket like this. Solomon would think it a fine toy. It's right here if you need it. I hope it's not a charm. I'm a God-fearing woman and don't like superstitions. Is there someone we can get word to?"

I shook my head, my cheeks burning with shame.

"Sleep, then. I'll make sure Solomon doesn't bother you. What's that you're trying to say?"

"I...like the cat."

"He sure seems taken with you. I was just teasing about Howdy. He's a good man. He'll be up later to say hello. He'll be glad to hear you're feeling better."

"Your...name."

"Goodness! I'm Gwenity Jackson. Howdy built this inn by hand four years ago. I'm what you call a mail-order bride. He wrote back East for a hard-working woman willing to share his life in the West. I was an old maid, you see. I always wanted a big family...I thought the West would be a good place to raise one. I wasn't so sure a man—a strange man—would take to me. I'm not much on looks and I'm pretty near flat..." She giggled. "But he thought I was fine. I was so shy! I expected to have a child the first year, but nothing happened. Then I was pregnant for a while...guess I wasn't meant to have children. We keep hoping, of course. One loss don't mean the end. I'm still practically a bride and only thirty-six. Never thought I'd see a Mrs. in front of my name! Gwenity. Can you remember that?" She smiled and slipped out, closing the door careful.

Later I heard piano music, but it wasn't painful to the ear. The gentle melody lulled me to sleep and I dreamed of Gwenity talking and talking. I felt safe and happy, but somewhere along the line she changed into mule-mouthed Effie Kennings and dangled a string and sponge before my face screaming, "Whore, whore, whore!"

Fourteen

Early Winter 1866

"You're supposed to be resting," Gwenity scolded.

"I feel a lot better, really. I ain't one for sitting around when there's so much work."

Gwenity scowled and pushed back her hair. She never did get upset for long. "Guess a little sweeping wouldn't hurt you," she smiled.

That's how I started out helping Gwenity at the Calico Inn Stage Depot. She had her hands full cooking and keeping up the few rooms Howdy rented to travelers.

"Howdy, I keep telling her serving is much easier," Gwenity would complain, "but she won't get her hands out of the flour barrel."

"Leave her be," he'd say. Howdy was a mighty nice fella for a man near three hundred pounds. He had a smile as broad as the valley and a heart as big as the western sky. If a miner come in hungry and broke he'd get a clean bed and a full meal for nothing. It was easy to see Howdy would never be rich!

"You're worrying my missus, young lady," he'd say, coming into the kitchen to sample biscuits or pie after a long afternoon of chopping wood or tending stock.

"She likes to fret," I'd smile.

Nodding, he'd say, "It's not right for the good Lord to keep children from a brood hen like Gwenity." And he'd pat my shoulder.

Right quick I had to learn to stop looking at men the way I'd come to. Especially Howdy. I knew his kind soon as I saw him the day he come to my room and said his hello. He was shy about it, but I saw his eyes go over me. I'd been holding my breath for fear I'd knowed this Howdy Jackson fella sometime or other. For once I was lucky.

I forced myself to forget everything I knew. I was back among the good and God-fearing, back where women didn't know nothing about sex and sure didn't take to it once they did. I learned how to blush—by wondering how Howdy looked in his johns ready to climb into poor skinny Gwenity's bed! The force of keeping back my smile would turn my cheeks the proper color.

The constant flow of travelers coming up the pass through a town where my name had been known by near every man worried me sick. I didn't want nobody finding out what I'd been.

"You sure are timid with strangers," Gwenity would say when I'd peek from the kitchen every time a load of coach passengers would come in, or a bunch of miners slept over, or a family traveling by wagon stopped to eat.

Gwenity never asked where I come from, never asked where I was going. To folks who asked about me she told the story she'd pulled from the air the day I woke up: that I got lost from my people during the storm. As summer ebbed and the aspens turned yellow, I did see a couple familiar faces. At times like that I'd take sick and lay abed, shivering with worry. Was it worth trying to forget my past?

The months slipped by easy and peaceful. My memories of Tempest faded with each sunset. I liked living and working at the inn, getting praise for my pies and breads. Ma's recipes did me proud. I grew plump and happy. Though I was always watchful of strangers, I felt safe. I enjoyed cozy evenings while Gwenity played her piano and Howdy looked on with a proper gleam in his eye.

Gwenity and me was putting up pumpkin one afternoon when we heard a far-off boom that rattled the windows. "I don't think that was thunder," she said, going out front to look.

I come up beside her and scanned the ridge. "I see smoke."

"I don't take to this blasting for mines nowadays," she said, shaking her head. "Guess the gold wouldn't be worth so much, though, if it was just laying around."

Howdy was hunting a stray just before supper and Gwenity was feeding her chickens in the packed yard when we first caught sight of a wagon coming down the road from the high country. "Put in more biscuits," Gwenity called, watching the trail of dust. "I don't take to miners much. A wild bunch, most of them. And they scare you so. Go on in, Angie. I'll see to their horses."

I didn't like leaving Gwenity to greet the men alone. She was more worried about me than her own safety. I knew what could happen to her even if she didn't.

Three men on horseback come in behind one driving a wagon. From the window I watched them hail Gwenity. I knowed where Howdy's rifle was and figured to use it if I had to. I didn't recognize the four faces.

Gwenity looked in the back of the wagon and horror crossed her face. I bolted out the door and was beside her in an instant. The men all tipped their hats, but I paid no mind.

"Mercy, Angie! They say this poor fella almost blew himself up!"

"We got us a small mine about ten miles up," one of the men said. "You figure you could clean him up some 'fore we take him down the canyon? I heard there's a doc in Tempest."

I looked up into the sunburnt wrinkles around his eyes. "You fetch the doc up here. We'll tend him 'til you get back."

Gwenity's face went white. "He looks dead, Angie."

Through blood and mud caked on his face I saw a muscle twitching near his eye. He had more hair than a buffalo, shoulders as wide as Pikes Peak was tall. I figured he'd bled near all he could without turning white. The men carried him into a small room that backed the kitchen's stone fireplace.

"What's the poor man's name?" Gwenity asked.

"Judd, Ma'am. Judd Rydell."

Gwenity and me sponged him. He had cuts all over his face. His hands was black from burns and his chest was near raw. I could pull away his bloody shirt and dribble boiled water over his wounds without it turning my belly. Gwenity near to fainted twice. "See about supper," I told her. "I'll finish him up."

"You can't strip off this man's drawers and wash his wounds! It wouldn't be proper. Go out of the room while I do it. Tear up the old linens for bandages."

"And leave you to fall on him when you pass out? It ain't going to bother me. It's bothering *you* plenty."

"Sometimes I don't understand you, Angie! You claim you're only nineteen, and yet you get on better than me sometimes."

"I figure I turned twenty this summer, so don't treat me like no child. Let me at that place 'fore you pull off all his skin."

She reeled and stumbled from the room, holding her mouth.

Judd Rydell looked to be in his early thirties. There was a fair sprinkling of gray in his dark brown hair. I couldn't guess at his features for all the soot and beard, but judging by eyebrows and nose, he had a fair chance of turning out handsome. I tried hard not to recall times when I'd laid with miners like him. Weren't easy.

Snipping at his bloody trousers with the sewing shears, pretty soon I had him naked and washed. Nothing of importance had been hurt. I was surprised to find myself relieved. Even unconscious and beginning to battle fever, he was a fine figure of a man. I wondered what sort of person he was under all that hair and blood.

He lay without moving 'til the next morning.

"I hear horses." Howdy pulled hisself from the bench by the door where he'd waited all night. I'd fallen asleep in the chair by Judd's bed, so I wasn't awake enough to run for cover when Doc Billy's boots thudded down the hall.

"Light the lamp, Angie," Howdy whispered. "The doc's here."

Maybe I could hide from Billy if I didn't look square at him.

"This here's Angie," Howdy said. "She works for me and my wife. I figure she done a damn good job on the fella's wounds. What do you think, Doc? Will he pull through?"

ANGEL

"Glad to meet you, Miss Angie," Doc Billy said.

I hadn't cried in a mighty long time, but tears sprang to my eyes just looking at Doc. Last time I'd seen him I'd hated him right down to the soles of his boots. Just then I could've kissed him. "He ain't moved since I finished with him. Is he dead?"

Billy laid his ear on Judd's chest. "Weak. Lost a lot of blood."

I could've told him that.

Billy poked and prodded, lifted a bandage here and there. Then he pulled bottles and salves from his bag and set to work. "Not much else I can do," he said when he'd finished. "No telling when he'll come around."

"Excuse me, Doc," Howdy said. "I hear my missus calling. This fella upset her stomach."

"Not surprising," Doc muttered.

After Howdy went out, the room echoed with my breathing. Doc gathered up his bag. Handing me a potion bottle, he said, "Give him this if the pain's bad. Whiskey, too, if you've got it."

"Will his hands mend?"

"A tough man might make use of them again. Keep the wounds clean. Boil all the water you use, and especially the bandages. Soak them in this," he said, handing me another bottle. "He'll need a lot of care."

I followed Doc to the door, busting with questions I was too scared to ask.

"You're looking good, Angel," he whispered. "I'm glad to see you're safe and well. Planning to stay on here?"

I nodded. "It's decent work and they need me. What about the...baby," I whispered.

"Don't ask. It's better you don't know."

By the time winter rolled down from the peaks, laying frost on all the sage, Judd Rydell had come out of his stupor and was mending fast.

"I'll tend him," Gwenity insisted. "You see to the meals. I

told you before, it isn't proper for an unmarried girl to care for a sick man."

Gwenity had growed pale during the fall. Now she tired easy and sometimes fell asleep over her mending. I took over more of her work. Though it wasn't exciting, I felt young and strong again. I carried water in from the creek, scrubbed floors, swept, changed linens, and cooked. Gwenity took the easy jobs, like serving the travelers, though there was fewer as the days grew colder. She enjoyed talking with the few women who come through.

Judd was an ornery fella on the mend. He fussed at Gwenity, sent back his supper trays polished clean of every crumb, but with complaints a-plenty. "Biscuits is heavy. Coffee is weak. Steak is tough. Pie is cold." I hardly ever saw the man and I'd had my fill of him. I boiled his bandages, though, and squirmed with curiosity.

"How's he mending?" I'd ask Gwenity.

"A mass of scars and scabs. Not much of a man to be filling your thoughts," she'd smile. "I pity any woman who marries him. He don't even know good cooking."

Gwenity did her best for him, though I could tell it was wearing on her. One night I woke to her cry and jumped out of bed, thinking maybe Judd had taken out his temper on her. I ran into the hall not knowing where to turn. She let out another small wail in the kitchen. I busted in to find her bent over the cookstove standing in a pool of blood.

She looked up, her eyes filled with terror. "God help me," she wept. "I'm losing another one."

I helped her sit on the floor and grabbed a clean stack of bandages from the table. "Lay back. Don't be scared," I said, pushing at her skirts.

"Almost five months this time," she wept. "Why doesn't the good Lord see fit to let me a have a child? I've waited so long. I've prayed so hard. I don't want to die, Angie. I don't want to leave Howdy."

"You ain't going nowhere but to bed for a long time. You should've told me." I pressed the bandages between her legs. She

ANGEL

gave out with another groan and there it come, a baby no bigger than my hand. It would've been a boy. I looked away hearing the inn shudder under Howdy's step.

"Not again!" he croaked. "God, Angie, what do I do?"

"Take her upstairs soon as I get the rest of this out. What can you do? I figure you can find somewheres else to take your pleasure 'cause the next time you get Gwenity pregnant will be the last."

Howdy's eyes popped. I didn't know or care if Gwenity heard me. All I knew just then was I never had seen a normal baby birthed. Gwenity cried against her arm as I finished up the business under her skirt. When she was feeling a little better, Howdy carried her upstairs. I sat on the floor for a long time with her weeping ringing in my ears.

"Don't you worry about him, Gwen," I told her the next morning as I spooned chicken broth into her mouth.

"He needs care. He complains so much," she said weakly.

"I'll do it. You just get your strength back. I'll bring all you need. Don't get up for nothing. Just get well. Please, Gwenity. For me?"

She patted my hand. "You're a good friend. Don't you let Judd get fresh with you now. He's getting well enough he might. If you're smart, you just might catch that man. I don't know what it is about you, Angie. You shy away from every stranger, but you got a bold eye. You're a good girl, I know that. You've worked hard to keep Howdy in line—don't be so surprised. Men are men. He can't help but like looking at you. You haven't once looked back. If you look at Judd the way you look at some of the men, though, he'll think you're fast. Keep your eyes down and don't let him touch you 'til there's gold on your finger."

Gold on my finger. Secretly I'd laugh over that. All Judd would have to do would be touch me and I'd hop across his lap. How virgins, old maids, and widows got on, I sure didn't know. I needed some loving, and here I was supposed to be so fresh and innocent I

151

couldn't even look Judd in the eye.

"You're a mousy little thing," he'd say, propped in his bed, stuffing cornbread in his mouth. His blistered fingers was healing up fine, but they was stiff. "Don't you ever say anything?" he'd tease.

I had a mighty hard time keeping my eyes down. I wanted to cuss him right proper. Times was I thought on spilling coffee in his lap. Finally one day he caught my hand and tried to pull me close. "What's the matter with my face that you won't look at it?"

"For one, you need a shave and proper bath, Mr. Rydell. And if you please, I'll take my hand and get back to work."

"You don't bring me late snacks now that I'm feeling better. Bring me some coffee and pie tonight."

I dragged myself away. Just the smell of him, tobacco, sweat, and a whisper of whiskey on his breath made me forget I'd had enough men in my time to last all my days.

For a spell, he left me alone. He'd look out the window toward the ridge and his mine for hours.

A nice Injun summer stayed through October. Gwenity mended but kept to her bed and wouldn't talk to me of the miscarriage 'cause she figured I didn't know nothing of losing a child. I could've told her plenty about sorrow, how the pain she felt was a sight easier to bear than if she'd lost a baby who'd sucked at her breast.

One morning I got up to golden sunlight playing along the ridge and a mist over the creek. I started coffee and snuck into Judd's room to empty the chamberpot—I didn't like taking it when he was awake. His bed was empty!

I stared a full minute before I ran out front. I don't know what I thought at first, that he'd ridden off in the night maybe. I would've called his name, but then I saw him near the creek. I come up behind him, mad he'd scared me. He was answering nature into the bushes. He turned and we stared at each other.

He'd shaved. He stood in that golden sunshine naked to the waist, his trousers open, his socks sunk in red dust. There was no keeping my eyes down no more. He buttoned his trousers, then stood looking at me with a kind of squint to his eye like he wasn't sure about me. I still wore my night dress and wrapper. The cold gravel stung my bare feet. My panting breath filled the air in front of my face with little white clouds.

I fixed my eye on him and let him know there wasn't nothing mousy about this female no more. "If you're well enough to be up and about, you're well enough to get in that creek and scrub off some of your stink. I'll go change your linens," I said.

"Worried, were you?" He caught my arm and pulled me close.

"Yes, damn your hide. Thanks to me, you got fingers that still bend and hair on your chest."

He spread my palm along the new curls breaking out all along his belly. A delicious shiver went up my back. Then he pulled me tight against him so we touched from chest to knee and arched against me as I tipped my face up just enough to be kissed.

Kissing Judd felt like cooking a fine meal and then not getting to taste a drop. I knew I had to pull away or I'd lose my chance at marrying up forever. I wanted gold on my finger more than I wanted him in my bed.

"Don't go," he said against my lips.

I looked into his fine dark eyes and had to bite back my words. As I pulled away, he closed his hands over my breasts. I sagged against him and let him kiss me again.

That was the strongest need I'd ever knowed. Its strength come from knowing I wouldn't be answering it. Maybe that was what ailed a whore's life, I thought. There weren't no chase, no hunt, no surrender. There weren't no excitement knowing the whore'd give in. At least, not for her.

"It's still early. Stay here with me awhile."

"I ain't going into no bushes with you."

"I'm a gentle man."

"Are you?" I longed to shed my clothes and feel the heat of his skin next to mine, but a thousand faces drifted across my mind. All my mistakes filled me with fear. This time, foolish and hopeless as it seemed, I was doing things right. "You want me, Judd Rydell, you'll have to marry me."

He exploded with a laugh.

So, I wasn't worth marrying, was I? I'd die before I'd let him near me again! I turned and marched back to the inn. From then on he never saw me that I wasn't buttoned to my chin proper as the old maid I surely was.

But oh, the ache…He'd touch my hand as I'd pass the milk pitcher at the supper table. He'd catch my eye as I served up bacon and beans. He'd fetch me to change the bandage on his shoulder and grin when my mouth watered for a kiss.

As the winter winds closed us in, Gwenity's advice wore mighty thin. Not many travelers ventured up the pass in the snow. Them what did wasn't much company. If Judd ever noticed how I hid out, he never said.

"He'll come around," Gwenity kept telling me, though she was poorly and couldn't get too worked up over my problem with catching my "first" man. "You need faith," Gwenity told me when I complained no good come from curbing my eye.

"It don't work with him," I'd cry.

"It has to," she said, her thin hands limp across her empty belly the day I sat with her, trying to find one good reason for going on with the foolishness. "There ain't no other way to catch a man. Some just ain't the marrying kind. Maybe Judd's one."

I went to sit by myself in my cold room. I looked across the snowy meadow, watching snowflakes dance through the air. Somewheres out there lay my ma with all her fight wrung out of her. I could see then why she would have stayed with Dalt 'cause there wasn't no more hope left in her. I figured that's what killed her. No fever done it.

I about made up my mind to let Judd have his way when he knocked. He'd never come to my room before. I felt like I'd conjured him up from my thoughts and the fear of that raised the hair on my neck. He dropped a load of wood by the potbelly and stoked the fire. I could just about see the muscles in his back, though he wore a thick wool shirt I'd just sewed for him.

"Shirt looks good on you, Judd," I said. I went ahead and

looked square at him. Gwenity must've cut his hair. Most of the burns and cuts on his face had healed leaving only faint pink scars that was darkening as he spent hours helping Howdy tend the stock and split wood.

He straightened and dusted hisself off. "Not bad. Thanks." Judd looked of a serious mind as he stared at me curled lonely in the rocker by my window. "Thought I might ride up to my mine now that I'm better."

Good weather for it, I thought disgustedly. I went back to staring at the ridge, figuring this was a goodbye. My throat felt thick.

He planted hisself on the edge of my bed. It was about the most familiar thing he'd done yet. His next question would be if he could have one time with me before he left. I expected my answer to be yes.

"I know you're mad about that day by the creek, but I swear I wasn't insulting you. I wanted you then. Still do."

I unfolded my legs from under me and rubbed a numb spot. I was feeling so much myself I forgot how much leg I was showing. Solomon decided to pad in then. I bent to pick him up but he kept just out of reach, being a cat who decided when he meant to be held.

Judd reached across the space between us and slid his hand inside my shirt. I'd forgot to close it when Judd come in. A charge went down through my legs. I knew my face was red and my eyes filled with tears. Easy as anything, Judd slipped across the space between us and knelt before me. He kissed me and his hand found a path up my skirt. I cried out, trying to get free of him. Not on the floor! I kept thinking. The door was still open. Gwenity or Howdy might walk by...

I pushed at his hand, wept without tears, and squirmed to be free. "Damn you," I said, falling out of the chair and scrambling into a corner. "This ain't no way to treat me."

"I want you!"

I pulled up my knees and held tight. He could see most all I had. Wasn't there no man willing to take me on as wife? Was "whore" branded on my face?

He stood and faced the wall. He needed me, did he? How surprised he'd be if he knew I was expert at easing that need in half a hundred ways. He rubbed the back of his neck and then jammed his hands in his pockets. "Get up off the floor. You got your price."

My eyes jerked to meet his. "What price is that?"

"I'll marry you. I don't promise it'll be good. Come spring I mean to work my mine. You won't be stopping me."

I pulled myself up, staring at him like I'd never seen a man before. He'd called marriage my price. When it come to marriage, was that all it was—being a respectable whore? I'd have none of it! "Go to hell."

"That's what you want, isn't it?"

"I want a hell of a lot more." I closed the door, then undid my buttons, spread my shirt and pulled down my woollies. Pressing myself against him I said, "Them breasts is fixed fast to a woman, Mr. Judd Rydell. This here woman ain't no feather brain. You marry up with me, you get more than bed. You better be for damn sure you want *all* of me. I ain't so sure I want all of you."

He took me in his arms so tight I couldn't breathe. I had to be crazy aggravating him. Them that gots, keeps. Them that don't... Did I want a husband or not?

"I do love you, Angie."

I hadn't hoped for love.

Fifteen

Winter 1866

"Ever been promised before?"

A tingle of worry ran up and down my arms as Judd turned the buckboard down the freight road. "Nope," I said, stealing an uneasy look at the man I was fixing to marry.

"Took you a minute to figure that answer. Some men would take you for a calculating woman."

"Never said I wasn't."

We crossed the meadow and headed into the canyon. Off to one side the foundation of Snowy Ray's cabin stuck up in the weeds. No wonder I hadn't seen it that summer; the place had burned down. Beyond it I strained to see the trail up to Dalt's cabin.

"See something?"

"A deer."

Judd slapped the reins across the horses' rump. "I watched you dress that buck Howdy brought down last week. You're no stranger to a knife."

"Been in the mountains a long time."

"How long? Am I entitled to know how old you are at least?"

"How old are you, and how come you're so curious all of a sudden?"

"I been curious since I first saw you pouring hot water over my burns. I wondered what kind of girl could do that. The only girls I've ever known would've squealed and cried."

"Where is it you knowed such no-account females?"

Judd laughed. "Sit closer to me, Angie. I knew them back East, before the war."

"Was you in the war?"

"Fought for our glorious Southern pride."

"I heard there wasn't nothing left of the South."

"Don't know. Never went back."

"All your people dead?"

"What people?"

I sighed. "Everybody comes from somebody. Even you."

"Most of mine are dead. Those that count. And you?"

"All dead, no-account and otherwise."

The buckboard groaned with the steeper descent. I felt older than Judd, as if I'd lived a whole lifetime in the past six years.

"Gwenity told me they found you half dead after the big flood. Were you running from something, Angie? Is that why you look so uneasy coming back this way?"

"Just myself," I said, wishing I could've talked Judd into going to Cold Water instead of El Dorado to find us a judge. Uneasy weren't the word for how I felt heading for Tempest.

"That's no kind of answer," Judd said.

"Is to me. You want me bad enough to take me as you find me?"

"Taking you is what I'm after, yes."

My first turn of luck come with the snow. Judd and me rolled into Tempest, looking no different from the rest of the folks trudging through snow with mufflers about their faces. We stayed the night at a small hotel on the down side of Tempest. The lodgers talked of nothing but the elections. Judd thought it odd I knew nothing of government and politics.

"I once knew a woman who could name every country and its capital," Judd told me over supper. "She could sing opera, play the piano, and ride to the hunt. She'd been to Europe, dined with kings, and almost married a duke. She was beautiful…but not as beautiful as you, Angie. Not nearly as nice to be with."

My heart warmed. "Never knew nobody like that. Was she a good person?"

Judd's eyes took on a peculiar sadness. "Most evil woman God ever put on this earth."

"Kilt somebody, did she?"

"Not that kind of evil." I think Judd shivered. He reached across our table and caught my hand. "You'd best go upstairs now or I'll be breaking a pledge I made with myself. When I touch you, you don't pull away because you want to. You pull away because you have to."

I took myself up those stairs fast as I could.

Before we left after breakfast the next morning, Judd read me the newspaper, front and back. The birthings and dyings didn't stick in my mind, just two names; Jim Lewis, Tempest's first mayor, and Russel Kennings, sheriff.

"You're not listening," Judd said, gulping the last of his coffee.

"Oh," I smiled. "I'm listening better than you think."

A good foot of snow fell during the night. Down the rest of the canyon our horses fought the drifts. The wind tore between the rocks and howled about us like a freezing white nightmare. By late afternoon we'd crossed the log bridge and headed down El Dorado City's main street.

"I'll get you situated," he said, helping me down in front of the best hotel. "Then I'll board the horses and see to the judge."

I pulled my muffler tight about my face and hurried inside.

"Two single rooms," Judd said, pulling forth a chamois pouch of gold dust. "And I'd like to reserve the bridal suite for tomorrow night."

The desk clerk smoothed his sparse middle-parted hair and squinted through the iron grate. "Won't be finding a judge hereabouts," he said. "He died last week. The preacher marries folks on Sunday."

"Figure you can wait?" Judd asked.

I nodded though I saw something in his eyes I didn't like.

Judd paid through Sunday night. He followed me up the grand staircase into a room that reminded me a powerful lot of Eloise's. "I'll be back," he said, rushing off to tend the rig.

After I unpacked, I opened a satchel Gwenity had given me before we left the inn. I lifted out yards of creamy lace—and a lump formed in my throat. A wedding gown! I couldn't believe my eyes! Holding it to my breast, I stood before the looking glass, gazing at my reflection. A wedding gown! I wanted to cry!

"Angie?" Judd called, tapping on my door. When he saw me his eyes filled with wonder.

"How many days?" I asked, laying aside the white lace dress and running to his arms. His body felt stiff as I hugged him.

"All the way to Sunday—unless you don't want a preacher."

"Why wouldn't I?" I asked, a coldness creeping over me.

Looking mighty unhappy, Judd began talking of where we'd eat supper, did I want to shop, would I mind if he went off to order Howdy's supplies. After he left, I set to altering Gwenity's dress to fit me. I didn't let myself think—not a bit.

By Friday night I was near out of my mind with impatience. Judd acted more peculiar by the minute. Times had been he couldn't keep his hands off me. Now his eyes skittered away whenever I looked at him. I felt certain something had changed his mind. Seeing me up against civilized folks, hearing my ignorant way of speaking and probably getting shamed to the bone every time I exclaimed over some new wonder, he must've realized what a low person I was.

"I could use a drink tonight," Judd said as we walked up the stairs after supper. "Would you mind if I went off a few hours? I'll say goodnight later. If it isn't too cold tomorrow, we'll take a ride through those red rocks."

"Fixing to gamble?" I asked, not meaning to sound cold.

"Thought I might turn a card or two," he grinned. "You're not fond of the sport, I can tell."

"We keep finding out more about each other," I said, feeling sick.

"Hasn't been too surprising, has it?" he asked, though his eyes had growed dark.

I just wished I could see into his head and figure what he was thinking. On the outside men was creatures easy to read. This business of love, though, it didn't have no physical signs. 'Course, I'd seen Judd's need for me often enough. Seems like I did all I could to provoke it 'cause it was comforting to understand *something* about him.

"Wish I could take a bath," I said. "Don't seem right to have this fine bathing tub in here, but no water."

"This little card says they'll bring it up. All you have to do is ring...Sorry, Angie. I forgot. Let me ring for you."

A half-hour later Judd took his leave. I closed myself in with a bathing tub full of sudsy water. The looking glass told me I'd growed plump under Gwenity's care. I loosed my hair and let it tumble free.

No mountain lake had ever felt so delicious as that tubwater. I lathered again and again, thinking someday I wanted to be rich enough to bathe every day. The hairwashing soap smelled of lilac and bubbled into my eyes. I rinsed away the tears wondering, would Sunday really be my wedding day?

Judd tapped a while later. "Can I come in and say goodnight?"

"I'll be just a minute!" I was just stepping from the tub when Judd walked in. Bubbles slid down my legs as I grabbed my wrapper.

"Don't!" I gasped as he caught me in his arms and forced me to kiss him. I couldn't have screamed if I'd wanted to.

"I shouldn't have come in," Judd said, looking solemn into my eyes. "I hoped to find you in bed. I want you, Angie. Now."

My heart and body cried yes, but I backed away. If I gave in I'd never see gold on my finger.

"You're not budging? Now even now?" He looked crazy with need.

I could've let my wrapper slip bit by bit. I could've walked to the bed and laid myself on it, parted my legs and smiled oh, so warm and wicked. But I knew Judd better than he knew hisself. He wanted more than just something he'd paid for. If I gave in, he'd change his feelings without even meaning to. I pulled the screen around me and waited 'til the door closed. Then I cried.

• • •

Our Saturday ride among the red rocks never come about. I waited 'til ten o'clock the next morning for Judd to fetch me to breakfast. By noon I was starving and called for coffee and biscuits to be sent to my room. I took off my traveling clothes and stopped watching from the window by four.

I didn't cry then. I just sat, remembering, cussing myself for being a fool. Somehow or other, luck had it I would be no man's wife. Men would go to no end of spending to get me, but when it come to just giving me their name and support, well, that was different.

I looked at my eyes in the looking glass. They was still gray, still round without a line or smudge of harlot's paint, yet folks saw something dark and mysterious in them that said I wasn't what I wanted to be. Lifting my eyebrows I tried to look innocent. Still it showed, a spark, a fire burning deep that would never go away.

By supper I felt wore out. I dressed for bed, remembering the night before, the quickening in my belly when I stepped from the tub with Judd's eyes on me. No knock come at my door all night.

Come morning—the morning that would've been my wedding day—I packed Gwenity's white lace dress back into the satchel, folded all my new dresses into my carpetbag and counted out my few coins. I felt about as cold and empty as ever in my life when suddenly, out in the hall, I heard a commotion. My heart stopped. I hadn't once thought Judd might've got hurt in a brawl, or drunk, or held over in one of them card games Dalt used to say could reap a man a life's fortune!

The door near to come off its hinges when Judd busted in! "Am I late?" His hair stood on end. He had a day's whiskers and looked like he'd slept in his clothes. He glared at me and I glared back.

"I figured you changed your mind and took off," I said.

"You weren't worried?"

"Some."

"Still want to marry me?"

"That's my price."

"Damn high one. Sight better prices at Eloise's."

Something kin to horror and surprise shot through me. "You spent more than a day in a whorehouse?" I sank to the bed, hiding my shaking fists in my skirt. Now I knew how Effie and Mary and Lizbeth felt. I looked up at Judd and felt awash with sorrow. I had no right to feel so mad.

"It's no use," I said, unbuttoning my bodice. "You don't want to marry me. I want to make you happy and figure I could if you'd just let me, but…" I pulled off my bodice before Judd's astonished eyes and began untying the ribbons of my new camisole. In seconds I'd start at the corset laces. "If I ain't worth marrying, then I ain't. I won't fight no more."

Judd stumbled across the room and grabbed my shoulders. He shook me hard and then yanked me to his chest. "You *are* worth marrying, Angie! I only wish…"

I waited for his reason, his excuse. He only gripped me tighter 'til I thought I heard a moan in his throat. "Put on that pretty white wedding dress, Angie. I'll be sober in an hour. The ceremony's at noon."

Fat snowflakes drifted from the sky as Judd helped me down from the buckboard. We went up snowy steps to a rough pine church built up one of the low hills around El Dorado. From tall narrow windows, morning sunshine spilled in yellow ribbons across the benches. A little boy wearing a red knit cap over his ears scrambled behind the pump organ and began working the pedals. A woman in a wool cape and scarf played the wedding march.

Judd knocked snow out of his hair, shed his coat and hurried up to the front, where a preacher with a curly black beard stood holding a Bible in his mittened hands.

I warmed my fingers 'til the preacher nodded. My breath made quick little clouds in front of my face as I began to walk. I tried not to let my boots show under my white lace hem. I felt as light and beautiful as one of them snowflakes.

A tear began down my cheek, rolling, tickling, growing cold. I brushed it away and smiled at Judd. I didn't hear a word the preacher said. Judd nudged me when it was time to say "I will." Then he turned and put a thin ring of gold on my finger.

I thought of nothing but giving Judd the secret part of myself I'd held back from all the others. I don't think he was sorry he paid my price.

Sixteen

Summer-Winter 1867

"Angie!" Gwenity's footsteps pounded across the veranda. "What happened?" she cried, bending over me.

I sat up, heat pulsing in my temples. Long rows of vegetable plants stretched out before me. The hoe lay across my legs. "I think I fainted," I said as Gwenity helped me to my feet. I laughed at her worried eyes 'cause I felt so foolish. "I'm all right. Stop fretting."

"Have you been working too long? It doesn't seem that hot. Come on in. I made tea."

Howdy waited by the door. He'd thinned a bit over the winter. Hunting had been bad and we'd been snowed in near two weeks in March. "Hurt yourself?" he asked, rubbing his eyes.

"I'm fine," I said, edging past him. "Too much sun."

"She fainted! Draw some fresh water," Gwenity said, leading me back to the room off the kitchen. It was cool and quiet. A shaft of sunlight fell across the bed. I felt so befuddled, I didn't struggle when Gwenity sat me down and unlaced my boots. That feeling, like I wasn't quite myself, lingered. I'd been hoeing and the sun had felt so good and warm on my hair, kind of friendly. I liked working in the garden and had been thinking...

"I haven't seen your face so white since you were sick last summer," Gwenity whispered. "Howdy'll fetch Judd." When she was worried, Gwenity looked like her teeth hurt. "Was it the sun?"

I no more would've told Gwenity what I'd been thinking than I would have told her about my past.

She sat herself on the bed and wiped her forehead. "You scared me! I looked out and saw you on the ground. For all I knew you were dead!"

Something cold touched my heart. Ringing come in my ears again like a high painful scream. The room faded and I began to feel heavy and cold again. Rows of wooden crosses rose from the darkness...and I heard hoofbeats.

"Angie!" came Gwenity's voice from afar. "Wake up!"

I was half on the floor, shivering with cold sweat on my forehead.

"What's the matter? You're worried about Judd I'll bet. He's been gone too long. Howdy, you best fetch Judd right now!" she shouted, though Howdy probably couldn't hear her out by the well. "Angie's sick."

"It ain't nothing," I said. "Don't go bothering Judd. He's got his work. He'll be back when he's ready."

She got up and paced. "You weren't married six months and he was off to that fool mine. Don't you want to be with your own husband?"

"I guess there's no use keeping it from you. I'm pregnant."

Like a roped calf, Gwenity turned, her eyes wide. Her face filled with wonder. "Oh Lord, Angie! Is it true? Are you sure?"

"I ain't got out the rags since April. Don't that put me due around January?"

Her hands was cold and trembling as she took mine. "I'm so happy for you! Don't know why I didn't guess. Maybe when you didn't get pregnant right off I figured you were like me. Lord, I'm happy for you!"

I had to look away. Gwenity didn't know the cold fear laying deep inside me. I'd lost one baby and miscarried another. I'd worried so long on not having babies I hardly knew how to think now that I was expecting one and it was legal and proper. A lump of hope and fear big enough to choke me stuck in my throat. I guess I was happiest just knowing whether it lived or died it wasn't no bastard.

"January," Gwenity said, beginning to pace again. "That's enough time to make you the prettiest quilt! Now we'll have to send for Judd!"

I hadn't thought to send for Judd just to tell him the news. I'd figured his gold fever meant more than me 'cause it was for certain we'd scratched every other itch between us! "I was waiting to see if everything went right."

"Don't you worry," Gwenity said. "You'll carry this baby!"

Judd had gone back to his mine in April. We'd got on real good at the inn 'til then. After our first night together, I'd made an effort to act like I didn't know nothing about bedding. Judd never did ask how I'd come to be the one married-up female in the world who liked bedding.

I loved laying close to Judd at night and hearing his snores. I loved waking to see that scarred up sunburnt face pressed tight against his pillow like he was scared it'd get away. He'd wake and see me looking down on him, my heart plain in my eyes and he'd reach for me. All the gold on earth couldn't compare to that.

After Judd left and my monthlies didn't come, I waited each day, wondering if my dream would disappear in a flow of blood. May come and went. June…Still I didn't let myself believe I was going to have a baby I could hold and love and just plain be glad about!

What with the corral full of horses for the stage to tend and seeing to the summer travelers, Howdy didn't have the time, but finally he struck off for Judd's mine to fetch him back a couple weeks later. Gwenity already had cut the pieces for the quilt called the "Jackson Star."

Judd had been gone near four months without so much as a how-de-do to tell me he still breathed. I'd settled in, working at the inn like before, though I missed Judd. I'd been alone a lot of years, though, so I'd come to expect a man to go off from me when he was done with me.

A couple days later, Howdy come riding back—alone. He had a bit of a time coming down off his horse, being near as big around as a steer. He led his horse toward the corral, looking like his bones was broke.

"Did you find Judd? Is he coming?" Gwenity ran after Howdy like a pup, her skirts flapping.

Howdy left the horse for her to brush. "Judd's doing good," he said to me, leading me in the inn. "He's got a couple new fellas working for him."

"I hope you didn't get on him about coming back before he's ready."

Sighing with exasperation, Howdy rubbed his jowly cheeks. "If you didn't mean for him to come, why the hell did I go up there? That's some ride up that trail, Angie! I won't be able to set a horse for a month."

"I figured to spare you the grief of telling me he ain't coming."

"Well, that's it, for sure. He said he'd come if you was sick or hurt, but he's got to work every waking minute."

"Figured as much."

"I can't understand some women," he said, shaking his head and eyeing me. "Got any coffee made?"

"Since when ain't we had coffee?" I looked sideways at him. "Did Judd have much to say at all?"

Howdy turned. "You know, it was kind of funny. When he said he wouldn't be coming back for a while yet, I figured I'd better tell him your news. Didn't at first, you see. Gwenity figured you'd want to tell him." Howdy laughed a bit and shook his head. "He looked like he never heard of women expecting. He just went right back to work."

"If he's of a mind to come back," I said, "he'll come."

Gwenity walked in then and washed. "When's he coming?" She went to the pie safe and pulled out a golden-crusted delight. "I baked this in honor of Judd's return."

"He'll come when he's struck gold, or when he ain't," I said, and ran for my room.

Autumn turned them aspens yellow as sunshine. October winds stripped them, leaving dark pines against gray and red rocks. I found myself sitting on the veranda on cool afternoons and going to bed right after we swept up from supper—Gwenity insisted. I'd fall asleep to her piano playing and dream of my pretty new baby. Her music talked to me, comforting me. I didn't much like playing second fiddle to gold, but that music could fill me with peace, like the babe turning and kicking in my belly.

One cold night in October long after we'd turned in, a horse drew up in front of the inn. I lay abed, listening to Howdy get up; there weren't no mistaking him when he was about. Gooseflesh tingled up my arms when I didn't hear his usual laughing greeting. I slipped from bed and peeked down the hall to see moonlight spilling in the open front door. Don't know if I thought bandits had come upon us, or what, but I was reaching for the rifle when I seen him.

Judd looked so like a ghost I almost screamed. He stood in that unearthly pale moonlight, his clothes in tatters, his face in shadow, his wild hair and beard growed long like I'd first seen him. "Angie?" he whispered, coming to me slow. He laid his hands across my belly and kissed me soft like I might break.

A mighty lot of things to say come to mind as I threw myself into that dusty mess of whiskers, but I bit my lips to keep them in. Didn't need to go angering the man when he'd come back to me.

"You're not mad I took so long?" Judd asked, kissing my cheeks and forehead and eyes. He sounded like he already knew I wasn't, not enough to speak of, anyhow.

"I expect you either got cold or you struck your mother lode."

"Would you be very upset if we were to be rich soon?"

"You need a bath and shave, Mr. Judd Rydell," I said, pulling him into our bedroom. "You'll do for now, though. Rich? Not much chance of it, is there?"

"I'm afraid so," he said, beginning to grin. Them teeth gleamed bright as the moon. The moonlight from the window caught his eyes. I laced my fingers in his matted hair.

"You found gold?"

"Just came from the assay office in Cold Water!"

I squealed and let him dance me around.

"I'm going down to Tempest to order ore cars and track soon as I've done you justice. Sorry I didn't come with Howdy in August, but I figured you could do without me awhile longer if it meant a good future for our baby."

"I expect you're right."

"Tell me what I can bring you from Tempest. It'll be a long winter. I've got to stay at the mine, you understand. I can't leave it after ordering the cars. Come spring…"

"I don't want nothing from Tempest! I don't mind being alone all summer, but you ain't leaving me to birth this baby alone! If you're going back to that gold mine, I'm going, too."

Judd looked mighty surprised. "There's no place to live!"

"Planning to turn yourself into a bear, are you?"

Judd ran his fingers through his tangle of hair. "I'll put up a lean-to if I get cold."

"Timberwolves is fond of lean-tos," I snapped. "The smell of fresh meat gets through the chinks easy."

"Then I'll build a cabin!"

"Long as you're at it, take an extra week to make it fit for me and your child." I kissed him and pulled my nightdress over my head. "Come to bed."

With Howdy's help, Judd raised a cabin by November. They wasn't pleased to be doing it since a foot of snow fell before they got the roof done.

ANGEL

"Are you sure you're doing the right thing?" Gwenity asked as we readied to leave. In the wagon we had stores enough to last four to five months.

I took Gwen's hand and smiled. "Don't know if we'll make it back for Christmas, but we'll be down by January."

"You've gone longer than I ever have. I'll miss seeing you come to the end of it."

Finally Judd was ready and we struck off. The trail was easy 'til we topped the ridge. Near all day we struggled up through them pines over rocks and gullies to the mesa. Three sides of the mesa fell off into canyons, and along the edges was big boulders, pines and stands of naked gray-white aspen. The far side lay against a low mountain that blocked Pikes Peak. The higher we got, the less of the high peaks we could see, but when we turned, the vista was enough to steal my breath.

A powdered sugar dusting of snow lay over the valleys. The pines looked like burrs on a coverlet, stretching far, far into the distance to faint gray peaks. The air was cold enough to make my lungs ache.

"The mine's over that way, near the spring. I panned a couple hundred dollars out of the creek two summers ago. Last summer the Wilson boys from Cold Water helped me dig for the source of the float I found. Leroy and us dug a shaft ten feet in. That's when I tried the blasting powder."

We followed a steep creek toward the mountain. "I want to show it to you," he said, his cheeks red with excitement.

That face made me shivery. He'd let me cut away some of his hair, but he'd kept his beard. With his lips pink and smooth against the brown whiskers and those twinkling eyes staring from pockets of sunburnt wrinkles, I thought he looked about as fine as any man in creation.

He stopped beside a little rise. I saw the tailings hid under the snow, two big boulders beside the entrance and a dark hole, like a mouth, that give me a chill. Judd helped me down and led me up a path that skirted the tailings. I kept slipping in the snow and didn't like spotting my best dress.

When Judd stepped inside all I could see was his grin and I thought of Pa. He'd dreamed on such a mine all his life and never saw a one. I felt sad and sorry. That gold fever was mighty troublesome in my estimation, but I smiled for Judd and stepped into the darkness with him. I intended to give Judd full rein.

"Wait 'til your eyes get used to the dark," he whispered. "Feel how warm it is in here? In the summer it's always cool and damp even if it's hot and dry outside." The rock walls was knocked smooth here and there. The floor was beaten dirt and sloped as we stepped deeper inside. "We're coming to a step now," Judd said, his voice all but swallowed. He sounded small with the earth pressing all around him. It was as near death as I cared to get.

Judd held my hand as I stepped down again and again over wide smooth rocks. When the floor leveled, the ceiling hung so low Judd and me had to stoop. By then it was midnight dark. I'd forgotten the sun and the crisp-smelling air. All I knew was the damp odor of rocks, red dirt and time.

Axes, shovels, and hammers lay at the end of the shaft. Judd struck a Lucifer match and held it close to the walls near one yellowish-red streak.

"That's it?" I asked, feeling a bit disgusted.

"That's what we found once we cleared away the debris from the blast. Imagine what we'll find when we try again?"

"More scars on your face where whiskers won't grow."

When we stepped back into the afternoon sunshine, my eyes stung. The cold bit my cheeks. Once up on the wagon seat I turned to stare at that hole. Like people, no telling how deep it went or what lay inside just by looking at the outside.

"We built the cabin over here because the wind isn't so bad," Judd said as we edged around a stand of pine. The cabin lay like a shadow in the drifts. Ridge poles near two feet long stuck out from under the roof. It had two leather covered windows and a door of unstripped pine. Snow covered the nearby stumps and mess left from fitting the logs.

ANGEL

Up to the roof, the chimney was mud and rock. Above that was crisscrossed pine branches chinked with clay. "I know it's not much," Judd said, lifting down the first bundles. "We didn't try the fireplace, so I don't know how it'll draw. We'll have a good view of anybody trying to jump my claim, but they won't see us 'til it's too late." He threw open the door. The fading afternoon sunlight fell on the snow inside. "I'll start shoveling as soon as I get a fire going." He looked anxiously into my face.

"It's a fine cabin," I said, grinning.

Judd's face lit with wonder. He lifted me into his arms and carried me inside. We was home.

Seventeen

Early Spring 1868

"She can't stay on her feet much longer, Judd," Gwenity cried, wringing her hands, her eyes wild with worry.

"She'll lie down when she's ready." Judd went on stripping bark from some pine branches. He was making a stool.

I leaned on my broom. "I feel fine," I said, though my belly tightened to a sharp knot and my legs softened like dough. I didn't want to lay down. Gwenity was afraid something would happen if I didn't climb into the bed and birth my baby proper. I was afraid something would happen if I did.

All afternoon Gwenity had been laying hot stones on the bed tick. Her and me had been sleeping there a week. When Howdy brung her up right after the New Year the snow had been three feet deep in places. Howdy rigged runners on his buckboard and it worked pretty fair, except they near to slid into a gully.

"Come on," Judd said, putting his arms around me. "I'll lay by you and keep you warm."

My belly knotted again, harder, and my back ached like an arrowhead was twisting in my backbone. A fullness between my legs puzzled me. I didn't figure I'd been working at the labor long enough to be ready to birth. Moaning deep in my throat, I hung onto Judd as my knees gave way. The fullness got greater.

"Let me lay you down," he whispered, a fine spray of sweat laying across his brow.

"Not yet," I panted. "Not yet."

"She's not making sense, Judd! Bring her over here."

"Not yet!" I shouted, I felt a pop. Something warm puddled in my boots.

Judd held up my skirt as Gwenity stripped off my drawers and woollies. My teeth began to chatter. Judd helped me waddle toward the bed. I stopped when my belly knotted again and bent over grunting. It was so different from before! I wished I could tell Gwenity and Judd it just wasn't time yet. I'd probably lay all night screaming, my insides coming undone, the world a red haze of pain.

"One last kiss," I said, pressing my face into Judd's whiskers.

"Don't be a fool, Angie. You're wearing yourself out. Just lay down and give a little push."

I laughed. To show him what he knew, I bore down as my belly knotted again. "*Oh!*"

"Judd, carry her! She doesn't know what to do."

"Don't move me! Oh, damn! That does it." I staggered back and gripped the edge of the table so hard the bark on the underside pressed patterns into my fingertips. The fullness got awful. I threw back my head and let a sharp, piercing scream fill the cabin.

Gwenity tried to pull me toward the bed, but I wouldn't let loose of the table. My eyes stretched so far open I could feel the muscles pulling all along my cheeks. I squatted lower. Everything I had down there was hot and throbbing like a soft angry heart. Then, suddenly, the pain eased. "Judd!" The heavy feeling got deeper still.

We all heard a cry. Judd and Gwenity pushed up my skirts. "My God! It's half out!" Gwenity gasped. "Lay back or it'll fall. Judd, take hold of its head! Oh, Lord have mercy!"

"It's a girl!" Judd laughed.

One by one my fingers came loose of the table. Gwenity eased me to the floor. The cold soaked up through my shoulder blades and ached against the back of my head. I saw snow sifting through the chinks in the roof and falling soft as sugar into little piles on the bureau.

The lusty cry of my newborn babe filled the winter silence.

"No, tie it there, like that," Gwenity was saying, running for a blanket. "Go ahead. Cut it."

Then beaming, Judd lifted our daughter. Her eyes was slits, her skin red as fire and oh, she didn't have black hair! She had brown, like Judd's. That had to be a good sign!

They carried her to the cradle by the hearth, exclaiming softly over her beauty. I eased to my feet. The floor felt uneven and soft as I waddled toward them.

"Mercy, Angie!" Gwenity cried. "Haven't you got any sense at all? Judd, make her lay down!"

I felt drunk and silly. "Bring her," I laughed, as Judd helped me into bed. He laid our babe in my arms. She surely did look little!

Silently I said to her, *I ain't never going to let you down.* I'd broke enough promises to guarantee me a place in hell, but to that child I spoke a solemn oath. *You'll never be hungry or afraid or ashamed.*

Gwenity began weeping. Joy had changed her from plain and awkward to a glowing beauty. She looked on my child as if it was hers, her hands clasped in front of her empty belly as if in prayer. So help me, I felt ashamed before her and didn't know why. "What do you think, Gwen? Does she look healthy and strong to you?"

She smeared her tears across her flushed cheeks. "Don't pay any attention to me. These are tears of joy, Angie. I'm so very happy for you!"

Judd bent and kissed me. I saw a touch of sadness in his eyes.

"She looks good, don't she, Judd?"

"The most beautiful baby ever born. Thank you."

A shiver of happiness went through me. Judd and me was going to raise her up to be the very best. Just Judd and me—and luck. She was my chance to undo every mistake.

"What will you call her?" Gwenity asked.

What a comfort it would've been to hear Sara's name live again in a sweet smiling child, I thought, but Sara had knowed mostly sorrow, from a mean and empty childhood to a mean and empty death. I could no more give my child Sara's name than my own. To deny her that would be to deny forever her chance of turning out like us.

"Lillian, after my ma?" I asked Judd.

"My mother's name is Elvira," Judd grinned. "A great lady. Born to wealth."

"Or, Cornelia, after a woman who was kind to me. Or Gwenity, my friend who saved me," I said, smiling.

Gwenity touched trembling fingers to her lips. "Not my name, Angie. It's after my grandmothers Gwendolen and Serenity."

My beautiful babe squeezed her face into a pout. "I guess them names is a lot to heap on her," I said.

"Then call her Lillie, simple and beautiful, like she'll be someday," Gwenity said.

"And you'll teach Lillie to play the piano? Please?"

"Of course she will," Judd said. "Lillie Elvira Rydell. Does that suit you, Angie?"

Hands of darkness pressed on my drooping eyes. "Sounds like a right proper name." I held up my newborn babe for Gwenity to take. Her eyes rounded with wonder. She took the precious bundle to her breast and smiled like the sun. Her love burned for my child as fierce as my own. "Don't sleep," I whispered. "'Til I've rested. Ain't nothing going to happen to that child." I looked deep into Gwenity's eyes. Surely, as she nodded over that downy head, she knowed all that lay behind my eyes and my words.

There ain't much to say about the first months of a babe's life. We all put up with a lot of crying and fussing that ought to have sounded like music, but sometimes didn't. That little bundle of muscle and grit could bring on more fears in us three weatherbeaten big folks than a plague of wild Injuns. Gwenity called it colic. I called it plain stone-headedness that made that child decide night was day.

It suited me, though. I wasn't about to sleep while that babe lay in the darkness. I took to staying up with her 'til the sky glowed with dawn. I was destined to live by moonlight.

I hoped Howdy had no great need of Gwenity just then. For a childless woman, she knew a heap about them. I became expert at bringing down my milk 'til I felt like a milch cow. For sure, it was a joy to see that babe grow chubby and pink.

Come March, Judd chipped the last of the ice from our wagon and readied the shaggy horses for the trip down the mountain. When we took to the trail everything was muddy and red and smelled of soggy pine. Snow slept in hollows. Sunshine sparkled through the pines and glinted off pure white peaks.

We stayed two nights at the inn and then went on alone to Cold Water for our supplies. The road meandered higher and higher through brown meadows, past lakes smooth as a looking glass, around mounds of red-gray boulders flecked with silver, agate, and quartz. Each vista was more beautiful than the last.

The best was when we looked down on Cold Water City laying in a narrow valley. The town got its name, o' course, from the nearby creek. Cabins was sprinkled along the bank. That was how a town ought to look, I thought, not climbing up a mountainside like some creature trying to free itself from a trap. We followed Main Street into town and would've stopped at Cross Street to wonder at the stores but the fiery-tempered driver of a logging wagon behind us let loose with a string of cuss words that brought a grin to my mouth.

"S'pose we'll get a bath while we're here? Remember how curly my hair is when it's clean?"

Judd laughed. "I'll buy the hottest water and best soap in town." He wheeled us in front of the hotel. "I'll be right back, Angie. Sit tight."

Cold Water City wasn't no mining town—more a crossroads— so the usual string of saloons and dancehalls was missing. Everything I saw displayed in the store windows, from a shiny tin coffeepot to a brown calico dress, I wanted.

"We're all set, Angie," Judd said, and I jumped. Judd reached up, grinning. "We'll shop tomorrow. You'd like a new dress and bonnet, wouldn't you? And boots and drawers and a silk chemise like the one you wore under your wedding gown. Remember how I tore it?"

ANGEL

"Sh-h-h!" I hissed, mindful of a group of men eyeing us. My heart gave a start. Did any of them know me? I didn't dare look. I slipped into Judd's arms. "A new dress, yes, and new johns and shirts for you. And a featherbed!" I hugged him. "But first a bath— and sleep."

Being in a town put me in mind of so many forgotten things. Judd walked me down a long hall to our little room with a window looking out over the bubbling creek. He smiled down on me with that need in his eye. I'd healed up quick and was eager to get back to bedding. I figured on more children, a whole brood of them!

We found us that bathhouse the next day. Then Judd led me to the ladies' emporium and turned me loose with ten dollars. I swore I could outfit myself and Lillie twice for that—all the while remembering when I paid that for a single dress.

"Afternoon, Mrs. Rydell," a prim little thing buttoned up in black all the way to her chin said when I stepped in. "I'm Lisa Simms."

"Do you know me?"

"You and your husband are the first settlers to come to town this spring for supplies. May I see the baby? Cathy McGuire is expecting in the fall. She's got two boys and is hoping for a girl. Oh, she's sweet! How old is she?"

"Three months, or thereabouts." My heart swelled. "Do you have any children?"

"I did. A boy of three, but measles came through last summer and we lost him. I'll have more if the good Lord sees fit. Come over here by the stove and tell me what I can do for you. I have some lovely things I think you'll like. I made most of them myself. My mother knits the shawls. You'll find they're very warm."

Mrs. Simms didn't have much in the way of underthings, but I did find me a new petticoat. She didn't have no silk chemise.

"I do hope you and your husband will come for supper this evening," she said when I was done picking through her wares. "All the ladies will be over. We're working on a quilt for Bonnie Newbaker. She just got married last week. The circuit judge was on his way up to settle all the trouble in Eagleton. We fed him dried apple pie so he'd stay long enough to marry the poor thing.

"I guess you wouldn't be up on the news," she went on. "My mother does. She was educated at one of the finest ladies' academies back East, you know. She read in the newspaper about the raid in Eagleton. Were you around here after that terrible massacre in '64? Why, you've been in these mountains a long time then. Do you have people living near here?"

"All my people died early on," I said, hanging my head to look as if I couldn't speak of it no more. "I worked for Gwenity Jackson awhile."

"Of course!" Mrs. Simms smiled. "You're the shy thing she had working in her kitchen. I heard about that flood. Heard half of Tempest got washed away."

The little bell over her door tinkled and in walked Judd. "There's my pretty wife. Morning, Mrs. Simms. I've been to the bank, talking to your husband. Doing mighty well for yourselves these days. I remember when you sold felt hats and suspenders out of a tent."

Mrs. Simms's face turned a pretty red. "We've been lucky with most things."

"Sorry about your boy."

"Lots of dealings at the bank, I take it," she said, her eyes swimmy.

"Panned a little gold dust and exchanged it for cash. Angie, have you picked out all you need?"

"Why, I've just talked the poor thing's ear off," Lisa laughed. "It's so good to have somebody *new* in town. She hasn't heard all my stories twice over! Mrs. Rydell, I recall this fella coming to my store for a hat a couple summers back. We wanted him to meet a young lady who was here with her uncle at the time. He wasn't interested in nothing but gold then." She laughed behind her hand. "Always does my heart good to see a man give in to a pretty woman. You *will* be by for supper tonight. Please? The ladies would love to see your pretty baby. Say you'll come. The husbands not working will be there, Judd. You'll enjoy it."

"We'd be honored, Mrs. Simms. Is there anything we can bring?"

"Just yourselves! Take care in that hotel, Judd Rydell. Don't let them charge you for the view!"

I was so excited to be invited to a respectable home I didn't have time to worry. Soon as we walked in, though, all them eyes went over me. I got to shaking so bad I could hardly talk. Five or six ladies sat around a quilting frame in the front parlor. Back in the kitchen I heard men laughing.

"Go on back and make yourself to home, Judd," Lisa said, giving him a smart push on his back. "We'll look after your wife and baby. Ladies, meet Angie Rydell."

They all smiled and nodded, their eyes sharp as thistles.

"Sit by me," said one with her blonde hair in a knot.

"Let's see the child," said a crone in black, rapping the floorboards with her cane.

They clucked and cooed over Lillie and admired her pretty white dress tinged pink along the edges. After a bit Lillie fussed and my milk come down. Lisa showed me to an upstairs bedroom where I could nurse in private. As Lillie took that first sharp tug on my nipple, I leaned back in a handsome rocker relieved to be alone awhile. Them eyes wearied me.

The room had a four poster, a bureau, a wardrobe eight feet high and a pretty hand-braided rug. One painted picture of the old lady in black and three family daguerreotypes hung on the dark papered walls. Drifting up from the kitchen came the sounds of men laughing. One of them laughs belonged to my husband. My heart got so full I wanted to cry.

When Lillie finished I tiptoed downstairs, fixing to be sociable even if it killed me.

"You never can tell," one of the women was whispering. "You wouldn't think she'd be the type for *silk* underthings. I was so embarrassed! Imagine, asking for such finery!"

"You suppose her people were rich Southerners?" another

whispered. "Judd's a rebel."

"She told me she was here when the uprising first started. She must be older than she looks."

"Look here, Bonnie," the crone said. "See if them men are ready to clear out so we can put supper on."

I was ready to step forward before they could start in discussing me again, but I was too slow.

"Hush, that's not nice, Cathy. She can't help being pretty. And Judd don't have a big claim. If he did, my husband would know. I don't think she's the type to marry for riches anyway. It's plain she's rough stock."

"She looks like baggage to me. You saw the way she watched us."

"Being pregnant ain't done nothing for this girl's disposition," Mrs. Corbet, Lisa's mother, sniffed.

I waltzed in. "Lillie ought to sleep peaceful now," I said as if I hadn't heard a word. Them cats smiled back as if they'd been talking the price of calico and pickles.

"Lay the babe right here where it's warm. Hand Mrs. Rydell a needle, will you, Vi? You're handy at stitching I'll bet. Made that pretty baby dress, didn't you?"

"That was a gift from a dear old friend," I said, hoping I sounded charming. I felt like cussing the old biddie, but I meant to make a place for Lillie in respectable society. I started stitching.

"Wonder what's keeping that Bonnie," one skinny woman called Netta said. "Did you tell Angie about her?" She whispered to Lisa.

Lisa smiled. "There's a girl for you. She and her first husband came to town, oh, a year or so ago. He caught the measles and died. Hardly a year went by and she's married a fella old enough to be her papa."

"Was she the one married by the circuit judge?" I asked.

"Did you tell Angie about *that* already?" Netta asked. She had a sharp face and strange eyes. "About the raid on Eagleton, too?"

"Don't go scaring the girl," Lisa's mother scolded. "She's got to live up on that lonely mesa, remember."

"All the more reason to tell her," Cathy said. She was the

pregnant one and reminded me of Effie.

"I'll get the newspaper and she can read about it for herself," Mrs. Corbet said.

My belly turned cold.

Bonnie, a short, bright-looking girl, come back form the kitchen smiling, her cheeks red. "They're ready to clear out." She took up stitching beside me as the other ladies went to the kitchen.

Old Mrs. Corbet come downstairs, holding a newspaper sheet and stopped to speak to Lisa in the hall. "She's bringing me that to read," I whispered to Bonnie.

"The article about the uprising?" Bonnie asked when Mrs. Corbet turned to me. "Read it aloud, for us, Maude. You have such a fine speaking voice."

"Pish-tosh," the crone said, but smiling. "Very well. This is dated March, 1868. Saunders must have gotten there before the bodies were cold. He's got a nose for blood, that one. He writes too much of it for my taste."

"The article, Maude," Bonnie smiled.

"'The Utes struck in bloody rebellion at the Eagleton Indian Agency, killing Ray Johnsie, his squaw daughter-in-law, and two missionaries sent by the Love of the Lord Church and Missionary Society based in Philadelphia.'" Maude Corbet paused to clear her throat and look down the bony distance of her nose at Bonnie and me. Then she shook the paper out a foot or so in front of her face and went on. "'Johnsie, a speculator and trader, had been agent two years, assigned to provide for the Indians while they learned farming and Christianity. Supplies promised by the government, however, were never delivered. Ill with measles, the tribes' leaders begged Johnsie to open his storehouse but, according to a few surviving Utes, the stores were for whites only. The missionaries were easily overcome. The bodies of the agent and missionaries lay untended only yards away while the Indians ate their fill and the wives were held captive. This reporter's arrival helped effect release of the captives, one of whom was hysterical, having been repeatedly assaulted. I can only say that if Johnsie indeed cheated the Indians,

SAMANTHA HARTE

he paid a high price. Possibly his son survived the attack. He was hunting but hasn't been seen since. Clearly, an investigation will be necessary to determine what disciplinary action must be taken.'"

"Can you feature that?" Bonnie said softly, her arms in gooseflesh. "Killed one of their own women 'cause she'd married the agent's son."

Maude handed me the paper and went to the kitchen where the women was chattering like chickens. I looked at all them little black marks and shuddered. "I can't read a word."

"Don't let that bother you," Bonnie said, knotting another thread. "You know, I haven't been pregnant yet. Was the birth hard? Netta helped Cathy with her last and just about killed them both. Don't know how Cathy can go on having children after what she's been through."

"I guess a woman has as many babies as her husband gives her, or risks losing him to a…" I wanted to bite my tongue.

"To a what?"

I accidentally stabbed my finger and spotted the quilt. "One of them…women."

"A couple of years back a whole wagonload of harlots come through here. We all stood down at Cross Street with our husband's rifles and forced them right out of town."

"Bonnie? Mrs. Rydell? Wouldn't you both like to come in the kitchen with the rest of us?" old Aunt Vi called. "There's plenty of work."

"If we don't, they'll just talk about us," Bonnie whispered. "They're good women, really. Any time you need anything, they're right there to help. I don't know if it's because they're such good Christians or they don't have nothing better to do. What I do know is, they love their gossip."

"What'd you think of them?" Judd asked as we walked back to the hotel that night.

184

"I guess they took to me pretty good, though they had plenty to speculate on." Once in our room I fixed Lillie on the bed and began undressing.

"Before we settle in," Judd said, caressing my shoulders, "I got something I want you to sign." He spread an impressive bunch of papers on the table. "This is legal title to all the land I claimed up on the mesa and the mineral rights. Here's my name. Here's yours. Here's Lillie Elvira's."

I took Judd's pen and my fingers went stiff. "I ain't made my name in a long time." I dipped into the ink and labored over each letter. They come out looking big and ugly on that fine legal paper.

Judd folded them, bound them in a leather packet and handed it all to me. "The mine belongs to Lillie now. I know you're wondering why I didn't sign it over to you. I don't mean to hurt your feelings, but I expect Lillie to be educated someday and handle the profits herself. The mine should produce a long time. If something happens to me, you'll say who works the mine, which bank the gold goes to and how the money's to be used. You look pretty bewildered, Angie. Do you understand what I've done? I manage things 'til I die, but , men don't last forever. It's all I have to give my daughter."

"Stop!" I cried, shutting out his voice and pressing my face hard into his chest. I didn't see how paper could make that hole in the mountain belong to a babe when it was plain her papa had put his heart, soul, and a good share of his flesh and blood into it. "I don't never want you talking like that again!"

Eighteen

Late Summer 1869

Judd and me worked like horses our first summer on the mesa. Judd lay track into his mine, while I tended to our cabin and garden patch. Judd started a corral and barn so we'd have a proper place for the stock come winter. Once a month, regular, he went to Cold Water City to bank his gold.

When Lillie celebrated one year of life she had three teeth and smiled like the sweet little devil she was. She did all the things mothers dote on and filled my days with perfect joy. Marrying up with a miner, though, wasn't one of the smarter things I'd done. I got a mite aggravated that Judd spent near all his waking hours in that hole. Those men he hired had more say with him than me.

Preparing for the day Lillie would learn her letters and numbers, I took to practicing my name on the brown paper wrappings off the goods Judd brung me from town.

"I could use a good picture of the land we own," Judd said one night before he pulled off his boots and poured two piles of red dust onto my fresh swept floor. "I'll label the boundaries when you're done." And, like most other nights, he fell to snoring.

I was mighty pleased to think he took my pencil scratchings serious, so I set at the table by lamplight, wondering how I was at rendering cabins and pines. Lillie toddled over from her bowl of corn mash for a long pull at my breast. Near a year and a half old, she was a real armload by then. I loved the gulping, sighing sounds she made. Her little hands would curl and uncurl. Her eyes would droop so's she'd almost put me to sleep a-looking at her. She could already say Ma and Papa.

I looked across the room at her papa and wondered at myself. After two years I knew no more about him than the day we rode down Buffalo Pass to get married.

"If I thought it was important, I'd tell you all about where I went to school and who I knew and what I did. All Lillie ever needs to know, though, is right here in this cabin," he'd say.

So, I could look at the man I bedded with such contentment, and whose ring I wore so proud, and not know what state he'd been born in! Not that it mattered. I didn't know what state I'd been born in! His past was as empty and dark as my own. He never asked about me, though sometimes as we sat talking of buying a milch cow or such like, I'd see him look at me with a question in his eye.

I drew the cabin and corral and the half-finished barn behind it on that brown wrapping paper. Behind everything I put the mountain and pines protecting us from the wind. At the far side I drew the outcropping where the mine was, drew the tailings growing longer with each passing month, added the rail line when the boys got it finished.

When Judd wrote in all the details, I marveled at the pretty curls and spikes he claimed was longhand writing. My letters gouged the paper into ruts.

"Tell me what it all says," I said when he'd finished signing.

"This is a good drawing and may save Lillie a lot of legal trouble someday. Next time I go to town I'll have this registered. In the sky part I've written, 'This drawing is meant to be a proper record of the land and mine claimed by Judd Rydell, legally given to his daughter, Lillie Elvira Rydell. 1869.' Along the sides I've marked the boundaries. I found the first float here. Of course, this is the mine."

"Sounds mighty impressive. What you got writ across

the bottom?"

"I've christened our home 'Angel's Mesa.'"

Oh! the pain that struck my heart when he spoke my other name! I must've smiled, though, 'cause Judd looked pleased.

"Call it Lillie's Mesa. It belongs to *her*," I said, my throat thick.

"I first thought of 'Mesa of the Angels,' but there's only one angel here. You've made my life happy, Angel. It's best to name it after you."

I went to Judd's arms and clung tight 'til he loved me. Luck had smiled on me near three years, but if ever I believed in omens, it was then.

Judd made a sudden trip to Cold Water City in late August of '69. I didn't mind being alone. I kept the rifle handy. Judd had hired quite an assortment of men. There was old Cabe, a sinewy varmint who tasted his first gold out in California. The chaw he kept packed in his teeth made him look like a woody squirrel.

Young Leroy Story had a clutch of dusty brown hair permanently squeezed into the shape of his old hat. He was hungry and hard-up for work. Judd claimed he was his best miner.

There was Woolsie and Chopper Wilks who wanted to partner with Judd. They was still a mite peeved to be only rock-busters. And Steven Riley—I suspect he was loose of the law. As long as he worked hard and didn't pocket too much gold, though, Judd kept him on.

Judd got back from his trip as sudden as he left, turned up for supper and then took off for the mine 'fore the sun could go down on him. He hardly brushed my cheek with a kiss as he rushed out. He was like that in the fall, feeling the cold coming on and knowing the snow would near to stop his production.

"I'll be back before too late," he called across the yard, having not even taken off his hat as he ate.

I took Lillie out while I pulled the last of the wash from the ropes slung behind the cabin. Lillie busied herself wasting the soap bar on the scrubboard. Someday I wanted to be so rich I wouldn't have to haul water all the way from the creek. Judd had picked a sheltered spot all right—about as far from the creek as he could get. I had it in mind to speak to Howdy on it next time I saw him. Seems he could've steered Judd a little closer.

My garden patch looked real fine, near all harvested of squash, potatoes, and pumpkins. Lillie still found wild flowers to pull up. 'Course, I had to keep her from eating them. I sat on the stool, wondering how the place would look with cattle lowing in the corral, a goat maybe, and plenty of chickens…

Old Maude Corbet had said Lillie could board with them when she started her schooling. I couldn't let Lillie do that. We'd just have to build us a cabin in town, maybe a real house with a picket fence like Lisa Simms had, and the inside all done up in ruffled curtains, striped wallpaper and hand-braided rugs.

Lillie waddled into my arms, smelling as warm and pink as the day she birthed herself into this world, carrying the proud name of her father. Already she was a landed lady and how she did carry herself like a little queen, though her hands was always dusty and her knees red with Rocky Mountain dirt. She fit so tight in my arms not a chink of light got between us.

I heard running footsteps, a stumble, a grunt. The footsteps rounded the cabin…Leroy, his hair undone of its hat-shape by the wind, gasped for breath. Blood dripped from his cuff.

I stood up and pressed Lillie's face into my shirt.

"Better come, Miz Rydell! It's bad!"

Lillie felt so light as I bolted after Leroy I thought I might lose her up in the air. Over sage and cactus, around boulders and through wildflowers I ran. That yawning hole with the chin of tailings and tongue of iron rails sticking out still belched smoke and dust I heard a man's scream. Then nothing! In that settling dust I felt such awful, dreadful surprise.

"They're all in there, Miz Rydell! I couldn't get at them. They're all in there!" He screamed almost as high as a woman.

I set Lillie near a pile of timbers and scrambled up the tailing, scraping my knees and palms, taking comfort in the pain, wanting to bleed so I'd know I wasn't dreaming. One of the rails had buckled. At the mouth of the mine a carload of ore sat crooked as if one of the men had just gone off to right the rail.

"Don't go in!" Leroy screamed, his face squeezed in pain and terror.

I whirled. "Get Howdy! If he can't move these rocks, nobody can!"

Leroy threw hisself across the nearest horse and disappeared down the trail in a hail of hoofbeats. Then silence such as I've never known settled over the camp, silence colder than the dead of January—numbing, deadly, terrible silence.

How could the sun still hang in the sky red and peaceful when men lay crushed back into the dust they was formed from? "Ashes to ashes, dust to dust," they'd said over Becky. That's what the whole world was—ashes and dust, tears and bad luck.

Lillie started to cry when I called Judd's name. "Hush! I can't hear him! He could be dead. Your papa could be dead!"

I backed away as another rumble brought a fresh cloud of dust from the mine. I tumbled down the tailing and lay on my back at the bottom, crying without tears 'til it sounded more like laughing. I felt plumb crazy. Forever after folks would say poor Mrs. Rydell lost her senses the day her husband left her a widow—a woman alone.

I jumped up and started throwing rocks into the mine, throwing and throwing 'til my throat burned from screaming and my whole body ached with grief. Then, at last, I heard Lillie sitting in the dirt, her world a flattened dream, her good name as fragile as her little body. I knelt and pulled her against me, wincing when she shrieked in my ear.

"Take away the pain!" I cried. "Hold tight, little girl. Never let go of me." I leaned hard on her and, had she been any smaller, her legs would've buckled under her ma's grief.

• • •

Never once did the welcome darkness swallow my mind. Cold and certain through the next two days as every man for forty miles worked to clear the mine, I stayed awake 'til they found the four of them halfway back, sprinkled with gold dust, christened with blood.

Judd had laid a charge of some powerful new blasting compound to break through the mass of rock that had blocked their way all summer and dropped just a bit.

The rescuers found a vein so wide they could light their way by the shine. Speculation soared to how soon each man could claim a piece of the gold mesa. I would've given the land away, but Howdy directed them greedy bandits to Cold Water City's assay office if they didn't believe my baby child didn't own the whole kit and caboodle.

"Which one's Judd?" I asked as they brought out the blanket-wrapped bodies.

"Don't look, Ma'am. Where should we dig the grave?"

"Behind the cabin." One of Judd's boots fell off and I put it back on his bloody foot. "Step careful there," I said. "If you drop him, I'll cut out your heart."

The places where whiskers wouldn't grow. Nails always red with mud and flecks of gold. Arms like the rocks he broke...and that broke him...I wanted to empty the memories from my mind and be free of pain, but my heart beat on. I faced my future alone, always alone, save for my child. Finally I took the whiskey we kept for snake bite and downed it, hoping I'd die quick. All I got was a bellyache that burned as fierce as my heart.

Nineteen

Winter 1869

"Try some stew," Gwenity said, heaping more on my plate. She seemed to think eating would cure me.

I shifted Lillie to my other knee and mashed up another potato. She kept spitting out the lumps and grabbing at the tablecover 'til my nerves felt ready to snap.

Gwen and Howdy jabbered like jays, trying to keep my mind off my sorrow. I'd thought being with them would keep me from going crazy, but the inn was too crowded. Howdy was building another wing. He'd hired hisself three men. One was married, and his wife helped Gwenity in the kitchen.

Howdy had taken up smoking since I'd married. I watched him sprinkle tobacco across the little white paper. His trembling pink tongue licking the edge sent shivers up my back. I jumped up, handed Lillie to Gwen and ran for my room.

"Go after her, Howdy. She still isn't herself."

I hung my head out my window, sucking in lungfuls of sharp night air, watching clouds gather all across the ridge. I'd meant to stay at the cabin so I could be near Judd's grave, but I wasn't about to let the horses freeze or let Lillie take sick. So, before we got snowed in, we come back to the inn.

Howdy peeked in my door. "Let us help you, Angie."

"You can help find me another man to marry up with," I said, pulling my hair loose of its pins and brushing it 'til my scalp tingled.

Howdy looked a mite pained. "Somebody will come along. You just wait."

"I ain't got time." I threw down the brush and almost started unbuttoning my dress before I caught myself. "Men come through here every day. Not one gives me a look."

Howdy crossed the room to flick the cigarette butt out my window. To the darkness outside he said, "Anybody that looks at you knows you're hard grieving. No man wants to step in on that."

"That widow Bonnie in Cold Water City had men after her 'fore her husband was in the ground!" I snapped. I heard Lillie fussing in the kitchen. Gwenity would be in soon to bed her down. Since Judd's dying, Lillie hadn't been herself. Sometimes, as much as I clung to her, she grated on me.

Howdy's eyes slid up to meet mine. He smelled good, kind of sweaty and warm and smoky from building up the kitchen fire. When he took hold of my shoulders and pulled me close, I didn't resist. I laid my head on his chest and, for just a second, felt safe. "I wouldn't want you taking up with just any man," Howdy said. "Me or Gwenity couldn't stand having you leave. You know how much we love Lillie…Angie, if there's anything I can do. If you ever need me…for anything…" His voice went soft like he didn't want nobody to hear but me. I understood his meaning clear and was tempted to oblige. If, just once, I could get back that feeling Judd and me had shared…If I could only kiss him again…

I pulled away, unable to meet Howdy's eyes. "I won't be doing nothing that would hurt Gwen. She's been too good to me."

"You said yourself not to get her pregnant again. I need *someone.*"

I didn't say nothing. After a minute Howdy slipped out. There might not be much harm in easing Howdy's itch, I thought, though a good woman wouldn't think such a thing. I guessed I wasn't so good.

Gwenity come in then and dressed my child for bed. "Hold still there, Lillie honey," Gwenity was saying. "Go to your mama and get some milk before Aunt Gwenity tucks you in."

"Ain't no use. I cried away all my baby's milk," I said.

"I haven't seen you cry once," Gwenity said.

I scooped Lillie up and pressed my face into her feathery curls. "I cried plenty after all them helping hands that kept helping theirselves to Judd's ore took their leave. Suppose Leroy can handle the mine alone?"

"If he can't we'll find someone who can. You'll need the income. Howdy wants to build you a cabin down the hill. Wouldn't you like living near us? That mine will produce enough for you to live in comfort the rest of your lives."

"I hadn't thought on it," I said.

In the spring, though, I did think on it. My dreams come flooding back. I'd move to Cold Water where folks was tolerable and have my pick of husbands. I remember saying in May that I was finally over Judd's dying. I said that to Gwenity the very day a man smelling of the East come to the inn and set his carpetbag inside the front door.

He was lean as a fence post and looked about as kindly. His eyes spoke of breeding, high places, and culture. He wore a city suit, tailor cut and black as the inside of a mine. Looking about the inn, he picked a speck of road mud from his sleeve. "I'm going to Cold Water City, which, I'm told, is another day's journey from here," said the post.

"Can we get you some coffee and dinner?" Howdy boomed.

I stood watching from the kitchen doorway, never careless with my child's future.

"I wonder," said the man lying his hat on the table and drawing a wallet from his breast pocket. "Did you see this news item in the *Colorado Territory News* a few months ago?"

Howdy took hisself a chair. "Are you from Denver City?"

"No, sir. My name is Archibald Bromley of Atlanta, Georgia. I represent the family of Trulane Harvey, once quite a landed family of the Southern aristocracy. Of course, since the war, General Trulane has had difficulties. He is denied the right to vote or hold office under the terms of Reconstruction. This is, of course, irrelevant to my purpose here in the West."

"And what is your purpose, Mr. Bromley?"

"This article refers to the death of one Judd Rydell. I wonder if he is the Judson Rydell I knew in Atlanta."

I joined them. "You knew Judd?"

He stood right up and bowed. "Good evening, Madame. Did *you* know Judson?"

"I'm his widow."

His eyes narrowed as they swept over me. "The man I knew—this was in '59—was thirty, brown hair and eyes, educated. He disappeared during the war and was presumed dead by his family."

"That sounds a lot like Judd. What do you think, Angie?"

"Do you have a picture, Mr. Bromley?"

He pulled a daguerreotype from his wallet and handed it to me and Howdy. Seeing Judd's face again twisted my heart! He looked elegant in a butternut-colored uniform coat trimmed with a dark sash. A saber hung at his side, so long it reached the ground. Oh, that fine face, that bewitching smile. I could almost feel his touch again and hear his laugh…A cry sprang from my throat, but it wasn't just 'cause I was seeing him again, seeing him as he looked before I knew him.

What held me spellbound was the other person in the picture. She was almost as tall as Judd, dressed in a hoop-skirted wedding gown with a train so long it swirled around in front showing off all the embroidery.

"When was this made?" I asked, my voice unsteady.

"June, 1861, just after the war broke out," Mr. Bromley said, returning the picture to his wallet. "Then we are speaking of the same man? You're certain the man in this daguerreotype died in the cave-in last year?"

"That's him," Howdy said.

"When did *she* die?" I asked.

Taking a notebook from his pocket, Mr. Bromley said, "Might I have your name and the date of your marriage? I am here to settle Judson's estate."

"I'm Angela Rydell. Jacobs, before I married up with Judd. We met…when was it, Howdy? '66? '67? We was married that fall."

"And *where* were you married?"

"El Dorado City, by a preacher, in a church."

"I'm sorry to be the one to tell you, Madame, but Leona Harvey Rydell did not die. That makes your marriage to Judson Rydell null and void."

"You're a lying snake!"

"Not I, Madame! Judson obviously assumed his first marriage would never be discovered in this…wilderness. I can only hope he left you something in his will."

"Did Judd leave a will, Angie?"

"I don't know! Git out of here! I've had enough of claim jumpers. That mine and mesa belong to my child. No fancy Eastern lawyer is going to change that!"

Ain't no describing how I felt after that blue-blood took his leave for the bank in Cold Water City. "I hope he gets caught in a blizzard! I hope renegades steal the buttons off his johns!"

"Settle down," Gwenity said. "It's not that poor man's fault. Why, I almost had to laugh. You had him so scared he almost ran out of here."

"This ain't funny."

"Sit down and have a sip of whiskey," Howdy said, pouring hardly enough to dampen the glass.

I grabbed the bottle and poured a dose that would quiet the voices screaming in my head. "I could've gone just fine never knowing I wasn't Judd's legal wife. Now everybody will know!"

"It wasn't your fault, Angie. Folks'll understand."

I looked on Gwenity and for the first time saw her for the innocent fool she was. I felt like laughing. Folks wouldn't understand. *I* didn't! I'd married up with the first man to come along and thought myself smart in the bargain. "What am I going to do? Not being married legal makes Lillie a bastard child! Do you know what that'll do to her?"

"You've got to believe folks will understand. It's not Lillie's fault. Angie, please calm down! Maybe the lawyer was wrong."

"Don't see why he'd make up such a story," Howdy said.

Gwenity gave him a hard look, but I didn't mind him speaking the plain truth. Soon everybody would know I was just a damn fool woman born to no good. Lillie'd never be able to hold up her head in no school or get courted by decent fellas.

That snake Archibald Bromley showed his face again about a week later on his way back from Cold Water. Gwenity knowed he was back 'fore I did and tried keeping me busy in the kitchen making extra bread. While I didn't relish seeing his slimy eyes again, I was mighty curious to know what he'd found at the bank.

Soon as he saw me, he started sweating. "I won't be subject to any more of your abuse, Madame!" he said, ready to bolt for the door.

"Did you get your hands on all Judd's money?" I was acting tough, but I felt like mush inside. That man held my child's future in his skinny white hand.

"Judd Rydell did, indeed, file a change of ownership with the bank and district claims office. Twelve acres to be defined by map and landmarks plus mineral rights to the Little Angel Mine belong to Lillie Elvira Rydell. Indeed, future proceeds are to be handled by you, Madame. If you will forgive me, I will call you Miss Jacobs so as to be accurate. You have sole control over the banking and use of the proceeds until your child reaches the age of eighteen. 1886, I believe, is the correct year.

"The Bank of Cold Water City had three accounts listed for the Rydell family. You, Mrs...Miss Jacobs, have one in your correct legal name, not your incorrect married name. The total amounted to five hundred six dollars deposited, I believe, at the time your daughter was christened. I am not able to provide you with this sum because, of course, only you can withdraw on your signature."

"What's them other accounts?"

"The second is listed for Lillie Elvira Rydell, over one thousand dollars deposited during 1869. I arranged for co-ownership until 1886. I hope that meets with your approval."

"That sounds fair, don't you think, Angie?" Howdy asked.

"I don't know nothing about banking."

"I assure you, I'm doing the best I can with a difficult situation. The third account was in Mr. Rydell's name and must, of course, go to his legal widow and surviving relatives. Since I did not anticipate an estate of any magnitude I failed to acquire power of attorney before venturing West. Therefore..."

"What's that you said? You ain't got the power to be an attorney out here? What you doing settling all this money business then?"

"I cannot *sign* for the legal Mrs. Rydell. She must withdraw it in person. I sent a telegraph message. She'll be here within a month. I'm going back to meet her train in Denver. The line from Cheyenne may already be complete. Her journey will be most comfortable."

"That woman is coming here?"

"Madame, calm yourself! There's no reason for you or Leona Rydell to ever meet."

I walked out of the room. Gwenity stopped me from taking up the butcher knife and hacking the fresh baked loaves to bits. "She's coming here! All them gossipmongers will see her! I'll have to take Lillie away!"

Gwenity grabbed me. "There's no reason to run! No one with a Christian bone in their body can blame you or Lillie for this. Just hold your head high. If there's talk, it'll die away soon as you look people in the eye."

"I hear a good deal of talk on Christians, but I only met two in my life. One was so damn good God decided she ought to die of a cancer. He almost took you with a miscarriage."

"You mustn't talk like that. God doesn't punish the good with death."

"Well, he sure don't punish the bad with it, neither. God ain't done nothing but kill every person I ever cared about."

"He gave you Lillie," Gwenity said softly. "No matter how good I try to be, Angie, no child will ever drink at my breast. You're blessed with God's greatest gift and you have the gall to curse Him. I know you're hurting, but if you turn your back on God, He'll turn His back on you."

Gwenity stood trembling with tears rolling down her cheeks. Her words scared me. If she believed them, they had to be true. In my judgment Gwenity was a true good person, but what she believed from crackling old Bible pages and what life dealt me year after year just didn't go together.

Howdy and Mr. Bromley come to the kitchen door about then. I turned on that man dressed in black. "I don't suppose it's any of my business to know how much *that woman* will get."

Mr. Bromley cleared his throat. "Over ten thousand dollars, Madame."

"Well," I sniffed, turning away. "I figured it had to be a fair sum for Mrs. Leona Rydell to come all this way *herself.*"

News spread far and wide that Judd Rydell's true widow was coming to claim his fortune. Maybe folks knew the whole story, maybe they didn't. I didn't much care. Howdy set to work on my new cabin soon as the weather warmed. I knowed Gwenity was scared I'd take off with Lillie. She loved that child and had near to taken over the mothering of her while I fretted. I went along with their plans since I didn't have none better. I helped in the kitchen, did up rooms, and hung out wash in the spring wind 'til my arms ached.

I was out getting snapped in the face by the wet washing the day a handsome black carriage come down the freight road from Cold Water City. I hadn't seen a rig like that since Sara's funeral. It shined in the late afternoon sun as the driver pulled up in front of the veranda. I shook out another sheet and pinned it to the line.

The lady in the carriage held a pink ruffled parasol. Her escort got down and helped her to the ground. A black maid carrying a bulging carpetbag got down by herself. Howdy marched across the yard, first holding his hand out in greeting. When he gestured back toward me, a peculiar itchy feeling crept into my belly. Mr. Archibald Bromley stood a-twitching with discomfort as I crossed the yard.

Wearing a jacket and gown unlike anything I'd ever seen, Judd's true and legal wife stood before me. "Y'all must be Angela," the bitch said, extending a dainty, lace-gloved hand.

I felt like crawling off to some dark place. My patched brown calico looked scruffy and my hair flew about wild like it was alive and crazy. I felt like them sorry-eyed alley dogs that used to roam near our shanty.

That brought my chin up. I looked at her from the corner of my eye. "Now that I see you," I smirked, "I can't figure why Judd couldn't bring hisself to go back to you." We matched snapping eyes.

"I just couldn't come all this way without meeting y'all. Mr. Bromley tells me y'all married Judson in a church. That's just plain crazy. Judson loathed churches. To my knowledge he never set foot in one."

"Not even when he married you-all?"

"*Our* ceremony was held at my father's home in the garden with over four hundred guests." She smiled like a rattler.

"I guess marrying up just before a war is *one* way of catching a man."

Her pink lips twitched. She turned to Mr. Bromley. "Isn't her speech quaint? She sounds almost like a darky. May we come inside now, Mr. Jackson? We do have one important piece of business to discuss. And, Mr. Jackson, I'd like to see my accommodations, if you please. You *do* have someone to carry up my trunks, don't you?"

Howdy stepped back, nodding dumbly. He lumbered up the stairs to show the bitch and her maid his best room. I sank to the lowest step, burning with a sourtasting, hopeless hatred. "Thought you said I wouldn't have to meet her, *Mister* Bromley."

He jumped and looked about, sick to discover he was alone

with me. "I understand you have a map of the land your child owns. May we examine it?"

I stood up and gave a little curtsy. "I'm sure you're doing your best with a difficult situation." My voice was purely Sara's and brought a wild look of surprise and terror to old Archibald's face.

I found Gwenity in my room, playing with Lillie to keep her quiet. "She's here! I expect that *lady* will rest the rest of the afternoon. I'd like to pin that snake Bromley to the line by his…ears."

"She can't hurt you, Angie."

I pulled my drawing from the blanket chest. "I ain't said nothing right yet. Keep Lillie in here for me, please? I don't want that bitch to think up some mean comment. Elsewise I'll have to scratch up her pretty pink face."

Gwenity sagged with shock.

Howdy tapped at my door. "Mr. Bromley and that woman are waiting in my office." Howdy's office was a corner of the dining room where he kept the cash box and his ledgers. I took me a deep breath and went out to face them.

"I brought proof of my marriage to Judson," the bitch said, handing me a scroll tied with a blue ribbon.

I dropped the ribbon and unrolled the paper. Mr. Bromley kindly pointed out Judd's signature and matched it with the one on my marriage certificate and Lillie's title to the mine. There weren't no mistaking we'd both married the same man. I handed them my drawing. "I'll take that back soon as you're done."

"Is this legal, Mr. Bromley?"

"Here's the district seal. I'm afraid, Mrs. Rydell, the land and mine do, indeed, belong to Miss Jacobs's daughter."

"The child could be anyone's. Surely you can see why Judson married this person. I demand to see the little girl!"

"I can vouch for Angie myself!" Howdy blurted. "My wife assisted in Lillie's birth. That baby is Judd's all right. Soon as he saw Angie after his first accident he couldn't think of nothing but marrying her."

"For obvious reasons."

"You'd be wise to curb your tongue, Leona. We are guests here."

"Wouldn't bother us none if you was to take your leave," I snapped, grabbing back my drawing.

"If this child is, indeed, my husband's, I feel it only right that I take her back to Georgia and raise her as Judson would have wanted."

"He wanted no such thing! You got his money, so git!"

"Surely y'all can see it's the only possible solution to the child's predicament. Y'all realize, of course, she's illegitimate. I'm offering her a future."

"Howdy, shut her up 'fore I get the shotgun and blow a hole in her face!"

"What a crude little creature," she said to Mr. Bromley. "Inform your chef I'll be dining in my room, Mr. Jackson. We'll leave in the morning. I can see this creature is too ignorant to understand the future I offer her unfortunate child."

Howdy grabbed me just as I was fixing to rip out her tongue.

She gave me a look of pure disgust and headed for the stairs on the arm of her lawyer. She talked to him in hushed whispers. They edged into a shadow and argued.

Outside it had growed dark and strangely silent. No stage was due and only three people was booked into rooms. They was probably sleeping. Howdy's helpers was down the way in their cabins.

I tore free of Howdy and ran back to the kitchen. I found the black maid fussing over a china teapot. I took it from her and dropped it, nice as you please, in the middle of Gwenity's fresh scrubbed floor. That maid didn't say a word.

Gwenity peeked out my door, her eyes full of worry and alarm. Lillie ran into my arms. "Ya dropped it, Ma!" she squealed. "It's all a mess!"

"Hush," I whispered, pressing her to my chest.

"Is she Master Judson's chil'?" the maid asked, her dark eyes wary.

"Her name's Lillie Elvira and *nobody's* taking her from here!"

"My mistress, Miz Elvira, that Master Judson's mama, she tol' me Miss Leona would be finding a child out this way. She tol' me to give her this. Since she's such a little tyke, I'll give it to you." She handed me a little box wrapped in white paper. "Don't tell Miss Leona 'bout this. She wouldn't like it."

"Judd spoke kindly of his ma," I said. "Thank her for me."

I was just turning the heavy little box about in my hand when something in the dark front hall caught my eye. I thrust Lillie into Gwenity's arms and dropped the box into her apron pocket. "Put Lillie to bed. Now!" I pushed Gwenity and the maid into my room and fixed them with a stern eye. "Bar the door!"

Out front, two masked bandits stood silhouetted in the moonlight. One held a pistol in Howdy's side. Mr. Archibald Bromley and the Georgia bitch cringed in a shadow.

"Bar the door and don't come out for *nothing!*" I pulled the door closed to Gwenity's horrified face. Just as I heard her push my bureau in front of it, another masked man busted in the kitchen from the back.

"Well, well, well, well," the bandit chuckled, a kerchief over his nose muffling his words. "Get yourself in with the rest," he said, crossing the kitchen, pointing the way with his shotgun leveled at my belly.

I edged backwards. I heard one of the others say, "Turn over that ten thousand and we'll be on our way."

Howdy watched me creep down the hall. His face looked as round as a full moon. Though he knowed his wife was in my room, he never once looked at my door. That's when I knowed Howdy wasn't stupid and wasn't no coward.

"Where's your money?" the bandit wearing a blue kerchief over his face said. He had familiar eyes.

Leona saw me looking at him and stepped forward. "That tramp is behind this! She knows them! Y'all stop her, Mr. Bromley! I'll have the law on you until your dying breath!"

The bandit in the blue kerchief brought her up short with the tip of his rifle barrel. "If you don't hand over that money I'll look for it myself—in your corset."

"Y'all wouldn't dare!"

Mr. Bromley tried to fade into the wall but he met with a pistol and froze.

"I suggest you turn over the money, Mrs. Rydell," Howdy said. "These men mean what they say."

"I need it!" she hissed. Finally she lifted her hem and mounted the stairs with Howdy at her elbow. The bandit in the blue kerchief leveled his rifle at their backs and followed them up.

Swaying, Mr. Bromley flinched when he heard scuffling and a sharp scream upstairs. Something fell and the inn shuddered. He looked up and the third bandit struck him on the head. Mr. Archibald Bromley collapsed like a wet sheet.

After that bandit went upstairs, the one standing over me motioned toward the door. "Outside, sweetie."

"Whatever it is you want, you can take right here," I said. If I kept him busy he wouldn't notice Howdy's cash box.

He pressed his shotgun against my neck, pulled down his red kerchief and kissed me. I'd forgot what an empty thing a stranger's kiss was. When he pressed his hand against my dress front, I whimpered 'cause I knew that's what he wanted. He backed me against a table and leaned his shotgun against the wall. With both hands free he found his way about me easy.

I played so hard at getting away he had a terrible time with his trousers and johns. With one hand tight over my mouth, he pressed his flesh between my legs. It was mighty peculiar to feel strange flesh against mine again, to hear the groaning and under-breath cussing of a man taken over by his itch. I did a good show of struggling and screaming quietly into that grimy, sweaty palm.

When the other two bandits scrambled down the stairs I waved my arms as if for help, knowing full well I might just get more of the same. They was half out the door before they spied us.

"Hey!" one yelled, bringing the fella up short by the scruff of his neck. "You crazy?"

Faking sobs, I pulled free and half fell, half ran down the hall, holding my skirts high so they'd have plenty to look at. I intended to lure them out to the shed. No telling how long Gwenity could listen to all that commotion without opening that door!

They looked at me. I looked at them. I dropped my skirts and clutched at my near bare bosom. Then I tore open the door. The one who wanted me grabbed for his shotgun and started after me. The other two collared him, cuffed him about the head and dragged him out. Their horses pounded away into the night.

Really crying then, I slid to the floor and sat spread eagled staring at the broken teapot, the shadows beyond the door and Mr. Bromley's shoe sticking out past the bottom step. Then my sobs turned to laughing. The fool hadn't even got in me. That's how far I'd come trying to be a good woman. It was a fool's journey and I was tired of it!

Gwenity stuck her head out the door. "Angie! Are you hurt? Did they…" She flew out and crouched beside me. "Oh Lord! Where's Howdy? I'll send him for the sheriff!"

"No! No sheriff! I'm fine. See to Howdy and leave me be. I'm just catching my breath."

She clattered down the dark hall. "Lord, Mr. Bromley! You're bleeding. Wake up! Howdy? Howdy!" She clattered up the stairs.

I staggered out back and held tight to the railing. If they sent for the sheriff, that would be Rusty Kennings hisself!

"Angie! Where are you? Howdy's all right. Luckily his head's thick."

"Mr. Archibald looks dead," I said.

"The poor man. Howdy will have to fetch a doctor, too. That woman was out cold." Gwenity's voice got low. "I…covered her. They tore off most of her clothes! I saw a few greenbacks still sticking out of her bustle. Do you suppose they…"

"Oh, I hope so! I truly do."

"You're upset. God forgives you."

"No, he don't. Gwen, shut up a minute. I want you to promise me something. Swear on the Bible."

"I'd never break my word to you."

I took hold of her cold hands. "You're a good woman and the best friend I ever had. You've looked after me and my baby and never asked a word of thanks. Now, I'm telling you, if that sheriff from Tempest comes I *can't* be here."

"Don't be a fool, Angie!"

"I am a fool and can't help myself. I got to leave. I'm just bringing you and Howdy trouble. You're good people. I like you so much I want you to take Lillie. Take her and teach her to call you Ma. Teach her to read so's she can go to school in Cold Water City and get church-learning in a real church. I want my little girl to be like you, Gwenity. I want her to be good and honest and decent, like my ma wanted me to be, but I ain't such a fool that I don't know I can't teach her them things. You got to do it for me."

"You don't know what you're saying!"

"I'll put my name to paper if you want. Get some and write, 'Angela Jacobs Rydell gives her child to the Jacksons to be brought up proper and respectable.'"

Oh, the temptation in Gwenity's eyes was a wondrous thing to see, 'cause as much as she didn't want to hear me saying such things, her heart ached to take my little girl as her own.

"I know you want her, Gwen. If one of them men kilt me tonight you'd take her quick as anything."

"You know I would, but…"

"That bitch and her lawyer kilt me. I ain't nothing without Judd's name. Lillie ain't going to grow up no bastard child. She ain't going to find herself in a dancehall when she's sixteen. Take her and raise her up as your own. Don't *never* tell her about me. Give me your word of honor!"

Gwenity's eyes glistened. Suddenly she grabbed me, her thin shoulders sharp and shaking against me. "I'll take her 'til you come to your senses. Where will you go?"

"Back to Tempest," I said 'fore I could think.

Gwenity looked into my eyes. "You have my solemn promise I'll raise Lillie to be the fine young woman you are."

I kissed Gwenity's cheek. "Tell everybody I'm dead. Make Lillie forget me. She's little. She will."

I plucked a cape from the pegs along the wall and ran for the shed. As I saddled one of the horses I wanted to go back inside just once to say good-bye to Lillie. I remembered how she looked, running out of my room after I smashed Mrs. Leona Bitch's teapot. Her face had been round and pink, her brown feathery hair flying about her face, her plump hands holding out to me. There she was just a bit more than two and she could talk so good...

Something cold squeezed my heart and bent me double. I couldn't do it! I saw again little Becky hanging limp in Ma's arms and the screams echoed fresh in my head. I could still picture that lonely marker way back by the river, my little sister dead so many long years. If I left Lillie, she'd be dead to me, too. I couldn't go!

I let loose of the reins and cried against the rough flank. I felt as cowardly as old Archibald. My dream of Lillie growing up fine and decent sounded mighty pretty, but I couldn't really go off without her. She was my little girl, my one good thing in a lifetime of bad. She was my Judd's daughter, owner of twelve acres and a gold mine folks traveled two thousand miles to haggle over.

A laugh filled my throat. Rusty would come up to see about the robbery. Leona would claim I'd been part of it. Folks would always remember and talk.

I got my foot in the stirrup and yanked myself high atop the horse. Pictures danced through my mind—Lillie alone after I died, Lillie searching for work, Lillie getting looks from low men...

I sank my heels into the horse's flank, and he bolted into the darkness. I hung on tight, squeezing tears from my eyes 'til I realized I was headed down the canyon. I reined and pranced in circles on the freight road, trying to make a plan, trying just once to do something right. If I went to Tempest, Howdy and Gwenity would come after me. So would Leona and her lawyer.

I knew too many folks in Cold Water. The only place a strange woman could make her way unnoticed was in wild towns, like Tempest had been ten years before. I'd keep to myself, make no friends. I'd just make money and send it to Gwenity...

No, I had to be dead to her, too. If I thought on what I was doing, I might forget the future—Lillie's future—and take what I wanted now, the feel of my little girl's arms around my neck, her voice clear as a winter sky, her face a little mirror of her pa's.

How I *hated* Judd for dying!

I urged the horse around and passed the inn at a full gallop. I hugged the horse's powerful back with my knees, my head down, my eyes closed. Miles fell behind me like tears.

Suddenly the horse stumbled and I went flying. I landed on my back in a clump of sage and stared up at the stars, wishing with all my heart I could just be dead. What a relief it must have been for Ma to close her eyes that last time.

Part Three

Part Three

Twenty

Summer 1870

From my shack I could see down the gulch to the creek and across to the tents and haphazard buildings that made up the little town of Timberline. Some five hundred men and sixteen women lived there. Far beyond, distant white-capped mountains blended with the pale sky. Some miners claimed we was so close to the divide we could see the sky over California.

I'd been there a month and rented the best crib, which wasn't no prize, and there I stood, watching the sun melt the night's snow from a stretch of boulders. All I had on was a woolly nightdress and didn't give a damn who saw me—not that anybody cared to look that time of day anyhow. Some days I wondered if I was living in a dream.

Dalt's cabin had had wind through the pines, the chatter of wood chipmunks, and the howl of coyotes. The mesa had had wind racing across the sage, hawks calling up the mountain and, of course, the cry of my newborn child. This place had a silence so big a person would think he was dead. The sky pressed on the boulders and sage like a hand to a mouth. Only sometimes could I hear picks striking rock or a miner yelling. Even the wind was quiet and it could freeze a man in an hour.

After that horse throwed me I spent the night in a shed near Cold Water, helped myself to somebody's stores and paid them with a thin gold band that gave me only the slightest twinge of pain to leave behind. Just before dawn I lit out again. Come noon, a stage caught up to me.

"Where you headed, little lady?" the driver had called down from his high seat. He lifted his hat so's I could see his craggy face.

I guessed him under thirty. Since I couldn't smell him, and admired his fine boots, I smiled. Back to work. "Lost my horse in the night," I said. "Sure could use a ride to wherever you're going."

I rode with the stage driver, Rudy McCabe, near a week and earned my passage good and often. I took my leave of him in California Gulch, which had a sizable church-going population. Giving me ten dollars to get out of town, Rudy promised to look me up next time he made the route. I traveled on 'til I found Timberline. By then I was wore out.

I took up residence in the one room crib and paid my rent by the day, which was five dollars. I charged five, sometimes eight dollars for a half hour roll on my rag tick. When a miner couldn't pay in cash money, I charged a pinch of gold dust; a pinch being worth probably ten or fifteen dollars. While that was good for my cache, I won't say what kind of men I earned it off of.

I had to haul my own water from the creek so it took near all my mornings to fill a whiskey barrel. If I laid six or eight men, it'd be gone by dawn. I couldn't get no lemon juice or alum thereabouts, and I'd run off without a bit of sponge. So I tied a rag in a knot and left it to soak in whiskey, using that to ward off babies.

I suppose I should say I was sorrowful to be back at work, but I wasn't. I ate fair and kept warm best I could. It did me good to see them miners troop across the log bridge with their gold, silver, and greenbacks—and best of all, their eager eyes. I only thought of Lillie when I was sober.

'Long about the end of June I heard tell of a big celebration planned in Ore City. That seemed like a good excuse to move on again. Ore City took a coach ride of two days to reach. I come into the camp on July third and already every man was whooping it up for Independence Day. I outfitted myself in a fine red silk gown with a draped bustle. I didn't take to a corset after so long and didn't fit into the size I'd once wore, but I looked a sight better than most my sisters.

Come the next afternoon I ventured into the street, mindful of drunks shooting in the air and horses running wild from firecrackers. A dandy playhouse had just been built down from the hotel. A hawker stood out front, announcing the grand opening that night. He was a good-looking brute in a derby and long coattails. "See Annie Collins herself play the beautiful Juliet. Thrill to the first Shakespearean play south of Denver City and west of St. Louis."

Just when I thought I couldn't listen to him go through his spiel again, a man in a black buggy heavy with silver trim and doo-dads pulled up. "Benjamin! Come eat with me. Save your voice for tonight," the man in the buggy called. I hadn't seen such a man since Silver Stan Sampson. He wore a silver gray suit of the finest worsted wool. The clasp on his bolo sported a gold nugget as big as his nose. His face gleamed from a fresh shave and his roan-colored hair was slicked down to either side of his face so shiny I could smell the oil.

Benjamin, the hawker, climbed down from his box and mopped his doughy face with his eyes on me. "You've been watching me, my lovely. Can it be we're old friends?"

"By tomorrow we might be," I smiled, relieved he'd noticed me.

His laugh showed a mouthful of teeth surely meant for a smaller man. "Tell me your name. Then I'll introduce you to Mr. Hannable Sheever, the richest man in the Rocky Mountain West."

"Just call me Angel," I said, linking arms with him.

An hour later we was in a meadow outside town where somebody was making a fiery speech. Children and dogs ran races. Feats of marksmanship, chopping, digging, and other such showing-off sports took place. Respectable ladies slaved over long checker-clothed tables while certain other "ladies" in our satins and silks sat on the arms of rich gentlemen and promised special pleasures with our smiles.

Long about sundown Benjamin went back to hawk at the playhouse. I stayed with Mr. Sheever 'cause we was having a fine laughing time, drinking his whiskey and eating such wondrous food as I hadn't seen in ages. Come nine o'clock I waltzed into that new playhouse on his arm.

That place was a sight to behold. Fine paintings of ladies with half their charms spilling out of gauzy dresses hung along the lobby walls. Hundreds of candles glittered from the chandeliers. Blood-red velvet drapes enclosed the theater. Mr. Sheever let me peek inside before we climbed the marble steps upstairs.

We took our seats on a little round porch overlooking the stage. Another little porch perched across the way. Grand folks filled the seats below and sat staring at the ceiling, where some brave soul had painted clouds and naked babies with wings and bows.

Mr. Sheever patted my hand. "We'll have a late supper in my hotel suite after the performance and then…retire for the night."

"My pleasure, Mr. Sheever. Who do you suppose had a place like this built right here in the middle of a dirty old mining camp?"

He laughed and his hand strayed to my knee. "Who else but me, my dear? I own most of the town, including the hotel and three mines."

I considered myself lucky to have met up with him.

I was glad he had the forethought to refill his whiskey flask 'cause that Romeo and Juliet play left me feeling sad. Most of the time the respectable Hannable Sheever tried to get his hand up my skirt or down my bodice, which just proved no matter how rich a man got, he never outgrew his itch. I let him touch enough to keep his mouth watering, but he knew enough to pull away 'til gold touched my palm.

After all that poisoning, sobbing, and thunderous applause, Mr. Sheever pulled me out of the theater so fast our chairs almost overturned. His hotel was just up the street so he didn't even wait for his buggy.

The Ore City Hotel was near as pretty as the new playhouse. We didn't dally in the lobby long enough to see the wonders, but I did fancy the gold carpet and colored glass windowpanes.

'Fore I knew it, Mr. Sheever was locking the big double doors to his suite. The biggest bed I'd ever seen, with posts near as thick as my leg, stood across the room. All around it hung lace drapes pulled back with fat satin cords.

"You live here?" I asked, watching Hannable tear off his shirt.

"When I'm not in Denver. Please, my dear, feel free to undress. That's a lovely gown, but I prefer what's under it."

I smiled oh so innocent. "Why, Mr. Sheever. I'm not just any working girl. I work very hard at what I do best."

He struggled with his boots. "How much?"

I began with my bag and gloves, then my buttons and hooks, exposing just enough to pull his mind from money. "Depends on what your special pleasure is, Mr. Sheever. I know so many."

The sweat I expected didn't break out on his forehead. Now Mr. Sheever moved more slow, watching me with steady black eyes. "I've paid as much as one hundred dollars for what I like best," he whispered.

One hundred dollars.

His hands slid into my bodice. "I won't really hurt you, and you mustn't scream, but I want you to make me believe I am. I must *believe*."

I looked into his eyes. "One hundred dollars," I said thickly. "More if you really do hurt me."

He turned away and laid a stack of gold coins on the washstand. Then he went into the next room and closed the door. I counted three times and gave up. It looked like a hundred.

When I'd readied myself, I dimmed the lamps and crawled into that big, cold bed. Afar off the comforting sound of the honky-tonk and laughter filled the night air. Firecrackers still popped here and there in the distance. The wind whispered by the window as if warning me. I could hear my heart beating loud in my ears.

I pulled up the cover and shivered as the door creaked open. A shaft of yellow light fell across the carpet. If I hadn't knowed Mr. Sheever was going to steal in like that I might not have heard him. All I had to do was pretend I was a little …asleep, he'd told me.

I didn't move as he crept closer. His breath smelling strong of whiskey brushed my face. The covers slid away 'til I lay curled naked. His warm quick breath traveled all over me and near to drove me wild.

To ease my cramped muscles and to add to his game, I pretended to stretch. I rolled onto my back, making sleepy noises. Maybe his game wasn't so bad. Then he commenced to poking and prodding 'til I couldn't see no use in pretending sleep no more. I opened my eyes and gasped. His hand came down on my mouth. I struggled and faked quiet screams. Before I knew it he had ropes around my wrists.

When he had my ankles fast, he got up and paced. In a low voice he talked on how I must never tell my mother, that I mustn't scream, that I had to do what he said, all he said, no matter how bad it was. After he got hisself into a good working stance, he mounted the bed and set to handling me in ways I'd never knowed.

The more I writhed, the more it pleasured him. After a good two hours my skin hummed with rough use. He took his final pleasure in my mouth. The cries he made was from a man so deep in his satisfaction he didn't know nothing else.

He crouched over me only a few seconds before he stopped sudden as if he heard something. Like the law was after him he undid my wrists and ankles, threatened me again never to tell a soul, then covered me, slinking out as he'd come in.

I waited a mighty long time to see if he had more in store and near to fell asleep. When I heard his snores, I looked in on him sprawled in another bed, looking as harmless as a baby. I wondered if he'd ever really raped anyone. Shivering, yet pleased I'd pleasured the richest man in town, I dressed, gathered my coins and took my leave.

Quite a collection of handsome gentlemen watched me come down that grand staircase. They was talking in groups, smoking long stogies and smelling of expensive whiskey. I thought on planting myself on one of them little velvet lobby chairs 'cause my legs felt weak. I didn't spring back quick as I once had.

The doorway to a darkened, smoky saloon beckoned across the lobby. A polished bar, gleaming brass spittoons, and softly glowing lamps reminded me of the Silver Star. And I had a flaming thirst for a stiff double whiskey. I lifted my chin and shook out my hair. When I walked in, every man turned.

One man come up to me and bowed. "We meet again!"

It was so dark I didn't remember him at first. Then I recalled when I'd first seen his face and felt surprised at how much he'd changed. "Mr. Saunders!"

"You're the pretty girl I saw in El Dorado City that day back in '64."

I laughed. "And once before. You still don't remember?"

"Come sit with me and help me remember. You are free to have a drink with me, I hope."

"I sure will make time," I said, wishing I knew how to talk fancy.

When the barkeep come to our table Mr. Travis Saunders ordered hisself a whiskey. I asked for the same.

"Not sherry or champagne?"

"Whiskey's fine. I ain't much for elegant things."

He leaned back, smiling. "I wouldn't know it by looking at you. Tell me, before some catastrophe separates us again, what's you name?"

"Call me Angel."

"Why?"

My face grew hot and I didn't like that. "'Cause it's my name."

"Do me the curtesy of telling me your real name. You know mine." His face had growed full and soft with the years. His paunch was considerable though he wasn't fat. He looked at me low and casual, tipping back his chair like he was toying with me.

I took a gulp of my whiskey and let the fire roll down my throat. Mr. Saunders watched 'til suddenly he snatched my glass and drank from it. He looked startled. "It really is whiskey!"

"I don't drink tea, Mr. Saunders. My real name is Angel... Appletree."

"How long have you know Hannable Sheever?"

I met his eyes. This man who had always struck my fancy didn't like me! "Since this afternoon."

He set down his glass. I don't think he expected the truth. "I saw you come downstairs just now. Couldn't you agree on a price?"

"We settled things just fine, Mr. Saunders. If that's upsetting to your sensibilities I'll drink with someone else."

"You're not worried about angering Mr. Sheever?"

"I don't anger men. I pleasure them! You're a clever man with an ear for the truth. You once said you was in search of stories to please reading folks back East. Don't you remember the first time you saw me? I was fourteen and wasn't no whore then."

He looked a mite uncomfortable. Well, I'd met up with his kind before. He wanted to shame me and nobody could do that now. "Another whiskey," he called to the barkeep.

"Whiskey looks to be your good friend," I said. "Mighty comforting thing, whiskey. Quiets voices, eases pain, keeps a body warm. I like the laudanum potion, too. I'll get me some next time I find an apothecary."

"There's one just up the street."

"I ain't had time to shop. Working takes a lot of my time, and then, o' course, I can't read them signs. One of these days I'm going to learn to read. Then I'll know what fellas like you say about folks."

"Where did I see you? I don't remember."

"Back in Denver City. Me and my ma had just come into town. Ma was a widow and couldn't get no respectable work. You was looking for us and called us beggars."

"That was ten years ago! You're twenty-four?"

"Thereabouts. Hope I don't look older."

He bolted his whiskey. "How long have you been working in Ore City?"

I counted on my fingers. "I been here one whole day. I been earning my own way now seven years."

"More whiskey, Angel?"

"All you care to buy."

"Tell me what happened since that day I saw you in Denver."

I laughed. "You ain't so clever, Mr. Saunders. You think I want my life writ up in one of your newspaper sheets? No, sir! What I done is my business, though what I could tell you about towns and men would be considerable. Don't suppose it'd set too well with a respectable gentleman like yourself."

"What makes you think I'm respectable—or a gentleman?"

"Just the look in your eye, Mr. Saunders. Just that look in your eye. And don't go thinking I find that something to admire."

He was just beginning to smile when a commotion started out in the lobby. We turned to see Mr. Hannable Sheever waving his arms and shouting at a fella wearing a gold star.

"If Sheever thinks you belong to him now, you do," Mr. Saunders whispered.

"I don't belong to no man! There ain't a man this side of heaven what can be trusted, including you and that varmint. You could write yourself a blue-blazing story about him if you knew what I do."

"But your 'honor' as a hard-working whore prevents you from telling."

"Something like that."

Mr. Sheever and the sheriff stormed into the saloon. "Arrest her!" He waggled his finger at me, his face lighting up just a bit. "She stole a thousand dollars from me."

"Really, Angel. Fleecing him was foolish."

"I ain't no thief!" I yelled, standing. From my bag I pulled the coins he'd paid me. "That's what you paid and that's all I took. If you say otherwise you're a damn liar."

"Come along peaceably, young lady. We run a clean town here," the sheriff said. "We don't allow your kind in respectable places."

"One thousand dollars in greenbacks is missing from my room," Mr. Sheever yelled. "Search her. Bauds always hide it on their person!"

The sheriff marched me out back. "You're making an unnecessary spectacle, Mr. Sheever," he hissed. "Leave her to me. I'll get at the truth."

Mr. Sheever sneered. "You didn't earn half that hundred. Jed, I expect you to take her up to that jail of yours."

The sheriff grumbled but pushed me along in the dark with Hannable close behind. I cussed myself for being such a fool. I could've gone to sleep up in that fine bed and stayed out of trouble.

We stumbled along behind all the buildings 'til we come to the top of the street. Then we followed the road 'til the town's lights was far behind. "I should've brought a lantern," the sheriff said. "We're liable to fall in a gully."

"I hope you had brains enough to bring your keys."

"Aw, Mr. Sheever. You don't expect me to throw this girl in jail. You're just trying to scare her." He watched Mr. Sheever shake his head with slow determination. "How long you mean to keep her in there?"

The jail stood on a little rise solid and black made of the heaviest square-cut logs I'd ever seen. The sheriff fumbled with the rusty bolt and then swung the door wide. The inside smelled like a spidery root cellar.

"Mr. Sheever, I'm real sorry I made you mad!" I cried. "If you want more I can pleasure you in so many ways you'll…"

"Where'd you hide my money?" He was smiling.

"I ain't never stole from a customer!"

"Strip her, Jed."

The sheriff thought on that a minute and then I guess he decided I was guilty 'cause he took hold of my bodice and pulled. We commenced to struggling. A fist hit my face. I got pushed down. A hand pressed so hard against my mouth I feared my teeth would come through my lips.

"You sure it was greenbacks, Mr. Sheever? I don't see nothing."

"It must be under her corset." A knife blade slashed at the laces. Then a blinding pain cut through my head. I didn't know nothing more.

• • •

Not a star showed above me. Not a flicker of light come from down the hill, though I could still hear music. As I sat up, my belly crawled into my throat, my head throbbed and my eyes burned.

I touched myself all over to see if I was cut or bleeding and wondered just what they did after they knocked me out. I don't guess it mattered except that if men was going to use me I wanted to know what they was about. Except for the fact that I was stark naked, I seemed to be in one piece.

I got to my feet and ran right into a log wall. I was in the jail! Feeling along the walls, I found the door. Sure enough, it was bolted fast. I found plenty of low spots along them walls where other prisoners had tried digging out. Finally I curled into a corner and waited. Just before dawn a hush fell over the town. A cock crowed, a wagon rattled by, paused and went on. Hammering echoed off the mountains. I could've been back in Tempest for all I knew.

I expected morning light to come through the chinks, but scarcely a flicker told me when the sun come up. Soon the sun warmed the roof, though, and I stopped shivering. Before I knew it sweat began breaking out under my hair and dribbling down my back. By afternoon I was hungry, but I'd knowed hunger, so it wasn't too bothersome.

The day's traffic eased off about the time that jailhouse felt like a bake-kettle. I slept most of the time, but I'd dream of things and come awake with a start. How long did Mr. Sheever expect to keep me there?

Pretty soon the saloons opened their doors to the cool night air. A hundred frantic thoughts scurried inside my head, wearing at my sanity, filling me with terror. To calm myself, I recalled peaceful evenings at the inn with the supper dishes done, me and Gwenity before the kitchen fire sewing, Lillie sleeping in the next room.

I thought back to silent nights on the mesa, winter wailing outside and Lillie at my breast, Judd by the fire whittling and looking toward me, smiling, wanting me, waiting for me to turn back the cover, all the while knowing a wife waited for him back in Georgia, and me knowing he wasn't my only man.

I pulled myself into a tight ball. The jailhouse cooled.

As long as Judd and me didn't know the truth about each other we'd been happy. He was lucky now; he'd blasted hisself into eternity, leaving me behind to this hell. I weren't no high-class, high-paid whore. I was just one of the bauds men hated or wanted as it suited their purpose. If I ever got out of that jailhouse I'd figure a way to pay them all back. I'd hurt them the way they'd hurt me—if I ever got out.

When darkness returned my belly felt a bit pained and my tongue felt rough as a cactus. I moved about just to keep from turning to stone. When I couldn't wait another second, I left a personal gift for the sheriff, or next prisoner, to remember me by. After a bit I didn't notice the smell and sat back down to wonder on my fate.

Now and again a shivery fear would begin in my chest. "I ain't going to get out. I can't get my breath! My heart hurts, it's beating so hard. I'm going to die and nobody cares! When they find me that Saunders fella will tell everybody my name. It'll get back to Gwenity and Lillie that I died a naked whore in a jailhouse."

I jumped up and held back a scream with my hands. Finally I slid back down and wrapped my hands around my own shoulders. I didn't have nobody…but me.

When I woke I couldn't tell if the hours was passing at all. It was some time the next day I heard a wagon pull up outside. I was dizzy from the heat, mixed up and hungry. "Mr. Sheever ain't going to like this," somebody grumbled outside. "I'm telling you, I shouldn't let you do this."

"He can't keep the incident quiet forever. How long do you think he means to keep her here, until he figures where to hide her body?"

The sheriff laughed. "You've been around too many desperadoes, Mr. Saunders. Mr. Sheever wouldn't kill that tramp. She ain't worth it."

"One hundred dollars seems like a lot for an ordinary session with a whore. I don't believe for a moment he lost a thousand to her or anyone. Sheever's keeping her quiet because of what she knows, because of that one-hundred-dollar favor. Don't you wonder what's worth that much, Sheriff?"

"I guess maybe I thought about it a little."

"Other folks might like to know, too. They might reconsider his suitability as governor someday."

"You ought to talk this over with him before you…"

"There's no need. I can see he pays you well. Do me this little favor, Jed, and I'll forget my curiosity. You don't think I'm just paying my respects to the lovely little tart, do you?"

As his key slipped into the lock, the sheriff chuckled. "I had my eye on her myself. She's a good-looking piece of baggage all right. If I hadn't been so busy last night I would've brought her something to eat and…"

"No food or water since you locked her up?"

"Well, you got to be firm with prisoners."

The door swung out. I covered my eyes when the sunlight hit my face and pressed myself back in a corner feeling mangy and ugly. I tried to open my eyes to see the men looking in on me. A bit of fresh air broke past the blanket of heavy sour air that had been locked in the jailhouse with me. I took a deep breath and let out a cry. I'd been dying!

I could just make out Travis Saunders's silhouette against the blinding glare. He stood very still and seemed taller than any man I'd ever seen in my life. I think if I'd believed in God, he would've looked like that—big, black, and still.

"What did you say your last name was, Jed?" Travis asked quietly.

"Just go on in! I'll guard the door and take my turn later," the sheriff said nervously.

"Don't you want to be remembered as one of Colorado's upstanding citizens?"

"It's no secret. I'm Jed Wraith, ready to help you any time."

"Then hand me those things laying in the weeds. This girl's naked."

"Ain't she something? Looks just like that painting in the Ore City Playhouse. I figure Mr. Sheever won't want her no more, her being a thief, so I'm fixing to keep her somewhere outside town. She could bring a man a fine income. Pleasure, too."

"Doesn't Hannable Sheever pay you enough?"

"Ain't never enough for an ambitious man. What you want her old clothes for? They're torn and dirty."

Travis held out my chemise. By then I could see his face clear and it wasn't belonging to a man who meant to use me. When I was covered I lifted my head and looked square at them.

"You want me to shut the door now?" Sheriff Wraith said.

Mr. Saunders reached into his coat and pulled out a stubby pistol. "I want you to turn around. Angel, there's a blanket in the wagon. I wouldn't have known you were still around if someone hadn't stolen your dress from the weeds and put it up for sale in town."

I ran wobbly-legged for the wagon.

"I swear this was all Mr. Sheever's idea!" the sheriff whined. "I didn't want to put her in there. We've never put a woman in jail. Mr. Saunders, please! I'm a fair man. Go ahead and take her. I'll tell Mr. Sheever she escaped."

"Has any man ever escaped?" Mr. Saunders jabbed his pistol deeper into the sheriff's back.

"I'll tell him someone stole her!"

"You're full of good lies, aren't you, Sheriff Wraith? After you searched her, did you rape her, too?"

"She's a whore! She don't care."

"I'll be sure to write an article about you and Mr. Sheever so everyone will know just the kind of honorable men you are."

"You were buying her drinks. You're no better. You came here to…"

"It may have seemed that way to you since your mind works in that direction. Just be glad I came when I did. She could've died. Then I'd be writing about your hanging."

I pulled the blanket around my shoulders. "A buggy's coming up the hill like the devil's on its tail," I called.

"Get down!"

"Better lock up that no-account sheriff first. He might like sitting in the dirt on his bare ass, too."

"You heard the lady," Travis chuckled. "Better hurry."

"You can't make me!" he squawked.

"He had to knock me out," I called from my hiding place under the blanket. "Knock him over the head. After that buggy goes by I'll make use of him. He won't know the difference."

That sheriff tore off his clothes right down to the last stitch! Mr. Saunders locked him inside the jail, kicked his clothes back of the weeds and ran for the wagon.

Fifteen minutes later when Travis was sure we hadn't been followed, he stopped. "It's safe to come out now. I brought food."

I tore into the hamper and stuffed biscuits in my mouth so fast I couldn't talk. When he held out the jail's key I grabbed it. The road overlooked a grassy valley with a blue ribbon of a creek waving down through the boulders. I flung that key high in the air over the edge and watched it disappear into a tangle of pine tops. Then I sat back and drank of a pot of cool lemonade. Before I realized what was happening, I couldn't swallow no more. My throat closed and I broke into a sob.

Travis touched my hair. "Eat up. It's a long ride to the next town, and you need a bath."

"I don't need reminding, Mr. Saunders!" and I dashed the tears away.

"You could call me Travis and, you could thank me."

"I know my manners! You could've got me out of that damn jailhouse sooner!"

He threw back his head and laughed 'til his voice echoed through the hills.

Twenty-One

Winter 1870-Spring 1871

I found myself living in a room, scarcely big enough for an iron bed, over a saloon in some half-dead mining town somewhere between Ore City and Cold Water. If I remember right, the place was called Cramer Park after the first and last fella to strike gold there.

The saloon was run by Eb Frazer, a wiry old fella with eyes as hard as garnet stones and a face like a rock. The only reason he was there was to fill his pockets. A small crew of girls come and went upstairs—Chinees, Mexicans, and some that couldn't speak English—broken or otherwise. I had the high-handed notion to feel sorry for them and spent half my time listening to them cry and the other half showing them how to use whiskey and a sponge.

I had next to no money. Every bit I earned I spent on liquor. My brown bottle potion was hard to come by that far in the mountains. Travis Saunders had driven me to that miserable place, him and them words he could put to paper.

We'd escaped Hannable Sheever's justice easy enough. We stopped in Colorado Creek, a nice little town with its share of saloons and the like and took connected rooms at the hotel. I kept expecting Travis to visit me in the night, but after several days I knocked upon his door to find out what he was about. "How long you going to stay shut up in your room?" I asked.

"Don't bother me now. I'm working." There he sat, dipping his pen and scratching away 'til I thought he was part field mouse with them writing noises.

"What you writing?"

"Hannable Sheever's epitaph."

"You fixing to kill him?" I thought it mighty flattering Mr. Travis Saunders hisself was so riled by what that varmint did to me. I'd never had a protector before—well, there'd been Dalt. The only other folks who ever cared a whit about me had been Cornelia and Gwenity—but a lot women could do about such things when you thought honestly on it.

"I'm killing his political career. Colorado, when it becomes a state, doesn't need a man like that in its capital."

"You suppose he really had a thousand dollars stole from him, or was he just angered I left him 'fore he'd had his fill of me?"

Travis had set down his pen and leaned back. His lips could look like a smile was coming on, but then they'd just stay that way, not smiling, not serious. I don't blow just what I found so stirring about that going-to-seed face, and it scared me to think he didn't find me as stirring. "I haven't met many women like you, Angel," he said softly.

"I've been told I'm one of the best in the West."

One corner of his mouth turned up and he shook his head. "I didn't mean that." He rubbed his eyes and sighed. "Go on. I must get this written. You've given me a potent weapon against Sheever. I only wish you'd tell me what he paid a hundred dollars for."

"You want me telling every fella who asks what I done with the ones I was with before?"

"Might be amusing."

"It ain't always been so funny, Mr. Saunders."

"Then why do it?"

"Oh, I hate hypocrites! I met up with your kind before."

"*My* kind?" He laughed.

"I been with near every man in this damn territory. I could tell you some secrets. You ain't no different and no better."

"Except that you know I won't be crawling into your bed."

"Don't see why not. I've bedded my share of pious old goats.

Come some lonely night, you'll find me to your liking."

"I'm thirty-nine, hardly an old goat."

"You're old. You got the look. Last fella like you I ran across was preaching virture to his neighbors the morning after he raped me."

"Tell me more."

"Go to hell! Ain't you worried about *me* sleeping in the room next to yours? Ain't folks liable to talk?"

That aggravating smile twitched on his lips. "You're strong and fierce and I admire that, Angel, but only two days ago you were huddled in a jail and looked like a frightened animal. I'm sorry I had to see you like that. Those others you speak of see you as beautiful, but remembering you in that jail, naked, doesn't spark my desire. I don't remember your breasts. I remember your eyes. I don't long for your lovely thighs, I see marks on your abdomen. You've borne a child. Tell me who you really are."

"Ain't no use in that."

"Go back to your room then and leave me to my work. The only woman I could ever want would have to be mine alone. You'll never qualify."

As he turned back and dipped his pen he became a blurry shadow. I closed the door. A weight so heavy it pulled me to the floor settled deep in my belly. I held myself tight and stared at the floorboards, fixing my mind on the wood grain, recalling other burning belly pains and aches in my heart. Would I ever feel anything for a man again except hate?

That night I drank my fill of whiskey. Come morning I walked out of that town. Down the canyon road I picked my way up a gully where I could watch the traffic passing below. When Travis's wagon bounced down the road I headed up over the hill and angled across 'til I met with a narrow track that took me to Cramer Park.

"The nearest doctor's twenty miles away at least. Don't fret so much, Angel. Bad meat'll pain you every time." Eb Frazer, owner of that fine, cold saloon I lived at, sat across the table from me, polishing off a mess of beans and bearsteak he'd throwed together. He could turn perfectly good food into slop. If I hadn't been so sick I would've throwed him out of his own kitchen and done it myself.

Not long after getting to Cramer Park, I took sick. Considering the men I took up with, it wasn't surprising. The burning and swelling got so bad I could hardly sit. I finished eating and swallowed an eye-watering gulp of rotgut whiskey.

"Women always have plumbing problems," Eb muttered, disappointed 'cause he wouldn't be collecting no rent from me that week, cash or otherwise. He sucked the spaces between his teeth and eyed me. "I had it before. It comes and goes as it wants."

"Well, I'm fixing to find me a doctor," I said.

A week later a traveling medicine show man come to town. Soon as he set up his wagon over by the whiskey wholesaler, I wrapped myself in a blanket and made my way down there.

The tall fella with the handlebar moustache smiled down at me. "Got yourself a toothache, little lady? This fine substance will cure gout, rheumatism, impotence, dyspepsia, influenza, and melancholy."

"I got belly pains," I said. "If you take too much, is it fatal?"

"Most things are." He came around from tethering his horse. "My name's Elizer Webster. Doctor Elizer, they call me." He hiked up his trousers. "A pretty woman's a rare sight in these hills."

"Call me Angel. I'd like to buy some of your fine elixir. Suppose we could work a trade?"

"How many bottles?"

"All you're willing to sell—all I can carry, anyway. You fancy your own elixir, Doctor Elizer?"

"Never touch the stuff. Never a sick day in my life! I'm very strong for my age. If you're willing, little lady, I'll trade five bottles for an hour of your time."

I curled my fingers about his lapel. "Fifteen bottles and I'll spend the whole night."

That night I took my own supper in my room. After two

spoonfuls of Dr. Elizer's elixir burned down my throat and set my veins to singing I felt a sight better. By the time I went to meet the medicine show man in his wagon I'd polished off near half a bottle. I needed it to get me through the night.

"Come in, my dear," he whispered, his black eyes twinkling. His wagon had wooden sides with windows and curtains and his bed had fine linens and woolly blankets.

We got down to business after a goodly amount of small talking. I ain't exactly sure when he finished with me—I was near dead drunk. Sometimes a stab of pain would open my eyes and paint stars before them. I recall waking near dawn when he was at me again.

After he left for breakfast, I drank the rest of my first elixir bottle and fell back asleep. I woke once to hear Elizer pitching his spiel behind the wagon. When he climbed inside later that day I was still abed. "Much as I enjoyed your company last night, Angel, I must bid you farewell. Necessity requires I travel, and I must be on."

"Take me as far as the next town," I said.

"Delicate ladies and respectable gentleman wouldn't buy from me if they knew I traveled with a woman of your calling," he said, frowning.

"I'll keep inside and won't trouble you. I just got to get out of this town."

"What have you done, my dear?"

I smiled a bit and waved my fingers lazily. "I'm bored."

"A temptress to the last," he chuckled. "Very well. I'll wake you when we've found a campsite."

I traveled with Dr. Elizer four days. I guzzled his elixir all the while and got so confused I didn't know night from day. One night I woke to find him in a fit of rage, shouting at me and throwing my clothes out the back. "Dirty whore!" he was yelling, yanking me up by the shoulders. "You gave me your filth!"

He threw me and my box of bottles to the ground. Gravel rained on me as he beat his horse and rattled away into the dark.

If it hadn't been so cold I wouldn't have knowed I was half

naked. Finding two bottles unbroken, I dressed and took them along with me down the road 'til I come upon a little town and a house with a picket fence. I settled myself beside it, waiting for Ma to come along and take me home. After finishing them bottles I felt darn good as I fell face first into the red dust.

Dr. Peabody, who lived in that house, give me the cure for the clap, which was a vile looking salve of mercury and an even worser potion of it to drink. Three times a day he applied the salve. I remember still the sight of his balding sunburnt head bending over me, his expression equal to one who worked over all manner of unpleasantness.

He was also the town's undertaker. Twice, while I resided in his back room I watched him ready a body for the ground. We was in a part of the mountains where graves had to be blasted from the frozen earth. First time I heard it I near went crazy. Dr. Peabody had to beat me into silence.

The day come at last when I was called cured. I could answer nature without crying and sit a chair in the normal fashion. I could do a day's work—and the doc did work me. I scrubbed his floor of blood, cooked, swept, and listened to his gruesome tales of bullets, babies, and bodies. I was fixing to bid him farewell the day a dance troupe come to town for the spring festival.

I liked all the dancing, singing, and carrying on. One fella read some famous man's sonnets and brought the miners to their feet clapping. Everybody threw coins. I was on my way to the next town when their wagon come up behind me and they offered me a ride.

Pembleton, the sonnet reader, had delicate hands and pretty eyes. I sat between him and David, who played the violin. Three dancing ladies slept in the back of the wagon. We was sisters in the same trade, if my guess was right.

After their performance the next evening we went to a small eating house where the ladies smiled at miners, working men, and the faro dealer from the saloon. David took his leave early when the cook wouldn't bring him a better beefsteak. I was glad to be alone with Pembleton, who looked to be well off. Giving him my most suggestive smile, I said, "Spending the night alone?"

He blinked them pretty eyes and dabbed his lips with a white kerchief. "Surely you're not suggesting we spend it together."

"And why not? You're a handsome fella."

"That may well be, but I must confess you're too old for my tastes."

I felt like I'd been kicked by a horse! "I'm only twenty-four!"

"Dear, dear, then you *are* in a bad way. I would not be intentionally cruel, but...I can see most plainly you've been ill. In one of your trade, the illness is well known and justly avoided. You've been pleasant company, Angel, but let's not venture into business."

I swallowed hard. "I need money."

"I'll lend you a dollar then."

I stood up fast, my head reeling. "I can have any man here!"

He looked about and smiled weakly. "Have you gazed into a looking glass lately? The sight might quiet you." He paid for our dinner and hurried out.

I sat down with the men at the nearest table and smirked. "Must be something wrong with that one."

The faro dealer gazed dully at me. "I don't need your trouble, either."

The owner of the eating house come up to me and whispered, "I'll have to ask you to leave. You're annoying my customers."

"Just doing business!" I snapped, my heart pounding.

"Not in my place, not your kind anyway."

"Look at this holy joe! He'll be the first to sniff around me come midnight."

He took my arm and escorted me to the door. "Don't come back!" He tried to push me out, but I held fast to the door and went out dignified. One of the girls from the troupe lent me her arm when I stumbled and near to fell off the porch. "Steady there. Can you make it?" she asked.

"I could have any man in there!"

"Sure you could, honey. Quiet down now, or we'll have trouble."

"I'm just trying to earn money. I got to work!"

ANGEL

"I heard there's a house outside this town. I'll walk you down," she said. "You'd best lay off the whiskey. It's killing you."

"Let loose of me! I don't need your damn help."

She held tight and moved me along 'til we come to a lone house hidden in a stand of pine. The windows was lit up bright enough to hurt my eyes. The piano music pained my ears as she led me 'round back. I couldn't feel my feet touching ground no more and wondered if I was already dead.

When I opened my eyes the next day I stared up into Big Bess's frown! Her face sagged like heavy saddlebags and her hair was near white. "*What* have you done to yourself, Angel?" she snarled.

"I want work," I said, near to crying for joy at the sight of her.

"Not in my house! Have you seen yourself?" She lifted me out of bed and propped me in front of a looking glass out in a hall. "Take a good look, Angel. It might be your last."

The gilt-edged glass was lit by a dim oil lamp. I knowed the reflection was me 'cause I knowed a looking glass when I saw one. I stepped closer 'cause I couldn't believe what I saw.

I was old.

My silver-streaked hair was tangled and dull. I couldn't remember the last time I'd washed it or cared how it looked. Most of the curl I'd always hated was gone, leaving it limp and sorry looking. Pulling my nightdress to my neck, I stared at bones and valleys where plumpness and beauty had once been. My thighs was narrow, my breasts near gone.

I dropped the hem and stared at my face. My skin was an unnatural yellow. The plumpness that had once spelled youth had worn away. I was as plain as Gwenity, my eyes marked with purple circles, and a kind of haunting sorrow lurked in them that sparked no desire. I whirled and fell into the mushy softness of Bess's bosom. "I ain't got nothing left! I can't take no more!"

Bess didn't say nothing as she dragged me back to bed 'cause there weren't nothing left to say. I saw in her eyes the truth she'd lived with since her body left her old. A whore's livelihood was her beauty. I was a whore no more.

I held myself and cried from the pit of my belly, from the inside of my bones. Where could I go? Who could I turn to?

"Stay as long as you want, Angel," Bess said. "But, like it or not, you're through working."

"I'll go back to Dalt!" I whispered.

Bess stopped herself from saying something. "Give yourself a few months, then. We'll get you some good clothes, tend to your hair...Yep, Jack will be glad to see you all right." Her eyes told me she was lying, but I didn't care. In the spring I'd be beautiful again.

Twenty-Two

Spring 1872

"Won't you sit down, Miss Jacobs? I'll get the necessary papers and your money. Are you sure you want to close your account?"

"I know what I'm about, Mr. Simms," I said, looking about the office of the Cold Water City Bank.

"Everything's in order. If you'll just sign here..." He spread the papers before me and fussed with a kink in his watch chain while I clamped my teeth and got the pen just so among my fingers.

"Good weather for April," he said, looking out the window and polishing his spectacles. "My missus is hoping to get her garden in early."

"How is she?" I asked, blowing on the wet marks I'd made.

"Fine, fine. My boy will be two next month. Didn't you and Judd have a child?" He slid a packet of greenback dollars across the desk.

"You know my child and husband is long since gone from me, Mr. Simms, so don't pretend otherwise."

"Just making conversation, my dear," he replied innocently.

"I expected to see Cold Water a-buzzing with trade when I come into town this morning," I said, eyeing him. "Seems things ain't going so well here."

"We're expecting a boom when the railroad comes through. They've graded as far as Snowy Ray's old trading post, the one that burned down. It got struck by lightning, I think."

"Didn't know that," I said. "Did he set up trade somewheres else?"

"Why, he was killed, you know, at that agency near Eagleton. Scalped to the bone."

I shuddered. "Mr. Simms, since you're late for your supper I won't be keeping you. You're a decent man. I can see it clear. You'd do most anything for your new son, I'll bet. Well, you're the only man hereabouts who knows I ain't dead, so I got to ask this favor, and I got to have your word on it. Don't tell nobody I was here."

"That will be difficult come accounting time, Miss Jacobs."

"Men are good at figuring ways. I ain't asking for myself, you know. I'm asking for my child. I just need this money to go back East, for my health." I lined the bills up before him. "Count this for me, Mr. Simms."

"I assure you, it's all there! One, two, three…"

"This here is worth one hundred dollars all by itself?"

"Yes, Ma'am. Clever thing, paper money."

"Will you keep my visit secret, Mr. Simms?"

"Like I said, the accounts…Why, Howdy Jackson is in once or twice a year, asking if I've had word from you. I always tell him I can't do anything about his daughter's account—your daughter's."

"She ain't mine no more. What about that account?"

"You must cosign for any withdrawals, my dear. No matter how badly Howard needs it, I can't turn it over without proper authorization. I wish I could lend him more, but since his fall…"

"If Howdy Jackson needs money, you give it to him!" I said. 'Fore I knew it, I signed more papers to make Howdy co-owner of Lillie's account. Then I gathered my money. "Do I have your word, Mr. Simms?"

He rounded his desk and took my elbow. "Howdy will know you've been here."

"Howdy can keep a secret. Can you?" I pulled a fifty dollar bill from the wad in my hand. "Don't your boy need a pony, a fine suit of clothes, or a rocker horse?"

"Miss Jacobs!"

I pulled another fifty out and tucked them both in his fat

hand. "I love my child more than life. I want your solemn word as a gentleman you won't tell nobody about me. Make up some fancy story to convince Howdy that account is truly his. I can't threaten you, Mr. Simms. I'm just asking your help."

"You have my word of honor."

"I'll hold you to it."

I slipped out the door into the dusk. At the post office I put three of the hundred dollar bills into a letter Bess had writ to herself and dropped it through the slot in the door. When it come to getting her money back, Bess was expert.

My buggy waited nearby in a stand of scrub oak. I lifted the heavy silk of my new black dress and climbed aboard. My white horse had cost Bess plenty. I owed her a good deal more than three hundred dollars—I owed her my life. "But you can't very well pay me back for that," she'd laughed when I took my leave. I tapped the reins across the horse's rump and rolled silently out of town.

Bess had taken good care of me over the winter, though she wouldn't let me have no whiskey or potion. I ate good and began to look human again. The curl never did come back to my hair and it had thinned so much I had to handle it careful for fear of turning bald as Dalt. I had three loose teeth thanks to my mercury cure and, though I scrubbed with salt, my mouth didn't get free of the stains for months.

Now I had the same sinewy arms and raw-boned look to my face that Gwenity and Cornelia and so many other women of the West had. It come from plain hard work and, I suspect, a good deal of fear and sorrow.

As I headed toward Buffalo Canyon I could see lights from the Calico Inn but turned my face away. When I rolled within sight of Tempest the next morning, my back ached and so did my heart. The canyon looked so different I hardly knew it. A narrow gauge railbed hugged the far side of the canyon wall. I could see three short tunnels, and around the next bend the crew was laying track.

In another mile I saw Tempest itself. The old main street still climbed the canyon walls, but growing up this side was a new street lined with more stores, hotels, a stone bank, three liveries, and a carriagemaker. The number of houses among the trees had doubled. A white church steeple peeked from behind some rocks farther down. "So, ol Jim finally got it built," I muttered, smiling and shaking my head.

"Don't suppose you could tell me if Jack Dalton still lives hereabouts," I asked the smithy at the first livery I come to.

He propped his boot on my footrest and smiled hello. "Everybody knows Jack Dalton. I'm Denver Smith, Ma'am."

"Glad to meet you. I thought Denver was a city."

"Big enough name for both of us. Jack Dalton's one of *the* men in Buffalo Falls."

"Where's that?"

"You're in it, Ma'am! Best little town in the West."

"This here's Tempest! I lived here long enough to know that."

"Town council voted to change it. We figure to improve the image. Jack's up there." He pointed up the East slope. "He owns the Silver Star."

"Damned if he didn't do it!" I laughed. "Where's the road at? Everything's so growed up I can't see it." I followed the direction of Denver's sooty finger, spied the road and was off.

The sun was high when I reached the mesa. The Silver Star didn't look quite so grand as I remembered. It was still beautiful, but I just wasn't quite so admiring of such a place no more.

A groom come 'round and saw to my buggy. As I walked inside, I lifted my chin. I was a mite scared to be facing Dalt after so long. In the dining hall a Chinee was setting fresh linen and silver. Through some double doors I saw one of the gaming rooms. When I heard that familiar "Heh-heh-heh," a tingle went up my back.

Two men sat at a table, playing out their poker hands. The one in the ruffled shirt looked up. "Another of your ladies, Mr. Dalton?"

Dalt counted out a number of chips from the fine stack in front of him. Then he looked at me, and his smile sagged. "The time for looking at ladies was hours ago, Lord Waxmore. The time to finish this game is now." He turned back to his hand.

My knees near to give out. It appeared I'd walked away from Dalt once too often. Maybe he didn't even remember me. I sank into a chair in the dining hall too tired to even cry. I think I dozed there, 'cause the next thing I knowed, Dalt was pulling me to my feet.

"Morning, Madame," Dalt's friend the Londoner said, bowing over my hand. "You have my deepest thanks for getting me out of that nightmarish game. I'll return tonight to win back my money, Mr. Dalton. You are a most accomplished gambler. I salute you." He swayed, the marks of sleeplessness and whiskey gouging his eyes.

"Good night, Lord Waxmore," Dalt said, his voice rougher than I remembered. The Londoner headed toward the staircase and Dalt let out a sigh. Then, without a word, he led me down a hall to a dark door. The walk seemed to tire him. New furrows crisscrossed Dalt's brow, and a deep crease cut his face from cheek to chin. Silvery stubble grew along his jaw. When he turned the door handle his hand shook. Then he closed us in his room as if he was shutting out wolves. I braced myself for his laugh.

Still he didn't say anything. He just put his arms around me and drew me tighter against him. His lips felt dry and hesitant against my cheek. "Angel," he whispered. "Angel...I've missed you."

I hid my face in his coat so he wouldn't see my tears.

With the drapes closed against the late afternoon sun, Dalt's room had a rich rosy glow pleasant to wake to. What a pleasure it was to curl against the back of a man again, a man whose name I remembered and whose face lived in my memory from when I was a girl. We'd said next to nothing since I got back. We'd just fallen into bed and held each other.

I put a little kiss on his shoulder. Dalt snorted and rolled over. He pushed hisself upright and commenced to rubbing and kneading his whole head 'til he was awake enough to stagger to his feet. He'd lost muscle in his chest and arms; it was plain he'd not get it back. His legs had shrunk to narrow posts and looked a bit comic 'til he stepped into his trousers. "I thought I dreamed you," he said.

"I'm here to stay if you'll have me," I said, still not sure he wanted me.

Still sleepy, he turned up the lamp and studied my face. "I didn't recognize you at first. Marie told me you set out for the cabin. You been there all this time?"

"I never made it," I said. "Tell me about folks around here. Is Jim Lewis still mayor?"

"Same high and mighty jackass," Dalt grinned.

"And Rusty Kennings?"

"The sheriff? He's his own joke. I forgot you knew him. He talks like he's trying to close the saloons, but he ain't. We pay him too good. A born politician, that one. Lies up both sleeves and smiles while he's doing it. Him and Effie got four or five kids now. Would you believe it? Some say Effie is tetched. Jim, you remember, is a widow-man. All the old sows love him and call him Jolly Jim, one of the founding fathers of Tempest." He snorted with disgust.

"Does Davey Whitehouse and his wife still live here?"

"Sure. They've got a few kids, too. He's a deputy, you know, with his weak belly, too!"

"What about Ben Corning…and his wife?"

"I was afraid you'd come to them. Ben has a shack up in the trees. He only shows up around here a couple times a year. There's a fella playing with half a deck."

"And Lizbeth?"

Dalt rubbed his face and swallowed. "Rotten business, the pox. Doc Billy said her baby died in her. One morning Ben found she'd shot herself."

I curled against the pillow and stared at the wall. Darned if I didn't feel sorry for her. And she kilt my friend, too.

After Dalt went off to tend to his business, I dressed and took my buggy into town to find an apothecary. I was dressed sober, so I doubt folks knew who or what I was. They stared curious, but didn't cross the street at the sight of me—the womenfolk didn't—and the men didn't let a twinkle shine in their eyes.

ANGEL

By the time I got back to the Silver Star it was near dark. I'd forgotten to eat, so I took a table in the dining hall and ordered up a fine supper. "Where you been?" Dalt demanded when he come out of his gaming room and saw me.

"You wasn't worried?" I said, feeling terrible that I'd worried him.

"What the hell was I to think?" He sank into a chair beside me and rubbed his neck.

"I'm sorry. I been alone so long I forgot you might wonder what I was about."

"Good evening, Mr. Dalton. And the beautiful Angel," Lord Waxmore said, joining us. He'd sobered from the night before and gazed on me with watered blue eyes and held out a bony white hand for me to shake. It give me a start 'cause the only such hands I'd ever seen belonged to babies or corpses.

"Meet Lord Sedgwick Waxmore," Dalt snapped.

"From England, are you?" I said.

"Northumberland. Join us between hands for a drink later, won't you?"

"I won't be playing tonight," Dalt said, his eyes low. "Miss Angel come a long way. I'm seeing to her needs."

"Indeed! Perhaps we could go riding some afternoon, my dear. I haven't met a lady of true character in this town yet."

"Hope you do soon," I said, turning back to my meal.

"I meant you, my lady! Your modesty is charming. Surely, Jack, you could spare her for a few hours. She's truly lovely."

"That's mighty kind of you, Mr. your lordship," I said. "But I come just to see Dalt and wouldn't feel right spending a single minute away from him."

Dalt just grinned.

We spent the rest of the evening in Dalt's room, laughing over Lord Waxmore, discussing the sorry state of affairs in Tempest and just generally getting to know each other again. That night as we lay in each other's arms I didn't know if I'd let Dalt have his way with me. I hadn't had no contact since the medicine show man and didn't know if I ever should again. Soon it was plain, though, that Dalt didn't mean to have me.

As the days went by, Lord Waxmore did a good deal of insinuating and chuckling about my long "private" visit, but the fact was, Dalt had no interest in bedding at all. "I'll tell you why if you promise not to laugh," Dalt said when I finally asked about it.

"I don't promise nothing to nobody no more," I said. Dalt kept his face turned away. "For more than a year I've kept three... sometimes four women here at the Silver Star. I pay them good and like my reputation..." He quieted me. "I'm trying to tell you I paid them for silence. Winter before last I had some kind of attack. Bill Granger helped me through it. He said I got a bad heart."

"Not an old bear like you!"

He chuckled. "After that I sold my holdings and had so much money I figured to retire. This place fell into my lap. I'm a big man now. Remember John Harrington? He runs everything for me. When the town council wanted a schoolhouse, did they go to Lewis or Kennings? No, they come to me, so I'm one of their damn town fathers, too. On the books, anyway."

I kissed his cheek. "So why's Lord what's-his-name want the Silver Star so bad?"

"He wants to turn it into a casino—but he hasn't got the cash since our very first game together." He chuckled. "He's been waiting three months for a draft from his London bank. If I sell the Silver Star I want to build a place like I saw in the South one time, a social club, I guess you'd call it. I bought some land down the canyon. John'll run the place. We'll bring in a few very fancy ladies. You could be the madam. How about it?"

"Me!" I laughed. I wasn't so sure I liked that idea. I didn't see why we couldn't just live at the Silver Star.

That night Lord Waxmore showed his face again before we'd finished half our supper. "I thought perhaps you two had run away together," he smirked, setting hisself down without invitation.

"Got your draft yet?" Dalt asked over a foamy beer.

"I would've beaten down your door if I had. I was just at the post office this morning—nothing. Not even in the unclaimed box."

"That's for folks who don't want to answer to their rightful name," Dalt said.

"I thought perhaps the oaf sorting letters might've put mine in there by mistake. A good deal of Tempest's population must be answering to aliases because that box is overflowing. Some letters are more than two years old. No less than four await the attention of one A. J. Rydell! I was tempted to take them myself. My curiosity was piqued."

"I've heard that name before," Dalt said, squeezing his cheeks as if they hurt. "A couple years back, in the newspaper. The Savage wrote it up. Some Eastern widow got herself robbed of ten or twenty thousand dollars. Her name was Rydell. Remember that, Angel?"

"You know I can't read a word."

"Indeed, my lady?" the lord said. "What a curious affliction. Did the woman recover her money?"

"Nope, but they figure they know who done it and put up a reward. I seen it posted at the bank. Remember Snowy Ray's breed, Angel? He's become one of the worst renegades in this territory."

"Not Pike!"

"Yep, took up with a couple outlaws after that big massacre. He's robbed enough to make quite a name for hisself. I heard he hid out for a while and settled with his pa at the agency, took hisself a squaw wife. Then the Injuns turned on them and killed the squaw. She was pregnant, too. Can you beat that? He robs anybody now and is worth a thousand dollars." Dalt looked at me and wiped his mouth. I couldn't eat no more and took myself off to our room.

I was still awake when Dalt staggered in after playing cards 'til the sun come up. "You got to take me to town!" I said, jumping from my chair.

He sagged against me. "Don't let me get talked into playing with that man again, Angel. I'll sell the London bastard this place, but I won't lose it. I can't lose it."

"Dalt, please! I got to go to town before that lord gets my letters. I'd get them myself, but I don't know the name Rydell from fly specks. You can read. Get my letters for me!"

"You wasn't robbed," Dalt muttered.

"There ain't time to explain! Just come with me."

He sighed heavy. "Send the boy for my carriage."

"Quiet down, Angel," Dalt said, turning his carriage away from the post office a while later. "I figured you didn't want the whole world knowing you got that name A. J. Rydell. Otherwise you would've spoke up last night."

"Can I just hold them?" I said, pressing close, not even knowing what a letter looked like.

He pulled four folded papers from his vest pocket as he turned down the freight road. "Thought you might like to see my land," he said. "It's a nice drive, and private."

A half-hour later he eased his carriage off the road to the creek, where it flowed between the aspens. "Are you going to tell me how you come to be this A. J. Rydell?"

"After you've read the letters."

Dalt arranged them in order and opened the first. *"July, 1870. Dearest Angie, I write, not knowing if this will ever find you. I still cannot believe your beautiful little daughter is mine. I pray every day, hoping you are well and happy...I am, by your instruction, teaching Lillie that we are her mama and papa now.*

*"Sometimes Howdy has bad headaches, thanks to that ruffian who struck him. Leroy is working the mine and doing well with it. Howdy pays all he can. The profits are in the bank, so I hope you'll send along a letter giving us permission to use the money for Lillie. Our very best wishes go with you wherever you are. Your friend, Gwenity Jackson...*If that don't beat all," Dalt said. "You had another baby, and gave her to this woman."

I nodded and looked away, blinking fast.

"Got yourself a mine, too."

"Lillie does. Her pa give it to her. The Jacksons are good people, Dalt. Read the next letter."

"November, 1870. Howdy went looking for you in Tempest when he ordered supplies. He found only one man who remembered your name. Tempest is a wild place and I hope you've moved on, though I will keep writing you there. Each day with Lillie brings me more joy than I could ever put into words. Your heart must be breaking without her. A letter from Mr. Bromley brought news of a lawsuit. I cannot let myself worry over that. Hope you are well. Howdy sends his best..."

"What's a lawsuit?" I asked.

"Don't worry about it. This letter's two years old. Want to hear another one?" Dalt asked, breaking the seal on the third. *"January, 1871. We celebrated Lillie's third birthday today. It's so cold my ink is nearly frozen. Howdy took a spill off his horse last month and hurt his leg...I can only guess at where you could be. Mr. Simms says if we do not hear from you in seven years Howdy will be able to use the accounts...My prayers are with you as always, Gwenity."* Dalt rubbed his face. "Here's the last one, Angel." When I didn't answer, he read on. *"July, 1871. I think of you often... Sometimes I fear you'll return to claim your child. I've never known such joy... Lillie calls us Mama and Papa now. She stands so tall you wouldn't know her. She's very smart. Leroy promised to work the mine all summer though we can't pay him anymore...I can only guess you're not getting my letters, but as always, we send our love..."*

"We'd best write that woman," Dalt said. "I know a man at the bank who'll help."

I fell against his shoulder, my heart indeed breaking.

At the bank that afternoon, I had to tell Dalt most all my story in the process of explaining about Lillie. My signature gave Howdy permission to hire a mining company for the Little Angel mine. And Dalt included some of his own money in my letter in case the Jacksons needed it for the settlement. My letter said simply, *I just now got your letters read to me. Write the Tempest bank if you need help with that snake, Bromley. I'm sorry he's been a bother. I'm alive and well and have been traveling. Give Lillie a kiss for me. I do miss her, but she belongs with you. I done the right thing....*

"Promise you'll never tell a living soul about any of this," I said. "And pay your bank fella for his silence, too, 'til I can do it proper myself."

Dalt chuckled. "How do you think he affords the best rig in town right now? Don't worry. If he can't shut up that Eastern lawyer, nobody can."

"If killing Mr. Bromley would keep Lillie safe, I'd do it," I hissed.

Dalt closed the office door and looked close at me. "I think you would. I guess now's as good a time as any to ask you this, Angel. Would you consider marrying me?"

I busted out laughing. "I thought you weren't never going to marry."

"A man can change," Dalt said. "You'd be rich, honey. There won't be nothing you can't buy."

"Excepting one thing. Sure, I'll marry you, Mr. Jack Dalton," I smiled, hugging him. "I kind of like you after all this time."

Twenty-Three

Fall 1873

"There she is, reigning queen of Tempest, Angel Dalton! Angel, come down and meet my friends and bring your girls."

I lifted my black silk skirts enough to show the fine lace on my French petticoats and started down the stairs of the Mountain Club, as Dalt had named our new house of pleasures. My stockings was of a clever weave of flowers and stripes. My high button shoes reflected all the candles in the chandelier. Men from as far as Ore City and Denver watched as I come down. When Dalt handed me a goblet of champagne, I held it high. "To all of you," I said, drinking it down.

One by one my girls started down the stairs. "This is Annie, from Kansas City," I said. As many men as possible gathered around her and she led them into one of the parlors. "This is Charlotte, from Tennessee." The blonde in blue silk come down the stairs all smiles and dimples. She was a fair reminder of Sara, but not near as pretty. She led off a bunch of them fellas, too.

Jenny, Lula Jane, and Virginia come down more slow, being new to their trade in a quality house. Dalt and me had picked them from the saloons in Tempest. The others we sent East for. Dalt said we'd have more in time.

"Let's say hello to all the folks," Dalt said, offering me his arm. He led me down the hall to the office. John Harrington sat at the desk and lifted his hand with a smile as we passed. He surely did look fine dressed in a tailored black suit. John still worked at the piano if he was of a mind, but he was our manager now.

We had two parlors, one done elegant, like the playhouse in Ore City, and the other more like the Placer Saloon, only done up with a polished mahogany bar and brass candle lamps.

Off in the corner of the "ballroom" men with fancy fiddles made music like I'd never heard in Tempest before. My girls danced and laughed and pretty soon was heading for the office, where their customers could pay John for a brass check. Dalt learnt about them checks back East. "The girls can't cheat or get robbed using them," he told me.

Half a dozen rooms beyond the ballroom was for private games or dinners. Downstairs was the liquor stores, kitchens, and rooms for John and the others we needed to run the place. Dalt and me had our apartments in back, nothing fancy, but enough to remind me I was now a rich woman.

Upstairs was ten bedrooms. Dalt had picked the carpets, papers, and drapes since my tastes in colors wasn't so good. It had taken near a month just to carry up all the furniture.

"This place looks right proper," I said, and Dalt give me a little hug.

We'd gotten married in the Silver Star the year before and lived high while the carpenters labored over his dream. I gorged myself on every kind of food Dalt could dream up to buy me and had dresses made by the dozen, only to put them away when I got a little meat on my bones. I had enough silk drawers, camisoles, petticoats, and chemises to fill a room. My corsets was of the finest whalebone and linen, covered with enough lace and ribbon to be worn just by theirselves.

My wedding dress had been a sensation. It even got wrote up in the paper, though the town ladies thought it was a sin. Dalt bought me a diamond necklace and put a band of gold on my finger, so thick and heavy I had to take care I didn't get my other fingers smashed when folks shook my hand.

"Well, look at that," Dalt said as we come out of the ballroom.

"There's Mayor Lewis hisself. Bet I know what he wants. He's even got his fine son-in-law and that sidekick Whitehouse with him. I'd better see to them."

"They mean to close us down the first night!" I said, following Dalt into battle.

"They'll try," Dalt chuckled. "It wouldn't look right to folks if they didn't. I got enough, though, to keep 'em quiet a few more weeks."

Dalt went right up to Jim Lewis who had growed into a stooped old codger and asked him flat out what he wanted. Jim just frowned like always, while Rusty did the talking.

Rusty looked better than ever. That wide jaw was still sharp, and made me remember those long ago days at the Placer Saloon. I caught him watching Annie leading a customer upstairs.

I would've gone on gazing at him forever, except that who should walk out of the office just then but Travis Saunders. He was grinning from the tail-end of a conversation with John.

My blood began to race. I lifted my chin and adjusted my gown so the cut of it would capture his eye. I intended to show him I wasn't the scrawny whore he'd rescued from the Ore City jail no more. I was *madam* of the Mountain Club, Mr. Jack Dalton's respectable wife—or as respectable as I ever cared to get anyhow.

"Mr. Saunders!" I exclaimed, ignoring the others—it always paid to let folks know just who was important. "Whatever brings you here?"

I weren't one for gloating, but when he turned and saw me, I gloated plenty. His eyes didn't pop. His mouth didn't even drop open. I don't suppose nobody knowed he was surprised to see me, but he was. He couldn't find nothing to say right off. And he swallowed, looking a bit off-balance, like the tilt of the floor didn't quite suit him.

I tucked my hand through the crook of his elbow. "Ain't this something? I got all my favorite gentlemen together in one place. Hello there, Jim. I ain't seen you since the rainy night you..."

Jim's face drained. His eyes near to shook in their sockets. He took one step back with his lips twitching. Rusty steadied him.

"How's all them grandchildren? Good God-fearing babies, I'll bet," I said. "And Rusty! How's Effie these days? Have the years been as good to her as you? Why, there you are, Davey! Remember the flowers you used to bring me on Thursday afternoons? Remember?" I didn't mean to go on and on, but I couldn't seem to help myself. "You all know Mr. Travis Saunders, here, don't you? He writes all them newspaper articles. Mr. Saunders, I've always wondered how it is you're always right where the trouble is. Got mystical powers?"

Having found me there, I could almost hear his pen scratching across the paper as he wrote "soiled dove of the West," "lady of the town," or "maid of all pleasures…" to describe me.

"You ain't said hello yet, Mr. Saunders. Run out of words?"

Oh, he could make his eyes hard. "It's nice to see you again, Angel. I understand Jack Dalton is one of the richest gamblers in all of Colorado Territory. I suppose if you can't earn money yourself anymore, it makes good sense to marry it."

With the force of a dynamite blast, Dalt hit him square in the face! Travis staggered back against the front door. Before Dalt could deliver another blow, John grabbed him.

"It's all right," Dalt panted, his face filled with a rage I'd never seen before. "It's my place and I can bust it up if I want. Saunders, if you got business with one of Angel's girls, you can stay. Otherwise, clear out. Get your stories someplace else. You got a nose for blood. I don't need none of it around here. We run a peaceable house. We don't need none of your kind."

Travis picked hisself off the floor, letting the blood from his trouble-hungry nose stream onto his shirt front. Darned if he didn't look dignified even so. "What's the going rate in this place?"

"Five dollars, Mr. Saunders," I said. "Buy your check from Mr. Harrington here and take your pick of my girls. They're the best."

He paid for one of our checks. "Good for one screw" was printed on the back of it. A smile tugged at his lips as he read it and then pressed it into my palm. Something like lightning went up my arm.

"I ain't available, Mr. Saunders, not to you, not 'til God Hisself says to me you're a man worth laying. And since I don't know no such God, I don't expect He'll ever speak to me."

Travis tugged at his coat sleeves and turned toward the door. "You're out of your element here, Angel. You'll never be more than what you were two years ago in the Ore City Jail. Nothing."

"Don't go after him!" I said as Dalt lunged for the closing door. "All he's got is sour guts and them fancy words he throws around." Looking around, I laughed. "Don't everybody spend a day or two in jail? It's a good place to catch up on sleep. And I sure need that! Come on, fellas. The drinks are on the house. Stay as long as you like. We're open all night, and, down here in the trees, won't nobody see what time you head for home come morning."

For a full week we did a booming business. Every night the parlors was full to busting. My girls was up and down them stairs as fast as dressing and undressing would allow. Dalt and me stayed up 'til all hours, drinking with our customers. Then we'd fall into bed with a fearsome weariness pulling at our backs.

On the eighth day of our grand opening I slept straight through 'til ten o'clock that night. When I showed my face in the office Dalt sat propped behind the desk, too tired to even smoke. "Kennings was just by with another warning," he sighed, rubbing his eyes.

"Wants more money, does he?"

"The son of a bitch says the town's in an uproar. They don't want just my hide now. They want yours. I don't know, Angel. The Silver Star wasn't this much trouble. Come here, honey. You look tired."

"I'm plumb wore out and I ain't done more than make fancy talk all week," I said. "Virginia is thinking of quitting. What'll we do?"

"The West is crawling with girls. Give me a kiss, honey. Seems like I never get to see you now that we've opened this place. You still glad you married me, Angel?"

"You know I am. About time, too, considering all we been through."

He smiled a bit and nodded. "Heard more from that woman up the pass? How's the kid?"

"The *kid* is doing just fine. She'll be five come January. Don't that beat all? My little baby, five years old."

"Want to see her some time?"

"Ain't never going to see her," I said.

"Aren't you curious?"

"Don't aggravate me! She's never going to know me."

He slid his arm about my waist. "That can't be easy for you."

"Easiest thing I ever done. One of the few right things, too. I ought to know. I've done a heap of wrong things."

Our conversation fell off after that. We sat thinking, holding hands, and making tired smiles now and again. Dalt looked like he needed a good rest and some of my best loving. I was in the mood for it, too—not a lusting mood, just a need to be close to him and feel good. Our sojourns together had been few and far between since our wedding.

"Let's forget all this and have us a few peaceful hours alone tonight," I said. "I expect John can handle things just fine without us."

A grin spread across Dalt's face. "What you charge, Ma'am?"

"It's on the house. Whatever pleasures you most, that's what I do best." In a minute we was hurrying down the back hall to our rooms, eager as any customer and girl.

"You're still so beautiful," Dalt whispered as we lay entwined, our hearts drumming, our bodies a-gleam with sweat.

"You still got stamina," I laughed softly, though I knew Dalt was trying too hard. The pleasure that had once come so easy to him now ran ahead, taunting him. I did everything possible to bring about his release, but he was just plain tired. He pumped away, his arms trembling, his knees buckling, his face red enough for me to see even in the dark. He seemed about to reach his peak when suddenly he dropped his full weight on me.

I gave a grunt and rolled him onto his back. "Darned if all this high living don't tell on a body," I sighed. "I just ain't no girl no more. I remember when I used to bed ten or twelve a night and afterwards, if the right fella come along, I could go another round."

Dalt lay stiff, his hand clutching mine, his head pressed back into the pillow.

"It's hot in here! I don't know if I can walk to open the window. You really wear a girl out." I finally did roll out of bed and pushed up the sash. Across the way the parlor windows was lit up and smoke spewed from every one. The violin music was fast and lively. Plenty of laughter filled the air. It was for sure our club was a success.

I crawled back into bed and curled against Dalt's side. Running my hand over the curls on his chest, I said, "You was my first man. You're still the best."

I expected that to give him a lift, but still he didn't move. He did seem a bit more relaxed though. I leaned over to kiss his cheek. I lingered there above him, able to see that fine bold face in the dim light from the window. Though I didn't often hear coyotes no more, they was yipping a mournful cry up in the hills. I kissed Dalt's cheek, holding my lips against him a long time, like I couldn't quite pull myself away.

Then I got up. I felt bone weary, dull and heavy as if I'd drunk too much, worked too hard, and lived too long.

I commenced to dressing; first the chemise, then corset and drawers; stockings, garters and shoes; petticoats, bustle, skirts and jacket. It was my best outfit, made special all the way from New Orleans.

The diamond necklace lay like ice about my throat. I brushed my hair loose, and though it was wispy, it still made me look like first-class baggage. I walked to the door and turned the gold knob. "Good night, Dalt. Sleep good. There ain't never going to be nobody else besides you."

I closed the door and walked down the hall toward the music.

The closer I got, the more I hated it. I hated the club, the fancy carpets, crystal candle lamps, and golden frames around paintings of plump, half-dressed ladies.

I found John in the office.

"I thought you and Dalt called it a night," he said, looking up from the ledgers, his face furrowed, his deep black eyes glittery in the lamplight.

My mouth began to twist down. I pushed back my hair, looking all about as if words would come easier if I didn't look John in the eye. Then suddenly a sharp laugh come out of me. "He up and died on me!"

"Who?"

"Just when things was going good for us, his heart quit. It ain't fair. It just ain't fair!"

Twenty-Four

Summer 1874

The narrow gauge steam locomotive chugged up the Buffalo Canyon line, disappeared into a tunnel and come out seconds later, belching white smoke high into the air. "You ought to be on that train," I said to Mr. Travis Saunders who sat by the window, nursing a whiskey. "Ain't some story waiting out there for you?"

Travis went on staring into his whiskey glass. He'd been warming my chairs the better part of the year now. In all that time he hadn't writ a word. He just drank and pestered me. "What time is it?" he mumbled.

"Don't know and don't care," I said. "Go eat something 'fore your insides figure to die on you."

He pushed back his chair and pressed his broad-brimmed hat into place. "I think I will go. I can't stand your nagging."

"Glad to be rid of you!" I laughed. "You're bad for business. Look at yourself. You done made yourself into an old man before your time. I don't know what's so terrible about running out of words. You seen near every tragedy in this territory first hand. You made yourself a name and plenty of money off it. Can't you just put your pen away now?"

"I'm waiting to hear *your* story, Angel. I'll dog your steps 'til you tell it to me."

"I'm a sight younger than you, and I learned a while back a human body can only stand so much pain and abusing, so I'm healthier, too. I'll outlast you just like I done everybody else. You been drinking all day, Travis. Give your gullet a rest and go sleep it off."

"Is this how you nagged Dalton to death?"

I edged up to him real careful and trailed my hand from his cheek to his belly. "I've a mind to punch you," I said through my teeth. "I ain't never heard tell of you writing about something good. All you're good for is causing a body pain. You're a snake and varmint of the worst variety."

"The opinion of a whore always carries weight with me," he muttered.

"I thought name-calling was Mayor Lewis's speciality. It don't bother me after all this time."

"It should."

"You smelly drunkard, you're dirtying up my place. I own this saloon and got the say who stays and who don't. Maybe if I slip Rusty Kennings enough, he might throw you in jail. That would quiet you."

"I've seen jails before."

"Not dry ones. You got a dangerous friend in that whiskey bottle."

"If you really hated me," Travis said, turning and fixing a bloodshot blue eye on me, "you'd hope I'd drink myself to death."

"And if I was so wicked you'd find yourself somewheres else to waste your days. Go, Travis. You weary me."

I went out and watched the night come, while Travis plodded up the walkway toward his boarding house. I'd never seen such hot weather. Not a drop of rain had fallen since spring. Even the winter had been mild, which suited me. Travis Saunders was aggravation enough.

John and me had closed the Mountain Club for a week after Dalt died. I moved out after the funeral and took a room in a small hotel. John took over running the club. Right across from my hotel on the old main street was a little saloon with big front windows and rickety stairs leading to the one sleeping room on the second floor.

One afternoon I went in and bought the place for six hundred cash out of my handbag.

And there I stood, near a year later, watching the sky blaze orange. Jodie's cooking smelled tasty. She was an old whore who couldn't get no work in town 'cause Doc Billy said she had pox. I made her take the cure and, though it didn't make her feel much better, she cooked and swept for me and called her life her own. I liked the salty ol' girl.

A ragged girl lugged a toddler on her hip and picked her way down the rutted street. I knew right off she was headed toward me. She come right up to me, her face set, tears standing on her cheeks. I figured her for some angry wife. "Are you Angel?" she asked. She was smaller than me with lank brown hair and a hollow face. Her baby weren't pretty with health.

I drew her inside. "You got business with me?"

"I need a job real bad," she whispered. "But nobody'll take me with this here child. What kind of town is this? I'll work! I'll work hard. Some fella told me to find Angel. Is that you?"

I escorted her back to the door and hissed, "Come 'round back after dark." Then I gave her a shove. "Don't you come looking for your no-account husband in my place!" I said that loud enough to be heard clear across the street, and a goodly number of folks was watching, too. "Even if he was here, I wouldn't tell you."

Scared and furious, she stared at me and then hurried off. Tempest was a hell of a place to be a lone woman with no money.

An hour later, looking a mite better, Travis showed his face again. "I heard you're throwing young wives out of your place now. Doesn't a woman have the right to find an erring husband?"

"Are you here to drink or talk?"

"I'll have a whiskey, thank you. You could at least be civil to decent women. Or do they make you feel cheap?"

One of my regulars sidled over. "Saunders, you got no call to talk to Miss Angel like that. Want me to throw him out, Ma'am?"

"Don't let it bother you, Willis," I said easily. "Mr. Saunders forgot how to be a gentleman a long time ago. He's so low-down he's got to make sure somebody's always under him, at least in his own estimation. If you wait, you can help Abner carry him out later. Go on now, Willis. Have yourself a beer on me. We're all friends here—leastwise we try to be."

Seeing Jodie motioning to me from the back door, I wandered back that way, laughing a bit with my customers over the local drunk's behavior. Then I slipped into the kitchen.

"That girl's out in the weeds, but she won't come in for me," Jodie whispered, her seamed face puckered into a pout.

I walked out back as far as the privy before I saw her. "Get inside 'fore somebody sees you! If folks think you're looking for work whoring, that'll do you for all time," I said, hurrying her into my spare room. "If they figure you've been deserted by a no-good husband, they'll take to you just fine."

Jodie brung food, put water to boil, and lugged the bathing tub inside. Starving miners, a whole family of penniless Chinees and a half-Injun whore from El Dorado City had all slept in my spare room at one time or another over the past year. "Where you from?" I asked, as the girl chewed meat and biscuits and fed them to her baby.

"My people settled down in Little London. I got mixed up with a fella who left me to go prospecting. When I started to show I lit out and got a job caring for some widow-man's children. He wanted to marry me, but I didn't want to be nursemaid to them children forever."

"You don't want to work in no saloon, neither."

She pushed back her dirty hair. "It seemed like the only thing left."

"Plenty of men in this town will take to you if you give 'em half a chance. Don't tell nobody else what you just told me. You can sleep here 'til you get set somewheres. Take what you need as long as you need it. Door's always open."

"I might not be able to repay you," she said.

"I don't expect nothing."

She was starting to protest when her eyes jerked to the doorway behind me. Travis stood there grinning. "I'd heard rumors about your back door."

"Knowing you," I said, shoving him out, "you figured me to be working on my back far into the night. Go back to your bottle. If you say anything about this, I'll have your tongue. I might even shoot you."

"I'll bet you would," Travis laughed. "You don't fool me, Angel. I know just what you're trying to do."

"Good. Then, come morning, I can count on you to hunt her up a job and get one of your respectable friends to take her in."

"I'll be busy with Founder's Day tomorrow."

I made sure Travis went all the way back to his spot by the window. "What the hell is that?"

"Didn't you know? Tempest officially becomes Buffalo Falls tomorrow. On the pavilion across from the Silver Star, the mayor will give a speech. Even the territorial governor will be in on the afternoon train. There'll be picnics and racing, prizes for the children, and ribbons for the best baked pies. The whole town will be there. No, Angel, tomorrow is no day for me to be placing waifs and orphans."

"Got yourself a fancy article to write, I suspect. Got to hob-nob with the governor and get yourself drunk in front of everybody."

He grinned. "Too bad you can't go, Angel. I'd offer you a ride."

"Oh, I'd be there if I wanted. Ain't I the wife of one of the founders? But I wouldn't want to be seen with the town drunk. Might give me a bad name."

Travis stood, his mouth set hard. "You'd best take care who you rub the wrong way, Mrs. Dalton." And he left me in peace the rest of the night.

"Jodie's going to ride you over to the picnic grounds," I told Carrie Baxter, my latest secret lodger, next morning. She looked right pretty, in a poorly sort of way, wearing my oldest traveling skirt and jacket.

"This isn't going to work," Carrie whined, fussing with an old bonnet I give her. "Everybody'll know I was here all night."

Jodie come in dressed in her best, which weren't much. "Did you finish all them pies already, Angel?" she asked, looking over the assortment cooling on the sills. "Folks ain't going to believe I baked all that."

"It don't matter. It just gives you a good reason to go to the picnic. Take them along now, Carrie, and see to that tasting contest. I don't expect they'll win anything, but them fellas who like home cooking will remember you. Get along now. Remember, you're Jodie's niece just in from Missouri."

Carrie's little daughter Janie looked a sight better dressed and fed proper, but she was a dull little thing with hardly enough meat on her to keep her alive. A chill went up my back as I watched Carrie take her out to the wagon. My Lillie could've looked like that.

I hadn't heard how Lillie was getting along since I told Gwenity to stop writing. Too much pain went along with her letters and, besides, I didn't want nobody at the post office getting suspicious. I wasn't the first whore to be hiding a child somewheres.

Long about noon, after I'd had a bit of a nap, I stepped out on the stairs landing and looked across the canyon. I couldn't see nothing of the picnic, but fancied I heard cheers. I thought on going up there in Dalt's fine carriage to show off my matched horses, fine clothes, and diamonds, but the day was too pretty to spoil. I'd growed weary of folks' low opinion of me anyway. I didn't see them helping strangers who was down on their luck. Like as not, they'd just kick 'em lower.

Later that day when my customers trooped in, I had beans and biscuits warming for them. The place lay quiet as a sick dog without Travis around aggravating me. Darned if I didn't miss him sometimes, though when he did show his face I wished he'd just stayed away after all.

"I couldn't eat another bite," Travis groaned when I offered him a biscuit. "The ladies elected me judge of the pie baking contest!"

"Much in the way of baking there?" I asked.

"You've never seen so many women hoping you'll choose their pie as best," he said.

"No, that ain't been one of my bigger problems."

"Hardest job I ever had. It was nice of your cook to help that …" He lowered his voice to my warning look. "I gave one of her pies second place. Carrie claimed it was hers and folks thought it was nice Jodie let on it was, too."

"I'm glad to see you didn't drink yourself ugly. Folks got a lot of respect for you."

He laughed. "Jim Lewis made quite a speech. He described how the canyon looked the first year he settled and emphasized the importance of establishing a decent, law-abiding community here at the gateway to the Rockies, where the buffalo used to roam. All his talk on driving out every painted lady, gambler, and claim jumper got everybody pretty excited. Strong stuff from a man boiling in his Sunday best. I expect him and Rusty'll want a handsome price to let you stay open."

"I wish you'd write them up," I cried. "What happened to the fella who tore apart Mr. Hannable Sheever's career 'cause he wasn't suited to government? Jim and Rusty are no better."

"I realized one day my articles did no more than sell newspapers," Travis sighed. "I doubt I'll ever write again."

"I'd sure like to set things straight in this town. Don't know why I stay. I got enough money I could go anyplace."

"Planning to disappear into the night like you did last time?"

"Might. Ain't a soul here who'd care. Nobody thinks on my feelings, least of all you, drunkard that you are."

"How come you don't call Rusty your pretty names! He was so drunk today Jim sent him home. There's a belligerent son of a bitch. He tried to lock up everybody."

"How'd Effie like that?" I giggled. "I ain't seen her but once when she was coming out of Doc's, and then she wouldn't even look at me."

"She's confined again."

"That must make six at least!" I cried, though Travis didn't seem to see nothing important about birthing that many babies unless it took place out under a rock during an Injun raid.

It was about four that morning when I woke to a knock at my door. "Who's out there?" I whispered, pulling my pistol from under my pillow.

"Let me in before somebody sees me!" Rusty slipped in when I unbolted my door and stood in a shadow, watching the street below. He smelled so high of liquor I would've taken him for Travis in the dark. He laid his head back on the door and drew a ragged breath. "Can I trust you?"

"More than I can trust you, I expect. I paid all I'm going to this month. So, if you want to close me down, do it. This town's wearing on me."

"I've got to have your word you won't tell anybody about this. I need your help."

"What kind of trick are you pulling?" I hissed. "Why should I help you?"

"No trick, Angel. She's dying, and I can't think of anybody but you to help. Everybody knows you can keep a secret."

"Yep, I got so many secrets in me I hardly fit in my corset," I snapped. "Who's dying?"

"Effie."

I dressed quick and followed Rusty to his horse. He lived across the canyon behind the Silver Star. I didn't know what the hell I was doing, riding off into the night to help a woman who'd hated me from the day we set eyes on each other. Still, I held tight to Rusty's back and, as he rode, I tried to keep my pistol from banging too hard against my leg. I'd hid it in my skirt pocket. I weren't no fool.

Rusty brought his horse to a teeth-jarring halt at the porch and dragged me down. The house was tall and pretentious with fancy window trim and a round copula on the left. He pushed open his front door and let me into a house as dark as a grave. Upstairs, a skinny boy stood in the shadows. "Todd, get back to your room," Rusty hissed.

I stopped and stared. Had I been in the mountains so long Effie's first born was near as tall as me? Another couple years he'd be drinking in my saloon!

"In here," Rusty said, pushing me into a dark sleeping room. "I said, get back to bed!" Rusty yelled again and, when he turned, Todd shrank from him and shut hisself in another room full of weeping children.

"For pity's sake, light a lamp," I said, leaning over the body in the fancy four poster. "Effie? Can you hear me?"

Rusty brought a lamp near, though he kept the wick so low I could hardly see. "It's hives," he whispered when I gasped at the sight of Effie's face.

"It ain't no goddamned hives!"

Effie pulled the sheet over her face and rolled away.

"Rags," she moaned. "More rags."

"You done this!" I said, shaking my finger at Rusty.

"Keep your voice down. I was drunk. Can you help her?"

"Why don't you help her first off by not beating her?"

His lips drew back over his teeth 'til that fine face I'd always admired turned ugly as a timberwolf's. "I brought you here to help her. Now, help her!" He raised his fist.

Though my belly had turned sour, I stood fast. "I got a mighty lot of customers who'd sure be curious if I showed up with a face like hers this evening."

"What makes you think you'll leave if you don't help?" Rusty smiled. "I can't kill her, but I'd take pleasure killing you. Would you like to know how I'd do it?"

I couldn't get a deep breath. "Them things Marie used to say about you was true!" I whispered. "You are an Injun killer, a squaw killer! You was with that regiment years ago. Marie once told me you claimed to have cut up squaws and that you carried the pieces about with you. You took your pleasure with Marie, remembering what you'd done. I didn't believe it!"

He grabbed my throat and pressed his thumbs into it. "Think your boy will...sleep through digging two graves?" I croaked.

Rusty shoved me against his wife's bed. "If she dies, you die. I'll kill you the way I killed those squaw whores."

I pulled free and turned to Effie's ashen face. "Fetch more rags," I said, reaching under the bedcovers to see what was ailing her. I pulled out my hand bloody to the wrist and thrust it in Rusty's face. I shook it 'til thick red drops hit his cheeks. His nose flared and he backed out.

"He done this, didn't he?" I whispered, pulling up Effie's nightdress and wiping her legs with the embroidered coverlet. "Look here, the bleeding's let up. You ain't dying on me, Effie. You ain't dying."

"I won't die and not because of you. It's just a miscarriage," she hissed. "I won't leave my children to him."

"Next time he lays a hand on you," I said, shaking, "kill him."

She coughed like she was laughing. "Let up on me there, Angie. That hurts."

"Why don't you tell folks about this instead of hiding?"

"Who would I tell?"

"Your high and mighty pa, for one. He'd kill Rusty sure if he could see you right now. I'll bring him 'round myself."

"Pa's old, and he's been sick. Leave him be. Sh-h-h. Here comes Rusty."

By late morning I had Effie sleeping in a fresh, dry bed. Considering how much blood she'd lost, it was a wonder she was alive. She twitched in her sleep—from pain, I guess. Rusty must've beat her good and often to account for all them bruises I saw when changing her nightdress.

"If she's better," Rusty said, coming up silent and scaring me, "I'll take you back."

"Not in daylight, you won't," I said, spreading my skirts for him to see the blood stains. "One way or another, you're paying for this. Effie ain't deserving such a life."

"She's an ugly shrew, and I never did want her."

"Then leave her! You can't hide something like this forever." As one of his hands curled into a fist, I pulled myself out of the chair, walked right up to him and stared into his eyes. "It's time you started paying me, Sheriff Kennings. I ain't got enough whore's honor to keep quiet about this, but you know whores—they'll do anything for money. So you pay me as generous as I've paid you and I'll forget about Effie and this here hell hole. I'll forget all about them Injun squaws you mutilated, though that'd make mighty fine reading for all your friends. You know what a good friend Mr. Travis Saunders is to me."

"Instead of all that, I'm just going to kill you," he smiled. When I didn't cringe, his smile faded. "Aren't you afraid?"

"Some. Only killing me ain't going to be near as easy as you think. I'll take a good piece of you with me when I go." With my hand in my pocket, I nudged my pistol into his crotch. "Git on out of this room 'fore I send you to hell right now."

I sat with Effie all day 'til she come around and took some broth. Her daughter, who was eleven or so and looked the spit 'n' image of Cornelia, come in to tend her. They had a Chinee cook, too, so I wasn't needed no more. After dark Rusty took me back to my place with no trouble.

Letting myself into my room, I sagged against the table just inside the door. I felt so old and tired I wanted to sleep forever.

"I thought you left," come a voice in the darkness. I whirled and my back slammed against the door. "Who let you in?"

"The door was open. Aren't your doors always open? I should call you the prostitute philanthropist. Tempest's own angel of mercy. Where have you been?" Travis said low. As he rose from my easy chair by the window the planes of his face gleamed in the stifling heat. He come 'round my bed slow, like he was trying to unnerve me.

"Get out of here and don't never come back!" I cried. "I ain't got the belly for you no more!"

"Who were you with?"

"Ain't I got money enough that I got to keep whoring? Ain't it never occurred to you I do something other than open my legs? What's grieving you is I ain't never opened them to you and ain't likely to."

"You flatter yourself, Angel."

"Then what're you doing up here? This is my place and I don't invite nobody in."

"Jodie thought you might be sick." He come face to face with me. "I was worried. Once before you took off after I said something stupid."

I laughed. "I *figured* you was hanging around for a reason. I still ain't available, Mr. Saunders. You ought to get your money back for that brass check."

His hands closed around my arms and he tried to pull me close. "You're trembling. I won't hurt you."

"You can't hurt me. Don't knock at my door again 'cause I'm liable just to shoot you and be done with it."

He shook me. Then, suddenly, he pulled. I fell against him. My arms went about him and I held tight. I turned my face up just so my cheek could touch his, just so I could smell his skin. He pressed his lips to mine and left me breathless.

I let him kiss me again 'cause it had been so long since I'd been held and I was so damned scared. When he let go, my arms fell at my sides. I felt drained and stumbled to my bed. "If I could tell you where I was tonight, I would, but I gave my word and I'd like to think it's worth something."

Travis lit my lamp and crouched before me. His eyes was clear. His breath didn't reek of liquor. When he discovered the blood on my skirt he didn't say nothing. He just pressed me back 'til I was stretched out on my tick. Then he dimmed the lamp and turned toward the door.

Travis watched as I pulled my pistol from my skirt pocket and dropped it on the table. Then he went out and closed the door. I turned on my side and pressed my face into the pillow. Of all the men who'd ever held me...

Twenty-Five

Spring 1875

"The drought's killing this town," Abner said, wiping the bar. He'd wiped it so often that afternoon the dust hadn't had time to settle. "These mountains is tinder dry. We're liable to go up in flames any day."

"Nice thought, Abner," I laughed, sitting there with my legs showing up past my knees, fanning myself with my skirt. "Ain't enough business to keep a body alive these days. I thought changing the name of this no-account town was supposed to transform it into a booming paradise."

"Everybody's up in Ore City these days. There's more silver there than we ever had. Tempest is dying."

"I don't like seeing it happen." I wiped at a dribble of sweat running down my neck. "Where's Travis? I ain't seen him all day. Ain't it something how you can miss a body even when they grate on you?"

Abner rubbed at his side whiskers like he was wondering how much he could say 'fore I'd take offense. "I think the Savage has looked for trouble so long he's finally found it."

"Whiskey'll do it. He sure ain't getting no hot stories in this town," I said. "No brawls or gunfighting. Ain't had a good claim-jumping in a year. Last trouble we had was when them renegades shot up the place. Remember? Shot out both my windows. Damn near got you."

They had been the same ones who robbed the Georgia bitch. The fall before they'd taken a stage at the pass and killed the driver, a family man from El Dorado. After they shot up Tempest, rampaged up the pass and set fire to a store in Cold Water, they robbed the bank in Eagleton, held up half a dozen more settlers, and looted Waverly after it burned.

"Did you hear they got caught? Sheriff Kennings is bringing them back to our fine jail to wait trial. We're liable to have a hanging." Abner kept polishing my bar. "That'll step up business."

"Just what we need. Who's that coming in? Hey, Doc! Ain't seen you in a while. Got yourself a thirst? Good weather for it."

Doc Billy looked mighty distinguished in black coattails, a turquoise bolo, and shiny new boots. "Just a beer, Angel. I'm on my way up to the Kenningses' to check on Jim."

"How's he doing these days?"

"He's talking better since the stroke, but he won't be able to walk without help anymore. I figure that's the end of being mayor for him. Rusty's already talking of taking his place."

"Rusty ain't fit," I said, sitting across from Doc.

"I didn't come all this way just to talk politics. How you and Saunders getting on these days?"

"Same as usual. Like two mules."

"You got much feeling for him, deep down?" Doc curled his clean fingers around one of Abner's polished glasses.

I stared out my window at the heat waves rising off the dusty street. "He's a hard man to like. I ain't taken a man to my bed, paying customer or otherwise, since I married Dalt but Travis still calls me a whore. Can I care much for an ornery cuss like that?"

Billy took off his spectacles and peered at me through one lens. "Perly Thompson wanted me to check on Travis earlier today. Seems one of her lodgers complained about the noise he was making. He's locked hisself in his room."

"The only noise Travis makes is swallowing," I sniffed.

"I wouldn't stick my nose in where it's not wanted, though I suppose I do sometimes," Billy said. "I know a lot about folks and their problems, though, and like to help."

If he knew so much, how come he didn't do something about Effie?

A gust of wind scattered papers and dust across my floor. Abner took up the broom. Suddenly a man come in, squinting from the sun and swept off his hat. "Sheriff Kennings is back with them renegades, Doc. One's beat up pretty bad." The deputy bolted out holding his hat against the wind.

Getting up, Billy said, "You might look in on Travis. He'll have my hide for saying this, but he needs you."

The only men who ever *needed* me had paid me, I thought disgustedly. Like an ache, though, them words stayed with me long after Doc left and I'd eaten supper and settled my few customers at their tables. That Saunders who'd learned his letters on the ruler-edged knee of a tutor, who had gold stamped papers from universities, and knew politics, religions, and words I'd never understand, couldn't need the likes of me.

I went out back and looked across the canyon at the dry sage rustling in the wind. The pianos rattled softer than the old days. The laughter never got as high 'cause the stakes wasn't what they used to be. Even so, I stayed in Tempest 'cause I couldn't get no closer to the Calico Inn and wouldn't move no farther from it. Tempest had become a dull place full of respectable folks. Their hate for me grew more painful each year. I wondered how many folks knew, or cared, I was now the richest woman in town.

Travis lived in his boarding house and took his meals at various restaurants or homes of certain genteel folks who thought theirselves important, but he hung around me 'cause I might make a story good enough to rekindle his writing habit. I'd been telling myself that long enough anyway.

Upstairs, I changed into an old calico. Couldn't call on Travis in business clothes, though his reputation wouldn't have suffered none. Men was entitled to their vices. Travis could drink enough to melt gold with his breath and still folks would talk on him like he was a president or king—Mr. Saunders this, Mr. Saunders that…

How come you wasn't up in Leadville for the boom…Where's your articles on cheats, charlatans, massacres, and the general state of troubles in Colorado Territory…

Suppose ol' Savage Saunders sent Billy to fetch me. He'd kissed me a good many times. One time as he held me, he whispered, "Whoring has turned you cold, hasn't it?" But even a challenge like that hadn't gotten me into bed. Not insults, not blows, not silver or gold would ever get me into bed with a man again. Widows, virgins, and old maid spinsters I didn't know; but old whores, we was beyond temptation!

"I heard Travis is sick or something."

Perly Thompson was dozing behind her desk. She blinked and straightened, wiping sweat from her brow. "Something's wrong. Ever since that telegram…"

"Bad news?"

"Must've been. About an hour later I thought he was having a fight, except he was all by hisself. I sent for Doc, but he couldn't get a grunt out of Travis. I'll get my keys." Perly rustled up behind me. "If it was anybody else but you, Angel, I wouldn't do this, you understand."

"Chances are he'll throw me out anyway," I said. The smell of smoke and liquor rolled out to smart my eyes as his door creaked open. Travis lay sprawled across his bed in his stocking feet, his shirt open, his mouth gaping. "Could I trouble you for coffee later?" I asked Perly.

She made a disgusted face. "I'll bring it up before I turn in."

I flung the windows wide to the hot night air. Travis had broke a chair across the dresser and smashed his wash pitcher, but otherwise the room was in one piece. I picked up his good hat, his polished boots and found the crumpled telegram paper on the floor.

"What the hell are you doing here?" Travis muttered as he sat up and squinted at me. He slid off the bed and stood careful, like he didn't trust the floor.

"Perly's bringing coffee."

He ignored me and took up a bottle from the bookcase, drinking long throat-stretching gulps.

"Got a good suit of clothes hereabouts?"

"I'm in no shape to go anywhere," he said.

"Should I order up a standard pine box then, or one a bit longer?"

"This stuff won't kill me. I've tried."

"It's after you've sobered up and decided to give life one more try that it hits you. What's wrong with you today?"

"It's there in your hand."

"I can't read it."

"Then you'll never know my secret just as I'll never know yours."

"If I told you my so-called secrets, would you stop calling me whore?"

"I don't call you that!" He put the bottle down.

"Once a day for over two years you've called me dirt in one way or another. Sometimes when you're sober and lonely you kiss me, but when you've had enough to loosen your tongue, it always comes to that. It galls you I ain't pure."

"I'm supposed to close my eyes and say, go in peace, I forgive?"

"I don't want, or need, your damn forgiveness! If I was smarter I'd know why you're still coming to my place, calling me names and inviting yourself up Sunday afternoons for supper at my table."

"Go away."

"Is it 'cause you need me, Travis?"

"A slip of a thing like you?" he laughed. "You don't know how many men you've had. You couldn't count that high! I visit your fine drinking establishment out of pure curiosity. I only want to understand you."

"You shouldn't need to. Others have taken me for what I am. I think fondly on them."

"Not me?" He looked hurt.

"Nope. I don't care to be judged by the Savage."

"Then leave me to drink myself to death. You can shake your head over my grave."

Why not, I asked myself, or did I want him to think me worthy of his caring? I lowered my eyes. I already knew Travis's judgment of me. If I'd been decent, I would've killed myself rather than become a whore. Honor or death, them was respectable values. All I had was a working girl's values. Virtue was for fools, like love and dreams. "You don't need me, Travis," I said, turning to take my leave. "All you need is yourself."

He grabbed my arm. "You talk mighty high, Mrs. Dalton. Do you practice what you preach? Do you take me for what I am? No judgments?"

"I don't put myself above nobody but liars and hypocrites."

"Then I have good cause for drinking, because I, dear Angel, am a hypocrite of the highest order. I am a liar." With great ceremony he took the telegram from me and smoothed out the wrinkles. "Before you go, I'd like your crudely innocent opinion of this."

"Keep it to yourself. I got enough sorrows."

"I need to tell someone…someone I can…trust."

A trembling started in my toes and went up through my legs and belly to my heart. Oh, he was clever with words! I think I would've bedded him just for that, for trust.

Travis cleared his throat and straightened his back like a politician readying for a speech. His face grew long and grim. Then, by thunder, he started crying! *"To Mr. Travis Saunders, Tempest, Colorado Territory, from Charles Peterson, director, Abingdale State Asylum, Abingdale, New York. Dear Mr. Saunders: Regret to inform you of Elizabeth Saunders's passing on May 18, 1875. Condolences…"*

Travis took a breath that come out like a sob. The paper fell from his hand. He grabbed the edge of the bureau and sank to his knees. I crept up behind him and touched his shoulder. He fell hard to the floor and bent over 'til his forehead struck the drawer pull. I put my arms around him.

He seized my hands and pulled me to the floor with him. "Do you know who killed her? I killed her. I wouldn't go see her.

I couldn't. I was a coward. I couldn't look at her. I got sick to my stomach and couldn't go. She died alone, year after year, and still I didn't go. Now she's in the ground. No one will ever see her face again—except me. That face will haunt me. I'll die with it burned on my eyes. I should have comforted her, but couldn't even do that. I've seen slaughtered families, mutilated Indians, babies dead of fever, every form of horror and death imaginable, but her face will follow me to my grave. No amount of whiskey blots it out."

I pulled him tight against my bosom 'til his tears soaked through my dress to burn my skin. I knew such pain, but Travis never had. He'd never let hisself face it. For that, he was weak and helpless, a step from his yawning grave.

"She was so good," he wept. "They came west with the first immigrants—before the gold in California. I was twelve."

"Your mother?" I breathed.

"I saw an arrow sink into my father's chest and watched him die. I heard her screams and could do nothing. God, forgive me, I couldn't save her! They threw her across a pony, like so much chattel, and rode off. They took three women into the hills, white legs kicking, prayers to a deaf God. I lay under a blanket stupid with fear."

"But she escaped."

"She was rescued. One woman had died. Another had a child; the rescuers left her behind. My mother they saved. I was seventeen when they brought her back. I had been in school; I was raised by my grandfather. I had wanted to find her. When they told me, I went to see her. They sent me into her room without warning me, and I screamed. I was seventeen years old, and I screamed. I never went again. Not in all these years. I sent money. I wrote letters. I tried to find a story worse than hers—and failed."

"It wasn't your fault!"

"But she was my mother! She died alone, in an asylum. If I was a man, I would've gone to see her no matter how she looked."

"Did they scalp her? I've heard tell of folks surviving it."

He was long in answering. Chills danced along my backbone as

I waited. "The squaws, they tell me, were jealous." He sounded as if his belly was crawling in his throat. "They cut off her lips."

I seized Travis and rocked him against my bosom. I saw into his soul and knew, here was a man no stronger than his sharpest words. I wanted to soak up his pain and free him of it, 'cause I knew I had the guts for it. I kissed his tears and held him and cried. After a time I think he slept.

Twenty-Six

Late Summer 1875

"What do you want?" Sheriff Rusty Kennings asked, coming out of his jailhouse and propping his boot on the iron fence. His eyes looked narrower and meaner than ever.

"I come to see Pike," I said, stepping down from my buggy. "I'll strip down if you want to search for weapons." I smiled a bit, though my mouth was sour. I'd tucked my silver-handled derringer in my sleeve, figuring if Rusty did search me, he'd never think to look there. Abner had given me the little pistol after vigilantes tried burning my place earlier that spring.

"No visitors," Rusty snapped. "Pike Johnsie's a condemned man, and I'm fixing to hang him first thing Monday morning."

"I never heard of a prisoner so dangerous he couldn't even have visitors. Leastways, Doc Billy says he ain't dangerous. How is it Pike's so poorly?" I asked. "Maybe bruises and broke ribs is his ailment. Do folks know how you treat prisoners...and your wife?"

"Johnsie's a thief and killer. A breed, too. That doesn't leave him much in the way of human rights." His eyes flashed ugly as he stepped aside and let me in. "Johnsie," he shouted. "You got a caller."

Pike looked up from the cot in his eight-by-eight cell. His hair was long and ragged. He could've been wearing the same buckskins I'd seen on him last. Welts and bruises twisted his face. His wrists was raw and leg irons kept him close to the cot. The past fifteen years reflected in his bottomless black eyes.

I grabbed the thick black bars between us, forcing myself not to scream. I'd been such a fool! I didn't know right from wrong, good from bad, easy from hard. Why had I let him go? Was anything I did right?

"Can we be alone?" I asked, expecting only a mean laugh from Rusty.

"I don't care if you lay together. Just quit plaguing me with your threats." Rusty took his rifle and stalked out.

The jailhouse fell so quiet I could hear the creek rushing a hundred yards away. "Did you do them things they claimed at the trial?" I asked.

Pike stared empty-eyed at the wall. "Some."

"It don't matter. I'll get you another lawyer." My throat thickened, though I'd sworn I wouldn't cry. "I won't see you hanged!"

"I heard you're a whore."

"I don't work no more," I said. "My looks went, my health. Now I run a saloon."

"Why'd you do such a thing?" His voice was soft and angry.

"I had to! You was raised up proper. Why'd you go bad? Was it 'cause of me?"

Pike smiled. "To be honest, Angie, I'd forgotten you. The judge said because I had loyalties to no race he sentenced me to hang instead of shutting me away to rot like the other two. He's right." He chuckled, but winced and held his ribs. "After the massacre I hated whites. I would've killed you or anybody. I was Indian then, not breed. My world was straight. When the bounty hunters got too close I went up and settled with Pa, took a wife, made a child…" He swallowed and studied his hands. "Pa was selling off the supplies. One day while I was hunting, the Utes took care of him. Only they killed her, too, emptied her of my child. What was I to do then? Cut my hair and pray to a white God again?" Pike made two very white, very tight fists. "After that I accepted what I was and I accept what's happening now."

"But I can help! The judge was wrong!"

"Leave me be, Angie. The breed boy you knew fifteen years ago is gone."

"I can't watch you hang!"

Pike pushed hisself to his feet. Without wincing, he dragged the cot after him with the leg irons. He stuck his nose between the bars and looked at me, first with one bruised eye, then the other. "I'm glad I saw you once more."

I pressed my lips against his 'til the bars bit my cheekbones. Then I pulled away, arching my head to hold back the tears. "This ain't right!" I'd expected to hatch a scheme with him to escape, but what could I do if he didn't want help? When I looked, he was smiling.

"Good-bye, Angie. Take care of yourself."

I tumbled out the door into sunshine so hot it pained my eyes. My tears dammed in my throat, solid and cold. Rusty smirked at me like a low-minded greenhorn kid. How I hated him! I hated his face, his smile, the cruel streak that lit his eyes with a wicked fire.

I threw myself into my buggy and lashed the unsuspecting horse so hard he near to pulled me into the creek. Rusty's laughter followed me all the way back to my saloon. Once in my room I felt smothered and crazy. The good was bad. The bad was good. Nothing made sense!

I heard Travis tramping up my stairs. "I saw your rig, Angel…" He paused in the doorway, a cheroot hanging from his lip, his smile fading behind a curl of smoke. "Thought you might be hungry."

"Pike don't want my help!" I felt so hot I thought I was dying. I began tearing at my clothes. "Rusty's still going to hang him!"

Travis come in and shut my door behind him.

As I tore open the buttons of my blouse and pulled my skirts up to kick my shoes at the walls, I felt like screaming. "I could've married Pike! All these years I could've been respectable and had friends and neighbors coming to me for help. Instead, I came here. All I've ever wanted was to be good. I was once, too. I had a family, a home. When I lost that I didn't want to go back to whoring, but I did 'cause I had to. Travis, get away from me. You muddle me."

Travis came 'round to where he could look close at my face. "I've waited years to see you like this, Angel. Since I got you out of the Ore City jail, since that night I got the telegram, I've waited." He took me in his arms.

I pushed him away. "Have you forgotten I'll never be good enough for you?"

His face hardened. "That's not it at all! You don't think I'm good enough for you. You don't trust anyone."

I pulled down my stockings and threw a ruffled garter at him. "Git out of here."

"You don't even trust yourself," he said.

"Who else can I trust, if not my own self?"

"I don't know. Everything you believe in is backwards. You won't let me love you because once I hurt you, but I know you want me just as I want you. I understand, Angel. I've wanted you so much I couldn't stomach myself for being such a fool. I want you because you're soft and giving and beautiful."

"If you're done speechifying, I'd like to take a bath. I'm clearing out. I ain't watching Pike get hisself hanged. I'm sick of this town and its holy joes and nose-in-the-air women. I'm sick of you and the way you muddle my head. Did you ever figure I don't welcome you to my bed 'cause I'm sick of bedding, or maybe 'cause I'm being true to a man who took me in when I needed him?"

"Dalton? You married his money."

I reared up and struck Travis full in the face! It felt so darn good I swung again and, 'fore I knew it, I was raining my hate on his chest. "You dirty snake! Everything else is spoiled, but you're not spoiling that."

Travis pinned my arms. "I'm sorry, Angel. I never believed you cared for that old man. Stop crying. If you loved Dalton, I admire you for it. He was lucky. The only woman who ever loved me was my mother. I betrayed her."

"I got no more sympathy for you! You're a mean snake and you deserve to rot with the rest. I hate you all."

Travis held me tighter. "I've been back at writing a few weeks, working on my mother's story though I never thought I could do it. Would it help if I wrote up Pike's story?"

I slumped against his chest and didn't really care if he tried. It was enough he wanted to.

By Sunday I was packed and ready to go. After giving Abner my saloon and John the deed to the Mountain Club, I went to the bank and collected cash and drafts enough to see me all the way East. I would've gone, too, if I could've got my buggy free of the snarl of rigs around my place.

Every person for a hundred miles around with an itch to see a hanging had come to Tempest. They wasn't desperadoes and loose women, either. They was families—sober men and sweet-faced women with babes and children, sunburnt and excited. Customers packed my saloon to the walls. Jodie had gone to the wholesalers for more stock, but wasn't likely to find much left. The town was crazy, worse than Founder's Day and Independence Day put together—all for the hanging of a breed renegade.

Travis had closed hisself in his room two days to write up a fiery article to save Pike's neck. I seen him run some papers over to the newspaper office earlier that day. Now three boys was hawking them up and down the street. Travis was at the telegraph office, sending back and forth with the governor.

I was just saying my good-byes when Travis come into my place, his face hang-dog. "The telegraph just went dead. Somebody cut the line. I won't be able to get through to Denver again."

I sank back into a chair. "Maybe if I told what I know about Rusty..."

"That wouldn't change the fact that Pike Johnsie's guilty of murder and has to hang." Travis touched my hand. "There's nothing more we can do. My article just fanned everybody's excitement. A train's leaving soon. Let's be on it."

I figured I couldn't rightly leave town with Pike still in jail. So after a good deal of arguing, Travis and me decided to spend the night at the Mountain Club.

All that night I tried to think of some way to help Pike, but as the sky grew pale with dawn, I knew Pike was going to die. No amount of whiskey could save me from it.

"Go rest," Travis said, watching me drink from a glass that near to rattled in my hand. "I'll wake you in time to get to the depot."

"It weren't right to kill that stage driver or rob them banks," I said, having thought it over a thousand times. "But I just don't see that hanging Pike is going to set it all straight. We got to get back to town, Travis. There's got to be something I can do!"

"It's no use!"

"I ought to be there at least. Don't you think I should?" I cried.

"We should catch the ten-thirty to Silverton."

I rubbed my burning eyes, knowing it was hopeless. "I'll drive myself back then. If Pike's got to die, at least he can be looking at me when Rusty pulls the lever."

Around each bend for as far as the eye could see, rigs and teams choked the canyon road. "We'll have to walk," I said to Travis as I climbed down.

"Be careful," Travis said. "I'll stay with the buggy and meet you later."

A quarter mile up, I met a man on a saddle horse. "You got a powerful need to see that hanging, mister?" I hollered.

"That renegade put a bullet in my leg a couple years back." He jerked his hat brim lower and urged his horse around a wagon and eight-mule team.

"A hundred dollars would buy your horse easy," I said, panting, cussing my corset, swearing I'd never again wear heeled shoes.

"Would, at that."

"Two hundred would get you down off him right now."

He reined and stared down at me, his lower lip pink and wet

like Judd's used to be. I handed him two greenback bills marked a hundred each, and he swung down.

"You can buy my rig, little lady," a grimy-eyed muleteer behind me called over a chaw.

In good time I was looking on the church steeple a-ringing loud and cheerful in the morning sun. Wagons and buckboards stood everywhere. Some folks was still at their campfires. The smell of coffee watered my mouth and shamed me for even thinking about food.

I maneuvered that horse as far as the old main street. Up past Smith's livery the jail sat proud and ugly. I could picture Pike in there, drinking his last cup of coffee. The boy who'd lived in the mountains, trapping and hunting to stay clear of folks, was soon to be Tempest's main attraction for the day.

My heart beat unsteady and hard as I prodded the horse through the crowds. I got as far as the back fence of the livery and then couldn't go no farther. I could see the jail plain from there and the buckboard standing out front. Afar off in a field of yellow grass stood the gallows. A short ways beyond that was the graveyard. They wouldn't have to carry Pike far.

Up by the gallows Doc Billy paced. Jim Lewis sat close by in his chair with wheels. Effie with all her children, from fifteen-year-old Todd on down to her newest little one, sat in a surrey-topped carriage close enough to hear Pike's neck snap.

I climbed down from the horse and pressed through the crowd. I near to smothered between those folks straining for a good spot where they wouldn't miss a bit of the show. Elbowing a few steps closer, I could see the shadows inside the jail, moving about. Suddenly the door opened. The sun caught Rusty's gold hair as he stepped out. Pike's hair gleamed blue and snapped black as agate as he followed, still in irons.

A couple men ahead of me turned and stared at me funny. I was screeching, shaking my fists, kicking and shoving to get closer, trying to touch the man who'd first touched me, to comfort one who'd once comforted me.

Oh, but Pike's face was hard. His eyes was empty as a mine shaft. And angles of his face looked like they was carved of Pikes Peak granite, not so red as they used to be, more raw, the color of Colorado Territory dirt or pale blood—the color of an Injun already turned ghost.

When Pike caught sight of me, Rusty did, too, and his face twisted as if his belly hurt. He pushed Pike onto the buckboard and the crowd began to hum like a riled bee swarm and growl low in its animal throat like a timberwolf smelling prey.

Eyes strained to see Rusty lay on the whip and turn his rig toward the gallows. When he reached the pine platform he spoke to a man nearby, and that man went running up the trail to the graveyard. Checking on the grave, I figured. Rusty steered his prisoner toward the steps. Pike leaned back against him a bit, his back arched and awkward, his chin high, his hair streaming from his face.

The air smelled like hot breath. The ground trembled under impatient feet. I couldn't reach him! Men stood on every rail of the livery fence. Here and there a boy sat atop his pa's shoulders. A child stood on a wagon seat next to her bonneted ma. 'Way across the creek, under the shade of a few fluttery aspens, a hefty man pointed out the gallows to a little girl on his knee.

Pike placed his feet on the trapdoor. That rough inch-thick rope slipped around his throat, itching his Adam's apple, pressing against his ear and holding his head cocked to the side just a bit. It creaked softly on the timber overhead, danced with tension down and across to the spot where Rusty had it tied fast to the rail.

A preacher's voice droned across the suddenly silent herd of spectators. Coughing, shuffling, the creaking of saddle leather, a child's soft question, wind whispering low and gentle through pine boughs...I was trying to see, trying to boost myself higher on some fella's shoulder to catch sight of—not Pike—that big man near the aspens!

It couldn't be! Howdy wouldn't bring her here, not for this. The other men, maybe they'd let their young ones watch a man die at the end of a rope. "That's what'll happen to you if you grow up and break the law, son," they'd say. But not Howdy!

"Turn loose of me, lady," the man said, swatting at me.

I looked back at the gallows. Small, thin, not quite real, Pike tiptoed at the end of that rope. Suddenly, the canyon echoed with a quiet crack. The rope quivered taut.

I screamed!

Pike went out of sight under that trapdoor, but I could see him clear as if I could see through the wood. I threw myself against the men in front of me. "Let me through!"

The crowd's gasp echoed in the silence. I saw eyes round with horrible excitement, hands flexing, wiping mouths sour with death, knees weak with relief…These was respectable folks. These people was the kind I'd trusted my Lillie to. Something wild exploded in me, and I howled.

The crowd parted. Folks stared open-mouthed at me as I pulled my horse up the path. The poor, scared beast began trotting ahead of me. Grabbing the horn, I threw myself up across the saddle. In seconds I was galloping toward the gallows, screaming just like an Injun.

Effie, wearing a heavy black veil, was just turning her carriage and was headed straight toward me. All her children was still twisted around, staring at the swaying rope.

I saw Doc Billy climb under the gallows to get Pike. Rusty was helping Jim back into his buggy. They looked up when I reined by Effie's carriage and held the horse in one nervous spot long enough to look her in the eye.

"Get out of her way!" Jim shouted, still able to lay a whip to his horse's back. "Let my daughter pass."

I leaned over and grabbed the surrey. Effie raised her whip to drive her team on, but I slid aboard and pulled the rig off balance. One of her horses reared and her children cried out.

Just as Jim pulled up on the other side of the surrey, I snatched the veil from Effie's face and ripped it clean away. The morning sun was none too kind to her bruises. Jim saw what I meant him to. So did a goodly number of other surprised folks nearby.

That's when the first clouds of smoke curled over Tempest's rooftops. It took me a minute to realize it was coming from the old main street where my saloon was. I turned loose of the surrey and began running.

Doc Billy, Davey Whitehouse, and Rusty was just carrying Pike from under the gallows by his hands and feet when the smoke plumed dark and ugly, and flames began snapping high into the air. Everybody started running toward town, shouting. The smoke rose higher, thicker. Flames danced first over one rooftop, then over another.

Behind me came angry shouts and shrieks. I heard children screaming, and the cry of a spooked horse...and glanced back to see Jim staring at Effie's battered face.

Doc Billy was yelling as I reached them. "There's patients in my office," he yelled, dropping Pike's leg and bolting along the path. He looked down on the fire spreading along the street. His lips curled back as he ran out of sight.

Davey had both Pike's legs now and staggered with Rusty up the hill toward the graveyard 'til a new burst of flame lit the canyon bloody red. "My house!" he yelled, taking off. Rusty staggered under Pike's dead weight and then let him drop. I fell across Pike's body, screaming and crying, kissing his sightless eyes.

More shouts come from behind me. I turned and saw Jim bringing his buggy around. His whip snapped high in the air. His horse reared and leaped forward, bouncing his rig across the ruts toward the gallows again. Without hesitation, Rusty drew his gun and fired over my head!

I squawked and ducked as the bullet zinged by.

Jim's rig floundered. The horse pawed the air as flaming debris landed in the brush at his hooves. Jim half stood in the seat, one hand holding the reins taut, the other up in the air with a pistol. There was a flash of surprise on his face as blood burst across his chest. He hung there like a bird in midair. Effie screamed. Then Jim's rig toppled beneath him, pulling him down into a puff of red dust.

I sprang straight over Pike's body into Rusty's chest, hitting him solid. He tried to crack my head with his gun, but we started sliding down the slope beyond the path into a yucca and some boulders. Fire rained on us steady as we struggled in the weeds.

"Now I can do anything I want with you or Effie," he hissed, his breath hot on my cheeks.

He jumped off me and pulled me up by my jacket front. I stumbled ahead of him down the hill toward town. He pushed me so fast I sprawled once in the gravel, but he had me up in seconds and forced me on, jabbing his gun in my shoulder blades.

As soon as we was out of sight I expected him to shoot me. Rusty was sure to be mayor once I was out of the way. As we come 'round behind one of the higher buildings, I pulled up my skirt to cover my nose and mouth from the smoke. Rusty slid one arm around my neck. "How does it feel to know you're going to die, Angel?"

Folks was darting into stores, trying to save goods, only to be driven back by fire. From the upstairs window of a saloon a woman was waving and shrieking. At last she jumped, but no one ran to help when she hit.

Some men had formed a fire line from the creek to the bank since it was the only building worth saving. Each bucketful was about as useful as tears. Most my money—Dalt's money—sat in that bank. My traveling cash was sewed up in the ruffles of my petticoats, and my bank drafts was up at the depot in my trunk. I would've given it all just then to know Travis wasn't in my saloon.

Orange flames was swallowing my place. The windows looked like blackened eyes. The heat scorched my cheeks and singed my hair and roasted my eyes as Rusty pushed me ever closer. I twisted around to catch sight of him and he was smiling like the devil hisself. Rusty liked the heat, the screaming, the stench of burnt horseflesh close by in a livery.

He let me go suddenly and holstered his gun. Sure and steady, he stooped to pull a bowie from his boot. He meant to carve me up! I plunged headlong into the smoke. I didn't think I could get through the flames to the freight road. Already my skin was stretched like it was frying, but I did manage to double back. Rusty nearly missed me.

Up toward the depot I ran, holding my skirts high to free my legs. I heard Rusty's footsteps coming and ran faster though my lungs burned. For each building I passed, my chances got better. He wouldn't kill me so long as anybody might see.

I was going to make it, I thought! Rusty would never catch me! Then, suddenly, I lost my footing and fell. When I could take a small breath and see clear again, I pulled myself up and stared straight into the windows of the building that had once been Big Bess's dancing salon. I couldn't remember why I was running.

I got up and staggered across the walkway to the door. Inside, one wall was already on fire. A few tables stood scattered about. I was about to turn when something hit my head from behind. The floor floated up and kissed me smartly on the cheek. As I lay against the cool rough planks I fancied I heard dancing feet. The rattle of old piano tunes jangled in my head. The old days drifted through my mind like jittery dreams.

I rolled over, and there, looming over me, was the smiling face of Effie Kennings's golden boy. His pretty blue eyes laughed and flashed.

Suddenly I saw everything clear. From the shadows of my past I heard Jim Lewis calling, "Run while you can, whore!" I saw silhouettes of naked men, bloody sheets, and pine limb crosses stuck crooked in snow. I heard explosions, cussing, creaking beds. Rain beat my face as I lay in mud. Darkness smothered me in a log jailhouse, and I saw a hag in a gilt-edged looking glass.

Rusty's eyes glowed bright through it all. If it hadn't been for him...

His teeth flashed white. His lips went wet with spittle. His skin flickered orange and yellow with the dancing flames nearby. I saw it all and lay very still, remembering my life as one struggle after another, one sorrow leading fast and sure into the next. My head cleared. I knew where I was and understood why I could smell Rusty's breath. I knew why his eyes burned like one sick of a fever.

ANGEL

I let my hands fall back limp on the planks above my head. I watched easy and unafraid as Rusty ripped opened my bodice and tore at the camisole. The blackened fingers of his other hand curled around the bowie's handle. Up, up, he drew it as flames danced along the keen blade.

He tensed for the plunge. His breathing turned to a rasp. The knife hovered high, its tip aimed for my quivering heart laying like a snowhare beneath the cold flesh of my breast. Curling his fingers again and again to make sure the curved blade would sink clean through and pin me to the pine floor, Rusty Kennings took a deep breath.

He didn't see me slip my hand into my other sleeve. One quick twist and a soft squeeze of my silver-handled derringer's trigger blew a neat, black hole into Rusty's temple. The knife tumbled from his frozen hand and grazed me high on one shoulder. His blood rained on my face as he fell and pinned me breathless under him. Crackling flames crawled across the floor toward my head. I pushed and pushed, thinking I'd never get free of him, 'til finally Rusty rolled away.

Dense smoke hung in the rafters. Orange tongues licked the walls. I was tired, so very, very sick and tired I wanted to lay there for the rest of my life. But the stench of Rusty's blood on my face made me crawl to my knees and drag myself out. Then the blazing roof caved in.

Twenty-Seven

Late Summer 1875

"Have you seen Mr. Saunders?" I shouted above the roaring crowd in the train depot.

"He come in just 'fore the fire," the harried clerk behind the ticket window yelled back. "I ain't seen him since."

I got jostled back against the wall as the folks trying to buy passage out of Tempest smashed against the clerk's window. When I couldn't get back to the door, I just picked up my dirty skirts and climbed out a window.

Finding me a spot along the platform, I sat and stared down at the steel rails. I felt an urge to lay among them cinders and sleep awhile. Up in that fierce blue sky the sun hung like a hot yellow ball. My throat was parched, but I couldn't move a muscle to fetch a drink from the rain barrel nearby. Smoke still hung heavy in the air. A few blackened timbers stuck up from the ashes of the old main street. I couldn't tell from one pile to the next where the stores and saloons had once stood.

A swarm of smoke-dusty men buzzed out of the depot and stood at the far end of the platform, pointing this way and that, saying they didn't figure a horse or rig was left in Tempest. They was wrong, a-course. The whole town wasn't burnt up, just the part I'd knowed. They spied Denver Smith's livery over by the creek and headed down that way.

I wished I had the strength to get up. Somebody was bound to come for me sooner or later, but I'd be too tired to explain how I'd come to commit murder.

Oh! I was tired, so tired and bone-weary and wore out I didn't really care if I got hauled off to jail. I understood, suddenly, how Pike felt after that posse'd caught him. I wished I could know no more trouble would find me, that the sorrows dogging my heels with each turning of the seasons was done and gone.

I couldn't take no more. I didn't dare wonder if Travis had died in the fire. Maybe I didn't care. Maybe I just wished I did. I could always pretend he was someplace close behind, soon to be pestering me with those questioning eyes, trying to kiss me though I was weary of kissing.

I chuckled over a lump in my throat. That liquor-soaked, cynical-eyed, hard-smiling varmint—he probably did get hisself burnt up. He probably ran down to my saloon, while I was making a useless effort to right an injustice according to my own values and now, along with being an old whore, I was a killer as well.

It was high time I accepted the world for what it was. It didn't make no sense. It didn't follow no code except look out for yourself and let the rest be damned. I didn't need book-reading and church-learning to figure that out. It's just that some had set store by them things—like Ma. She wanted me to be better than her, and in some ways I was. Leastways I had some money.

A man in a soot-smudged suit come up to me about then. He held out a kerchief. "You're bleeding, Miss. Can I get you some water?"

Sliding his kerchief under the rip in my bodice, I realized I was near to hanging out for all to see. I let out a weary snicker, thinking I sounded drunk. So, that's why all the folks in the depot let me get to the window.

Like a prim little lady, I pulled together the shreds of my bodice and nodded to the stranger. He brought me a dipper of water and watched while I drank. He probably expected a pretty thanks, but I didn't even look up as he put the dipper back in the barrel. Destruction all around, and still some fool could figure his chances with me!

I burst into a sorry laugh. Then I was laughing harder, laughing 'til tears streamed down my cheeks and I thought my sides would split. There weren't no difference between good and bad!

Good *was* bad. Bad *was* good. I didn't give a damn no more if folks understood me. Maybe Jim Lewis and Rusty and Dalt and Davey Whitehouse and Ben and Judd was all to blame for my sins. Maybe I'd suffered more than my share, but being good was no guarantee of happiness neither.

Cornelia had died of a cancer. Gwenity was barren. Effie got beat regular by her no-good, legal, proper, upstanding and respected husband. Jim Lewis had some kind of stroke attack and had to ride in a wheeled chair the rest of his no-good life; Judd blowed hisself into dust; Travis—that snake—screamed at his poor ma's mutilated face and cussed hisself into a life of torment and guilt. That weren't no better fate than my own. In fact, I wouldn't trade it.

I laughed 'cause suddenly I felt free of a pain I'd nursed near all my life. Always I believed I was low-class and dumb-ignorant. I'd never felt good enough to be called decent. Now I felt like getting up and telling everybody Angel Dalton was just as good, if not a damn sight better than most! I was proud of every little thing I'd done 'cause it took strength to do it, strength and a solid mule head and guts, which was more than most had.

Finally I did get up. I wanted to find my trunks and set myself to order 'fore I got on that train. I tossed back my hair to clear my eyes, lifted my chin, and straightened my back...

Coming up the road, like a man dragging rocks tied to his heels, was ol' Savage Saunders hisself! His shirt was torn and near black with soot. He walked with his arms limp and his shoulders bowed under some great invisible weight.

I watched him come 'round the corner of the platform and wipe the hair from his smudged forehead. Never in all my life had I ever seen a face so racked with grief! I recognized the granite-heavy sorrow crushing his shoulders and felt the same pain, the same emptiness, and hopeless anger writ on his face.

I hadn't never felt like that before, like my lips couldn't grin no bigger, like something hot and tingly was alive in my belly. Travis Saunders knew a lot of words and put them to paper fancy, but nothing had ever convinced me that he cared for me more than the way he rubbed his eyes there by the platform. He loved me. He loved me!

I found myself running. I flung my arms wide. Travis looked up and gasped as if I was a spook. "Angel!" He vaulted onto the platform, caught me and swung me high. Then he held me so tight I couldn't breathe. I never wanted him to let me go!

Our ride up Buffalo Canyon on the narrow gauge was short indeed compared to my first trip in a wagon. "There! That's where the road camp was," I said. Travis only nodded and went on clutching my hand. "Over that way was Jim Lewis's homestead. Up in the trees was Dalt's old cabin. My ma and my first baby are buried there."

From the look on Travis's face I couldn't tell what he thought. I fell back in my seat with a shuddering sigh. He hadn't said much since we found each other except to tell me how he'd pulled a woman's burned body from the flames near my place. His face was still sickly with the memory.

I pulled his hand into my lap and patted it. I hated to heap more grief on him just then, and had waited all the miles up the winding rail line, but now I had to tell him. "When we get into Cold Water City," I whispered. "I mean to get off this train. I got to see someone. Will you come with me?"

"I doubt you could get rid of me now, Angel," he said.

I hardly recognized Cold Water as we stepped from the train about four that morning. It was built up just like a real city. When the train pulled away, the silence pressed around us. I took comfort in it. My life in the Rockies was at an end. In another year or so Colorado would be a state. No telling the changes then. I looked around and felt an ache in my heart. Colorado Territory had sneaked into my heart and now called itself home.

Travis rented a rig and, by dawn, we was headed down the freight road for the Calico Inn. "You're probably itching to know why we're coming back this way," I said, my heart pounding harder with every mile.

"Knowing you, I'll have to wait to find out," he grinned wearily.

I laughed. "I lived here once. Over that ridge is a mine called the Little Angel. I lived on that mesa near two years."

Travis just eyed me as we jostled shoulders on the buggy seat. The morning sun weren't easy on his red eyes. I leaned over and kissed his prickly cheek. Then the inn come into sight. I wasn't sure what I was fixing to do. I just knew I had to see her. I had to know if Howdy had taken Lillie to the hanging.

I could raise Lillie myself now, I thought. My values was good as anybody's. The idea sounded so pretty I began thinking over gentle ways of telling Howdy and Gwenity I meant to do the very thing they'd feared all these years.

A fence surrounded a proper barn and stable now. A store and smithy stood across the road. As we pulled up in front, I couldn't breathe. Travis got down. Just as he reached to help me to the ground, there came Howdy just like always, smiling broad and holding out a welcoming hand.

I hardly recognized him! Folds of flesh hung at his neck, adding ten years instead of the five I'd been away. The man I'd seen at the hanging had been big. Howdy had growed old…and thin! I rushed past Travis, my arms outstretched. "Howdy! Don't you know me?"

"Angie?" Howdy whispered, talking my face in his hands. "What have you done to yourself?"

"Is that any way to talk?" I laughed, kissing him. "I look good, considering. This here's Travis Saunders. Did you hear Tempest burnt to the ground yesterday?"

Howdy shook hands with Travis. "Nice to meet you. I've heard of you. Come in. There's coffee. I been up near all night with the folks fleeing Tempest. What happened down there?"

Already the smell of bacon filled the air. "Gwenity's still getting up with the sun, I see," I said, dancing around, touching the tables, near to crying with the joy of being back. "Don't you never give that woman a rest?" I edged toward the kitchen doorway to catch a peek of her. I hoped to see Lillie at her side, mixing up the flapjack batter.

When Howdy didn't say nothing, I turned. His face looked like his bones had suddenly turned soft. "Gwenity died last winter."

Travis was at my side in a second. He took my elbow and supported me as he eased me into a chair. Then he edged away.

"I'm sorry, Angie," Howdy was saying. "I should've broken it to you more gentle. I'll get some coffee."

The pretty morning suddenly felt gray and cold though the sun still burned bright out in the yard. Howdy came in with a tray of cups. An old woman followed with the coffee pot. I didn't know her, but I liked her face. She was as plump as Gwenity had been lean and looked a good deal like her. Howdy sat hisself on the edge of a chair and kneaded his knees with wide, bony hands. "She went quick. No pain or much, they told me. Some ladies from Cold Water were down to help..." His ragged voice trailed off.

He didn't speak again 'til he began kneading them knees. "Sometimes I think I still hear her...when Lillie plays the piano..." He cleared his throat. "I go out to the barn and work it off. Funny how a woman can haunt you." He looked at me so earnest his eyes pained me. I supposed he forgot Travis was listening. "I killed her, Angie. I loved her and I killed her with my love. I made her pregnant again...and it was just like you said it'd be. At the end she said she didn't mind going so much. She'd had all the happiness any woman could want. She said to tell you..."

Travis was looking at Howdy, his mouth tight, his neck corded.

"She said to tell you thank you." Howdy got up fast and turned toward the coffee. "Mr. Saunders? Ella makes good coffee. Angie, coffee?"

"I could use a good bolt of whiskey," I said.

Howdy grinned weakly. "You always was a puzzle. For years we thought you were dead. Then you wrote out of the blue…I've meant to write and thank you myself for all the money and lawyers…The mine keeps us comfortable, as you can see. Are you hungry? Ella's a fine cook, too. Don't know what I'd do without her. She's Gwenity's sister, you know. We've got us a real nice little settlement here now, not so lonesome like when you lived here. I'll have to be careful in another couple years what young fellas I let come around…" His eyes skittered across the room and met mine. "Lillie." Her name hung in the air like the peal of a bell.

Travis opened the door. He looked as if he'd never seen a ridge quite like that one out there, hadn't never seen the morning sun glow in a dusty yard like that. The more Howdy talked, the harder Travis looked.

"I thought she might be boarding in town now," I said softly.

"We talked on it, me and Gwenity. We probably would've sent her in this year, but…but I figured to teach her from Gwen's books a year or so more. Then…I don't know. She's gathering eggs right now. Plenty of chores for a young lady around here. I ain't slackened just 'cause her ma died. She plays the piano regular, does her lessons. Only after that can she ride or play. She doesn't lack for anything 'cause Gwen died."

I felt hot and uncomfortable.

"I didn't write because…" He spun around and faced me. "You fixing to stay long?" His voice was high and loud.

"Did you call me, Mr. Jackson?" Ella said, hanging her head out the kitchen door. "Don't know what's keeping the little miss and her eggs."

Howdy waved her off.

I pushed myself out of my chair and laid my hand on his arm. "One night. That's all."

He didn't look convinced.

"I'll get your trunk," Travis said, launching hisself onto the veranda.

The air in the dining room hung thick with things unsaid.

ANGEL

Howdy couldn't bring hisself to ask what I meant to do about Lillie. I couldn't tell him he had nothing to fear.

A moment later Travis lugged in a small leather trunk trimmed in brass. A slight child in a blue cotton dress skipped in at his side, her gray eyes round and curious. "We've got a trunk like that upstairs in my room. I keep my treasures in it. I'd keep these eggs in it if Pa'd let me! Aren't they big? We've got the best hens in the valley." She held eight eggs in her upturned apron and smiled when she saw me. "Morning Ma'am. Sorry I took so long, Pa. The kittens were all into the roost and I thought one was lost. Breakfast will be on in just a bit." She gave a little curtsy and clattered into the kitchen, her black-booted feet as loud and quick as hooves.

I felt faint! My head pounded so hard I couldn't see nothing clear. My baby was so beautiful! My baby...my baby...and she had...I clutched at Howdy for support. She had a blue ribbon tied up around her curly black hair!

Howdy steered me toward the stairs. "You look tired, Angie. I have two nice rooms in the new wing, where you can rest. Let me carry that, Mr. Saunders."

"Thanks, I'll manage. I could stand a razor if you've got a spare. Everything I owned went up in smoke yesterday."

"I'll get whatever you need at the store. Your credit's good. Any friend of Angie's..."

Like a person made of the finest, thinnest glass, I tiptoed up them stairs. Any minute I might shatter.

My baby, my baby! I laid down to calm my heart. Two nights with no sleep left me more than tired. My baby...Sleep took me like death's own messenger. Instead of hurrying back to see that little girl so tall for her age, so bright, so lively and easy with strangers, I slept like I was dead.

The cool afternoon shadows cast my room in twilight before I finally staggered from the bed and washed. I was almost done

295

dressing when Travis knocked. "You look better," he said, letting hisself in.

"I didn't want to sleep so long! You look better, too."

"Angel...Angie..." He pressed his lips together. "What is your name? I thought I knew everything about you and had accurately guessed the rest."

I pulled on my shoes and struggled over the buttons. I was busting with words but didn't dare let a one out. After a bit Travis kneeled before me and helped do them up. "She's your daughter," he whispered.

"Her hair's lighter, but she has the eyes, the chin. Did you see her smile? Oh, she's a good girl, Travis! She talks proper. Ain't she pretty!"

"She's very much like you. She and I had a good long visit after I rested," Travis said, still stooped over my shoes. "She named all thirty-eight states and their capitals, listed the presidents, recited the Gettysburg address, quoted from the books of Genesis, Mark and Revelation. She's a remarkable girl. She's waiting to play for you." He cleared his throat. "Are you planning to take her?"

"Ain't I got a right?"

"Why is she here, Angel? You were in Ore City, Colorado Creek, Tempest—everywhere but here. Why didn't you take her with you?"

I jumped up. "If Gwenity was here I wouldn't take her, but Gwen's dead! I'm Lillie's rightful ma! I need her! Don't say nothing. I'm good enough! Ain't no reason why I can't do right by her. I got money enough for Lillie to live proper and go to a fancy dressmaker and have a good teacher..." I held up my hand to shush Travis. "My first baby—Dalt's baby—is laying out there in them mountains beside my ma somewhere. I was sixteen years old when I had her. I've lost everything more than once, and I sprung back again and again." I stopped and gasped for breath. "I gave Lillie up 'cause it was best—then. I ain't so sure now. Can't I do just as good as they done? Now that I got money, can't I?"

Travis gathered hisself into a tight knot. Though he stood only inches from me, he could've been clear back in Missouri for all the closeness left between us. I felt like I'd just slid over the edge of the canyon road. The yawning space in that inch between us grew so wide the whole sky could've fit in it. "Taking that child from here, now, would be wrong! Yes, you'd make her a wonderful mother, and yes, your money would buy her clothes, books, tutors, ponies—all the things you never had 'til you earned them."

"Throw that up to me!"

"I'm not and you know it. Haven't you lived your mother's impossible dream long enough to know you can't make Lillie live yours?"

"You don't know nothing about my ma's dreams, and you sure don't know nothing about mine!"

"Only three days ago you told me you wanted to be good. You are, Angel, as good a woman as I'll ever know. I'm sorry for all the things that hurt you, all the things I've said, but don't tear apart Lillie's life now. Think what it would do to her."

I turned my face to the side. My mind was made up. Easy as that.

Travis's boots echoed across the floor. "If you take her…" His voice became quiet and hard. "You go alone."

A hot bullet of fear cut into my gut. I didn't want to lose him, but I held my arms stiff and wouldn't look at him. "What can it matter to you?"

"Before I knew about this I'd hoped…" Travis sighed. "Never mind, Angel. Do what you think is best. I shouldn't have said anything. Of course you should have her. You deserve every happiness." And he went out.

I ate supper that night at the same table with my Lillie. The dining room boomed with talk from all the travelers waiting for the next stage, but I didn't hear a word. All I saw was my baby. I basked in her chatter as if she was the sun and I had been long sick and in need of healing warmth.

"I'll be eight this winter. Pa says I'll be old enough to ride a big horse then. I have a pony now. Pa brought it all the way from Denver. Have you ever been to Denver, Mrs. Dalton?"

I nodded, not trusting my voice, afraid I'd start to say something and say instead, "I'm your real ma."

"I must be dribbling again," Lillie giggled, ducking her head into her shoulders and blushing behind her napkin, embarrassed by my stare. She spooned the soup more careful, like a little lady, but easy, like it come natural to her, too.

I couldn't get over how Judd's smile could come again to that child's mouth and be blended with my ma's chin and eyes and my too-curly hair. It was like seeing ghosts—much-loved ghosts, to be sure.

"If you're ready now, Mrs. Dalton, I'll play for you. I don't get to play for fine ladies very often." She twisted her skirt ties and pranced like a colt when I nodded.

Spinning the stool 'til it near to come off the stem, Lillie arranged it before the piano. She looked so little perched atop it. Her feet barely reached the pedals. Her dainty fingers curled just so over the keys. *Thank you kindly for all you've done for her, Howdy…*I was thinking. *I know I shouldn't, but…Now that you're alone I think it's better I…*

The tune "Beautiful Dreamer" floated out of that piano box as if by magic. How good and simple it sounded after all them years with the honky-tonk. It brought to mind so many things I'd fogotten: Sara bent over her garden patch; Davey's face the first day he asked me to dance; Travis sitting atop his Appaloosa, grinning like all the world was his…

I looked over where Travis had sat through supper in silence. He was gone! Moments before he'd been sopping up gravy with a biscuit! Outside the open front door I saw the glowing tip of a cheroot.

Lillie's fingers danced over the keys like little birds. Her hair was coming loose of her plaits, wiry as mine had once been. I longed to touch it. She scowled at them keys and reddened when she went back over a mistake. I would buy her the best piano…

When she finished, she hopped off the stool and sent it spinning crookedly. The folks clapped. Howdy smiled and patted his knee. Lillie crossed the room like a leaf on the wind and landed in his lap as if drawn there by force. She wound her arms around his neck and smiled the most joyful smile.

Howdy kissed her nose and set her down to straighten her collar and cuffs. "You played better tonight than I've ever heard you, Lillie. Your ma...would be proud. Tell Mrs. Dalton goodnight now."

"Did you like it, Mrs. Dalton? It's the best one I know." She stood before me eager as a pup.

"I never heard better," I said and went hot with shame that I couldn't talk better. "Goodnight," I whispered.

"Tomorrow I'll show you my treasures. I have a Bible, a map of Pa's mine, and all kinds of arrowheads I find when I'm out riding with Pa. And I have a real gold locket with pictures in it that came all the way from back East. It's very old. Mama gave it to me just before she died. It belonged to my grandmother. I get to wear it when I'm older." She was a step or two away when she turned suddenly and darted back. Her arms went around me quick and sure. Her little lips pressed sweet and cool as a snowflake against my cheek. "You're a pretty lady," she smiled. "'Night, Pa."

"I'll be up to tuck you in," Howdy said.

I looked back at the doorway. Travis was gone. I felt suddenly split clean in two, like a pine struck by lightning.

"Want to help tuck Lillie in, Angie?" Howdy was saying. "She likes you. She's already noticed how your eyes are the same color as hers. It won't be long and she'll guess the truth. Her life won't never be the same after that. We've had us a good life even though Gwenity is gone. Maybe if you stayed on..."

I looked up at Howdy. I couldn't hear Lillie's footsteps overhead no more. I couldn't see Travis. I was going to scream!

Howdy touched my arm as I stood. I searched his eyes, those gentle eyes tormented by the sight of me. I saw the fear crawling in his belly, felt his hand cold as death.

"Please, Angie." He closed his eyes slow. His lashes went wet. "Don't take her."

Out in the yard a horse snorted. Hoofbeats thudded in the

red dirt. There was Travis! He mounted a horse and turned in an uncertain circle as if waiting.

It wasn't fair! I needed more time!

I could stay, I thought, looking into Howdy's pleading eyes. Maybe I could even marry him and be my Lillie's ma! If folks found out about me, well, I'd just stand up to them and...

Now Travis began to move off slow, like he didn't really want to go. I couldn't see him no more, but I fancied I saw his face, a face scuffed like an old deck of cards, eyes sometimes hollow, sometimes hard, lips that could spout words hot enough to burn, lips that could tremble as helpless as a babe's...

I turned away. I imagined my child tucked snug under Gwenity's quilt, a quilt stitched in good faith that Lillie would be hers for all time. If I took her away, then for all eternity my one lasting, most solemn promise would be broken.

I dashed at Howdy and kissed him. I couldn't see him clear through my tears and forever after would remember him in a blue wash. "I don't remember much of my own pa," I said, feeling a worrisome nagging at my back. "I can't say I had much love for him. He was weak and selfish and made mistakes a-plenty. Maybe if I'd knowed him better I could've put my arms around his neck and...I could've been stronger all these years." I laughed a little. "I got a lot of money now, but I'd never be able to buy a father for Lillie like you. I thought I gave Lillie to Gwenity. You was just a man to provide for them and keep them safe. Now I see a man's more than just what he gives his family. It's what he is. I gave Lillie more than I ever knowed."

The hoofbeats died away. The night was silent. I kissed Howdy again, quick. "I didn't mean to scare you. It's just that...I love her."

Two big tears rolled down Howdy's cheeks. My heart hurt at the sight. "Take good care of her," I called softly as I ran out into the moonlight.

The mountains stood dark and quiet on the fringes of the

valley. Yellow lamplight spilled into the yard. I followed the faint sound of Travis's horse into the shadows past the fence. He was walking the horse down the freight road, slow.

I loved Lillie. If she had been alone, I wouldn't have turned away a second time, but Lillie had her pa, a good man, a good father. Howdy would give her what both me and Gwenity never could, a respect for men maybe I'd never had.

The truth of it was, Lillie didn't need me. *I* knew need like I knew a rib sore from a tight corset, like the bite of tight shoes, like the heat on a summer afternoon and the cold in a blizzard. I knew it with every breath, the searching and yearning for something with no name, and the hope that I'd find it before I died.

I wanted to fit somewhere, to belong easy and natural the way trout belonged in the creeks, the way the sun floated in the sky. I needed caring hands on me, eyes gentle with love on me, a heart aching to be by me. I needed to hold someone's head against my breasts and feel the comfort flowing back and forth like breathing, to search a crowd and find, as I had for the past couple years, eyes following me, eyes full of need, eyes that didn't turn away from what I was.

How had Travis opened my heart? With his tears, his sneers? Panting, I stopped to pull off my shoes. I wanted to catch up to Travis easy and say, "Get down off that horse, you stubborn varmint. I gave Lillie up for good and always this time. If it don't turn out right, I'll have your damn hide."

"Travis?" I called, aching with the fear that he'd never stop. I jabbed my fist into a stitch in my side 'til it eased a bit. Oh, how I hated being weak and used up. I wanted Travis to come running back to me, crying just a bit to make me feel strong and important. "*Travis?*"

The saddle leather creaked as he twisted around. Finally the horse stopped and he got down. The moon shined on his hair and lit it white. He stood still as I hobbled nearer. Couldn't he give me a sign? Did he still want me? He was the only man who knew everything about me from the blackness of the Ore City jailhouse to the dreams of upstanding respectability, alive and beautiful back in the Calico Inn. He was the only one…If I lost him there'd be no bouncing back.

"Travis!" I slowed enough to see the dark pockets of his eyes, the tight line of his jaw, the rigid angle of his shoulders. I pressed my fist deeper into my side and felt like weeping. "Wait for me!"

I crossed that yawning sky-distance between us. When I was a step from him, he put out his hand. Mine fit inside it just so.

As Travis pulled me close, I started to lay my head on his coat front, but he took hold of my head and tipped it back. His lips touched mine with only a moment's hesitation. Then I sank into a well of darkness and warmth, my lips one with his, my body tight against him and not a chink of light between us.

What Travis and I found there beside the freight road that night went beyond words and far beyond just physical loving.

I'd known all manner of men in my time. I'd even thought I'd loved a few. With Travis I found the real meaning of love.

I gave up all of myself, the secret and the not-so-secret, the good and the not-so-good. I expected nothing in return and found something instead, so beautiful, so mysterious I'm not sure many other people have ever known it.

Our bodies and souls became one. It was a kind of marriage of the spirit, the kind of happiness and satisfaction born of trial and sorrow, determination and love. We faced the future anew, bonded like air and wind, rock and mountain.

It was what man and woman were created for. It was what I had searched for. By the grace of my ma's fearsome God, it was what I found, and I would hold to it for the rest of my days.

Epilogue

Denver, Colorado
1890

Sometimes I wonder why I've written this for Angela. She didn't want me to. Her struggles seem so distant now I can see why she says they no longer matter.

I tell myself I have recorded Angela's life as she told it to me those days and weeks following our departure from Buffalo Pass because it was a story crying to be told. If Angela doesn't care if anyone understands her, am I not exploiting her as I have exploited the misfortunes of others? I'd like to think I've done more than that.

Angela Dalton lives in a sedate fieldstone cottage on the Northwest side now. Using the steady flow of interest from gold deposited years ago, she has insulated herself against the outside world. The fence around her property is open ironwork entwined with climbing roses, but the roses have thorns, and the fence is topped with spikes sharp enough to impale.

Her home is furnished simply and is a comfortable place to live. I'm proud to say I share her life there. While I've tried to maintain a vigorous male front all these years, I admit to needing Angel. I still bait her. I have found, to my horror, that I have often hurt her in my glib attempts to be bold and witty. She forgives me, though.

For a woman of slight build, who laughs at the wrinkles around her eyes and scoffs at the gray lacing her black hair, she is remarkably strong, likably cheerful, a person easy to be around.

My secretary has just come into my office, so I must set aside this manuscript and attend to the business of the Rocky Mountain Silver Dollar, a newspaper of some repute. Angela is intensely disinterested in anything connected with it.

After all these years she still cannot read or write. She wants to know only what can be seen from our upstairs windows or through the leaves of her rose bushes. I dare not mention a news story before she silences me with her eyes, those eyes soft and vulnerable, gray as a dove, which sometimes flash as cold and slick as steel.

Consequently, I conduct my work without her approval, only guessing at how she would feel. That gives me a unique outlook on all that happens in this great Western city. I am told my paper has a particular humanitarian slant that appeals to many. I must be satisfied with that.

"Mr. Saunders," my secretary says again, impatiently, from the door. Her white blouse is crisp, her gored skirt embellished with braid. She looks very much the educated woman of our time.

When I look at her I wonder what would she be doing if her father hadn't educated her as well as his sons. Our modern society hasn't changed much from thirty years ago. Saloons still litter the streets of every mining town from Colorado to Nevada. Houses of ill fame still abound.

A cold finger touches my back, and I lay my hand on the stack of papers, which represents Angela Dalton's life. I marvel that she now sits in her garden and laughs when I tell her I admire her. She takes my hand and kisses the knuckles. At forty-four, she is still remarkably young and beautiful.

I would marry her if she would have me, but, she says, while she has given me her heart, she wishes to carry Jack Dalton's name.

I think I must be satisfied, indeed honored, that she gives me as much of herself as she does. She knows something of intimacy I do not. I cannot imagine it, though it is often said I'm a man gifted with insight. I already enjoy an intimacy with her, that in her estimation, goes far deeper than sex.

She tells me all and holds nothing back. She cares nothing for my judgment. She simply talks about herself in a manner that speaks of trust. Can a woman value security—the security of trusting someone implicitly—above physical love?

"Mr. Saunders?"

"I'm sorry, Rebecca. I was thinking," I say.

"Someone is waiting to see you. She says her name is Lillie Jackson."

My head comes up abruptly. I have thought, up to this moment, I was beyond surprise. Then I laugh at myself. Have I not waited for this day? Surely Lillie Jackson could not be Angela's daughter and not possess a mule-headed desire to seek out her true identity.

Only six months ago I printed Howard Jackson's obituary. Being obliged to keep life's events securely locked among indecipherable words, I didn't tell Angela. Perhaps I am a coward as well as a liar and hypocrite.

"Mr. Saunders?" A young woman walks into my office as confidently as her mother once entered saloons. "I know you're busy. I won't take much of your time."

I rise and extend a hand that has gone clammy. My secretary closes the door, and I am alone with Lillie Jackson. "What can I do for you, Miss Jackson?" I tell myself I must remain casual. I cannot let this girl know I know her.

Though I have not seen her for fifteen years I do recognize her. She has her mother's eyes. Her hair is a soft brown whispering with gold highlights. It has a rebellious nature and is coming loose of the pins. She is a handsome creature with a smiling, open face. She has the look of an educated girl; inquisitive, bright, clever.

Her eyes do not flash as I sit across from her. She doesn't have that hidden core of steel, though I know she must be strong in her own way. She meets my eyes disconcertingly, smiling a bit. I wonder at the sort of young men who must match wits with these remarkable modern girls.

"I'm looking for someone, Mr. Saunders."

I fold my fingers and watch the tips go white. "How can I help?"

"I don't really know where to look and that makes it all the harder because I don't know just whom I'm looking for."

I chuckle.

"I'm from Cold Water City. My father died recently. My mother died when I was very small. I've been East in college, and that was hard. I was just a crude Westerner, you know." She laughs. I see she's getting nervous.

"And your father was…"

"Howard Jackson. When he died he left me a mine. He depended on it to keep the ranch going. I went to college on gold." She smiles a bit modestly. "I thought the mine was Papa's, that he prospected for it in the early days."

My mind races ahead, filling in her sentences, growing impatient.

"I found that I owned the mine all my life! It was staked by someone named Judd Rydell. I've been to the files, Mr. Saunders. You wrote an article about the man's death—in *my* mine."

"I've written about a good many deaths, Miss Jackson."

"But this one was special. Not long after, the man's widow was robbed. I've found scattered articles but nothing that tells me how it all came out. Do you remember?"

"How long ago was all this?"

"Twenty years."

I shake my head. I hate the discouragement gathering in her gray eyes. She pulls a box wrapped in white paper from her pocket and lifts a heavy gold locket and long thick chain from it. A stately man and woman are pictured inside. The man is garbed as a Confederate officer. The woman is lovely. Lillie has her mouth.

"My grandparents," Lillie says. Now her eyes do flash just a bit, but it's more the reflection of gathering tears. She inserts a buffed nail along the rim and pops the picture of her grandmother out. Behind the likeness, engraved upon the gold, is the name *Elvira Rydell*. "My middle name is Elvira. Rydell is the man's name who staked my mine and signed it over to his infant daughter in 1869. Lillie Elvira *Rydell*, not Jackson. Howdy Jackson wasn't my real father!"

"So it appears."

"And here!" She produces a thick ledger from under her coat.

"My mother's diary. It begins in 1862 when she first wrote to my father, Howard, and agreed to marry him. Accounts of her trips, her marriage, her life at the ranch..." Lillie flips through the pages.

How good it would make me feel just to tell Lillie her past and be done with it. Yet, her eyes shine so prettily I can't cheat her out of the solution to her life's puzzle.

"And look, Mr. Saunders. Here there is no entry for over three months. When Mother begins writing again she tells of snow on the *mesa*, how cold it got in the *cabin*. When I first read this, Mr. Saunders, I couldn't help wonder if Mother left Papa and went to live with someone else. I went up to the mesa after Papa died. I found the remains of the cabin. I found Judd Rydell's grave."

"It does sound mysterious. You said you were looking for someone? Do you mean Rydell's widow?"

"I'm so confused." She lets the ledger fall shut.

I rise and pour her a glass of water. I feel her eyes on my back. I feel cowardly as I lead her on, yet, I feel cautious and protective, too. I see a beautiful girl clever enough to have come to *me* for answers who may go all the way to Georgia before she's through. I've no doubt she'll find herself in Denver again before long, staring at an iron fence entwined with roses.

I turn back and wonder what she would think if she knew her quest would take her to a dancehall, a saloon, a jail? I sit and refold my hands.

"Mr. Saunders, I came here because you wrote the article about Judd Rydell. His widow's name isn't mentioned in any of the later articles about the robbery. My mother never writes of it."

How her eyes sparkle. She unrolls a map drawn on brown wrapping paper. I recognize Angela's bold pencil strokes immediately. Her name shouts across the bottom of the sheet. Lillie Jackson peers at me through her lashes. "This is my mine. Here is the cabin my mother stayed in. I was born there, Mr. Saunders. The question is, who was my mother?"

I watch her trace the map's markings.

"Did my mother bear me outside wedlock? Did my father take

her back when the man died?" Her cheeks flood a proper crimson. "Is that why no further pregnancies occurred until the last one that killed her?"

"I don't follow you." I followed her precisely.

"It took them that long to reconcile?"

I shake my head. "If this is all so, your father must've treated you harshly. Now you want me to reveal Judd Rydell's widow so you can go to her—for whatever reason."

"My father was wonderful to me! I don't wish to deny his love. I'm just so confused. How can I go on when those I loved are so suddenly changed? I remember enough of my mother to know what a strong and true person she was. I have only to read her diary to know how much she loved my father, to know all she did for those who stayed at the ranch. She often cared for injured strangers. During her second miscarriage she nursed my real father back to health. Once, she lent her own wedding dress to..."

She turns white. As she snatches up the diary and reads, my office grows hot and silent. I should ask her to leave, yet I sit calmly with my hand resting on a stack of papers to my right. I gaze at the daguerreotype of Angela standing so proudly beside my ink well.

I remember how in an attempt to extort love from Angela years ago I made her turn from Lillie. I shudder at my own callousness, my insurmountable selfishness. I have lived quite comfortably all these years, thinking Angela loved and needed me more than her own flesh and blood. Yet, there Lillie sits with such shining innocence on her face. I remember seeing it more than thirty years ago on her mother. This lone young woman would not turn to a dancehall for support.

Did I force Angela to make such an impossible choice after all? Wouldn't I have had her heart still if I had let her enjoy the remaining years of Lillie's childhood?

I am a fool. My thoughts turn to whiskey, though I will not betray myself. I watch a new, more complicated idea enter Lillie Jackson's head.

She claps the ledger closed. "Judd Rydell's widow was..."

"Leona Harvey Rydell, Atlanta, Georgia. You'll find her in the social register no doubt. I only know her name...I never met her." And Angela's name for her, I add to myself. "Will you travel that far to uncover your past?"

"I won't be put off so easily. I thought perhaps I was this woman's daughter—this Leona." Lillie's smile fills my office. "I knew I wasn't."

"Indeed?" My stomach tightens. I wonder if she plays chess because she has me in check.

"Leona Rydell would have taken me back East if I was hers. Gwenity Jackson was tall and had straight brown hair not so unlike mine, but our features were singularly different. What did Judd Rydell look like?" she asks.

"I never met him."

Lillie lowers her eyes a bit peevishly. Her finger slides across the map to Angela's printed signature. "Perhaps my real name is Angela."

How poorly I veil my surprise. "I don't think I can help you, Miss Jackson. I'm very busy." I take out a sheet of writing paper and title it, Epilog, 1890. I had thought Angel's story done.

"I copied this from the bank records in Buffalo Falls, Mr. Saunders," she says, producing yet another sheet of evidence. "You lived in Tempest until the fire."

I feel trapped and resent her for cornering me.

"These are records of money sent to my account, dealings with a lawyer. Look at these signatures."

"If you had all this to begin with, Miss Jackson, why bother me with it? The same child who scribbled across your map wrote on a bank ledger."

"Not a child, Mr. Saunders. A woman. I didn't make the connection before, but here it is in the diary. The wedding dress Mother loaned to a girl who married Judd Rydell. He was married to *two* women, Mr. Saunders. Someone else gave birth to me in the mesa cabin, *this* someone who wrote like a child, who disappeared and later lived in Tempest and sent my parents money."

"You think this Angela is your mother?" My tongue burns with the taste of treachery. My heart pounds. I feel a catastrophe lurking and merely sit.

How strong is Angela now, I ask myself. Is she strong because she lives behind iron and stone and veils her life with trees and thorny roses? Does she sit hours drawing, relaxing in the evening with a good whiskey because she is totally without fear?

"Mr. Saunders, help me. I'm so afraid you'll finally tell me she died."

I press too hard and empty my quill onto the paper.

"I'm not looking for money. A number of people have provided for me. You might be interested to know I inherited from my grandmother Elvira years ago."

"I didn't know."

"I'm a target for every money-hungry young man in the West."

"So, you seek out a woman who can scarcely make her name on paper?" I say. "Why?"

"Because I'm alone. I fear she's alone, too. Don't look at me so, Mr. Saunders. I'm sincere in my desire to find her, whatever her circumstances. If she had died, I think you would have told me immediately. You wouldn't torment me with false hope."

"Savage Saunders prefers to torment with the truth," I say.

"Everywhere I turn, the *truth* is kept from me. I was told many times she died in the fire. Was she so very wicked so many people wish to believe she's dead?"

"I can't help you."

She rises from her chair and gathers the shreds of her past. "I will find her."

"You've led a sheltered life, Miss Jackson. Are you aware of the type of woman who worked in boomtown saloons?"

"You have written extensively on the subject. I happen to know you sponsor the local Magdalene House."

I can't rise because my knees are quivering. "If you ever consider journalism for a career, Miss Jackson, I know a newspaper where you could work. Your investigation and presentation have been flawless."

She rounds my desk and stands near, her hands primly folded over her mother's diary. "I know what Angela was and why she disappeared. Must I also be punished?"

My mouth fills with the words she wants to hear, yet I cannot speak. I find myself looking at the daguerreotype, dumb with confusion. Angel has given me her trust. Though I am weak in many respects, I cannot bring myself to be unfaithful to her.

I see my reflection in the glass in the frame and, as always, I'm a bit startled by the heavy hand of time pulling at my jowl and the shine of so much silver in my hair. I live for my evenings with Angela, our quiet talks, our reminiscences, our easy laughter. I'm so very lucky to have survived to enjoy her company. She makes me feel young and cunning, and after fifteen years still has me believing I'm the best she ever had. I turn a resentful eye on this girl prying so confidently into that intimacy.

Her smile startles me. She has seen me looking at Angela's likeness. I've made myself into a lying fool and suddenly I feel quite good about it.

"Thank you for your help, Mr. Saunders."

"I did nothing."

She takes my hand and squeezes it. "I don't blame you for protecting her. I'm not at all sure how I'll feel when I find her. Everyone I've talked to has told me the Jacksons are my true parents and I know that, but somewhere there is a woman a little like me. Perhaps her eyes are the color of mine. Perhaps she can tell me if I have my father's smile…" She laughs and turns away. "I used to look at Mother's picture and worry. Why didn't I look like her? Why didn't I quite fit?"

I lead Lillie toward the door. My office has grown dim and sultry in the afternoon heat. I feel like a criminal about to bring off a clever crime. I look down on the curly brown head and feel a rush of fatherly emotion.

"Do you know how important it is to fit—somewhere?" she asks. Her voice is tender, tremulous.

"Miss Jackson, she'll understand even better than I."

• • •

Now Miss Lillie Jackson is gone. I return to my desk and dip the pen. Angel's story begins to live again across the pages. Though I crave to capture the feelings lingering in my office, a nagging need to hurry to Angela's side makes each word difficult to write.

Will I tell her Lillie is so near?

I look up, frowning at the darkening arch-topped windows. *Can Lillie find her?* As I blot up more spilled ink I have no doubt she will. Someday. She may even read my manuscript.

At last I set aside the pen and cover my face. I am tired. As Angela would say, the girl muddled me. I push the fresh papers in the drawer and lock it. I must be with Angela now. I don't know, though, if I go to protect, or to be protected. I only know I love her.

CACTUS ROSE

In the heat of the southwest, desire is the kindling for two lost souls—and the flame of passion threatens to consume them both.

Rosie Saladay needs to get married—fast. The young widow needs help to protect her late husband's ranch, but no decent woman can live alone with a hired hand. With the wealthy Wesley Morris making a play for her land, Rosie needs a husband or she risks losing everything. So she hangs a sign at the local saloon: "Husband wanted. Apply inside. No conjugal rights."

Delmar Grant is a sucker for a damsel in distress, and even with Rosie's restrictions on "boots under her bed" stated firmly in black and white, something about the lovely widow's plea leaves him unable to turn away her proposal of marriage.

Though neither planned on falling in love, passion ignites between the unlikely couple. But their buried secrets—and enemies with both greed and a grudge—threaten to tear them apart. They'll discover this marriage of convenience may cost them more than they could have ever bargained for.

AUTUMN BLAZE

Firemaker is a wild, golden-haired beauty who was taken from her home as a baby and raised by a Comanche tribe. Carter Machesney is the handsome Texas Ranger charged with finding her, and reacquainting her with the life she never really knew.

Though they speak in different tongues, the instant flare of passion between Firemaker and Carter is a language both can speak, and their love is one that bridges both worlds.

HURRICANE SWEEP

Hurricane Sweep spans three generations of women—three generations of strife, heartbreak, and determination.

Florie is a delicate Southern belle who must flee north to escape her family's cruelty, only to endure the torment of both harsh winters and a sadistic husband. Loraine, Florie's beautiful and impulsive daughter, bares her body to the wrong man, yet hides her heart from the right one. And Jolie, Florie's pampered granddaughter, finds herself in the center of the whirlwind of her family's secrets.

Each woman is caught in a bitter struggle between power and pride, searching for a love great enough to obliterate generations of buried dreams and broken hearts.

KISS OF GOLD

From England to an isolated Colorado mining town, Daisie Browning yearns to find her lost father—the last thing she expects to find is love. Until, stranded, robbed, and beset by swindlers, she reluctantly accepts the help of the handsome and rakish Tyler Reede, all the while resisting his advances.

But soon Daisie finds herself drawn to Tyler, and she'll discover that almost everything she's been looking for can be found in his passionate embrace.

SNOWS OF CRAGGMOOR

When Merri Glenden's aunt died, she took many deep, dark secrets to the grave. But the one thing Aunt Coral couldn't keep hidden was the existence of Merri's living relatives, including a cousin who shares Merri's name. Determined to connect with a family she never knew but has always craved, Merri travels to Colorado to seek out her kin.

Upon her arrival at the foreboding Craggmoor—the mansion built by her mining tycoon great-grandfather—Merri finds herself surrounded by antagonistic strangers rather than the welcoming relations she'd hoped for.

Soon she discovers there is no one in the old house whom she can trust…no one but the handsome Garth Favor, who vows to help her unveil her family's secrets once and for all, no matter the cost.

SUMMERSEA

Betz Witherspoon isn't looking forward to the long, hot summer ahead. Stuck at a high-class resort with her feisty young charge, Betz only decides enduring her precocious heiress's mischief might be worth it when she meets the handsome and mysterious Adam Teague.

Stealing away to the resort's most secluded spots, the summer's heat pales against the blaze of passion between Betz and Adam. But Betz finds her scorching romance beginning to fizzle as puzzling events threaten the future of her charge. To survive the season, Betz will have to trust the enigmatic Adam…and her own heart.

SWEET WHISPERS

Seeking a new start, Sadie Evans settles in Warren Bluffs with hopes of leaving her past behind. She finds her fresh start in the small town, in her new home and new job, but also in the safe and passionate embrace of handsome deputy sheriff, Jim Warren.

But just when it seems as if Sadie's wish for a new life has been granted, secrets she meant to keep buried forever return to haunt her. Once again, she's scorned by the very town she has come to love—so Sadie must pin her hopes on Jim Warren's heart turning out to be the only home she'll ever need.

TIMBERHILL

When Carolyn Adams Clure returns to her family estate, Timberhill, she's there to face her nightmares, solve the mystery of her parents' dark past, and clear her father's name once and for all. Almost upon arrival, however, she is swept up into a maelstrom of fear, intrigue, and, most alarmingly, love.

In a horrifying but intriguing development for Carolyn, cult-like events begin to unfold in her midst and, before long, she finds both her life and her heart at stake.

VANITY BLADE

Orphan daughter of a saloon singer, vivacious Mary Lousie Mackenzie grows up to be a famous singer herself, the beautiful gambling queen known as Vanity Blade. Leaving her home in Mississippi, Vanity travels a wayward path to Sacramento, where she rules her own gambling boat. Gamblers and con men barter in high stakes around her, but Vanity's heart remains back east, with her once carefree life and former love, Trance Holloway, a preacher's son.

Trying to reclaim a happiness she'd left behind long ago, Vanity returns to Mississippi to discover—and fight for—the love she thought she'd lost forever.

Printed in the United States
by Baker & Taylor Publisher Services